THE MYTH
OF
JADE AND BONE

THE FINALITY SERIES
BOOK ONE

THE MYTH
OF
JADE AND BONE

THE FINALITY SERIES
BOOK ONE

JJ LAFLIN

To those who listen and those who believe.
May we always find each other.

For my little sister Tay,
Who never let me quit – even when I swore I would.
Who reminded me who I was when the words got too heavy.
Whose belief in me filled the silence when I couldn't yet believe in myself.
This book is finished because you are here.
And in some way, I like to think you are a part of every page.
Thank you. For everything.
I love you more than ink can say.

THE FAR NO
SKEALL
THE TRACS
ISLA
TILIDAANS
FARIT
DAMIRE
ER RADA
TER
GRANDIA
JIDAANI TERRITO
FERACK

THE MOUNTAINS OF SIBER
THE BARRENS
THE STING SEA
SUNCE
SUNCE LANDS
BAHANI TERRITORY
KYR
MAJINKA
THE DEAD LANDS
DAHUE
MIRIT
JYNN
IDANE
MYDIZA
SADDLEBACK MOUNTAINS
BINE
TULA
SLAVE RUNNERS HOLD
ADEM TERRITORY

PRIOR

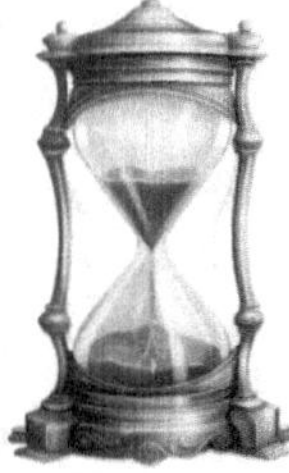

THEM

"There is no time. There will never be enough time."

Sand.

It swallows him.

Eroding granules grind against his skin as he sinks, the center of an unyielding hourglass threatening to devour him whole, crushing him beneath its weight. The deepening scent of the wet, swollen earth fills his nostrils, thickening with each strangled breath, mingling with the acrid bite of sweat and metal. An overwhelming heaviness grips his chest, caving his pointed ribs towards vital organs, threatening to pierce with one wrong move.

His world tightens, squeezes, traps him further; the sand is all consuming. He pries a hand loose, desperately reaching above the caving surface for something that is no longer there, something that perhaps was never there in the first place.

Had he been hallucinating it all?

The moments before rush through him in a blur of steel, of smoke.

Of... something else entirely.

No, no, no. Don't let me die. Not like this.

His thoughts expand, they threaten to burst, pounding against the walls of his mind before rapidly cooling into a strengthening focus. A new delicacy of fear lights as his fingers flex, struggling to grip the sinking ground around him. He attempts to push himself up once more, only to slip. His shoulder falters, trapping the upper half of his body deeper, sinking further – down, down, down, until the sand touches the belly of his chin. He will be entirely submerged within a matter of heartbeats.

The last bits of his vision begin to cloud right as the ground beneath him quakes. Dust billows, framing his face, blackening the empty sky above, no longer the welcome haze of what once was a new day. The hardened grains creep up to the base of his ear, his cheek. He spits the tiny particles from his mouth, a tang of dirt clinging to his tongue in its wake. The air thickens, suffocating him further. A strange sensation moves through the sand, pulsing through him, as though it were *alive*.

He is not alone here. A distance away, he watches the last bits of his vision drown beneath the surface; the sand melts, darkening further as it consumes him. It transforms into something too warm, too unbearably thick, a viscous liquid that sloshes and tugs against the weight of his sinking body.

Blood. Glorious blood.

An uncertain panic sets in immediately as he beats his arms up and down, finally freeing himself from the earthen grip, but now at the mercy of a violent, crimson ocean. It tilts and swallows, disorients, and confuses him. But the surface is within reach. He does not want to give up yet.

Thump. Thump.

He breaks past the space between life and death within those two heartbeats, grabbing a single swallow of smoke-rotten air before his body is jerked back downwards. Sharp claws prick at his ankle, clinging onto him as desperately as he is to the world above the terrifying sea. The slow kick he delves only forces the talons to dig in deeper, breaking the skin, tearing into muscle, caressing the bone. He cannot see what has a hold on him; the syrupy tides camouflage the unknown below. It does not matter; he does not care to open his eyes again. They burn.

Iron seeps between his lips, souring his mouth entirely. His throat tightens, choking out thick bubbles that assume the space around him, moving upwards in the direction he wishes he had the strength to go. He can no longer hold his breath; he is going to drown in this ocean of blood. The last mouthful rushes in through the gaps between his teeth, replacing the air in his aching lungs with the essence of death.

Let go.

There is that voice again. One that has washed through his mind many times before. It is... muffled, but he knows this voice. It drapes over him, coaxing and soothing, but the familiar feeling attached to it forces his eyes to snap open. His mind begs to scream that he is dreaming all of this, that it's only one of the nightmares that love to plague his near-sleepless nights. He does not know that this time, it's real. *Let go.*

The words are firmer, clearer now, accompanied by a swelling resolve that warms his bones. The panic slowly begins to dissipate. There is nothing left for him up there. He knows that. He can feel it in the emptiness of his soul. A strange, temptingly recognizable ease sweeps over his realization that holding on any longer will serve to be pointless, unnecessary.

Nothing left. Nothing more.

The softness speaks to him in a low, steady tone, with words he will surely never hear again. They shroud him; a blanket of tenderness telling him to blow out the heavy, blood-filled breath he has been struggling to reclaim as air. The pin-prick sensation around his calf releases on its own accord as though it, too, has acknowledged the finality of giving in.

It welcomes him.

Above, far from the surface, he swears he hears the sounds of the entirety of this life he knows belonged to him. It embraces him, replacing the dulled ringing in his ears with that of – concern. The creature beckons him to succumb to the dark, the tips of its claws grazing his calf.

A warning, should he choose not to listen. He does not know yet that he must continue fighting. For freedom is given only to those who are willing to change their fates.

ONE

ADESSA

"Listen to me, daughter. This is important."

"What the hell do you mean it's only worth twenty?"

I can feel the tension growing between myself and the cross-eyed merchant standing in front of me. I felt it long before I opened my mouth to sell. But there isn't a chance in this wasteland that I can allow myself to back down. Not with an insulting offer like that. I blink away the red that swirls around the corners of my vision. I'm becoming too desperate, and that could easily lead to making more mistakes. *He's lucky there's a barrier between us.*

I imagine how satisfying it would feel to reach over and strangle the trader before me; a nearly impossible accomplishment, surely, seeing how he's double my size. My fists tighten against each other, dirty fingernails digging into tough palms that leave behind dull, crescent markings etched in irritation.

Any attempt to end our deal the way I envisioned might not be fruitful. Still, I can't stand the thought of attempting to negotiate with him any further, seeing how bold frustration has already carved itself into the space between his sparse brows. I don't appreciate the way his left hand just moved to the inside of his sullen robes, either. My eyes remain focused on the folds of his tunic before taking a single step forward, pressing my hips against the edge of a hurriedly built storefront in the center of the alley path. An earthen scent of tobacco lines the air, pricking at my nose when I lean towards him.

What I wouldn't give to indulge in a cigarette right now. The smell of it makes me miss Farit more than I ever expected. At least that city had a well-established marketplace where a misplaced pipe or freshly rolled joint could easily be forgotten amongst such a diverse crowd. No silver needed; simple confidence was all that was required.

However, this – village – if one could even call it that, Er Rada, is the exact opposite of the city in the dunes. With its low, decrepit buildings, worn pathways blocked with dead ends perfect for trappers, and a marketplace that had all but been reduced to a narrow path behind the main street, they have the nerve to call this place anything other than a waste of desert. It doesn't matter if this place is technically *safer* than Farit. It makes me want to uproot everything I've done until now. It begs me to ask myself why I ever decided to follow the traveler's instructions. Sadly, there is no turning back now, not when I've already gone too far out of the way for any other viable option.

"I deserve more for what I went through to get this." I hiss through gritted teeth, sizing the man up once more. He stands well above my height, which is average at best, but I raise myself on my toes to match him while refusing to break the stare-down between us. I will not cower. I will demand. The merchant smirks, adjusting his gold-woven skull cap, no doubt hiding a patch of baldness beneath. His gravel-etched voice scratches my eardrums as he clears fluid from his lungs while speaking.

"You deserve nothing more than ten. You should be grateful that I am offering you twenty." His almost yellow eyes scan me from head to toe as he mocks my northern accent with that of his own desert-laced one. It sounds comically foreign on his tongue, but heat flares through my cheeks at the disrespect all the same. I picture my hands around his throat once more.

"Tainted shine." He scoffs, picking at a rogue splinter on the counter. "Clearly, what you went through wasn't as worth it as you thought."

Gnarled fingers pop the cork from the top of the stolen sun-faded jug I'd placed in front of him moments ago. The bottles at my back seemingly grow heavier at his accusation. A sickly aroma spills from the opening when he swirls the liquid around and around. I pinch my nose at the acrid tinge. *Damnit.* It smells of piss.

Swearing, I crack my bare toes against the baseboard of the canopy, forcing a corner of his merchant's flag to fall across the expanse of the fabric. All merchants are required to present markings like these, especially in owned territories, to announce the various tribes or clans from which they hail. It's a way to keep loyalties within the trading system and to guarantee that no one crosses a boundary to sell if they are not welcomed. Since Er Rada is in the territory owned by the most prominent clan on the continent, merchants of any rank can technically trade here as long as they obey the guidelines set. However, it is too bad that most of them are gone now; the stories of their competition on the routes are legendary on this continent. Although, they are the main reason why boundaries needed to be set in the first place.

This particular combination of colors is new to me, which isn't surprising considering the further I head south, everything becomes more and more unfamiliar. The markings on the fabric force my attention, screaming at me to remember them. Green against black stripes, sewn into the satin cloth in a horizontal pattern, glittering with a thread that matches the cap on the merchant's head. It's true that I have been on this side of the continent for less than a year now, not long enough to know the inner workings of anything other than what I experienced in Isla. Still, I've never seen anything with *gold* woven directly into the fabric. Let alone on a mere trader's flag.

The annoyed man grumbles, leaning to inspect his flag, and impatiently snaps his fingers. Less than half a breath later, a young boy, perhaps a handful of years old, appears from the darkened corner of the canopy. He rushes to my side and climbs the counter, breathing out a deep sigh of impatience while his tiny fingers work quickly, balancing steadily on his toes as he rights the corner of the flag, securing it back onto the nail above us. Straight once again. The kid turns back to me with a simple warning glance that fills his vacant eyes. I can't help but stare at the large, purple birthmark that covers the length of his face before he ducks back into the safety of the shadows.

"Let's get on with it then." The grumble directs my attention. "Twenty is my only offer, and that's mostly for the bottles the piss comes in. And for the fuel my fire will receive tonight."

I consider other options, knowing that I don't have any, and twist my body around to eye the line of people behind me. The same line that I had been forced to stand in for the better part of this morning. The heavy sun blares unforgivingly upon them all, showing clear signs of dehydration carved into many of the sallow faces ahead. I'm confident I look the same as they do, perhaps worse. Definitely worse. The desert is not kind, quite similar to home but in a different way. Besides, I would rather be warm.

Damn the Mystics. Damn them all.

I can't seem to shut my blaring mind off as I bury my foot into the sand to keep from letting out my rage on the stand. My hands find themselves placed flat against the splinters. I hang my head. A string of curses whispers violently from my chapped lips before I let out a breath that is on the verge of ending everything I've worked for.

What a waste of time. Getting to the compound before the sun began to rise this morning was a feat all on its own. Let alone finding the makeshift distillery that had been camouflaged among the bristle, only to discover it had been ransacked already. Then, hunting down the unarmed man who had stolen everything for himself and prying the bottles from his still-warm fingers – it had all been a complete – waste of time. Not to mention the additional hours it had taken to stand in this hellish line until the sun was high enough in the sky to blister each and every one of us. A warning to me that I had once again thrown away another day in Er Rada.

I knew it was too good to be true when I passed the boundary line and heard a whispered rumor that there was a still out this way. *Here? In the middle of the desert?* I'd thought to myself when I came upon this dry, vastly barren 'village,' knowing full well that there couldn't have been a nearby water source, which is essential for a still of any size to properly function. And seeing how everyone here is paying a transporter for weekly water rations, there might not be a well or river for at least a day's ride, if not more. My apprehension had grown even more when I hadn't seen a single wagon near the still nor any animal in sight that would be strong enough to carry the weight of a sellable haul. The wandering chickens wouldn't do it, and neither would the decayed body of an ox that had been half-buried in the sand. Which meant the 'shine' being produced was picked up by an amateur who had found the abandoned still and had no idea what they were doing.

There was also no indication that the alcohol was even semi-pure to begin with; I had let my desperation claw its way into my common sense. The top of this still didn't have any filtration hooked up, nor another tank to pour clean burn-off as I'd seen Tirma maintain herself every week back home when I was a child. Even the color of the shine itself was distorted, and I simply contributed it for sitting out in the desert heat for too long. I only knew what the liquid looked like in the ice storms surrounding our cave. Tirma always made her batches in the belly of our home, away from the light. It was always the color of the clear glass bottles she stored the shine in, no residue, no tint.

Damnit, I should have been more observant. Should have trusted my gut before blind fear tore me open. Before I killed someone over worthless poison.

"Are you selling or not? Some of us have families to care for."

Impatience in the form of a woman's voice chides behind me, interrupting the rogue thoughts that swim around my mind. I glance over my shoulder and then down, irritated at the blood caking my cuticles, flaking some from my thumb before sucking in a sharp breath. The merchant takes a swaying step backward, gesturing towards his servant boy.

Another unhappy scoff forces the crack of my neck. I spin on my heels to face her, matching my eyes with the deep-set pair across from me, carefully watching the frail, older woman cross her arms over her chest in an act of defiance.

She wears the same attire as everyone else in this desolate alleyway. Tattered clothing, covered in weeks if not months of dust, dirt, and sand, the dull pigments of a past life splattered into odd patterns on scratchy, one-size-too-big fabric. Loose threads from missing buttons hang along the outer hem. It's the kind of clothing the wearer might have looked fairly decent in once if survival hadn't transformed itself into outright starvation. The woman's tight-knit brows tell even more of a rebellious story hidden beneath assumed weakness. I can feel my heart squeeze.

These people. They will never be given the chance to stop fighting. Considering their circumstances, I cannot fault them for how they react to me or to one another. If I were in a different situation than the one I currently endure, I might behave similarly. I'm just grateful I had the forethought to wipe the blood that stained my skin from earlier today before I jumped into this line. If they only knew what I was capable of, what they were all daring to grunt and groan at. Wearing the stain of another's life would have gotten me in a lot more trouble than it would be worth.

The aging woman taps her foot against the hard sand, tsking her tongue as if waiting for a child's explanation. I smirk and look past her to the disapproving crowd in line, which now stretches past the block. Some hold children tightly against them, others wrap their fingers closely around the items they intend to sell, as if this *outsider*, with wild, unwrapped hair, would rob them in front of a crowd of unforgiving people if given the chance.

I would, but they shouldn't assume so quickly.

Since arriving in Er Rada a few days ago, I've been finding it more difficult, nearly impossible, to pry information from anyone who lives here. They are much less giving than those I had interacted with further north, and it seems here, they all react in the same way. Impatient and distrustful. In Farit, those who found homes there seemed more casual, more open with their knowledge and with their gossip. Probably because they were well-equipped and backed by the clan that ran their territory. The violence of the Tilidaans was well known in those parts; I know because of Isla. It allowed them the freedom to have a skewed sense of safety. They had their community. Unlike here, where peace is not something given, but taken.

As I approach the Red Line, it is becoming increasingly clear that the other regions of this continent have experienced a level of turmoil unparalleled by anything I have been subjected to in the north. As it has been since the time their bloodlines can hardly remember. Of course, they have every right to be untrusting of outsiders, especially towards one as disheveled as I look right now. Not knowing who to trust or where to go does make it challenging to find somewhere to sleep, something to eat, and a way to make myself more – presentable. But there's not much I can do anymore without my dagger.

I rub the back of my neck in remembrance of the hit I took from a solid block used for pounding dough only yesterday, with dried slabs still stuck to the misshapen wood. All for asking the owner what time the merchant usually showed up. Imagine what it has been like trying to get an entire night's rest. No wonder I haven't been thinking straight.

"Well?"

"Can't you see that I'm trying to negotiate?" I respond, tilting my chin to the side.

"Well, negotiate faster. Some of us have better things to do than stare at the back of your head all day!"

The crowd mumbles in agreement and I cannot help the flare of distaste in my eyes when I scan each individual person, acting as though I were committing their faces to memory. A tactic to intimidate them. But then my gaze falls on a young girl, well under my own age, standing three people behind the impatient crow before me. I immediately note her attire, vastly different from the rest. A clean, black shawl covers the width of her shoulders, wrapping up and over her head in a sleek shroud that hugs her hair. Bright floral embroidery dots its length, ending in simple frayed tassels attached to the hem. The material looks soft to the touch. The sun kisses the texture, caresses the fabric.

Is that silk?

The rest of the girl's wardrobe is equally clean, unlike the dust-coated shrouds and tunics around her. Either she has never stepped foot outside until this very day, or she's considerably well-off. Enough to have a rotating wardrobe, at least. The merchant seems to be reasonably wealthy as well, considering each of his large, swollen fingers are decorated in gold circlets that hold natural cut gems set inside each one. The fact that he owns a servant furthers the truth of his riches. His accent tells me that he isn't quite from the area and, like most merchants, most likely won't be staying long. I wonder if this girl is a foreigner like him.

My mind shifts, relying on the bits of information I pulled in Farit about the old wealth, cities along the Red Line once flourished in. Although sparse and desperate now, Er Rada was surprisingly included in that list. Which is precisely why I am here. Why I decided to follow this particular route, instead of cutting across towards the Barrens. Rumors of the Elites dragged me from my original course.

There isn't any indication of wealth in this village itself, besides a fully stocked farm near the butchers, with only a handful of camels and milking goats, but also a coop that didn't even have chickens. However, at the very edge of Er Rada's northern border, where I crossed, there is a cemetery with more than just erect sandstone bricks and dried palm leaves to mark the dead's final resting place, per tradition of Death Rites on these lands. There are also giant, hand-carved headstones of granite that take up many of the plots, too weathered to look recent. A telling sign that this area had once existed before the Cull. People had lived and died here before Er Rada was turned into whatever state it's in now. Which means the second rumor I heard could also remain valid.

A few others in line steal concerned glances towards the girl that I am analyzing, shuttering their eyes down when I match the stares that are racked with worry.

Do they know you? Or are you an outsider to them like I am?

Their quick glances suggest that she is also being judged.

The child shuffles her hands together, resting them at the base of her stomach in a nervous way, directing her attention anywhere but forward. I glance away briefly, only turning back after she shifts her hands, allowing me to notice her ring, which sparkles like the algae-filled sea near my homeland. I've never seen a stone this color before. It sits loosely around her slender forefinger; she keeps her right hand called into a tight fist as if not doing so would make the ring slip off entirely. *Interesting.*

I stretch my gaze back up to her features. I can tell that she knows I'm examining her. I mean, the whole line can tell. Her body stands tense and rigid, with the soft glisten of sweat lining her temples, leading to a sunken face that shows the same signs of vague starvation as the rest of this miserable flock. However, her posture holds a simple grace to it, unwilling to slouch, which easily separates her from the hunched crowd. She's no coward.

"Ahem." The annoyed woman finally clears her throat, breaking the passing curiosity that's been holding me. She reaches out to tap me along the elbow, but I snatch her fragile wrist and bare my teeth, throwing her balance off.

"I could break this." I hiss.

Fear takes hold, abundant in her wet, brown eyes. She backs up into the heavy-set man behind her, who had been holding a nearly dead goat this entire time. He pushes her towards me in defense. Her wrist is at my mercy, and she cries out when I use the push to force it back until it nearly snaps. The merchant behind us expresses another fluid-filled cough at the behest of his awaiting patrons, clearly annoyed that I've been taking up so much of everyone's time. I relinquish my grip on the wrist between my fingers. The woman cradles it against her chest, rubbing the swelling skin.

"If you wish for a fight, I will happily join." The trader bellows, forcing the line's attention back to him. He reveals the handle of a jeweled dagger from the inside of his robes, the weapon I knew he'd been concealing, and taps the tip of the curved blade along the wooden counter in lazy, rhythmic beats. The small boy appears once more at his side, holding up a whetstone brick between his palms in offering. His master slowly begins to sharpen the blade; a hissing sound of metal against the smooth stone pings the chatterless air.

He then proceeds to blow the metal shavings directly into the kid's face when he's finished, covering the birthmark in a sheen of steel. I glower, mostly because I know I won't be able to help the marked boy. I'm far too exhausted, far too weaponless to fight at the moment, and the distant memory of my bare fists pounding into soft flesh earlier in the day makes my stomach threaten to turn. I'm eager to leave this place; I wish I had done it sooner. I just need coins before I can.

"Fine."

My willingness to be done forces a raise of the merchant's brow, and a sigh of relief from the woman behind me. I can hardly care anymore, even though I really should. Still, I'd like to think I have some decency left instead of fighting an older woman over her impatience and wasting more time than I already have, which will just make me angrier when tomorrow comes. The tapping of the merchant's blade finally comes to a halt, making me realize I've made the right decision even though it's hard for me to admit this defeat. Especially when it comes to my self-proclaimed reputation of being able to negotiate competently on Arthur's behalf back in Isla. But the last thing I need is a knife in my chest.

"Twenty, for the lot."

My mumbling doesn't hide from my angered ego, strengthened more so by the smirk on the man's face. He nods. I nod. He places his freshly sharpened blade down on the countertop, a threatening remind-er, no doubt. If he only knew how motivated I could be. I surrender the sack of glass bottles tied across my back and push them along the torn wooden surface in a way that makes my neck tense.

"But I keep the sack."

My fingers grip the bag tightly, unwilling to let go. My own satchel has been on its last breath for months now, patched together by fabric torn from my ragged shirt and thread taken from one of the buttons on my jacket. For now, this shine sack will have to ease the desperation for a new bag. The cross-eyed man offers a slow grin, showing blackened, rotting teeth. He knows full well that he'd just gotten away with a successful swindle; the intact bottles should be worth at least a little more than what he's willing to give. But I know when to give in.

His large hands drag the bag across the counter, throwing its full weight at the boy beside him. The poor kid barely has enough time and strength to catch it properly, let alone maintain his grip on the whetstone in his hands. He half-drops the bottles onto the decorated rug in the center with a near-silent cry before setting the contents alongside the canvas. The merchant shouts hateful words at him in one of the continent's oldest languages, which only makes the child shake harder with fear. Small hands quickly empty the bag entirely before placing it in front of his master's frame.

His fingers barely reach the top edge of the counter before the rotten man shoves him away, forcing him back into the shadows with the hefty ceramic jug in tow. Oh, how I wish I still had my blade. I would slit this old man's throat right where he stands, not only for the blatant mistreatment of this child but also for the knowledge that he thinks he has the right to do so. It's something that I will never get used to. This continent is corrupted by slave runners, corrupted by those who are willing to own slaves, too. Corrupted by the clans originally established to safeguard their people, but now permits – all of this. I wonder if these villagers would have anything against me doing something about it. Would I destroy their fragile system? Or would they be grateful for being given the opportunity to raid his stand once he was dead?

I eye the golden dagger to my right and my palm twitches. It takes everything inside me not to be tempted to use his own weapon against him. He must sense it, too, because he slams his fist down hard enough to bounce the weapon off its surface, startling the birds that have found their way to the top of his canopy.

"Finally. Next!"

The empty sack hits me square in the chest. Calloused fingers press a small, tan canvas pouch into my palm. I weigh it in my hand and breathe out a sigh that's filled with more stress than relief. I haven't held this much money in months, yet still, it isn't enough. I'm waved off as the frail woman pushes past too boldly with her shoulder, shrinking away from my warning look. Only when she reaches the counter does she straighten, hiding her fear in front of the man who will decide her financial fate today.

"Out of the way!"

I hear someone shout at a distance, forcing the crowd of people to part, right as a wagon pushes through the narrow alley, disturbing lines of clothing that hang outside the open windows of buildings on either side of the alley. Its owner pulls his animal between the wall and canopy, enticing a slur of angry words from the merchant, before squeezing out into the space behind the tent, continuing its journey through the street.

Parchments lining the outer wall of the canvas flutter from the movements, forcing my attention. The yellowing pages hang haphazardly in rows, plastering the entire length of the makeshift wall. Red ink lines the parchments indicating the level of threat being presented, mainly in the area's First language. But many have been translated into the language I am most familiar with using here, written in small print underneath the larger symbols, for which I am grateful. These are all high targets, it seems. Some pages contain crudely drawn renderings of the people in question. Available contracts. The merchant must deal in bounties. No wonder he looks so unhinged.

I take a step closer, trying to identify any clan markings. Contracts like these used to pop up in Isla. However, I've never seen this many in one place before. Bounties are primarily meant for the territory clans anyway. Or the runners. Both chase after contracts for revenge or for sport, depending on the person's value. They aren't really meant for the locals, but they are valuable if those locals have information that would lead to finding the contracts. Sometimes, runners paid for questions answered.

The bounties typically paid out a decent amount of silver as well, especially for the ones who have five stars beside their names. Even the one stars used to tempt me more than a few times before I remembered why they were being hunted in the first place. Not even desperation has allowed me to find out how much their heads are worth, not at the risk of what it would cost – of it all. None of it would be worth the potential payout.

Those who belonged to a clan were the most heavily armed, skilled, ruthless beings on the continent. Even if they are featured on bounties, no longer protected by their own, whether it be true or not, there is a reason why they are marked. For that reason alone, I've never desired to confirm if I could take one on myself. I'd have better luck finding real shine before I'd ever be able to find a bounty worth accepting. Let alone be believed that *I* was the one to fulfill it in the first place. No one would think that a woman from the north would be capable of such a thing. Our bloodline is not well respected here.

But again, it is not something I will ever care to confirm for myself. I've tried very hard over these past years to avoid the clans altogether. My destination cannot be marked with distraction, and I'm running out of time. Although I almost want to laugh, considering I'm using the Red Line as my guide to the sea. I've never felt crazier than I do right now.

I squint at the poorly written pages, looking for any mention of the only clan that concerns me. From the stories I've heard, it would be ridiculous to think that a Jidaani would be on a simple bounty like these. That clan seemed to handle their affairs swiftly and internally. My fingers ruffle the papers around, peeling one from the top of another. There are some from the Tilidaan, and it is not hard to imagine why. Here, it says *"Nebil of the South"* from the slave-running clan.

I move another page aside. This one *could* say Jidaani, but I can hardly tell, given the way the red ink bleeds. There are a considerable number of stars, though.

How are people supposed to read these things?
My father taught me how to read and write in the universal language when I was a little girl, telling me repeatedly that it wouldn't be enough to just speak it. Driving the importance into my head with the stroke of my quill. Unfortunately, it's a trait that has slowly diminished over time. When all one can do is survive, reading and writing simply don't appear as important anymore. It didn't help that Tirma never learned and was unable to continue my studies as I grew up with her, seeing as she was born into the lowest caste in our village.

However, speaking properly in the language used by the majority is something I was never allowed to forget, and I am forever grateful for keeping that part of my past intact. Having the ability to speak in a way that makes me more than just a tainted outsider is a benefit to my journey, regardless of what I've had to deal with so far in Er Rada. I'm fortunate to have had parents who cared enough to beat words into my head. People respect that; at least, they do when I look – cleaner.

This other language, like the one on the bounties, along with other dialects in these foreign-to-me lands, is an entirely different story. I've only been able to pick up on a few words here and there over the years, mostly curses thrown in my or other's directions for prying too much. I would have focused on learning their languages if the universal one wasn't commonly used here and in most territories near the Tracs, close to my homeland. In a way, I suppose it's the one thing I can thank the world before the Cull for.

I scratch a fingernail against the ink, scraping some bits away before realizing that it's actually blood that lines these pages. *This merchant –*
"Next!"

His voice turns my attention back as the man with a dead goat walks away, rubbing two coins between his fingers. When he passes me, I smell rot clinging to his skin and choose to distract myself, fumbling around my sorry excuse for a bag, moving items from old to new before tossing the torn sack onto the street behind me. Someone will find a use for it, as I had when I first found it.

I look at the twenty pieces nestled inside the pouch before securing its top together and dropping it into the awaiting bag with a yawn. I'll have to walk. I feel my body slump as I make my way towards the busy street ahead. My original plan had been to receive enough money through theft, work or otherwise, buy a camel and get to Mirit. However, the only luck I'd come across was those stolen bottles. With enough money from *real* shine, I wouldn't have a single issue in obtaining an animal that would get me to the port. Now, I barely have enough to buy shoes to cover my swollen toes. Or food to fill my sack. Twenty pieces – that won't get me anywhere near the Dying Sea. I don't want to continue walking.

All the way to Darde.

The thought makes my heart clench with unease. I've been traveling far too many years on foot; at this rate, the group I'm looking for will be long dead. I'll never make it in time. The smell of roasting meat wafts towards me, forcing my stomach to buckle in response. I search the area past the street and pinpoint the butcher's stand, noticing the lack of saliva in my mouth, a good indication that I need water. Technically, I could buy something more substantial to eat now that I have some coins to spend. My body would thank me for it; the rice from yesterday sits like a rock in my belly.

Fresh meat, when was the last time I had that?

It's been longer than a year, at least, and it was the kind not nearly fresh enough to make it worth the price it cost me. I shudder, remembering the cold, sweat-filled night, the horrific bouts of vomiting that seemed to last endlessly. I've since given up on the idea of eating anything other than rice and the occasional root vegetable after that moment, just out of fear alone. Now, with the heavy aroma of crackling skin, I feel like I could potentially be swayed into forgetting my last horrible encounter.

My fists clench and unclench, knowing the slow answer that forms in my mind. *No.*

I need to save the coins. I can last for at least another month. I could last for an eternity if I needed to. My feet disagree, unconsciously turning in the direction of the butcher, allowing me to cast one more glance toward the growing line. The girl is next. I notice the sandals on her feet this time around, nice leather ones strapped to warm skin. She scans the area around her, eyes slightly widening when she realizes that I've moved my attention back onto her, then snaps her head back down. Dirty sand covers her feet as she buries them in place. I glare at my own toes in a mix of hatred and defeat.

My shoes had been worn down to bare ground months ago, so I had no other choice but to peel them off. What once used to be the scarf that kept dust from my face and hair now wraps the bloodied, half-healed, calloused skin in a feeble attempt to keep debris from lodging in my re-opening sores. After walking from Farit to Er Rada, the torn fabric has now become ragged. I managed to seal the ripped edges down with can-dle wax so I wouldn't have to waste more resources on re-wrapping them with clean linens, but they've been slowly falling apart entirely.

Any form of unoccupied shoe has been nearly impossible to find, and I am not willing to spend the amount that traders ask for a used pair. It isn't like I can just steal shoes from people's feet whenever I please either, although I have been tempted before.

Besides, no weapon meant no use threatening anyone, and I told myself that I wouldn't stoop to such a level anyway; no point in killing someone over a shoe that might not last long. At least, that's what I've been telling myself. However, curiosity can't help but get the best of me. So much so, that I find myself measuring the girl's feet in my mind. I crinkle my toes at the visual, imagining how the leather would feel against my skin. It would take time to get used to, considering I've only ever worn fur or cloth. Her sandals would fit, I'm nearly sure of it.

Another seller is sent away, disappointment speckling his face when he shoves a single shard into the pocket of his trousers. I take a casual step backward, leaning against the inner alley wall as I lower my gaze from the sun and out of view. I watch her reveal three bright orange containers from the inner lining of her dress and set them carefully on the faded counter. Much to the merchant's delight, he snatches them, grinning from ear to ear like the embodiment of greed itself.

I wish I knew what he was saying to her that makes her clasp the shawl a little tighter around her chin while a sack full of coins is placed unhesitatingly in her palm. She quickly tucks the bag away, and moves from the line, wincing at words the merchant calls out to her as she heads in the opposite direction from where I stand. The ring never left her finger.

The silk material around her head flutters against the wind when she hurries past, allowing me to briefly catch a glimpse of the hair underneath. A thick strand of it brushes past her cheek. Long, raven hair. *Shiny*, raven hair. It's clean, just like the rest of her. She burrows it back under the wrap, frantically holding her shawl to the apex of her throat with a wild look in her eyes as she peeks around to see if anyone noticed. Looks like no one did, save for myself. I can't contain the smile.

Shiny hair means that it's been washed. Washed means that there must be an accessible water source. It's well known that the wells in this area have long dried up, not having been able to survive the drought that lasted decades. And since there's no clear sign of where anyone gets their water from and how much they need to conserve, I can't help but wonder how a girl like her has found access to *disposable* water.

People don't bathe for weeks, if not months at a time out here in the desert. That's why many keep their hair shrouded with scarves or caps. That was quite a shock to me when I first stepped onto these territories. As someone who comes from a land of many abundant, albeit freezing, lakes and rivers, our usual concern was the lack of weather-hearty food and warm clothing. Out here, in the middle of the desert, washing meant having to walk all the way to wherever the water hasn't dried up yet or spend precious coins, waste drinking water, on something as silly to them as staying clean. People would rather have a full belly.

The girl is making it a point to conceal her hair from everyone around her in a way that most other women don't. Their loose shrouds are only meant to cover the mess of hair underneath, to protect it from dirt, not to conceal it completely. That could mean one of two things. The girl could be one of the Devout, something fairly uncommon in these areas but not entirely impossible. People usually stray from religion when suffering is all there is to be had, so I'm leaning more towards the idea that she's keeping her water source a secret. Which means my wasted time standing in a line all day is now being exchanged for an opportunity.

Once again, the rumors in Farit buzz in my mind. Old wealth used to have a home in areas like these, and the cursed houses of the past contained underground reserve tanks that were larger than any well we're familiar with now. I've grown up reading the stories. That was another thing my father made sure to raise me on. It was no secret that those associated with the Elites refused to give up their resources after the Collapse. They built massive tanks and now-empty silos in preparation before anyone else knew what was going to happen. The rest of their remaining funds had been funneled into a system that could maintain itself without the need for power. It had the ability to continue working even under the most severe consequences of war and eternities of drought. Of course, they were unwilling to share this resource with the rest.

If those tanks are in this area, that could explain the lack of abundant water in Er Rada's barrier wells, too. The water might be redirecting somewhere, not allowing the already established containers to fill up on their own. Maybe this girl knows exactly how and where it's hooked up.

I wait for the pair of soft hazel eyes to land on my mother's greens once more before she snaps her attention to the ground, absentmindedly patting the stash of coins near her ribs, then takes off down the street. I crack my knuckles and follow, mindful of the distance I need to maintain. The silk of her shawl is easy enough to follow between the sparse groupings of men and women. Its floral patterns jump from the fabric, beckoning me to follow.

I weave when she weaves and adjust my gait when she moves between a scatter of buildings with quickening steps. I can feel sweat beading down my neck, leaving track marks through the layers of dirt on top of my sun-worn skin. I long for a bath, a bucket of clean water, *anything*. At this point, I'd settle for a damp rag.

I'm growing tired of the whispers because of the tainted stain of blood on my skin, but the only water I have left is the disappearing amount inside the waterskin tied in a loop around my waist. I'd be damned if I used the last of it for anything other than keeping my dehydrated body from passing out.

My hair is covered in enough grime and sweat to make my scalp bleed from the endless itching. Part of it is now matted and too painful to untangle. I've resorted to tying it up into a mess at the top of my head, which has made it nearly impossible to brush my fingers through it anymore. It isn't like the people I've encountered recently have been pristine in any sense, but the ever-present stench that's coming from my clothing has become unbearable, even for me.

The remnants of oils I've rubbed into my dry skin while passing through the harems and opium dens of Farit are no longer preventing the stink from seeping out of my pores. That surely doesn't make the natives want to help me in any way. It's bad enough that the red of my hair screams that I'm not from these lands, not to mention my accent and general lack of knowledge of their bloodlines. I hate making it worse by *looking* like the outsider that I am.

I carefully dodge a group of clucking women as they glare at me, scornfully pinching their noses in a display of disgust, further proving my point of needing a bath before resuming their venom-tipped gossip. Another spin to my left avoids a cart filled to the brim with palm shrouds for the dead and empty ceramic pots overrun with offerings of rice. I'm soon led down a path of worn houses, forgotten and overrun with brush. The girl's silhouette practically glows under the shadow of the sun when she makes another turn, avoiding bits of fallen siding from an exterior wall. She takes a sharp right down another alley, then she disappears.

I quell the frantic thoughts in my mind, damning myself for only having fists to fight with, and sneak around the corner of the last building on the road. Covering my eyes from the blaring light, I squint, scanning the empty street ahead. There's an outcropping of three very out-of-place homes off in the distance, away from the border. But still no sign of the girl or her footprints.

She couldn't have gone anywhere else. She has to be around here somewhere.

I slowly begin to edge closer to the grand buildings ahead. All three are made of red brick. A clear indication of wealth here before the Cull. These houses look like they've been standing abandoned for quite a while. Judging by their size, the rumors may be actually true.

I'll ignore the other gossip suggesting that all the lands the Elites once fled from are now marked with death itself. A rumor that holds some weight. There are many superstitions regarding the Mystics, which explains why Er Rada kept this area bundled away from their borders. Even the buildings across the street are abandoned, as though the entire area is tainted.

At the time of the Cull, the Elites scrambled while society crumbled around them. They fled once they realized the angry rioters they used to rule over were not coming to save them. They were there to kill them. They had planned for the worst among their social circles, with their stock of resources and technologies we've never been able to reclaim, forgetting that their subjects were actually the ones to be feared. Many didn't survive long enough to cross the sea like others closer to the ports.

Their bodies were left stacked alongside their cushy brick houses, un-touched by the fires that burnt their owners alive. Their bones, swept away by the dry desert air. I'd seen some of those memories of the Elites in Isla, now overrun by the Tilidaan, who use the former rulers of the world's houses as harems, feast rooms, and prisons.

Maybe the girl had turned down a separate path, one that I missed. She *was* pretty quick. I wait, considering my options. I could search one of the houses and see for myself if there's any sign of a reserve tank or, at the very least, something worth bringing back to the merchant. It wouldn't be a waste of time if I could have something valuable enough to purchase that camel. At the very least, it might help me feel settled in my funds enough to restock my food supply a little more.

I'd be wrong to say a chill doesn't caress the back of my neck while I shuffle down the remains of a limestone path, feeling a cold shiver tingle the back of my neck. My stomach feels heavy. My mind is playing tricks on me. How can someone like me be afraid of death's shadow? If the Mystics only knew how much I laugh in their faces on a daily basis... maybe they already know that I do. Perhaps that's why they continue to punish me.

My finger bobs up and down between the three houses, counting methodically out loud before landing on the one that ends my rhyme. A silly, fate-tied game my mother and I once played, forcing me to choose between which of our three favored goats was the next to feed the family. That was near the end of our once peaceful lives in the Far North.

The selected house stands tall at the far end of the path, central to the other two that sit oddly on either side. In a previous life, it surely had to be a thing of beauty. The red brick is earthy and warm, replicating the shadows of a setting sun upon the dunes. Its stone pathway remains begin at the end of the limestone gate, leading up to a heavily damaged porch, most likely shifted around by past earthquakes that have destroyed much of the old landscape.

Broken pieces of decorative tile, with their dark blues and yellows, edge the base of the stairs, completely stripped and splintered. An enormous crack in the foundation splits the porch in half, leading up to a pair of giant double doors and weathered brass handles secured to the front. The first-story windows are boarded, similar to the other two houses, in the hopes of preventing scavengers from accessing the home easily. Not much good that does, seeing how the coverings have been torn to shreds.

I take another step, noting the faint whisper of footprints leading to the entrance. There hasn't been much wind lately, so these tracks could have been left at any point. Still, I'm cautious when I reach for the cold brass and turn my wrist. The handle doesn't budge. Maybe this place isn't abandoned after all. I shift my weight to one foot and lift my knee, kicking at the crumbling center of the door. Exhaling, I make the same swift motions a second time, hearing the frame groan beneath the force of my kick. The middle of the door splinters, spraying bits of blue paint everywhere on impact.

One more time, and the barrier finally gives way, allowing for just enough space for me to slip between the two knobs. I barely cross the threshold, brushing away broken segments of wood that snag my clothes before hearing a voice speak from the shadows.

"Stay right there."

The tone is even, slightly shaken at the tip, and very young. It's dark enough inside that my eyes have difficulty adjusting, but I locate the sound in the foyer before me. Her petite figure steps into view from the corner of the room, the barrel of a gun pointed directly at me.

TWO

ADESSA

"Hope lies in truth. It's unfortunate that there is no longer any truth to be had."

I've never encountered a firearm before, but Arthur used to tell me stories of the damage they can cause, especially in the wrong hands. Most guns have all but disappeared; assuming they had been used exclusively as the weapon of choice during the Cull, the ammunition needed for them to work properly is simply too difficult to recreate now. Besides, humans tend to choose a more – personal – way of protecting themselves nowadays, believing that the guns and explosives that were used by Elites and warmongers in the Time Before allowed for a coward's way to win. The justification is probably only an excuse due to lack of material. Who knows what the death count would be if the tribes had access to weapons from the past?

I reach my hand behind me to shove the door closed, offering us more privacy in case of wandering ears, but I kicked the frame in a little too hard. The crack I managed to squeeze through refuses to shut, filtering heat in from the outside. "I said –"

"Yeah, yeah." I spit, returning my attention to the girl with my palms raised in bored surrender. Her hands remain steady. She's threatened someone like this before. Maybe this had been her plan all along, making me curious enough to follow her, leaving unanswered questions to float between us, leading me to this house. What does she intend to do? Rob me? The idea of that makes me snort.

There's just enough light sprinkling in through the splintered windows of the foyer, casting an eerie glow around the sparse and dusty furniture in the room. This place's reflection of past wealth might have been pleasant to admire if I saw it under different circumstances. Unfortunately, there doesn't seem to be anything valuable left. My feet shuffle closer, eyeing an adorned cabinet to my right, gilded with remnants of gold that appear to have been scraped off over the years. The leftover flakes could sell for a small amount if I could figure out how to peel them off to stay somewhat intact. It may not be worth the effort.

"Don't move!" She screams, fingers twitching ever so slightly when she levels the barrel to my chest. Sweat gleams across her forehead, bead-ing down her soft, half-hooked nose.

"You don't –"

I *want* to say that she doesn't scare me, but she shuts her eyelids, scrunches her nose, and pulls the trigger. She's thrown into a panic when the gun doesn't go off like she planned, confusion sweeping her expression in a blaze. In a strange mix of relief, I release an uncertain breath, realizing what I dodged, then grab the moment with a few quick, pounding steps, closing the gap between us all while she hits the barrel with her palms. Aims. Fires.

The pellets blast into the peak of my shoulder, ripping through the material of my jacket and then burying themselves into my muscle. I stagger back in an agonizing amount of shock and pain, my hand grip-ping torn fabric, filling my palm with red. I can feel the hot skin underneath, bursting with fire-filled blood.

"Are you insane?" I blink back at the spots flickering in the frontline of my vision, holding myself steady against the wall. "Who – why did – you just shot me!"

My shouting seems unnatural, with equal surprise to see a weapon like that in action, to know firsthand the damage it can do. *How many shots are in a gun like that?* Not that it matters. She could use the damned thing as a bludgeon if she felt so inclined.

"Stop! Next time, it will be your face!" She shakes, raising her weapon again, clicking the lever back into place.

I refuse to miss my opportunity, snatching the belly of the barrel just in time, whipping it up towards the ceiling while she pulls the trigger again a second too late. It bellows, spraying tiny shards upwards, instantly shattering the remainder of the broken chandelier above us. The pop of glass makes both of us jump as glittering fragments rain down around us. I yank the blazing weapon from her hands, palms burning against the heat of freshly fired metal.

"What in the Abyss is wrong with you!" Cursing, I work my jaw as the continued ringing in my ears dizzies me. One eardrum finally pops back into place when I wiggle the tip of my finger around the inside with one hand and flip the barrel around to face her with the other, pressing the cooling metal gently against her forehead. She whimpers, backing up into the thin table behind her. The few items scattered on top fall to the floor. One of them, a vase, shatters from the height. *That could have been worth something!*

I glare at the broken pieces, then back to her. Wide, wet eyes burrow into mine, but slowly, the fear inside them dissipates. A surprised smile tugs at the corner of my lip at the slight change in expression. The girl swallows hard as she straightens, adjusting her head to center the barrel.

"Oh, you're a brave one." I snicker, noticing a glimpse of myself residing in her.

"Shoot me."

My brows raise at the immediate request, my shoulder throbbing in response, reminding me that there are pieces of metal buried deep. The adrenaline had been coursing through me too quickly to pay any mind to the pain that blisters me and is now making its presence known with a vengeance. The girl offers me a pained look, one that makes me believe she is much older than I previously thought. Survival inflicts that on people. Even children from as Far North to here have a certain disposition about them, due to the damage of this world.

"Please." She pleads softly. People beg *for* their lives. Can't say I've come across anyone who invited me to *take* it from them instead.

"I'm not going to kill you."

Her shoulders slump in response. I drop the angle of the gun, unsure of what to do with it, how to even work it properly. I've been begging for a way to protect myself since I lost my dagger, but I don't want anything to do with a weapon like this.

"Oh, don't look so upset."

Bending down slowly, I slide the weapon across the wooden floor, hitting the bottom of the wall beneath the window, and place my hands on my hips, groaning against the agony in my arm.

"The water. Where is it?"

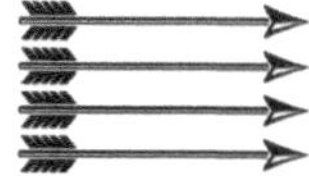

The rumors were right. They were actually right!

I would never have believed them if I hadn't seen the setup for myself. There are reserve tanks under all three houses. The second-floor bathroom has pipes and tubes that are hooked up from the underground to the actual bath that pours clean water from above, all tucked away in the corner of this unassuming, tiled room. This is the first and only time I will ever thank the Elites for what they've done.

I make sure not to dwell on it for too long as warm water, I've never had *warm* water to bathe in, splashes down around me. Even the sea near Isla was never this warm. The liquid turns black as soon as it washes over me, hitting the bottom of the chipped porcelain tub. Months of sweat, dirt, and blood gurgle down the opening in thick, greedy swallows.

"Still alive out there, right?"

I call out, hearing slight movements against the closed door that I tied the girl against. She fought me the entire time, both before and after

I had her show me how to turn the pipes on. Had to stuff her mouth with a rag just to get her to stop arguing.

I begin plucking the first pellet from my skin with my fingernails, hearing the metal clink against the basin when it finally pries loose. There are three more of them embedded into my shoulder. The trickle of crimson darkens when I pull the second out and let it fall to the drain, reminding me of my first encounter with death long ago. Reminding me of Tirma.

She had found me in a state much, much worse than this one, my body covered in an inch of freezing snow, with four arrows embedded deep in my stomach. Too deep for someone to survive. Too deep for anyone to *want* to survive. The old woman dragged me back to the caves she'd been forced to hide in by her own neighbors years prior, far into the Mountains of Siber.

That was the first time I realized that I couldn't be killed. And Tirma realized it too, hiding me for far too long in fear that my luck would run out. If she only knew how badly I craved that very thing to happen. How incessantly I once begged for this life of mine to end.

"I guess I'm lucky you didn't aim for my heart." I grumble, fighting against the urge to gag when the third pellet drops. The pipes above sputter and slow, reducing the water flow to a mere trickle just as I finish pushing the final piece through a particularly tough section of muscle.

"Damnit." The Elites had been smart enough to set a limit on the tank. It makes sense; conserving water in an unforgiving, drought-suffering climate had to be a priority of theirs. Even if the idea alone makes my blood boil. I sigh, reaching for one of the towels I'd seen resting on the outer handle of the glass door, giving it a good sniff before wrapping the rough cotton around my body and tucking in the folds before stepping out onto the cold tile. I dry my hair with its mismatched partner and stare at myself in the broken mirror, clearing the steam away with my palm.

Pinching my cheeks, I attempt to rub life back into my pallid face. The girl watches me wring the water from my matted hair; she sits straighter once she sees me peek at her reflection in the foggy glass. I have to admire the blank expression she wears when, only moments ago, concern altered her features. She must not be as sheltered as I thought she was.

"Have anything I can cut this with?" I ask, holding up a chunk of matting that falls past my breasts. I should have cut it all off a long time ago, and I had been planning to, but my dagger had been broken in half around the same time I was forced to rip my shoes off. One half of my blade found itself embedded in the farmer's shoulder, the other fairly close to his eye. It was all a misunderstanding from both sides; I just hadn't woken up early enough to leave his barn, and he was clearly a man who would die to protect his property. I rub my ribs in memory of the fracture I had to live with for a few days.

The girl's small frame considers me for a moment before mumbling something between the rag in her mouth.

"Ah."

The callouses on my feet tap the tile while I make my way to her, crouching low to yank the stuffing from her mouth. She works her jaw, circling her head in a stretch. Vibrant, hazel eyes land on the four tiny holes in my bare shoulder, still oozing with bits of bright red blood. "Top right."

She knocks her head towards the mirrored cabinet above the sink. "Untie me." Her sight remains firm on my injuries before moving to stare at her tied wrists. She tugs them against the doorknob above her. "My wrists hurt."

I snort, drawing my attention back to the cabinet. Squeaking hinges reveal a pair of scissors hanging loosely on a nail near the ledge. However, that isn't the only thing my focus is driven to. The shelves are lined with bright orange plastic bottles. The same ones I saw the girl sell to the merchant earlier. They all have inkless labels, worn off over time. Something tells me that the contents inside won't match whatever the faded words say anyway. If there were containers for medications of the past, the actual pills would have been long gone before my First grandmother was born. Perhaps before even that, before everything collapsed.

I unscrew one of the ill-fit caps and squint at the powder inside. It's halfway filled with fine dust, the color of scorched wheat.

"You were selling these." I swivel around to face her, wiggling the open container. "What is this?"

She doesn't answer, only watches me, slightly wide-eyed, as I dump a small amount of powder into my palm. I kneel beside her while she turns her head slightly away, her nostrils flaring as though she's trying not to make it seem like she isn't holding her breath. "Hmm?"

I purse my lips as if to blow the substance into her face. She cowers, squeezing her eyes shut, pressing her back firmly against the door, giving me precisely the reaction I'd hoped for.

"I thought you had been wishing for death?"

"Not like that." She peeps.

"I didn't think I'd run into a poison dealer in a place like this."

She glares, but all I do is drop the contents back inside its container and wipe my hand clean against the towel. "I'm not –"

"What kind of poison is it?" The scissors are hacking away at my hair between the silence only a few moments later. Chunks of matting drop into the ceramic sink below.

"I don't know." She finally admits.

"How do you not know? There are at least twenty bottles here. Not including the ones you've sold." The sharp snipping breaks the uncomfortable sound of her sobbing.

"My mother never told me. She never wanted me to know." She glances at the floor, curling her fingers.

"Your mother?" I take an uneasy look around the room.

"She – isn't here. Anymore."

I keep myself from letting out a sigh of relief, noting the crumpled expression the girl wears. One I know I've shown on my own face. I don't know if I should continue to pry at this point. She sniffles, maneuvering her body into what I assume is a more comfortable position, and pulls on the bindings. "Please untie me."

I watch her eyes fill with water, her mouth curling downward. Sighing, I continue slicing the thick strands. "How did you find out this place had reserve tanks?" Curiosity gets the best of me, even when I know it shouldn't.

"Are you going to kill me if I don't tell you?" A playful spark brightens her pupils.

"Hm. I'm very confused as to what you want me to do. Kill you or not kill you. Fine, don't answer that. Answer this instead. What's the going rate for this nameless poison?" If I can sell these bottles, I'll be able to get a camel. This was not a worthless use of my time at all it seems.

"You can't have them."

I chuckle, leaning back and tearing through the final mat of hair. My fingers begin the tedious task of combing through the shortened strands.

"Why not? Looks to me like you made out pretty decent from selling a few of your own."

"Well, they don't belong to you."

I pause, looking down at my hands, at the blood caking my fingernails. The water shut off before I could scrub the remainder of my weeks away. "Sounds to me like they don't really belong to you either."

"Is that why you were following me?" Accusation tips her tongue.

"Not exactly." I sigh. "I knew you were hiding *something*, I just didn't know what to expect. Definitely didn't expect to be shot by a relic from the Cull, that's for sure." My brow lifts. "Is that why you baited me? Because you knew I was following you?" I glance back at her reflection.

"You're bleeding all over the sink."

"It'll stop soon enough." I retort, smearing crimson against the stark white. Metal clangs when I drop the shears, push the handle of the faucet, and bash it against my palm when water doesn't spill from the spout. I briefly wonder if I emptied the tank.

"So." I smile, swiping at the ends that rest above my shoulder. My features seem to soften. "Who else is waiting to reap the benefits of the trap you set for me?"

My question seems to confuse her until I direct my nod toward her hands. "The ring. It doesn't fit your finger."

I find myself shaking out hair splinters all over the floor. "Who does it belong to? And don't say it's your mother's."

The girl shakes her hands at me in offering. "*This* is what you wanted? Here, take it and untie me."

It feels almost too easy, but I must take advantage of small victories. I grab the scissors again and kneel, slicing the ties that bind her wrists in two precise snips. She rubs the red marks that have already begun form-ing on her skin, then yanks the ring off and chucks it across the room. We both watch it skitter along the cold tile, landing with a *ping* beside the bottom of the cracking tub.

I pinch my face and she crosses her arms in defiance, sneering when I bend down to pick up the piece of jewelry that better hold more value than anything else in this house. The towel around me polishes the end while I move to the hallway, towards the light.

"I think it's a stone called Jade." Her small voice struggles when she stands.

Flecks of transparent greens and bits of white flicker around the band. I've never seen a stone this color before. "Lucky me."

I might be able to get a camel with this alone. Not to mention the poison. The possibilities of my journey could be endless now. "No one is coming to look for this?"

The girl wanders out past the door frame too slowly, hanging her head in silence. I chide, pressing both hands into her shoulders, backing her up against the wall, demanding an answer.

"No. No one will. It was never mine to begin with." She stutters, shaking her head back and forth. "You can have it."

I stare at her for a moment longer before redirecting my attention back to the ring. "Do you know the person it belonged to?"

I rub the band between my fingers before slipping it around my thumb. It's loose, clearly never meant for my finger either, but it's tight enough to fit over my knuckle, so it will have to do for now. I'll have plenty of time to get back to the merchant before the sun sets anyway.

"I found it. I don't know who had it before me." She tilts her chin up, and I snort, backing away.

"Thanks for giving it up so easily then."

"Like I had a choice." She mutters under her breath. Snickering, I step back into the entrance of the bathroom and grunt at the dirty clothes I've left on the floor. They are covered in sand, and Mystics' know what else; the last thing I want to do is put these crusty clothes back on.

"You live here, right?" I peer over my shoulder. "Are those the only clothes you have?"

I spin around and head towards one of the three other rooms on this floor, not really caring for her answer. The patter of her feet follows behind me when I unlatch the door to the furthest room. It's a tiny space, with only a single bed frame in the corner, right across from the door. No mattress. The walls are faded, and chipped paint speckles the wood grain flooring. Broken blinds hang loose off-center across a lone window near a completely empty closet. The crumbling ceiling decorates the carpet below.

Another room offers very little as well. Palm-sized pieces of broken glass line the half wall below the window, like the room had been broken into from the outside. A light breeze passes through the crack, fluttering shredded curtains that hang dully at the sides. Remnants of old blood mark the far-left wall in strange patterns and lines that look like they were painted by fingertip. I glance back at the girl, who taps her foot nervously against the floorboards, picking at a cuticle.

"What happened here? Is this –?" I give it another scrutinizing look. "A map?" The etchings look very familiar, yet not, all at the same time. I don't recognize anything on it. Nothing from my own map of this continent, nor from the maps that were commonly used in Skeall, or Isla for that matter. She shrugs, unwilling to give away the clear secret that clings to the air between us.

"How old are you?" Her question is effortless in a way that makes me laugh outright. I pass her, trying to make myself appear unbothered.

What a silly thing to ask.

People don't count their years anymore. Why would anyone want to keep track of how long they've been forced to survive this misera-ble world? I briefly remember a time when my parents tried to celebrate my years when I was younger, but I credited that to them finally being able to have a child despite the decades and the neighbors who couldn't conceive one of their own. They felt it necessary to cherish me, to have something worth celebrating. That ended many, many years ago. All I know is that I've spent long enough surviving this curse of being alive, and that's enough tracking for me.

I pretend to count on my fingers, humoring the girl before giving up, cackling into my fist, then ignoring her while I enter the last room on the floor.

"I turned twenty last week. On the first night the air cooled." She pipes up, scanning the larger room around us in an almost nostalgic way. Prints of tattered machines from another time plaster the furthest wall. Shelves lined with rusted figurines of those same machines and other small trinkets sit crowded with dust. A past long forgotten.

"I don't usually come up here." I ignore the sadness in her tone.

The bed in the corner is stripped; this time, there is a mattress, albeit torn to shreds. A pile of what looks like children's picture books are all spread out on top, worn from the ages. To my right, an open closet, both doors ripped from their hinges. Remnants of a wardrobe hang from the wooden rods, but most of the clothing is scattered along the stained car-pet. Men's clothing, by the looks of it. I feel the girl's gaze on my back while she rests herself against the doorframe.

"A man lives here with you?" It doesn't sound like much of a question when the words leave my mouth. The ease of slight panic runs a chilling fingertip along my spine as I rifle through the material.

You should have been more careful. You should have just cleared the house before you got so comfortable. Just because she doesn't have her gun doesn't mean she is no longer a threat. That's why she's so calm. All you cared about was a damned bath.

I peek behind me, noting the subtle shake of her head. She toes an invisible object on the floor. I fail to hide the relief on my face, the steadying of my breathing.

"Not anymore." She shudders. "I think you and him would be the same age by now. My brother was –"

"What is it with you and ages?" My hands reach for a harsh gray tunic and dark harem pants with deep pockets on either side. I'm leaner than I was a few months ago, but the clothing might fit with a few adjustments. The large pair of leather boots in the corner of the closet will not. I eye the sandals wrapped around the girl's feet again and release an exasperated breath.

"You have a lot of scars." She whispers, noting how well-marked my back and arms are when I pull the tunic over my head. The hem rests just above the middle of my thighs, which I bunch into a knot at the side.

"Yeah, and thanks to you, I have four more." The skin around my wounds twitch in response. I can feel the tenderness of them slowly knitting back together, a process that I'll never be fond of no matter the kind of healing. With a huff, I twirl my finger around, grateful that she obeys, facing the open hallway to allow for some privacy so I can pull on my new pants.

"Why don't you care about how old you are?" *Is this kid completely oblivious to the world around her?* Her tone has the audacity to sound irritated with *me.*

"Why do *you?*" My response is equally laced. The pants are a bit big around my hips, but thankfully, the string sewn into the waist allows me to tie it snugly. When I'm finished, I shrug my frayed jacket back on, but not before I annoyingly finger the new set of holes torn into its shoulder. These patches won't heal themselves. My satchel finds its way across my back, next, the now full waterskin around my waist; thankfully I had the idea of filling it before cleaning myself.

The girl turns back around, scrunching her brows, daring to look offended. "Do my brother's clothes fit you well enough?" Her voice is quiet, watching me inspect the small closet outside of this room. "He never let me wear his clothes. Said I would look too much like a boy and be sold to work in the mines."

"Better than looking like a girl and being sold to the slavers?" I hiss, eyeing her own outfit.

"He said it matters. That they treat the girls better because we create *more*." I swallow down the lump in my throat, the implication of what that sentence means. I find myself wandering back to the cabinet in the bathroom.

"You can't have those." I ignore her, shoving two containers into my satchel and closing the mirrored door.

"Maybe I'll put them back if you tell me what kind of poison it is."

"I told you, I don't know. My mother said never to use them."

"Yet you sell them."

She stomps her foot. "I need to be able to eat."

"Yeah? So do I." I nearly grab for more, but the strings in my heart don't allow me to take her only source of a means to get food. Not when she only has eighteen containers left. I wonder how long that will last her.

"How many floors does this house have."

"There's no access to the third. The ladder broke a long time ago." She points to the hole in the ceiling, to the unreachable third floor.

"Then where do you sleep?"

"Downstairs usually." She shrugs, wandering to the railing. "Where are you from? You have a weird accent." I roll my eyes, moving towards the top of the stairs. She steps in front of me, preventing me from leaving.

"Somewhere much further north from here." I say, grabbing her arms and pushing her gently away.

"We were from the west. Near an ocean port. Damire. Have you heard of it?" *This isn't her family home.* "Are your people here too?"

The memories of my own family spark in my mind for a bleak moment right before I'm able to shove them back into the deep pockets of my thoughts. I offer nothing more than a shake of my head. I don't care to know how her family left her if they abandoned her for reasons not their own as mine did.

I sweep my eyes across the hall for a final time and take another step. The filtered light casts shadows on the first-floor walls. *No more wasting time.*

"You don't have to go. I can always -"

I turn to face her, using the railing as support. "Give me your shoes."

She backs away from the top step, covering one treasured sandal with the other. I can't help but laugh, grateful that my demand shut her up. "Don't worry, kid, I'm not going to take the ones you're wearing."

I'll need to purchase some new linens, even though the wounds have already stitched themselves back together, it's only a matter of time that the sores will reopen.

"Wait!" The pleas force me to grab against the wall. I don't turn around again to look at her. "Take me with you."

With that, I bound the rest of the stairs. "First, you want me to kill you; now you want to come along. I won't explain to you why I travel alone."

"Please!"

Rubbing my temples in circled frustration, I close my eyes and hear her dart to the top of the staircase again. "Please, I can't live like this anymore."

Pain lights her tone, slipping past her lips, saturating me. It forces me to twist around again. "Trust me, you wouldn't enjoy the way I live either."

"You don't know that."

I give her clean clothes a smug once-over. "Oh, I think I do."

But my hesitation makes me take in her stubbornness for a second too long. She notices it, too, bounding half the stairs. Guilt creeps up, tight in my stomach. *No.* She would only be another mouth to feed, another body to protect. I've been having a hard enough time taking care of *myself,* and unlike me, she would easily be dead from quite literally anything I run into. I'd give it a week. Maybe less. The plan is to get to Darde by any means necessary. She'll only slow me down.

"You have your shotgun. Trust me, I won't be taking it from you." I don't know how the damned thing works anyways, let alone where to get the bullets. "I hope the next time you shoot someone, it works in your favor." I'm so close to the door. "Do me a favor, and don't shoot me in the back with it when I leave."

The foyer seems darker than it was when I first entered; I have to keep moving. I cross the wide expanse, forgoing the gold dust on the cabinet, patting the satchel with my ringed hand. "Sell the rest of the poison before the merchant decides this place is too poor for him. I don't know when another one will come to Er Rada."

Visits by merchants across the territories have become fewer and farther between now that the continent rapidly grows more dangerous. It seems to be in the throes of what happened to my homeland with the destruction of the caravans. Of the burning of Skeall's market. Our clans wanted to gain complete control, just as the Elites had tried to accomplish years before the Cull. It never ends.

"It always repeats." Tirma's voice echoes around me. *"As it always has and always would."*

Her cryptic words etch themselves in the forefront of my mind. Perhaps the closer I get to the Red Line, the closer I'll be to more merchants. More opportunities. I switch my damning thoughts to something more hopeful, even though I know it all may not be true. I've heard too many varying rumors about the infamous trade route to even begin to expect a positive outcome.

"He'll question you when you try to sell it to him. He trusts me. I can help you sell it. All of it."

Although the offer is in fact very tempting, that amount of coin would only weigh me down. "No thanks, I can manage."

I quickly scan the floor for shoes to fit my soon-to-be swelling feet. "Be careful about the water tank. The whole 'cursed land' rumor is only good for those who care about that sort of thing. More and more people are getting desperate by the day." I shove my fingers through the crack in the door and pull as hard as I can.

"And make sure to buy as much meat as you're able. Dry it out, the sun – "

Why *am I helping her?*

Soft footsteps move behind me right as I squeeze through the splinters and out into the blistering heat. "Don't you even dare think of following me either. My kindness ends here."

She clearly ignores my orders, following me outside, shading her eyes. *Darde. Darde. Darde.*

The words flow in and around my head while I walk down the limestone path with my head held high. The road separating the block of abandoned buildings is within reach. I don't even try to go to the other two houses; it wouldn't be worth my time anyway. I'll run out of sunlight once I finish with the merchant if the line has remained the same length, and I've already overstayed my welcome here. The last thing I want to do is spend another night in Er Rada.

"I can – I can speak their language!" The girl shouts from the top of the porch, uncaring of who might be listening.

"I don't care!" I shout back and wave my fingers above my head in farewell.

"You really won't let me come with you?"

Darde. Darde. Darde. My ears are ringing.

"Good luck!" I answer back loudly, half-jogging down the road.

She doesn't follow me. I twist my neck, watching her stumble back inside her home. *Good.*

My finger grazes the new ring around my thumb, inspiring me to lift it up once more, watching the sunlight reflect throughout the transparent pieces dotting the inside. I spin it around and around, feeling nausea begin to creep into my stomach. I wonder who this ring belongs to and why the girl didn't sell it if it wasn't hers anyway. Why did she give up so easily?

The thoughts come and go as I make my way through the familiar alley past the butcher's before stopping at the back of the merchant's line.

"How in the Abyss can it still be this long?" I mutter, listening to the chatter ahead.

People whisper around me, pushing aside in curiosity to witness the disturbance at the stand; I join them. A broad man stands at the counter, the tip of his shaved head nearly grazes the belly of the merchant's canopy. His shirtless, leathered skin is etched with jagged whip scars.

He holds a fist full of parchment, shaking it into the face of a now-wearied merchant.

"What did I miss?" I ask the person beside me, who only looks down and sneers before moving his attention back to the front, along with the rest of us. Everyone seems to be getting a glimpse.

Bellowed shouting forces the crowd from a curious line to a scattered mob, pushing in every direction, clutching their items firmly to their chests to keep the advantageous from snatching them away in the chaos. A few children scream, mothers too. I make my way through them, hoping to be the first in line when the confusion dies down. I watch the merchant grab his dagger, holding it out to the stranger confronting him. The man simply knocks it away, annoyed, then lifts the merchant by the scruff of his neck as if he were a puppy and not someone already twice the size of me.

"Why post a bounty if you don't want to claim it!" He shouts, spit pelting the merchant's face.

"I – I don't want him! I don't even know how his name got –"

Not so tough anymore. I snort, crossing my arms, trying my best not to look like I'm enjoying the karma. The overbearing stranger throws the merchant backward into his tent and, with it, follows the sound of glass shattering. I watch the servant boy flee the canopy walls, hiding behind one of the barrels along the alley to my right. The madness forces the line to disintegrate entirely, with sellers pushing themselves into the narrow alley in a herd, knocking down flag posts and empty crates.

The man who started it all latches onto the merchant's black and green flag and rips it in half with a roar before turning back towards the now-empty street. I lower my chin and tuck myself into the shadows of the clothesline when he passes, catching his stature in secret; his fists clenching yellowed parchment, three triangle tattoos vertically lining his left bicep. I make a mental note of the symbols.

Once he's out of sight, I run to the tent, desperate to sell my items more than ever. *This is enough to get a camel. I can be in the next town by the time the sun hits halfway.*

"Old man." I whisper, peering into the shade. The merchant busies himself with salvaging broken bottles of shine and jugs filled with what looks like wine. The bloody color stains the sand.

He mutters to himself in a language I don't understand. "I'm not buying."

"Okay, but I have something that –"

He curses at me, curses Er Rada and the surrounding territories as he throws his hands up. Then, he stands, tossing the curtain of his canopy down to block me out with a crazed look in his eye.

"No! I need to trade with you!"

My pleas go entirely unanswered. I can nearly feel the ring burning into my finger, the powder begging to be sold.

"Mystics damn you!" I kick the baseboard, spit on his torn colors, and twist back to the street. The sky is fading into a darkened afternoon. I'm running out of time to get settled before sunset. My efforts to leave this dust pit are slowly thinning into desperation.

THREE

ADESSA

"You will never be safe here, little berry."

The wiry, abandoned road ahead seems daunting, but I don't stop myself from shuffling along, passing the farm where I'd last seen the camels. It doesn't look like they're even there anymore. Maybe they've already been sold. I continue onward, knocking loose pebbles out of my path with half-numb feet. My mind can't help but slowly wander back to the girl as another wave of defeat burrows deep into my chest. It's nearly strong enough to pull me to my knees.

She'd been brave enough to *shoot* me, and at close range, too. Which makes me think that maybe she wouldn't have been a complete burden if I brought her along.

No.

I couldn't take that chance. The path I'm on isn't something I would willingly drag another person into. There's no point in punishing a kid with my obsession anyway. I quicken my pace, remembering the look on her face when she shot at the chandelier instead of me. Was that regret or relief that made her make that look? Or was it the fear of almost killing someone? Has she killed before?

She would be in quite a shock if she learned that I would have survived any attempt she made on my life regardless. Something that few others have realized in the past. They didn't live long enough to spill my secret to others. Tirma was the only one who knew from the start. When she found me lying there in the middle of that terrible winter storm, she assumed I was dead. I had thought she was a witch from early stories I'd heard shared around the fires. A witch who brought me back to life on her own to trap me in her cave. There had been gossip about her in my village, about her losing her mind for the purpose of gaining a different kind of knowledge back.

I was naïve and too young at the time to know how true their rumors were. Most of my childhood was lived in fear and awe of the woman I assumed saved my life. But when it came time, I was late in telling her that I believed her side of the story more.

When I was nearly killed a second time, and then a third, and woke up without her help, I realized that it wasn't her doing like I previously thought. I was successfully, painfully, brought back each and every time by whatever curse plagues me. To this day, I still cannot explain it and am only left with gruesome reminders on scarred skin. And the emotion-al weight of knowing it will never end.

I rub my shoulder, where the holes from the bullets should be, now replaced with fresh pink scar tissue. If the Mystics truly are real like Tirma believed with every ounce of her being, like the crazed monks who used to roam the streets of Skeall would preach in strange murmurs believed as well, they are cruel. Preventing my death is a torture that I've never agreed to endure. I have no reasoning as to why I have to endure it in the first place. Tirma used to ramble on and on about how this gift was not meant to be a punishment, but each time, I would wave her off and avoid her mindless words.

I'd rather not be stranded here in this suffering, in a world filled with horrendous memories and an unforgiving and now foreign climate that offers me nothing but unrest. Maybe once all of this is over, They will grant me release. Once I finally make it to Darde, once I finally hold the severed head of the Lapis in my hands - by the Mystics, I'll force them to end my suffering. Perhaps I won't even have to strike a deal. Revenge would be enough to satiate them. I've heard they enjoy that.

The ring twirls around and around absentmindedly between my fingers, most likely in the makings of an anxious habit. The kid used 'was' when referring to her family members earlier. Something that I didn't want to relate to at the time but can't help but reflect on now that I'm alone. I hope the memory of them fades for her soon, if only to help ease that pain. There is no use in trying to remember the past. It's unfortunate that I can't forget my own; I'd take these physical scars over the mental ones any day. Sadly, I'm stranded with both.

I grind my teeth together, swallowing hard at my reason for leaving the Far North, reaching a shaded area with a cluster of overhanging palms. They've been stripped bare for Death Rites. Which means it may not be smart for me to rest beneath them, but the day leans so heavily on me that I find myself wandering over. The loss of not obtaining a camel is finally setting in. The reopening blisters on my feet throb, making the scabs itch as they heal. The hard sand is too much for them to remain bare for much longer.

I rushed out of the house too quickly, fearful that I would have given in. That damned merchant too. All of this wouldn't have happened if the shine ended up being real. I feel a twinge in my stomach; there are so few traders. The last one I'd seen had his wagon completely overturned and torn apart, and he was dead. Propped up against his cow's carcass, picked clean by hungry vultures, with a sign, written in what I can only assume was his blood, which stated the territory owners.

Jidaani.

He must not have had permission to trade here. According to my map, their territory reaches nearly half the continent, if he was unable to sell in this territory, who knows how many others won't venture this way. I don't know when I'll get another chance to sell to a trader again.

Leaning back against the narrow trunk of the palm, I inhale the sweet tang of the Earth, shading myself from the blaring sun. It's already near the horizon. My map marks a town not too far from Er Rada, but now I'm rethinking following the Red Line completely. If I head straight east, eventually, I'll come up on a river; at least, that's what my map claims. There will be settlements there if it hasn't already dried up. Give me time to resupply and maybe update my map for the moment I cross.

I take a swig of warm water, mindful of the amount I have left in my waterskin, and drift my hand to the opening of the satchel beside me, feeling the uneasy need to account for everything I have. It's not like it makes a difference if I've accidentally left anything behind; I won't be turning around anyway.

Inside sits the canvas pouch of coins, the two containers of poison, a small portion of uncooked rice, and mashed pieces of fruit that I'd impatiently dried myself weeks ago, and now they're showing clear signs of rot. Gnarled flint lays at the very bottom of the bag, one that's been used one too many times. My wrinkled parchment map is here too, hand drawn by the traveler who'd given it to me in exchange for a single night beside a warm body, marked further by my own hand when I could. My compass rests beneath it, the one that chooses to work only when it decides to, usually never when I need it to. Tirma's gift to me long ago. I brush my fingertip along the roughly engraved 'A' on the lid.

This is all I have left. I feel the urge to laugh; it isn't like I had very much to begin with, thinking back to the donkey I'd stolen from my neighbor's barn all those years ago in the Far North. How I lost him less than a week into my journey, along with the majority of my stolen supplies. I was ill-equipped and much younger than I am now – too young – and unsure of what to do when confronted by roamers. Even more unsure of my ability to fight back. I'd never left the outskirts of Skeall or the mountains before and wasn't truly aware of the cost of doing so. It's funny when you finally realize how little you have when you're made to survive with nothing.

FOUR

ADESSA

"As it always has and always would."

Exhaustion grips me like a vice as I wrap myself in a bundle beneath the palm. So much so, that I don't realize dusk had been swiftly approaching before it's too late. The days are like that now: shorter. In contrast, the nights grow tiresomely long. If I were back in the Far North, it would be winter; not like the snow ever really stopped coming down. I shiver at the thought of being back in those caves, huddling in the unsettling corners of the alcoves, to stay warm, trying to start fires with frostbitten fingers and drinking from obelisks of ice, or the occasional stream that had yet to freeze over. Cursing the Mystics for another night, time and time again.

I am at least consoled by the fact that I will never have to deal with a northern winter again. Stories of the East are promising, but that's all they are – stories. I hold tightly to the hope that neither snow nor drought plagues the lands the Elites once fled to. The Mystics had to have smiled down on their journey if they made it all the way to Darde, like it's claimed they had. They wouldn't have fled to an area that had worse weather than they were used to.

The sun waves its final goodnight by the time I finally have the energy to build a fire. Traveling in the dark, in unknown territory, no less, isn't worth the risk to me at the moment. Even if it means being exposed to the empty road ahead, my only option seems to be to stay under the grove at least until daybreak. I'll make a run for it in the morning to hopefully make up some time.

I peel back the bark from the nearly stripped tree behind me with chipped fingernails, adding strips to the fire a little at a time. *No distractions tomorrow. Early start.*

My mind's feeble attempt to soothe my nerves fails to comfort me once again. I haven't made nearly enough progress over the years; I spent far too long in Isla, which was filled with distractions of how I wished my life could be.

There is still too much ground to cover before I finally reach the sea and, beyond that, an entirely new continent to cover. Completely new problems. I squeeze my temples, trying not to hold onto the daunting journey ahead, and pull out the dried, questionable fruit jerky instead, instantly regretting not having purchased fresh meat from the butcher earlier. It might have been worth the money. I'd even settle for some rice right now, but I don't have a pot to cook it in, and I wouldn't want to risk using the rest of my drinking water to boil it anyway.

The soft crackle of fire begins lulling me into a skewed sense of security. Who am I kidding? No one is ever safe in the desert, no matter if I'm dressed in men's clothing or not. Despite all that, my eyelids can't help but feel heavy. I haven't been able to get proper rest in so long. I nestle my head against the bulky pack, tossing around the items inside to make it more comfortable, and wrap my jacket tightly as I inch closer to the flames like a feral cat desperate to keep warm.

My thoughts derail, reminding me of the death dealt but not received, of the missed opportunities that I can't seem to forget about. It seems to be the only thing I can focus on when I'm alone. The jerky turns to rubber and sours in my mouth. My nose crinkles when I force myself to swallow before throwing the remaining strips into the fire where they belong. The flames hiss and pop in equal repulsion, melting into the sand like wax from a candle.

Now I'm out of water, trying to wash the taste from my tongue. The shredded mattress inside that house would have been more comfortable than this rough sand. If I stayed, I would have had a roof over my head, a water source to replenish with. I left when I should have stayed, but I was in denial about befriending the girl. She was alone, too. Desperate, like me. I wonder how much more either of us can take.

Fresh start tomorrow.

I grasp the sliver of positivity but still feel the need to pinch myself a few final times in frustration. *I wish, I wish, I wish I didn't have to do this by myself. I wish I didn't have to do this in the first place.*

My mind takes me back to Isla, to the date trees that I used to climb, to the man who treated me like one of his own, to the life I wish I still had before that too, no longer belonged to me. Thankfully, sleep pulls me under, helping me push all of my troubles aside, if only for a few hours.

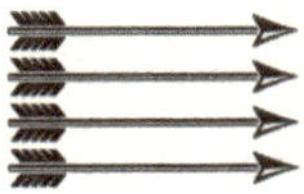

"Look! It *is* a woman!"

I wake suddenly to a rough kick against my feet and rub the sleep from my eyes, feeling my heart completely stop beating. A man's booming voice roars ahead of me. "She's awake! Grab her!"

Shit. This isn't one of my nightmares. This is *real.*

I push away from the burly man just in time before he's able to reach my ankles. My knee bucks, kicking at his face. He dodges it, latching onto my calf, yanking me flat on my back. My head hits the base of the tree as I go, fingernails clawing the bark behind me, then the ground, reaching for a protruding bushel of dying fire. The embers flare at the end of the partially lit mangle when I swing, meeting its mark – the stranger's face. Sparks fly. He yowls, releasing his hold on me, frantically patting the burning ashes that will surely blister the skin.

That allows me time to scramble to my feet.

I realize it isn't just him that I'm up against. There are two more flanked on either side of me. I hiss at them like a cornered animal. *Dammit, Adessa, how did you not hear them coming? Careless! Careless!*

The larger of the three runs for me, extending his hand out. It's scarred, with white lines deepening his forearm that are so raised and gnarled that I can see the curves easily under the light of the moon. Above those marks are three familiar symbols. It's the man from the marketplace. I dodge right before his fingers can brush against me. The man with fresh burns scrambles to his feet, shouting a string of curses at me with a mouthful of missing teeth. The third man chuckles. I'm trapped. Each one of them sheds the packs that are strapped across their backs, preparing themselves not to be weighed down.

I attempt to run around the trunk of the palm, but the tattooed one is too quick. His enormous hands latch onto a clump of my hair, and I'm thrown backward onto the sand. Blinding agony disorients me as my fingers move to the torn spot on my head, feeling the warm trickle of blood coat its tips.

"Fucking – asshole!" I swear, breathing heavily, frantically looking for a means to escape. The three men form a line in front of me, with the one in the middle pressing gently on his boiled cheek.

"Ack, this one won't sell. Look at her. Might as well do everyone a favor and kill her."

The man from the merchant's stand snickers, a sadistic smile plastering his face when he inches closer. I need to get out of here – there – the shorter one on the right staggers with a limp. He could be taken down. A distraction. I hold onto my senses and pull into a sprint before anyone can make a move for me, darting directly toward the staggering man, narrowly avoiding the outstretched hands of the other two. I fall to one leg, kick out with the other, right into his knee. He buckles inward, landing heavily on his side, crying out in a mixture of shock and outrage. I take the opportunity and book it.

The others howl and yip as they chase after me like a pack of dogs, not bothering to help their injured friend like I thought they would. I keep my sight trained on the empty space ahead. I *will* be faster than them. I have no choice. My thighs pump harder than they've had to in a long while.

Eventually, the labored breathing behind me quiets, sounding more distant. Still, I won't stop running, unknowing of the direction I've chosen, knowing that it isn't west but praying to the Mystics that I'm still heading east. Luckily, they didn't appear to have any animals with them and no means of catching up to me other than on foot. Clearly, I'm faster.

They have to have given up by now, right? What would the point be in chasing me all this way if I wasn't worth keeping alive anyway? *Sadists.*

I slow to a jog, grateful for the still-dark night that camouflages me while I continue to kick up sand until my feet are raw.

Finally, my hopes flutter when I see the outline of a small compound appearing along my line of sight just as the sun begins to greet the morning. My lungs feel weighed down with sand. I'm lucky the winds were low, but my feet, my calves, everything hurts with the soreness of a night spent running. I feel the wounds on my toes split open against sharp gravel the closer I approach the village borders. The fence that outposts the broken gate ahead beckons for me to come closer, if only to catch my breath against it. I reach for -

No, no, no!

I curse, feeling the space beside me where my satchel should be. I hadn't noticed that it wasn't strapped against my chest when I was running. I was too focused on getting away. Everything I need is inside that damned bag! I pat myself down, checking pockets that offer nothing but empty regret. I want to scream at the top of my lungs, uncaring who hears me. Instead, I let out my frustrations on the fence, punching the wooden rails until my knuckles bleed. I don't have a choice. I'll have to move on without – everything. The last thing I will do is confront those men, especially without any weapon. I barely managed to take down the one, I'd never be able to take on all three.

My coins. I want to weep.

FIVE

YOON

"Here lies the Lapis. May his bloodline end at the tip of my sword."

"What are you three doing out here?" I tug at the ropes attached to the trio of camels behind me. "I could have sworn Jax told you to wait for me."

My horse stops before them, stomping his hooves impatiently as the animals behind us rumble and groan. Aol and Burke flank either side of an injured Gunn, who rubs his knee in rough circles just before their – fire.

"What is that?" I ask. I'm unanswered. "Why does your fire look like that?"

The gnarled branches of dried shrubs rest in a burning teepee, unlike our usual way of burying the pit in the sand. Less smoke for signaling our location, less chance of being discovered. These three did not build this fire. Aol shrugs his shoulders, almost guilt-ridden. Burke stares at me with open distaste. Not unusual for him to do so.

I've just spent half the evening searching for these three, finally deciding that they chose to disobey Jax's orders to wait for me. It's a good thing I realized that a while ago; turns out my hunch was correct.

"What happened to your face?"

Aol gingerly taps his cheek with the last of our healing paste, smoothing it over watery blisters, playing off the fact that he looks like he's fallen face-first into the flames. "I –"

Burke shoves him, motioning for the other two to shut their mouths.

"What's that?" I question, hopping down from Hisan to better understand what Aol clutches in his lap.

"Found it on the road back there." He stands as tall as he can appear, lifting the gray satchel like it's a prize, making me have a tough time believing it had been 'found' without any of their involvement.

"I see." I grab it, giving it a shake. "And you three had nothing to do with this being – abandoned, huh?"

No answer. I tuck the sack into one of the camel's saddlebags, making a mental note to investigate it later. Not now, we're too out in the open. At least there aren't any dead bodies around that I can see. That offers some relief.

"Camels?" Gunn states, tiptoeing towards the animal to the right. It snorts, shifting to the side.

"Last three at the farm." I hand the leads to the man everyone calls Bonehead.

"How did you pay –" Burke starts. I hold my hand out to stop him, watching him glower at the slight command.

"We have Aol to thank for that." He starts immediately patting himself down. "Took a few of those gems you'd been hiding."

Aol gasps, realizing that the twin quartz he kept squirreled away in the lining of his tunic are no longer there. If he looks in his bag, he'll also notice the jasper is gone.

"What? Did you expect me to have us all *walk* to Jynn? Because if so –"

"You had no right!" He shouts over me, following a string of slurs that no one man should ever say to another, let alone the one who they once deemed to lead them.

"Oh please, they weren't yours to begin with anyway. Spend your greedy thefts on something useful. They're worthless if you keep them hidden."

"But you –"

"Shut it Aol." Burke smacks him across the back of his head, shutting him up immediately. "Remember what we've been told. Once we get to Jynn, we'll be *drowning* in wealth. You won't miss your stones. Isn't that right, *Qa'id?*"

He locks eyes with mine. I don't miss the apparent sarcasm lining his words. At the obvious lie I once told them that he has easily seen right through, but for whatever reason, the other two can't. They've always been blinded to the truth.

"But that was all I had left! We're completely out of – everything!"

Gunn tries to play off the fact that his knee doesn't buckle as he straightens, forcing my attention once more. "What's wrong with your leg?"

I breathe out, suddenly very aware of our situation. Something feels off.

"Bit sore. That's all."

My brows furrow, annoyed, but I make the easy decision to move from the topic. They're alive; maybe I wandered in on them trying to plan something, but as of right now, there doesn't seem to be an ambush planned. I must have caught them at the right time.

"Jax is meeting us in Teryal." I scan the men's faces. "I have a plan to make more silver. We won't be without for much longer."

The men groan.

"Then what? It will give us barely enough to survive the next week? We all know the road ahead, only this time, we are completely faction-less. We've barely had enough to scrape by to get us to Er Rada, and now you've taken the last of our funds to buy camels we didn't need yet. How will we eat? Will you feed us with your charm?"

Aol has always been too vocal. Burke watches our interaction in silence.

"You act as though you haven't lived through worse." My glare makes both Gunn and Aol shift in place. "Did you not see our names on the bounties?" I make it a point to drive the words into Burke. "They've reached Er Rada too early. We needed a faster way to Jynn."

"Well, I suppose we could sell your daggers if necessary."

My blood boils at the comment. "Touch my daggers, Aol, and you will never see daylight again."

I nearly feel the bone blades at either side of my hips begin to heat. I would sooner shove the tips into each of their hearts before I contemplated parting with them. "Trust me, I will get us enough silver, and I'll buy you meat and shine to make up for it."

Gunn licks his lips in response.

"Trust you!" Burke begins kicking sand over the makeshift fire with a laugh. "We'll see how much further this trust can carry us. You said the further east we went, the less likely we would run into bounties, even though we all knew it to be untrue. What happens if those contracts beat us to this precious city of yours?"

I keep forgetting that these three have never been sent to the ports. They don't know how it will be.

Before I can respond, he pushes past me, lifting himself onto the saddle of the largest camel of the three. I roll my eyes at the outright defiance, knowing full well that *he* was the one asking about the price of my head earlier. He isn't concerned about the bounties, not when he knows his means nothing when compared to mine.

This is my own fault, really; I'm dealing with the consequences of allowing these three to tag along. I did hope that they would only last as a distraction, a means to an end. At the time, I didn't care that I'd been toying with their own fates as well, and now, after nearly a year with them, I wish I had abandoned them in Farit. But where else would they go? They only know what our clan has given them. The lives they lived before joining have been entirely forgotten. So, sadly, I've already made up my mind that I would help them at least get out of Jidaani territory;

what happens after is out of my hands. I hoist myself onto Hisan to match the Damirian, who tries to outrank me every day.

"The bounties won't reach further. Bahani lands, remember?"

Aol fidgets with the drying clay on his cheek before joining us on the animal closest to Burke. Gunn follows quietly to the last pick. "Bahani lands." He mumbles quietly under his breath, forcing the air around us to grow tense.

We all know who is on the other side of those contracts, how easy it would be for him to plague any city, in any direction with the ideals of us being traitors. However, I find myself desperately clinging to the fact that Jynn is safe. Geal once believed that I would help her gain access to the Red Line. That I would help her with her war.

But that was before I left Grandia. I'm not sure if the news has spread that way yet, or if she's heard that I've become a traitor. I'm relying solely on the hope that she hasn't.

SIX

ADESSA

"And so, they soon took on other forms, disturbed by the unrest. War, Famine, Plague, Death. The world no longer knew peace." Excerpt from the fantastical writing of Hidaal, Copy Of Mystics, 2,400 T.A. Based from verbiage of The Script, Time Unknown.

Very few things frighten me.

The stories of the Blood Market is at the top of that list. That's where the rarest, most desired items are claimed to be traded within the walls of an ancient city somewhere off of the Red Line. Where the runners bring their slaves to be sold. Where visitors are not allowed in, not without permission. Where gold is used to tile the floors; due to sheer abundance, no longer being valued as currency but as a show of caste. The stories I've heard about this infamous market make my bones weary.

To be trapped there – it's a fate worse than death and not the kind of life I would be willing to suffer through either. I've always been so cautious, especially after realizing that I could easily end up in a place like that. If anyone found out about my ability to evade death, who knows what possibility they would consider.

That's my main concern with being followed by those men. They would surely find a way to sell me, market me at a price that would satisfy the slave runners. If they belong to a clan like I believe they do, thanks to the set of tattoos on the larger of the three, then they would have to know where the Blood Market is. Everyone on this continent seems to know about it. Arthur made sure I did, too. Unfortunately he forgot to mention *where* it is.

I suppose this is my own fault for wanting to travel along the Red Line, for putting myself in this amount of potential danger, but I've been told that it's the clearest path to the sea. Otherwise, I would have had to navigate the Barrens in the north, or the Saddleback Mountains in the south, and who knows how many craters and canyons formed by the Time Before would disrupt my entire route if I chose those options. The Red Line is reliable; one simple trade route from east to west. Easy enough. Hopefully.

The height of the morning wakes the little village beyond the gates. Maybe it's just irrational panic that forces an uneasy feeling to find a home in my belly. I've waited past sunrise, nervous to see three silhouettes on the horizon in search of me, but the men never came. Still, I can't help but wonder if this town would be a good place to stop in if they happened to be heading on the same path as me. They saw the direction I was running in, I didn't veer too far off course. I wish I had my map to know exactly where I am. I'm hoping it's Teryal. I am on the right track if it's Teryal.

I breathe out a flare of frustration, trudging past desert-worn buildings, in search of a place to lie low for a while longer, just in case. The smell of cooking oils in the air is too overwhelming for my empty stomach, especially this early in the morning. It forces me to weave behind a handful of sand-rotten houses, past a small, empty wagon, behind a yellowing building marked with a slanted wooden sign above the frame that reads 'Harmon's' in lazy painted writing.

Wincing, I gingerly peel back a large chunk of skin that hangs from the edge of my foot, an open blister. I'll need to wrap these again otherwise they'll begin to heal with sand trapped under the skin. Using my teeth, I shred the oversized shirt at the hem, stripping it, one for each foot and gently brush sand from my raw flesh. The wrappings go on easy enough, but the fabric is far too skinny to help in any way. It's all I can do for now.

My nose becomes distracted by the smell of food cooking inside the marked building, and my stomach roars with uncomfortable greed.

Fine.

I shush my thoughts, giving in to the temptation, and wander to the front of the steps. The dusty stairs lead up to a door covered in what are clearly old blood stains. The wall near the frame is riddled with holes. Still, I find myself stepping inside.

There are only two other people that I can see, locals, by the looks of if, sitting side by side at a creaky, oval table. The man, hair tied back into a knot at the top of his head, is deeply enjoying whatever meal graces his bowl, with a woman sat beside him. He plucks a cigarette from her mouth and peers up at me when I pass, piercing blue eyes following my every move. I notice his companion's head lower towards her lap in dis-crete obedience. Her own meal is untouched.

There's a quiet buzzing of flies hovering above the contents of what-ever is rotting inside the empty glassware that's scattered along the bar counter near the right side of the smokey room. I opt for a seat in the furthest corner, trying my best not to draw attention to the woman be-hind the bar. Before I know it, I'm in a chair that rests along one of the pillars, rubbing the dried patch of blood on my scalp. At least it's begin-ning to crust up.

With no money to pay for food, starvation really seems to be getting the better of me, seeing as my wounds aren't healing nearly as quickly as they usually would. I know I shouldn't be here but I can't help myself. I can't help the way my mouth salivates from the mix of salt and the sour-tinged blend of tobacco. It's enough to make my belly cramp with nausea. I try to focus on anything else.

I don't know how long I sit there, my chin lowered, arms crossed, leaning the chair against the back of the splintered corner, allowing my mind to wander as I stare bleakly at the edge of the table. Drumming up an impossible plan of my next move before the front door swings open and closed, turning my wild imagination into flames. It conjures up fears of seeing triangular tattoos, a blistered face, and a man with a limp cornering me in this bar. I lower my head further still, unwilling to look to confirm my terror. My face buries itself in the folds of my jacket. I can only hope that the dust covering the length of my body will camouflage me somehow.

The scraping of chairs at the table across from me settles my nerves ever so slightly, if only for a moment. It isn't them; they would have me in their grasp by now if it were, right? The hushed tones of the newcomer's voices draw my interest upwards instead. If I want to act naturally, I cannot stay frozen in fear.

"The traveler wasn't lying to us; I confirmed it before you got here. Darde is plagued with riots." His voice is low and hard to make out, but my ears prickle at the mention of the city in the east.

Riots?

The comment comes from a heavily armed man who has most of his back turned to me. He speaks in a much softer tone than I would have expected from his stature. Long, ebony hair falls in cords entwined with an assortment of beads that look like various shades of bone. On his back, a long broadsword is attached, and a quiver of arrows wraps itself along the outside of his upper thigh.

From what I can see, he wears iron cuffs on both wrists, large enough to make a clanging sound as they bang against the table. Thick leather boots, clearly worn, and a loose-fitting tunic a shade lighter than his own skin, deepened even darker from being out in an unforgiving sun with little cover. Paired with a sand scarf and heavily pocketed pants that match nearly all the same shade, his outfit tells me that this man is used to being out in the heat. From where he sits, it's hard to make out the features of the other person beside him.

"This could benefit –" He pauses, thrumming the tabletop. His braids swish along his back while he surveys the room. I miss the rest of his words, the blue-eyed man at the next table stops eating, forgoing the contents of his fork mid-air to watch me watch them, curiosity glazing his features. I've been observing for too long. I look away, distracted by an older woman, clad in a stained cotton garb, a yellow bandana tied around her neck. She steps out from the double doors behind the bar, making her way past the counter, to the pair ahead of me.

"We'll still be able to –" The stranger's voice whispers as the woman approaches them.

"Already here far tha bottles, eh? I din't expect ya tah be here til tonight."

I glance up, watching the men stand, bowing their heads before taking the pair of tin cups from her weathered hands. She steps back, crossing her arms, offering them both a frown as they settle back into their chairs.

"There was a change of plans."

A different voice, somewhat harsher than the other's, speaks while his partner laughs quietly, slurping down his drink in a single go.

"Fine. Give me an hour."

The other voice chimes in once the woman removes herself from their table, busying with a large pot that oozes with a deliciously sickening aroma of boiled vegetables. I sink into myself, as if doing so will make my accidental eavesdropping unnoticeable.

"We can trust Geal. I hope." There's a pause. "We can't trust them. And now, I honestly don't know if we ever were able to."

The braided man leans back in his chair. "Hm."

"You should have heard them today. My –"

"Don't say it." Iron cuffs clink as a hand raises. "Please, don't say it. You may as well tell me what this new plan of yours is, because I already know what you're about to say and now, I'm at a loss." A clearing of the throat. "You do *have* a new one." It doesn't sound like a question.

"Cut them loose."

That is all that's answered. He sighs, the tone of it forcing me to finally take a peek at who the voice belongs to. I shift carefully in my seat, adjusting my line of sight, but not before making sure Blue Eyes isn't still intrigued. He is.

Choppy, shadowed hair falls past the outline of the stranger's shoulder, loosely tied in the back, framing a rounder face with a tight jawline. I draw my gaze up, needing to scan the rest of his features and keep myself from gasping at what I see. A crooked, raised scar marks his sun-beaten skin, starting at the tip of his right eyebrow, across his eye and over the bridge of his nose, ending harshly at the base of his left cheek.

Something isn't right.

I feel heat blushing my cheeks right as his gaze begins wandering over to mine. My head shoots downwards, finding the uneven floorboards *much* more interesting.

"No."

He whispers, quietly enough for me to almost disregard it completely. His friend doesn't seem to notice. "What are you saying? I thought –"

There's a block of hesitation before the man with the scar finally answers. "Burke was asking about –" He lowers his voice, so much so that I can't make out the rest of his sentence.

"Bounty? He wouldn't do that."

The response is immediate. *Bounty?* I wonder if they've come from Er Rada as well, seeing as the merchant was the only one alive that I've seen so far, and with that many contracts on the canvas wall of his cano-py – I try to make a connection with the names and faces I briefly grazed over but can't seem to be able to. *Are these men hunting a bounty?*

A chuckle follows. "Jax, I don't know what else you want me to say. He's using us. Has been for at least the entire time he's been riding with us."

"Well, it isn't like we aren't using him too." His partner retorts; seemingly depleted. Their conversation slows at the sound of wooden legs scraping against the floorboards. I peer back at the silent tension that filters through the room and watch the man from the table behind them stand, dusting the crumbs of his finished meal from his pants.

He casually swipes at the mustache that's overgrowing his lips. His eyes lock with mine again.

He flicks the cigarette, aiming for his bowl. I see the woman beside him keep her head low, same as before, but I can feel her gaze centering itself on me as her companion moves my way, a tilted smile on his dirty face. I pretend that I am simply a part of the wall, squeezing even closer to the bare pillar behind me. If there's only one way out of here, the way we've all come in from, I'm screwed. Unless – there has to be another way through the back, or through the doorway behind the counter. I prepare myself to run, or to fight, shuffling my scabbing feet away from the legs of the table.

I knew I was already pushing my luck being in a place like this, no money to spend, no interaction with the woman running the place. Is he going to confront me about being here? He takes another step. A deep swell of panic blossoms in my chest.

"Let me see those eyes of yours, sweetheart." Blue Eyes coos, passing the other two at the table. Before his sentence is complete, the scarred one jumps to his feet, holding the tip of a dagger against the mustached man's throat. I didn't even see him unclip it.

"Turn around."

He says hoarsely, pushing the edge deep enough to prick stubbled skin. The bead of crimson is a stark contrast against the white-bone blade. Blue Eyes jeers, tucking a hand into his pocket. I can feel the thickness in the air, the steady silence that makes even the old woman take notice. He moves his gaze slowly between me and the stranger threatening him. The other man, Jax, leans back in his chair with casual ease, teasing the handle of the knife at his calf. His partner tilts his mouth into a morose smile, as if to say that starting a fight would lead to a life lost.

The lone man also seems to understand that concept, spitting a tarnished brown glob onto the ground a few inches from my poorly wrapped feet.

"All yours."

He turns back with his hands raised, roughly plucking the woman from her seat. She catches my gaze again, a sadness emptying from her expression while she follows him out the front door. It bangs against the frame loudly enough to get his point across. I can't help but know she isn't trailing behind willingly.

My attention roams back to the remaining two as the scarred man sheathes his dagger beside its twin. Both seem to be carved from the same material throughout from blade to hilt, the handle stained darker, nearly brown. The blade itself is a light bone color, contrasted against a single dark, moss colored stone centered in each handle. Something about them makes my heart flit a beat faster. I flick my eyes upwards to stop myself from being so entranced, only to end up holding the gaze of the man who owns them.

He centers his sight on mine so firmly, compelling me to swallow the lump in my throat. Finally, I notice that the pupil of his right eye is a milky white, while the other is a deep brown. *Is he – blind?*

I remember seeing an oracle wandering about the streets of Isla one afternoon when I was little. It terrified me. Her eyes were completely white. A cook in our kitchen ended up finding me hidden among the baskets of wheat, consoling my fears, holding me as she listened carefully.

"She has been blinded by the Mystics. So she can see. Do you understand?"

I remember her wiping my tears, sending me off with one of the pies Arthur's harem favored. The next time I saw the oracle, I wasn't afraid.

I look away from the memory as the decorated man rises with the soft motion of his partner's hand and find myself gripping the table so tightly, my knuckles beg for me to release it. A few nervous ticks go by before the two strangers finally leave their table. They don't move toward me like I feared, opting for the counter instead, where the older woman shakes her head, pouring a cloudy liquid into an enormous basin against the wall. She gives it a stir, whistling an unrecognizable tune to herself. The soft gurgle of it boiling follows a sweet aroma that wafts through the air, blending itself with the other scents in the room.

The scarred man motions his hand in my direction, his partner, Jax distractedly watches the exit. He moves in to whisper something to the woman when she leans over the counter, then nods in my direction as well, pinching her lips in a tight line when he places a small stack of coins in her hand. He takes a very slight glance my way once more, digging into his pocket, adding two more coins to the pile. Then, he simply leaves, his armed friend leading the way, shutting the door behind them with a click. I finally release the breath I'd been holding.

"Yah look a mess. All that sand."

The woman clicks her tongue, her sight following the path of dust I left in my wake when I arrived, leading up to where I sit. She steps out from behind the bar, a metal tray in her hand, swaying towards
me with age. "Relax."

Her voice is hoarse. She sets the tin down on the table, noting the white-knuckled grip I still hold along its edge. "No one will hurt yah here, so stop hurting mah table."

Her accent flares with a tone that I haven't heard on this side of the continent, or anywhere else for that matter. She reeks of tobacco, even more than the smokey room. My gut twists with need for something – anything – to satiate it.

I unlatch myself and stretch out my fingers, desperate to relax, to show her that I'm not a threat, and eye the meal in front of me. The tray holds a ceramic bowl of broth, with what looks like radish and what I hope is some type of cabbage floating around in the brown liquid. Next to the bowl is a fist sized portion of crusty bread, a metal cup nestled be-side it. The aroma of coffee oozes from its lip. She motions for me to eat, as if assuming that I don't have the ability to speak the language known by most, then pulls out the chair across from me and settles herself in silence.

Does she expect me to pay for this once I'm finished?

I hold the bowl up to my nose and sniff.

I'm sure I was caught listening in on a conversation not meant for my ears, is that why he was pointing in my direction? Is this poisoned?

It doesn't smell like it's been tampered with, but one can never be too sure. There are many tasteless poisons out there, especially when disguised with food. Botter, for one, has been used for centuries after the Firsts created it from runoff. Ligre, a horrible paste that forces one's body to seize has been utilized for much longer. And of course, the most unpleasant of them all – motte. I hope I won't be as unlucky to ingest something like that in this life.

It's a Blood Market poison, created by pure evil, some say by the Mystics themselves. It liquefies its victim's organs, turning them to a black sludge that leaks from every pore. I have no idea how the stuff is made, or what it even looks like. I've only heard of it being used once somewhere near the Tracs. It was enough to know how unimaginable it would be to die from it, let alone survive the effects, if one even could.

"Food's safe tah eat. Don't have it in me tah kill a young girl."

A firm line settles between her brows. Heat rises in my cheeks when she makes another motion for me to eat, so I force myself to nod a gentle bow of thanks. The spoon is light in my hand when I dip it into the steamy broth, holding the contents to my lips. It ripples thickly when I blow, the warmth tickling my nose.

"Not from around here I take it?" Her voice fades into the distance the moment the broth hits my tongue.

It's salty, but so very comforting and my stomach groans in pure bliss when the liquid slips down my throat with ease. My body almost hums in dramatic fashion, finally getting the sustenance it's been craving for *weeks*. The coffee is equally salty, the flavor tasting a bit more like burnt oil, but I am still so grateful for it. I tear off a corner of the flatbread and shove it into my pocket for later, using the remaining section to sop up the remnants in the bowl, leaving not a single trace of stew behind.

My tongue burns, draining the last bit of thick sludge from the coffee tin, warming my blood as it joins the food in my cramping belly. I allow only a moment to slip past me while I fully process the meal, the fact that this woman watched me eat the entire thing in near silence makes me not only uneasy but intrigued. She's patient. Probably waiting to be paid.

"Well! Ate that rather quick!"

"I – uh –" I start, rubbing my hands along the sides of my borrowed pants. "I appreciate the meal." I glance around the room, wondering how to get myself out of the predicament I now find myself in.

"The girl speaks!" She claps her hands, raising the corners of her mouth in entertainment. My foot taps the floor nervously, unsure of her reaction, of how to explain myself. I should have never wandered in here.

"I can offer –" I twist the ring around and around as my voice trails off, unwilling to let it go now when I was so willing to be rid of it not a day earlier. It could hold much more value in the future rather than merely being payment for such a simple, yet lifesaving meal.

The laugh she throws out turns into a hefty cough.

"Food's already been paid fahr." The woman rises from her seat. "Only wanted tah see yah sweat fahr a moment is all."

She stands with a hand slap to the tabletop, leaving me in my chair, stunned.

Food's been paid for? Is that why the scarred man was looking at me like that?

All yours. That's what Blue Eyes said to him before shrinking away with his tail between his legs. My heartbeat deepens. That stranger will be waiting for his own repayment no doubt. Nothing is free in this world, even if it's disguised as something that could be considered kind. That's a lesson I learned a long time ago. My eyes dart to the front door again. I don't have anything that he would want to trade with and I am not willing to – I shake my thoughts clear while heading toward the counter, bringing the empty tray along with me, setting it down before the woman who busies herself with pol-ishing an incredibly grimy glass with the inside of her apron. She grins at me, showing a single tooth that is barely hanging onto her blood-red gums.

"That man, with the scars on his face. Is he the one who paid for this?"

She gives me a once over, squinting. "Yah know him?"
I shake my head, not wanting to be associated with anyone from the area. My goal is to be a ghost, not attract too much attention, and get to the port on time.

"I see." Her weathered hand sets the tray on the ledge beside her. "Saved yah from Rust." A tilt of her head. "Yah're sure yah don't know him?"

I nearly recoil at her prying. She merely chuckles, shaking her head. "Rust." She repeats, leaning in. She tugs at the bandana around her neck when I don't answer. "Mister mustache." Her thumb crosses her upper lip in disgust.

"That isn't why –" I sigh. "Why do you think I know him? The – other man."

"Well, he stepped in. Doesn't seem the type tah meddle in another stranger's business is all now that –" She stops herself. "Anyways, good thing is all. Wouldn't want yah tah end up like that other girl. Poor kid. Her mother was kind."

I shiver at the implication of what her words could mean. I also don't know what else to say. My toes point towards the door, beckoning me to walk as fast as my sore feet allow.

"Need coin?" She calls out when I nearly reach the handle, watching me as I turn to face her with curiosity, waving with both hands to reel me back. Movements of her billowing sleeves reveals a matching pair of faded tattoos on the fronts of both forearms. Two arrows on each, four total, pointing in the same direction.

Only clan members have markings. To show their factions, even when their body lays to rot. *She belongs to a clan?*

"See this pot?" Her fingers wag at the steel basin behind her, redirecting my attention. I nod meekly. "I'm too old tah lift the damned thing nowadays. Have been fahr quite some time." She pauses, as if waiting for a reaction that will work in her favor. "If yah take it round' back fahr me, I'll pay ya. Fahr yah're – discretion. Whether yah know what it tis or what it tisn't."

A quick gesture to the back hallways shows the exit of an open door, bright light from the afternoon shining through the darkened corridor. I hesitate, waiting for a catch. When she meets my questioning face with only casual aloofness, I give in and hop over the counter to wrap my hands around the metal handles on either side of the tub. The bottom edge of the basin reaches below my knee, the top, well above my upper thigh. I glance back at her, measuring her height with that of my own. She's much shorter than I am, the size alone must have taken a considerable amount of strength out of her, especially now with her age.

The liquid jostles when I test lift the container. A familiar smell wafts towards me, burning the inside of my nose when I dip down at the knees for stability. I freeze, transported back to a memory. This is shine.

Real shine. Liters of it.

Craning my neck back to the old woman, she simply gives me a knowing smirk, rolling her sleeves tight below her elbows. Tattoos revealed. "Just out back there now. Mind the stairs."

Every bit of this could be a trap. Mystics around I need the silver. If I happen to run into the man who paid for me to eat, I will at least have something in my pocket to give to him besides a segment of crusted bread. I can't be caught without *something* to offer. I groan beneath the heaviness of the shine, bending slowly while lifting the wide basin from the stand it rests on. My muscles strain, forcing me to stagger a few steps so I can get the damned thing off the wall. I readjust so the bottom edge rests firmly at the middle of my thighs. It digs in but at least I'm able to distribute the weight.

Moving ever so carefully, I make it into the narrow hallway, fearful of splashing any of the shine on my clothes, not only in case of the potential added chemicals that would eat away at my new wardrobe, but if it's *real* shine like I assume it is, the smell of it on me could potentially attract unwanted attention. This stuff doesn't look or smell anything like the tainted shine I tried to sell off yesterday. It looks nearly identical to the shine Tirma used to make, and I know for a fact that hers was pure. Stuff like this is coveted.

Another staggered step allows me to finally cross the threshold of the back entrance, blinded by the heavy sun. The basin sways in my arms; I strain, keeping it steady, forgoing the warning of the stairs. I feel my foot fall, missing a step. It takes most of my strength to remain upright, but I still slouch forward, my knees buckling, giving out from under me. I drop the tub too far from the ground. Thankfully, it stays upright. I squeeze my eyes shut, sweating, nervous to inspect the damage I've caused, hoping I didn't make a huge mistake.

Sweat bleeds down the back of my neck, pooling into my collarbone. My fingers move to rub the droplets into my skin, eyeing a donkey that stands opposite me in front of a tall, enclosed fence. The surrounding area is bleak, save for what I assume is the donkey's water basin and a pitchfork of hay to satisfy his needs. He halts his chewing to stare back at me.

"Spilled a bit."

The voice makes my spine straighten immediately. I tilt my head to see who it belongs to, shading my eyes to prevent them from burning in this heat. My fingertips drip with the mix of sweat and spilled shine, coating my hand. I curse, finally realizing the error I've made. I glare at the man leaning against the side of the building, head turned down to the side, staring at my feet. I suck in a breath, moving my eyes down as well, past my torn toes. He's watching the shine get absorbed into the thickening sand around them.

Maybe a bottle's worth – or two – has been lost in my carelessness. I can only assume that payment is no longer on the table. Maybe I'll get a swift slice of a dagger across my throat as punishment. Or worse, maybe she'll sell me to Rust. Snapping myself from thoughts of a soon-to-be unsuccessful death, I scowl. First at my feet, then at the stranger. He deliberately meets my stare. One brown, one light gray eye gazes back at me. I pretend not to recognize him if only to keep my cheeks from flushing.

A rolled cigarette is tucked casually behind his ear, secured well, even when he pushes himself from the wall.

"Don't worry, Aya isn't the vengeful type. I'll say I tripped you. I've known her a while." He offers me a wink.

Squinting, I curl my lip in distaste. "I don't need your help." I spit, stating the fact a little less friendly than I intended. "Who are *you* exactly?"

I suppose I haven't had to interact with enough people as of late to remember to be courteous. He glowers at my response, scoffing outright.

"The man who paid for your first meal in what I can only assume would be –" He examines the length of my body with nothing but steady intrigue. "Weeks?"

I yank my jacket around me, hiding my scrawny form from him, then crack my knuckles, playing off the quiet thrumming in my head from his presence.

"And the one who kept you from –" His honeyed voice tapers off as his eyes land on my thumb. I tuck the ring closer to my palm, less concerned with him taking it and more concerned about what he would demand if I refused to let it go.

"Didn't I tell yah tah mind the stairs?"

I wince slightly when her footsteps stop at the top of the steps before moving out into the light. Her back hunches forward, pushing past me to inspect the loss. She clicks her tongue in the direction of the don-key, then gives me a side-long look. I feel my wrists cross subconsciously and hang my head in defeat, preparing for an onslaught of bad omens. She simply blinks once, twice, then moves her sight to the raven-haired man who steps up alongside me. He bows slightly at the waist. A scent of clove and cinnamon follows in his wake, surrounding him, and me. It stirs something foreign in my belly.

"Aya."

Her name is gentle on his tongue when he offers the cigarette he'd moved from his ear to his fingers, holding the joint out with a flourish of the wrist. The woman cackles with joy, plucking it from his awaiting fingertips, placing the filter between the crease of her lips. He produces a match from his pocket, which he flicks against the edge of the basin beside me, lighting the end for her. She draws in a heavy pull, holding the smoke in her lungs for an extensive amount of time, closing her eyes. The richness of tobacco fills the space on her exhale. My cravings for it brighten, just as they had back in Er Rada.

"Thought I told yah it would be another hour yet." She says, her stature instantly relaxing upon her next draw.

"Figured I'd wait out here with Harmi." The stranger admits with a sheepish grin, gesturing towards the donkey. I remain silent. *Waiting for what exactly?*

My jaw clenches with anticipation. Whatever it is, I don't intend to stick around to see. I clear my throat, attempting to muster up an excuse to leave.

"I won't take any coin."

"Nonsense." The woman responds on her next inhale, fishing around in her pocket.

"Give it to him. For the meal. I don't owe debts." I express wholeheartedly, not watching the man's reaction, but feeling it. I can tell I've offended him. His spine straightens, rolling his shoulders back. Aya waves her hand at me, expelling smoke directly into my face.

"Nonsense," Aya repeats. "He won't be getting any of yahr money, child. Yah earned it."

The stranger shuffles on his feet; out of the corner of my vision, I watch a smile curve the edge of his mouth. His eyes remain glazed forward.

"And if yah give him any of this, I'll cut yahr hand off. Understand?"

My distracted attention snaps back at her words. There is no doubt in my mind that she would be fully capable of following through on her threat. Her sleeves shake when she digs around in her pocket, revealing six coins. She holds them out to me, stern provocation written across her features. It's much more than I expected to receive.

She's paying you to keep you silent. Real shine, remember?

Still, the amount of silver is too much, even for that. I'd stay quiet for free at the possibility of her belonging to a clan. To *the* clan. Selling pure shine to heavily armed men under the ruse of running a bar. No point in getting tied up in the mess of a lawless territory.

Surely, she notices me hesitating because she quickly ushers the coins into my opening palm. I squirrel them away into my trousers, opposite the segment of bread.

"He's only paying fahr a crate anyways. A bottle's worth won't be missed much."

She winks at the man still beside me. I hear him chuckle under his breath, watching her walk to the opposite side of the basin, grabbing a misshaped ladle from a nail beside the railing. She dips the hammered edge into the shine, taking a hefty swig, tugging at the tight bandana around her throat when she swallows. She turns a raised brow up at the scarred one beside me, but all he does is raise a hand and shake his head softly.

"I'd offer yah some." Her gaze moves to mine. "But it would age a beauty like yahrself fahr too easily. Look what it did tah this body. All these human vices."

She tries her best to contain a fluid-filled laugh but fails, tumbling into a raspy cough. I want to laugh along with her. There are clear marking of a violent life speckled across my skin. Sun-beaten, dusted with freckles from the heavy rays, blistered beyond repair. A line has permanently creased my brows from the obvious stress of having to stay alive and I have enough mangled scars on my body that I've stopped recognizing my own skin years ago. In Isla, the women of the harem were beauties, sought after by everyone who heard of them. I've never been one to compare myself to them. A beauty I am not.

Besides, I wouldn't want a drink anyways. That's more implication, more reason to stay, more time wasted. More memories of Tirma's rage filtered tongue spewing hateful words in the name of the Mystics, of my own namesake, of Skeall. More memories of the blood on my hands from moments of outlandish aggression. Of the fact that I'd murdered a mere hobbyist over twenty pieces only yesterday out of sheer desperation. And I didn't even have the chance to spend my guilt on anything useful.

Aya begins grabbing a handful of empty bottles from an unstable ledge behind her, filling them up with the precision of someone who's done this a hundred times before. She sets them one by one into a wide, wooden box in rows of three. When she's finished, she swallows another ladleful, wheezing.

"Won't have any for yah next month, what with the well drying up and the other one past the farm being our only source left." Aya pauses, a trill of sadness lacing her tone. "And well, yah know, we may have to lie low for a little while anyway. Rust wasn't just here tah eat."

It takes me a few seconds to realize that she isn't talking to me. The stranger steps forward, bowing at the waist. "I'm afraid I won't be back for some time anyways, Aya."

He leans over, reaching for her wrinkled hand, kissing the back of it.

"Achk." She replies, swiping a gentle hand through the fallen strands of hair that frames his face. "May you be protected." She wipes her creased eyes with shaky fingertips. I can't help but feel like I'm intruding on a special goodbye. "Don't be joining Harmon anytime soon, yah hear me?"

The man nods once, deepening his bow before grabbing the bottom edge on either side of the box of shine. He turns, offering me a blinded wink. I roll my eyes when he passes, observing him unlatch and walk through the gate, turning towards the main road without another look back.

Aya doesn't speak for a while after that, only gazes at the empty space in the fence where he left. I shuffle my feet backwards, unsure if I should say anything, or just leave in silence.

"Are yah alone then? Or are yah clan owned?" She croaks, drawing in her last smoke-filled breath, burning the cigarette to its end before tossing it beside the basin. The ashes stain a circlet of sand.

"Sorry?" I blink back at her. The stranger's face still burns in my mind. There was something about him, something I can't shake. *Have I seen him somewhere before?*

"Don't know if yahr familiar with his type is all. Yah don't look to be from here. If yahr alone, I'd suggest getting in good with him."

I rapidly shake my head back and forth, an arrogant scoff finding its way from my mouth. "I don't associate myself with men like that."

Dealing with shine, with a weapon laced warrior for a partner – that horrific scar on his face. There's no way that man is a regular merchant. He has to be clan-owned himself. People don't just look that way because they can. Aya lifts a brow, eyeing my own scars that mark me, probably entertained by the idea of my distaste.

"Ah, so yahr only a traveler then. I'm sure." She clicks her tongue towards her donkey, who huffs, shaking his head. Her fingers find her way to her throat, fidgeting with the yellow tie again. A nervous habit perhaps.

"How do you know how to make this?" I whisper, knowing the consequences of my question. The entire area is filled with an intense smell of tobacco and oils, I can't help but wonder if the purpose is to solely cover the stench of shine being distilled inside. It's not in a secret area away from people, like most stills. Unless the other people in this town are all in on it as well.

"It's been passed to me."

"It's dangerous –" I slow my words, wishing they didn't leave my mouth. Her eyes spark.

"Tis' pure." A brief smile passes. "Gonna kill me fahr the rest of it?"

"No." I immediately object, unfurling the fingers that have somehow found themselves to tighten into a fist. She releases a hackled breath, wiping a speck of dirt from her sagging elbow.

"Nah. I don't suppose yah'd want me tah join yah yet. What with all the work yet tah do." She speaks into the open air, to no one besides her donkey. Her sight glazes over, as though she's experiencing an old memory. The donkey honks a few times, pulling her from her daze. I move my hands to the inside of my jacket pockets, anxious.

What am I still doing here?

"Name's Aya. But yah might have already caught on tah that." She doesn't offer her hand in greeting, instead, she turns towards the lowest step and pauses. I know what she wants, my name. I'm not inclined to give her one.

People will have power over you once they know your name.

"Rebellious little thing, truly. Hopefully that doesn't get yah killed one day."

If she only knew.

She taps softly at her tattoos, then at her neck, as if I'm supposed to know what she's hinting at.

"I'll be fine." That entices a snort.

"Where yah headed?"

My gaze shifts, wondering how impolite it would be to walk through the back gate without a response. My body sways back and forth with unsure anticipation, awaiting my decision.

"North?" She huffs when I don't reply, fingertips thrumming the railing. "Or south? Bine perhaps? Most wanderers eventually end up there." She clears her throat. "My husband, he hailed from Bine. I could tell yah –"

"East. I'm heading – East." I mute, flicking the tip of my tongue in annoyance. "Until the end of the Red Line."

"Are yah mad?" Her eyes grow wide. "Mirit?"

"Past that."

Aya's expression darkens, she squints at me long and hard, casting an uneasy glance towards her animal. Maybe she's thinking I'll steal it.

"Why would yah ever want tah go past that?" She clucks, squeezing her fist. "Any shipper worth thar salt will tell yah that returning after reaching those lands nowadays is nearly impossible. Been years since they've docked."

Returning isn't an option.

As if the information I'd given her wasn't already too much, I add. "I'm heading to Darde." *The gate is right there, Adessa, leave before you make another mistake.* My mind bleats ignored words.

"Darde? Why the hell would she want tah go there!" She begs the sky, throwing her hands up in defeat. "Ain't nothing for yah over there, child, not a damned thing! Yah hear me? It's all here. It's right in front of yah." She scans my bare feet, my oversized clothing. When I continue standing firmly planted before her, all she does is sigh.

"Please tell me yah at least left supplies with yahr animal. That yah have more on yahr back than just oversized clothing! That yah're not planning tah walk the whole way!" She peeks past the gate, as if hopeful to see that I might have left a means of transportation outside.

I swallow hard, unwilling to tell her that I don't have anything.

"Don't even have that, do yah." She leans back against the rail, acting faint. "This is what yah need tah do. Yah need tah ask that easterner tah trade with yah before he leaves town. He's got plenty of weapons." Her head dips towards the exit. "Ain't no way yahr gonna get across the Red Line without something tah protect yahrself. And I guarantee yah won't get tah a ship without something tah convince safe passage, if yah know what I mean." She takes another step.

She's right, six coins and a piece of bread won't get me very far.

My clothing suddenly feels too loose on my skin. Can't say my body will sell for much if I happen to become desperate enough. Before, I could use it to get information, like my map for example, but now, not so much. I know that there are larger cities ahead, so I'm not entirely worried that I won't be able to find *something* worth offering for transport across the Dying Sea. It's merely a matter of getting there in the first place that will prove to be difficult.

"What is the name of this town?" *Please, please, please.*

"Teryal." *Mystics' around. I didn't veer off course.* "Tell yah what. Yah find him. Yah tell him that I sent yah to look for him. If it costs more than another bottle – a crate even, for a weapon, that is, yah come back here and I'll personally make sure that he gives yah what yah need."

I pinch the center of my forehead. *Why would she want to help me?*

She must note the distrust written across my face because she adds, "My husband Harmon." I feel her nearly melt at the mention of his name. "That's what he'd want me tah do with yah. It's very –" She takes a peek at her donkey. "That eastern fellah, he's a good kid. Known him a long time. We have an understanding, me and him. Yah need to find him."

I snort at the use of her word 'kid'. And at the mention of him being good. When someone looks the way he does, I can't say 'good' would be a part of the personality description. I take an uncomfortable step back.

"Saved this old body's life once." She tugs against her bandana, making me believe that her survival has something to do with whatever she's hiding beneath. "He'll help yah. I know it."

"Why would you – why would either of you help me?" Being suspicious is an understatement.

Can't say that after all these years, I'm willing to accept the help of two strangers in one singular day. Arthur had been the only one to help me when I'd first arrived on the continent, and I only allowed him to because I was a child who didn't know any better.

"I told yah the reason. Harmon would want me tah. And yah seem like yah could use a kind hand. Go catch up with him. Shouldn't have gone too fahr, he's making his rounds. Probably at the blacksmith's by now. But if yah miss him there, he'll be up at my farm at the edge of the southwest border later this afternoon. Turn right when yah leave, yah'll hear the blacksmith's anchor dinging."

Yeah right.

I won't lose any sleep in knowing I refused to accept her offer, and she won't either. She'll believe I went to find him. That will give me peace.

"Be mindful of Rust. He'll be lurking around here, I'm sure."

"Thanks for your – advice." I won't admit to her that she's helped me immensely. I won't thank her for the coins I never asked for.

I raise my hand in farewell, then finally hasten my pace towards the back. Aya murmurs to herself, wobbling slowly inside. I know her eyes are still trained on my back. I make sure to latch the gate closed behind me.

SEVEN

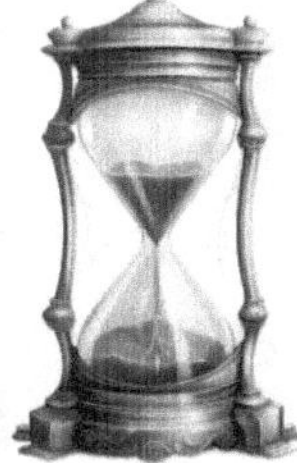

ADESSA

"Hold your head up high son, my caste does not define yours."

"You moron, grab the other end of the rope!"

Angry shouts rise over the fence line on my left, forcing me to quicken my pace. When I had the choice to turn right towards the blacksmith's, I chose left instead. Left, past the yellow-orange houses that appeared abandoned, if not for the occasional wail of a child or the clamor of pans being scraped after lunch.

Left, in the direction of a clear sky with an empty road sprawled out before me, the sun at my back. I won't beg for a weapon, no matter how desperate I am for one. I also don't want to put Aya out on the amount of shine she has when she could sell it to get by or use it for her own bartering chip. What if he demanded an entire crate in return for helping me? I'll continue to stick with my original plan; find shelter, maybe someone to redraw my map in the next town. I'm near the Red Line. I can do this.

I only hope that turning left wasn't a mistake, what with all the noise I'm hearing now.

"I have to get around her before – Bonehead, she's kicking me!" The male voices trickle between the wooden slats protecting the area they hide in, bouncing off the walls of an empty silo across the street. I lower my head, unwilling to involve myself.

Rust will be lurking around here.

I don't want to think about why Aya seemed so nervous when speaking about him.

"Come on –" A hard smack. A girl's muffled cries. That forces me to stop, feeling blood begin to heat my veins. With curiosity getting the better of me, I sneak towards the fence, unable to see through the barrier, but I press my ear against the woodgrain and hear whimpering. A fearful choke tips the end. It makes the hair on the back of my neck stand up.

I've barely made it out of the village. Maybe I should double back, find the blacksmith after all. I could try to convince him to let me barter for something, provide a service like I did with Aya. It wouldn't be begging. That would satiate my pride. Enough time has passed that he would probably be alone, without the company of that half-blind clansman.

The confidence of getting to the sea unharmed slowly diminishes the louder the voices shout into the open air. "She'll sell for a good amount! Look how clean she is."

The tone is enthusiastic. Sickening. *Don't involve yourself, Adessa.*

My gut screams at me. That's the cruel reality of this world. No one would help me if I was in this girl's position, which I have been a handful of times over my life, so I know full well the weight in which I cannot rely on others. Why should I feel so torn about not helping her? *Keep moving.*

Another fearful cry forces my feet to stop once more. I'm taken back to when I was little, listening to my mother cry out for my father as she was ripped away from the lands my ancestors had always lived. Away from me. My fists clench.

Alright, I'll bite. The comment on cleanliness piqued my interest anyway.

I reach a split in the fence, a broken slat that's been pushed off to the side, allowing me to see a bit of the enclosed area beyond it. My gaze lands on the back of a young girl, hands tied behind her; she's on her knees, being held steady by a man double her size while the other finishes the knot around her feet. My view is slightly blocked, pushing my desire to get a closer look.

The gate ahead offers me a clear enough view. There are three men in total. One joins the other two when he stands, pacing in front of the poor kid.

Walk away, Adessa.

My growing nerves make my feet turn, but my vision blurs at the sound of gnarled laughter. Maybe I was hoping that I didn't, but I do. I recognize these men. More importantly, I recognize the scarf hanging loosely around their hostage. I recognize the girl beneath it.

The only sound I hear is the throbbing beat of my heart between my ears. The shawl she wears is no longer in the pristine condition it was yesterday. It's coated in thick granules of muck. Her back hunches forward as she heaves deep, shattering sobs. She followed me. How did she follow me? I didn't see her anywhere nearby at any point the day before or even this morning. It's not like I had been paying much attention lately; I basically invited these men to sneak up on me while I slept last night.

But I thought she went back inside her home, back to where I would leave her and never have to feel the guilt of doing so again. How did she find herself all the way out here? I pinch myself in frustration. Did these men find her in Er Rada after losing the opportunity with me? Or did they happily pluck this wandering girl from the road while they were making their way to Teryal?

My mind bleats in warning. *They have my bag. My map. My compass. That's the only thing I have left from Tirma.*

It looks like they have camels with them now, one for each. If I'm careful and lucky, I could take one for myself. Maybe an opportunity has found its way into my lap. I have to play this smart.

I scan what I can see of the saddle packs, hoping to catch a glimpse of the brown leather straps that hold the entirety of my life. One sharp inhale erupts in my chest when I make the mistake of allowing my eyes to wander to the girl's profile instead. The right side of her face is completely caked in blood, tracked with tears that cut a clear path through, showing swollen skin beneath. Her lips are cracked and bruised.

"Gunn, keep an eye on her." The larger of the three barks his orders at the others. As I assumed before, he must be their leader. "Aol, finish unpacking the camels. Quickly. He'll be here soon with the rest of the supplies. We need to make sure he has no choice but to agree." His tone is one of a mocking grumble that fades as soon as he dips his head under the hooked doorway of the shed behind them.

Gunn, the one with the limp, begins swaying back and forth on his feet, taunting the girl with his knife. The other one, Aol, with fresh burns that are poorly covered in dark clay, heads for the tied-up animals in the corner. The kid wails, a sound that nearly makes my heart give out. I truly wish I never stepped foot here because now I know I cannot leave her. Satchel or not. I'll have to get her out before this other man their leader mentioned shows up. Three is – barely doable. But tak-ing on *four* would be out of the question.

I try to gain a clearer understanding of how far away she is from the others. I could pick one of them off like I did last night, then hope to take the other down – somehow. The camels aren't tied well it seems; I could slip onto one, scare the others into running. I've never ridden anything other than a mule before, but I guess there's no better time to learn than now.

My jacket shrugs off easily enough. I twist the dense fabric around my hands, pulling it taut. Clearly, the man to take down is, once again, the one with the limp. I scour the ground, searching for anything to throw in his direction and find a smooth rock resting against the splin-tered bottom of the fence. With a flick of the wrist, I chuck it towards my target. It bounces once, then lands softly at his feet.

He immediately picks his head up in confusion. I duck around the corner, slowly, long enough for him to be made aware of someone lurking outside their gate.

"Aol?" He calls out in the direction of my hiding spot.

"What, Bonehead." An annoyed reply from his comrade, who is busy tying rolled-up mats to one of the camels. I crouch, watching Gunn sway on his feet for a moment, considering. Another breath and he's made his decision, allowing his curiosity to get the better of him. Scooting back, I meld into the side of the gate, snapping the jacket tighter in anticipation. Another heartbeat and the beady-eyed man finally steps into view. I whisper a silent prayer to the Mystics that I'm not spotted by anyone else. He scans the road ahead, stepping further from the enclosure, dipping his chin to the right.

I immediately squat deeper into my left leg and kick out with the other, aiming my foot into the same knee that took him down before. He buckles. In that same breath, my jacket is thrown around his mouth. I pull as hard as I can, the fabric suppressing the brunt of his surprised scream when he hits the hard sand below.

Propelled by sheer adrenaline, I'm able to draw him backward, out of view, using the rest of my strength to yank his torso between my legs. I crisscross them around his waist, rolling the jacket to his throat, strangling the stunned man into submission. He wheezes silently, one hand to his neck, the other frantically searching for his attacker. Knobby fingers latch onto my uncovered forearm. Sharp fingernails dig in so hard; they break skin and slip on the blood that runs. I only squeeze tighter.

At this point, his entire body jolts, kicking at the ground in steady beats while dust billows around us, rolling over in struggle until his movement finally slows. His nails stop painting my skin red; his other hand has already fallen to the sand. Sweat bleeds into my eyes, coating my eyelashes. I give one last tug. With that, he crumples, unconscious.

My heart pounds with urgency. I'm on my feet in a matter of seconds, forcing the unmoving man from me, listening for an alarm from the others. I quickly throw my jacket back on and peer around the gate.

The camels seem to know that I'd just taken down one of their owners. They stomp the ground and throw their necks around while Aol attempts to settle them.

Good. Be distracted.

Gunn's mouth is wide open, but his shallow breathing tells me that he's still alive. Lucky man. I won't have time to kill him, not if I want to risk the few precious moments that I have in order to successfully save the girl, and myself.

Now or never.

I risk my chance and spring towards their hostage, stealing glances between the shed and the camels. A few more leaps and I slide into the sand behind her. She flinches at my lack of a greeting while I untie her hands from the rope that bloodies her wrists. The knot gives. I scramble to unbind her feet. Luckily the wrappings around her ankles are very poorly tied. I make easy work of it and jump to my feet, noting any change in our surroundings.

Thankfully enough, Aol still has his back turned. His hands are full with all three camels. They moan and stamp their hooves, pulling at the ties around the post behind them. It will only be a matter of time until he sees us if we don't hurry. I'm rethinking my plan of getting to one of the animals; doing so would mean taking him out too. I push the kid around to face me, her watery eyes spark with recognition. "You need to run."

My sight instantly looks to Aol, who has somehow gotten the camels under control much faster than I thought he would. His two hollow pupils bore into me, bewildered. Realization spreads over his face a moment too late. My legs are already moving before I can hear the girl's response. My fingers interlock with hers, pulling past the shocked man, over the unconscious one outside.

"Burke!" Aol's shout rings off of the metal silo across from us as I bank right. I can't lead them to Aya's, although something tells me that she would have no problem defending us. Regardless, I refuse to bring her trouble in exchange for all of her kindness. No, I'll lead them to the blacksmiths. I'll use his forge to set these men on fire if I have to.

"I know where we can go!" I yell between breaths as we sprint, veering right again in the direction that I should have gone before. My thighs are already threatening to give in, I can't imagine how she must be feeling. I push us faster, hearing her alarming cry, snapping my neck back towards her captors. The larger of the three has finally come out of the shed, barreling towards us like an unleashed bull.

"Hurry!" I scream, allowing my panic to force us forward. *Shit, he's so much faster than he was last night.*

We're almost to the main road. It's the middle of the day, surely there are people out here. We can make it. *For once, please be on my side.*

My prayers are always unanswered, but perhaps this is the one time they will take pity on me. If not me, then at least the kid. We leap over one of the decaying roadblocks, left behind from the Cull. The length of my pants wraps around one of the sharper edges, slicing through the fabric and into my leg. I bite back the splitting pain, dragging the girl up and over the same obstacle.

A tiny spark of hope flares through my aching chest when we make it over the blockage. At the apex of the road ahead, I watch the scarred man turn a corner. His gaze locks with mine. *You again,* his eyes almost say. His forearms are slick from carrying the heavy box of shine Aya gave to him, which rests on top of another crate that's tucked beneath. He brandishes a sword across his back, the golden, polished hilt rises from the crest of his shoulder. I see his brows raise in question the closer we get to him, the slightest curl tickling one side of his lip; but then his sight trains itself directly past us. The smirk disappears; his features turn to ice.

"Hang on!" I shout, lungs threatening to burst right out of my body. I can sense the girl is struggling even more so now, I can feel her resistance. I don't have time to react when I feel my body slip backwards. Horrified once I realize that she tripped, she drags us both down to the rough road. I'm unable to properly gain the upper hand and land on my wrist at a too-sharp angle, bracing myself for when my face smacks the solid ground. Iron coats my tongue as soon as my teeth bite down into it. My nose cracks on impact. The darkness threatens to swallow my vision in an array of watery clouds.

It takes me a moment too long to finally pull myself up to my knees, spitting out granules of sand and blood in a glob in front of me. Blood oozes from my nose, dotting the backs of my hands. Unyielding dizziness consumes me. As if in a haze, I sway to the harsh grip of the girl who clings to my arm. My free hand moves to my injured wrist, twisting it around cautiously. Not broken.

I lift my chin towards the sky, pinching the bridge of my nose in an attempt to keep the blood from flowing. It makes my throat warm, and my stomach sick. The crunch of footsteps ahead makes me alarmingly aware of our new situation. I desperately try to clear the disorientation from my mind. The shine dealer stops directly in front of us, setting down the heavy crates, observing us with a crumpled expression. His sight roams the entirety of my injuries, from my bloodied face to the streaks of red down my arm. His jaw works as if to say something, but he straightens and crosses his arms against his sand-tinted tunic instead.

My gaze falls to the pair of twin daggers kept at his side, clipped along a leather belt that's wrapped around to contrast his bone-colored pants. He's not close enough for me to reach out and grab one of the weapons with any ease. I wish wholeheartedly that I won't have to. His brows twist, expression darkening further when my eyes lock on his once more; he tears his gaze from mine, scanning the road ahead to the two who have finally caught up to us. I can hear them panting, one of them shuffles sand around as he stops, hard enough to pelt my back.

"Qa'id," One out-of-breath voice chimes in. *Qa'id?*

It sounds like one of the languages also used on this continent, unless this is his name. I sort my mind for any recognition I may have of it. My jaw crushes into my teeth. I knew I should have learned more from Arthur.

The man before me sucks in a sharp inhale through his nose, wiping his face from the sweat line dotting his brow, and pauses, circling us once, stepping over the splash of blood, etched in the sand by my injuries.

I refuse to be sized up like prey.

I latch onto the whimpering girl and yank her up, not allowing these men to see the tremor of my swelling wrists as I do so. The kid refuses to let go, gripping my arm so tightly that it threatens to pop from my shoulder.

"Where's Gunn?" Cold. Commanding. Nothing like the honey-laced tone I'd heard him speak to me with earlier.

"Alive. This one must have knocked him out cold." A firm hand pushes the base of my neck forward. I spin around, smacking Aol away from me, glaring. He merely sneers, forcing my body back to face front. The stranger's torn eyebrow twitches, examining me with a slight tinge of humor.

"Why were you chasing them?"

It isn't a question, it's a demand. His mismatched eyes remain firm on mine even though his words weren't directed toward me.

You aren't going to ask why we were running from them?

I feel freshly vulnerable. This can't be the same man I talked with back at Aya's. He *bowed* to her, a respectful gesture that's not common to see anywhere I've been. He was – warm. And now, there is nothing but cold, even out here with the sun blaring down against us. Aya told me I could ask him for help; perhaps she was truly wrong about his intentions.

Aol rubs the burns on his face, stepping alongside me with a dry cough. I hear the larger one groan as soon as he opens his rotting mouth.

"We found this one wandering outside the village borders." Aol gestures to the girl beside me. She presses her face into my bicep, as if doing so will make her invisible. It forces me to awkwardly balance her shaking legs to hold us both steady and upright. I wish I could scream at her to be stronger, to be that girl who shot me without fear. But her terror is justified, so I don't.

"Burke thought. We – we thought –" He checks his partner, who has positioned himself too closely beside the kid. "I mean, look at her, we could –" His sentence tapers off with a not-so-subtle growl from Burke. Aol clears his throat. "Found this on her too. I don't care about the gems you took. Not when we have a haul like this now." He presents the small leather pouch, shaking the silver inside.

"I swear I only had my back turned for a moment before I saw this one taking off with her." His gnarled fingers point close enough to my face that I wish I could bite them off. Pure disdain drips from his lips, sounding almost in disbelief that I could have been capable of running off with her. I wonder if they've recognized me as the one who got away from them last night. That could complicate things.

"If you're keeping the coins, then why –" The scarred man starts, getting interrupted by Burke.

"You know why."

The silence is enough to set my gut aflame. Aol releases a strange laugh, one that makes me question what might have happened if we hadn't tripped. If we were able to get back onto the main road like I had hoped. If we'd run into the person who helped me not that long ago, before he noticed that we were being chased by what seems to be his own men.

"You intend for us to keep them."

The words brim with disdain, a glimmer of loss in his tone. For a moment, I think he might help us after all, but my heart sinks deeper when he doesn't say anything more. I glare at his daggers again. What would happen to the girl if I tried to attack them?

"This one might be too much trouble to keep around." Aol spits.

Still, the shine dealer says nothing, only stares. The second it takes waiting for any answer feels like a lifetime; too swiftly followed by a quick wave of his ringed hand. I don't register what's happening until the girl screams.

"No!"

She's ripped from me. I reach for her but am instantly pulled backward by Burke instead.

"Let me go!" I shriek.

A rough hand claps around my open mouth. This *Qa'id* avoids my eyes which are so desperately searching for his help. He ends up leading the way to the enclosed area we nearly escaped from, leaving us to the mercy of his men. I cry out beneath the calloused palm that holds me tightly, struggling to free myself, watching the kid get dragged away in the same direction that I have no desire to go.

The cruelest of them all lifts me from the sand, proving that he's much stronger than I am and twice my size. I swing my body back and forth, whipping violently about, clawing at his hands. My legs kick back towards the only vulnerable place I can think of but he's as solid as a mountain. His arm tightens its grip around me, leaving painful divots, squeezing already tender skin. I clamp my teeth down on his meaty palm, unable to break through the tough exterior. His skin is like leather, leaving a metallic taste on my tongue.

"Oh, you are going to be a pain in my ass, aren't you? Won't be escaping a *third* time." He spits his venom, poisoning the air around us. *He recognizes me.* I'm lifted higher into the air, my back nearly brushing the underside of his chin. It's brief before he slams my body down, hard. My legs crush into the beaten ground. Agony tears through me, cleaving my spine in half. The intense pressure builds and bursts at the base of my tailbone. Pain splinters me entirely, rendering my lower half useless and numb. A cry slips out, though I desperately try to hold it in while I'm dragged limply across the sand. The tops of my toes burn against the sun-scorched granules that blister my skin. I am completely disoriented in Burke's arms.

All I can hear is the girl wailing, but I am barely able to lift my head to locate her. We've already made it past Gunn, who is sitting up against the edge of our soon-to-be prison, rubbing at the sore spot around his throat. He gleans, eyeing me like a crazed animal. My immediate regret for not taking him out for good prickles my newly broken spine.

The heat has reached the point where it's now unbearable. My skin feels like it's melting. The nausea in my belly from the sheer pain of it all is nearly too much to handle. The scarred man drops the crates off near the camels, nestling them between a divot in the coarse sand. The sound of bottles clinking together make me all too aware of the consistent ringing in my ears, of the trap I've allowed myself to wander into. This never should have happened. I should have never been here.

"What did you do?" The Qa'id asks, turning towards Burke, who still drags me halfway into the ground. I can't bear to look at him. At anything. I allow myself to disassociate, hearing Burke order the others to tie us to one of the palms as he hands me off. Gunn and Aol obey, tugging both of us along, the scratchy granules irritating exposed patches of skin. I'm forced into a standing position, a cruel joke. The men wrap secure bind-ings around our waists to hold us upright, and I wince when Aol ties an impossibly tight knot around my legs, so snugly that it constricts any possible feeling that I would have left in them.

I quiver beneath the rope, forced to grip my core in a way that causes the bottom of my spine to prick at my tailbone in the worst way.

What have you done, Adessa? Why couldn't you have let nature run its course?

There is hate in my eyes when I finally catch the half-blind man star-ing at me, setting his mouth in a thin line when he notices. His empty expression offers me no sympathy.

Aya said you would help me.

I know now that he won't.

EIGHT

ADESSA

"We, the People's Commission have agreed to a ceasefire. We are prepared to provide food, water and shelter to those who are in affected areas beginning tomorrow morning, 0800 hours. Standby for assistance. Help will come. Have faith in your comrades. Do not let the wrong side win." *-Excerpt from RAE, 2,100, two months before the Collapse.*

Dusk hits by the time the dizziness finally releases its solid hold on me.

I'm unsure if it's a good thing or not. Perhaps I've become so numb from the pain that I have no more capability left within me to feel at all. The time-worn haze that's passed over reminds me of how much my body has been broken. It threatens my concentration. My willpower. The stance I've been placed in makes it even worse, no doubt further punishment, one meant to upend me completely. It's working.

I can't believe how weak I am. My fragile spine – I can't feel the lower half of my body, haven't been able to the entire afternoon. Can't say this has ever happened to me before. Superficial injuries always heal fairly fast, give or take half a day, whereas bone breaks have taken a little longer. With an injury this severe, it's time that I don't have.

Unfortunately for me, being cursed with the fate of remaining alive doesn't mean that I don't feel the unyielding torture of my bones weaving back to each other. It only means that I have to survive it. I watch the circle of men, unable to feel the heat of their buried fire. They've spoken nothing more of their plans with us since I've been conscious. In fact, they hardly speak to each other at all. It doesn't seem like they enjoy each other's company in the slightest.

I want to know what clan they belong to; I've tried to think if I've seen the triangular markings before, the ones on Burke's arm. Now I know that Aol has them too. Two triangles center his chest. He sits shirtless with his back resting against the side of the shed, rubbing some sort of paste on his gums.

Although I can't tell if the other two have the same symbols, something tells me that their presence together isn't a coincidence. They are definitely clan-owned.

Jidaani. Jidaani.

That wretched name echoes in the folds of my mind. I hope to the Abyss that I'm worrying myself for nothing. If we were with Jidaani, I know enough from the stories I've heard that we would be in a lot more trouble than I could have ever thought possible. I know for a fact that they wouldn't be holding us hostage anymore either. We would be dead.

Maybe I actually, *truly* would be.

What I need to do instead of fearing the worst is to create a plan of escape. I've already run countless scenarios in my head, but so far, I haven't been able to plan anything that wouldn't cause the kid's immediate death. Regardless, there's no doubt in my mind that I won't be able to get away in the condition I'm in anyway. I wouldn't be able to crawl out of here fast enough even if I tried.

Soft, swallowed breathing next to me pushes another bout of cloudy gray from my mind. I swivel my head to check on her. Tears no longer fall from her swelling cheeks. However, her body still silently sobs.

"Kid." I test the level of quiet I'm able to speak with, eyeing the men to see if they can hear me. "Are you awake?"

When the four ahead don't make an effort to listen, I continue. "Kid."

Waiting, I softly clear my dry throat. "Are you dying?"

She finally notices, turning her chin carefully upwards, shifting uncomfortably on her feet. "I don't think so." Her tiny words are barely above a whisper. She blinks at the circle of men. No one seems to be paying attention to us.

"What the hell are you doing here?" I ask outright. "Why did you follow me?"

She sniffles in response. "I told you." Her throat cracks. "You left me. I told you that I couldn't live like that anymore. You should have just killed me when I asked you to."

My lips press into a seething line. I will not be blamed for this. For *any* of this. Sometimes I can't stand seeing my own gaze, *her* eyes in the mirror, reminding me constantly of the last moments of hate my mother had in her heart for her only child. All because I led them to their fate. She didn't know that I didn't do it on purpose. She got taken away thinking that I was the reason why her husband was lying dead beside our barn. That she had helped hide her love's murderer.

I don't think I can handle much more fresh guilt hanging over my head alongside all the other agonizing regrets. No, I won't allow a kid to blame me for her own poor decision.

"You should have listened to me and stayed where you were."

She bites back tears, quivering her lower lip. "But I didn't belong there anymore." Her throat shakes. She peers up at me with a sheen of sadness. "I saw those men try to take you last night. I'm sorry I didn't bring the shotgun. I could have stopped them. I wish I had stopped them. Maybe you would have let me tag along if I did."

I breathe a fresh breath out, relieved. Although it was truly a stupid decision for her to follow me, worsened by the fact that she didn't bring anything to protect herself with, I can only imagine how much worse it would be if they obtained a weapon like that.

"I hid for a while, I promise they didn't see me. I remembered the direction you went in and found some of your tracks. Maybe they found it too. I forgot to cover them up. My brother always told me to cover them up." She hangs her head, then immediately jolts back to meet me. "Is that why they're here? I led them here?"

I don't feel the desire to console her. I don't want to help her through this – the sound in her voice makes my heart ache.

"No." I say as gently as I can muster.

"You're from Damire, right? That's what you said back in Er Rada." Her eyes scan the ground back and forth before offering a curt nod.

"Are you familiar with their language?" Another steady nod.

"What does Qa'id mean?" I search her expression.

"Leader. I think."

Interesting. Their leader isn't Burke as I had originally thought.

"Their leader is the one with the scar on his face."

"I've seen him before." She makes sure to say it quietly. "I'm not sure where, but I recognize that scar."

"Have you seen him with the merchant?" She shrugs at my question. "I think they're shine dealers. He knows someone here in town who makes it. That's why they're here."

"Shine dealers? The man with the limp said they were going to sell me to the slave runners. Is that what shine dealers do?"

My stomach tightens. These greedy, horrible men. As if being a part of a clan isn't enough for them. "I think they are much more than that." I whisper, watching their leader focus on sharpening his blades.

The other three look like they're beginning to fall asleep. I wish my arms were free so I could slap myself. I should have just gone through the Mountains of Siber when I was leaving the Far North. It would have been much colder and offered me much less, but at least I wouldn't have had to deal with the clans until I wandered closer to Darde. I wouldn't have wasted half of my life in Isla. I wouldn't have to deal with the port in Mirit either. Although I'm unsure how I would get across the Dying Sea from the north. The Grand Map in Skeall didn't show anything past Majinka.

No. I needed the Red Line. I needed the path taken during the Cull. I didn't have much of a choice. In the Time Before, when the Collapse first began, the Elites tried their best to create laws on this land. On all lands, including the now-empty continent across the Great Sea. The rapidly forming clans refused to kneel to them again. Shortly after, the Cull swarmed the world in a death-covered blanket. The bloodiest moment in the Earth's history, according to my father. The Elites barely stood a chance, yet many tried to flee across the Dying Sea from the west. Only a handful were successful.

According to the writings of the Firsts, the eastern continent held those who were in support of the Elites before the Collapse. They were desperate for their guidance in a time when chaos reigned. Like the rest of the world, they had lost a devastating amount of their population and resources, but they were all in such despair that they welcomed those who started, and fueled the fires of unrest. They knowingly sought leadership from those who created the war that ended it all. At least, those are what the rumors state.

The newly formed groups drove the lands deeper into death. Desperation made its frigid presence known, as it still does to this day. The agreement to live this life came at a price. Join a tribe or die. Soon, survival became nearly something much worse than death. Many families were forced to sell off their own children as servants – or worse because they could no longer afford them. The cost of those lives meant a meager month's worth of food for the surviving family members. Or an old cow to pull their wagon.

Those who could afford servants became greedier once they realized there was a market for live humans. As well as any other tradeable item that was left among the brokenness of the world. That's when slave markets were formed. The Blood Market led the way. Routes were slowly developed, using the same worn paths created by the craters from the war and a large amount of upheaval over many decades. For many people's beliefs, it was finally the end.

Until suddenly it wasn't. According to Arthur, contracts were soon made between the First Clans, allowing freedom of choice. The territory wars led them to establish borders over mass graves, of leadership roles being introduced back into the collective's way of thinking. The Red

Line was developed, tainted in rivers of blood, following the same route that was soiled by the Elites as they scrambled to Mirit. The Jidaani were said to lead the charge in forcing them out, so they had a right to it. In turn, they established a functional way to get from one side of the continent to the other using that very route. Thanks to them, the ease of trade expanded, but at a cost.

When I first arrived on these lands, the stories of the trade routes sounded very similar to the events that took place in the Far North, so the concept of what happened here was not an unfamiliar one. I grew up knowing that slavers were something to be terrified of. My parents feared it above anything else; they would rather us all starve. Although, my people in Skeall never did see a single runner, the three of us on our little homestead on the outskirts were unfortunately the ones who welcomed in something very similar.

I suppose I'm grateful knowing that my father didn't live long enough to see his wife taken. I pray to the Mystics that he's unable to see what is happening to me now. I wouldn't want him to feel like any of this is his fault. It will always be my own burden to bear.

That's probably why Aya had asked me if I was clan-owned. Maybe thinking that I was would have given her enough relief. That I was protected. Or perhaps it was a silent suggestion that I should be. She tried to help me, but I refused. If I had taken her up on her offer, would things have ended differently? Damn my pride.

"Did you at least bring *anything* to protect yourself with? A knife?" *A glimmer of hope, perhaps?*

"No." My face falls. "I thought I would catch up with you before anything bad happened." I want to scream at her naivety.

"I confronted you unarmed back in Er Rada, did you really think that I would have been able to protect us both with *nothing*?"

She lifts her shoulders, clearly oblivious to the realities of this world. "I thought you would have gotten a weapon after you abandoned me. Didn't you sell the powder?"

The powder!

I completely forgot that I shoved those containers into my satchel. And now this clan has whatever is being kept inside. "No."

"No?" Her hazel eyes widen, panicked. "Where is it then?" She scans my pockets.

"Somewhere in this camp, I'd assume. It was in my bag. They have it." Her silence is deafening. It's making my stomach turn. "Why are you so concerned?" I lean in closer, watching Aol's head roll back, snoring deeply with his mouth open.

"Because – I..."

I can sense her anxiety rising, she fidgets with the rope at her waist.

"What's in those containers?"

Burke's head tilts ever so slightly, but it seems like he's only moving to throw sand across the fire, into the open mouth of Aol. The toothless man snorts and spits sleepily, but at least the snoring stops.

"Motte." She finally admits.

"What!" I squirm, desperate to keep my voice low, wishing I could break these bindings.

A clan can't have access to poison like that!

"You –"

"Shut up over there." Burke calls out, drawing everyone's attention to us. Their leader shifts his focus; I find myself lowering as deep as the bindings will allow, waiting for their interest to wane. No wonder the merchant was so eager to trade with her. That poison is worth more than anything he's ever paid for it. Now these men have it. Great. I wonder if they know what it is yet.

"Your mother –" I take a deep breath. "How did she get her hands on..." I mouth the next word.

"She wanted to heal people." Her voice is distant, pausing our conversation with the crackle of the fire ahead.

I'm not going to pry, even if the rampant thoughts I have are making me believe that this girl can't possibly be who she's making herself appear to be. Whatever her mother wanted to do, it was not to heal people. Not with a poison like that.

"I buried the rest of them." She releases a shuddered breath. "I didn't think it would be smart to take them with me. Or leave them for someone else." Then, "I'm sorry I shot you."

"We are beyond that now. It doesn't matter." My lips stifle the laugh that begs to escape.

"Yes, it does." She strains her neck, searching for the tear in my jacket where the fragments had punctured. "Do they still bleed?"

I shake my head, uncertain of why she's acting this way. So sincerely. Maybe it's to distract me from the idea of motte being in the possession of *anyone*.

"I'm Saedea."

No.

The back of my neck prickles. I have no need to know her name. I don't want to become any more attached to her than I already am becoming. I'd left her behind for this exact reason. How could she possibly think that now is an appropriate time to try to get close to me?

"You aren't going to tell me your name back?"

"No." I glower, watching the stifled smoke spread out low into the air. That must be why they bury their fire. I wish I would have known about this technique sooner.

"Why? My brother said that's how –"

"How you give the Mystics permission to use it?"

"How you make friends." Her soft tone nudges something profound within me. "The Mystics already know our names. Saying it out loud won't change it."

"Learning my name won't change our situation."

She sighs, settling back against the tree. "It isn't fair."

"Nothing is fair."

I can feel her pupils burning into me. "Then I'll guess."

What a child's response. I roll my eyes, ignoring her. Until she begins listing a handful of names I've never heard before. "Frieda. Kaar –"

"Shut up." I murmur, watching Burke and the Qa'id stoke the fire without any words between each other. Gunn picks idly at the hem of his pants. Aol seems to be fast asleep.

"Narella." *This girl.*

"Adessa." I whisper. "Okay? My name is Adessa. Look at me." She obeys. "Don't you *ever* use it around these men. Do you understand? And don't tell them yours either. I don't care what your brother said."

I had to add that to the end of my demand, just in case. A glow of satisfaction dots her smile. "Adessa." She repeats it, a little louder than I would prefer. It makes me flinch. I haven't heard another person say my name in a very, very long time. It sounds almost foreign to my ears.

"Sev would have liked you." Her throat sounds coarse. "He's a survivor too."

"I don't –" My words drift at the slowed movements in front of us. I'd been too busy, too distracted to notice the dark pair of boots stop ahead. My sight reaches that of the scarred man, who stands rigidly in front, hands tucked neatly behind his back. His hair hangs loose, the strands shake with gentle movements of his head as he flicks his attention between Saedea and I.

The expression he wears is – strained.

Putting a finger to his lips, he inches closer. I briefly catch the clove on his skin. It's all too familiar, in a way that makes my bones ache and my stomach cramp. I stiffen when he moves behind the skinny trunk of the palm I'm tied to and squirm when he starts to untie the rope around my legs. Blood instantly rushes back into them, rippling up my thighs, making its way toward my hips. It allows for some feeling to creep back into my veins. It's not much, but it's enough to heat my muscles, reminding me that this vessel is putting in the work to fix me. My body nearly floats. I would have fallen flat on my face if it hadn't been for the rope tied around my waist.

The pressure from standing on fractured bones for the better half of the day builds deep inside of me. I grind my teeth when the second knot is loosened. A careful hand finds itself on the front of my shoulder to help keep me upright. Their leader adjusts himself to face me again, tucking his other hand gently around my forearm, allowing me to sit at the base of the palm. The rope that was used to bind me is then wrapped around my wrists instead. He doesn't tie it tight.

"What are you –"

He presses two fingers to my lips, then gestures behind him to the others. A silent order for me to keep my mouth shut. He straightens my legs out one at a time. I blink through the mist along my tear line when he does so, muscles throbbing with a blend of unfamiliarity and relief. His limpid stare grazes my feet, unwrapped and bare from being dragged, crusted in sand and half-healed blisters. He tucks the end of the second rope around my calves, not even bothering with tying it. Like he knows I wouldn't be capable of leaving. I can't wait for my body to heal so I can prove him wrong.

Shortly after rising, he repeats the same process with Saedea, although not as gently, seeing as she doesn't need it. I hear her sigh with sweet release, wiggling her toes. Only her hands are tied as well, her knot equally less woven together than it had been.

"Thank you." Saedea muffles her gratitude, offering a brilliant smile. One that I've yet to see from her.

He says nothing, doesn't even look at me further. I keep my focus trained on his back when he turns away, eagerly returning to his comrades without another word. Burke grunts, picking his teeth with a blunt pinky nail, not bothering to hold his outright disdain as the one in charge sits across the fire from him. The two exchange a passive look, nothing more than that before the scarred one settles into himself against the shed.

I wonder why he decided to reposition us the way that he did. Is his guilt finally eating away at him? Good. It should.

What I wonder most of all is in what way we will be expected to repay this unwanted kindness?

YOON

"Every caste with a ranking of 4 or lower will now be responsible for the trench." –
Lapis Law #23 in the year of the Golden Cobra, 2,450 T.A

"There's two."

I try to cover the despair that haunts my tone. There's a knowing sadness in Jax's dark stare that nearly matches the heaviness I feel buried in my chest. We've been concerned about this exact scenario for months now after overhearing a private conversation one night between Aol and Burke. How they needed another source of making silver. How Burke knew of a slave running den further south of Er Rada. How they didn't trust our plan. That's when I started to become more aware that I couldn't trust *them* either.

"Burke will try to sell them. If he lets the other girl live at all." I know him well enough; he was never planning to keep them for himself.

We're incredibly close to the Red Line, so it will be easy for all of them to find someone to sell to. They'll only be waiting for the right moment, the right compound, regardless of how I feel about the matter.

"What's your plan? Let the girls loose and face the backlash?" Jax's head dips, matching my contemplation. I avoid him, flicking my attention to the space around us.

"We'll bring them with us to Jynn."

His mouth drops open slightly. "And what will we tell him?"

I am used to thinking on the fly. Usually, never having a plan works out for me – at least it has so far. "That they will sell for much more there. We'll make them believe we agree with their choice." I watch my friend think, more than likely comparing possibilities.

"And once we reach Jynn. Then what?"

"We let them go. The streets will be crowded enough for them to escape." I wait, considering my words. "I think Burke will try to use our connections against us if he finds out why we're really in Jynn. He could use the roost there to get word back to Grandia."

Jax crosses his arms, pushing a braided strand from his cheek. "Burke's name is on the bounties, just like ours, Yoon. Tyg never trusted him. There's no way he would ever allow him back, despite handing us in."

Jax has been my closest comrade, my *friend*, for most of my life, but Burke had once been under his direct orders. I will admit that Jax would understand his soldier better than I would. However, seeing what someone does when faced with only death or life is interesting. Especially when it comes to betrayal. Burke chose life when he ran. He'll continue choosing his own life. No matter what it costs him. Jax cannot deny that. He knows that Tyg offers the only style of life that Burke would ever want; clearly, being on the run is not the answer for him.

"Burke left because of a mistake. He doesn't think he deserves this punishment. Think about it Jax, why would he agree to follow *me*."

"Maybe it's because he had a moment of clarity and realized that Tyg actually was wrong for what he did."

We both try to hold back a laugh. Jax sighs, relaxing his shoulders. "I don't know, Yoon. I don't want to believe that he would willingly betray *both* of us."

My friend rubs the misshapen dent on his temple from the hilt of our Zaiem's sword years prior. In *Burke's* defense. It took twenty-one agonizing nights before he woke from his deep sleep. He doesn't – he can't heal like I can, and every day he was near death, I was tormented by the understanding of what his dying and me living through it would be like. Burke would never understand that concept, he would never have felt the same as I had. I don't think the man felt a single shred of guilt from the incident, or for anything else for that matter.

"He will give us to Tyg in a heartbeat if there's an opportunity for him and you know it. We've been riding with him for too long."

Which would ultimately lead to our death. Well, Jax's death. My – I don't even know what I would call the things Tyg would do if he caught me.

"What are you suggesting we do then? Kill him? What about the others."

"What we need is for us all to make it to Jynn first." He nods once. "And I'm not worried about Gunn. We'll show Aol the harem. Maybe he'll say the wrong thing there and we won't have to worry about crossing his path again at all."

I tap my chin, making it seem as though I've been thinking of this idea for a while. Jax always trusts me when he thinks I have a plan. "We can send Burke off early, with the fabrics." Jax side-eyes me, clicking his tongue. "Geal can be entertained by him until we get there."

"Entertained." He grunts. "We don't know the state of Jynn right now, Yoon."

I look past Aya's barn, the one we've been keeping Hisan and Tagan in to rest.

"We aren't being given much of a choice. It isn't, I can't - here."

I don't want to admit to him that I'm fearful of him staying around, even though I know he can probably sense it.

"He'll be fine crossing the border, no one will recognize him. All he has to do is cut through the northern side of the range and he'll be at Jynn's gates in no time."

I hand him a piece of torn paper with my own scribblings that I fashioned together before meeting with him.

"We'll give him this and send him off with the fabrics and a few bottles of shine. She'll see the note, and our hands will be clean of him for a while."

My friend sighs, unfolding the parchment. "This isn't your insignia." He laughs slightly, shaking his head in confusion.

"Exactly."

His smile fades, realizing. "You're setting him up."

"Ydir will take care of him and we'll still be able to maintain our relationship with Geal. It's a win-win."

"Ydir?" Shock clearly presents itself on his skin. "You can't be serious."

"I am."

He looks at me deep within the confines of my being, reading me so easily. I straighten awkwardly, wishing he didn't know me so well.

"This is about *her* isn't it." Not a question. "Eyes the color of moss."

He quotes my mother's words. Words that I confided in him long ago over a cask of Ferackian wine.

"No." My eyes twitch. He doesn't mention my reaction, instead, he grins.

"If this backfires, it's on you. I win the stash."

A chuckle slips at the severity of his words, reminding me of the deal we made the morning before we received our first mark.

I salute him, sarcasm lining the gesture, matching the lack of seriousness. If I'm lucky, the Bahani will get to him first the moment he crosses the territory. If I'm fortunate enough, Burke will never have to deal with Ydir at all.

TEN

ADESSA

"If you refuse this, you and your bloodline will be put to death."

I don't remember passing out last night. My efforts to stay awake bled the moment Saedea's deepening breaths and the quiet crackle of a dying fire lulled me into a heavier sleep than I intended. I'm exhausted. That's what this feeling is. Exhaustion. My body really picked the wrong time to shut down, which is probably affecting the rate at which my spine is healing, because I still can't feel my legs.

I remember years ago, I'd fallen from a rotting almond tree I'd been climbing to gain a better vantage point on a farmer's wagon supplies, and I shattered two bones in my arm when the branch I thought would have supported me... didn't. Although I was much younger at the time, that injury had only taken a full day and one afternoon to heal.

How many more days will I have to endure this?

I stretch my shoulder back as far as the loose restraints will allow, taking in the scene ahead of us. The men have been busy packing up their camp, heaving equipment onto the camel's backs, rolling mats up and tucking them into pouches along the saddles. I see Gunn try to shove his mat into a bursting pack, shouting angrily when his camel shifts to the side, forcing the nestled items to spill to the ground in a heap. I scan the items rapidly, landing my attention on a pair of brown leather straps.

My satchel.

They have it. I can see the familiar tear on the canvas, screaming for its presence to be known by me. Gunn hurries to snatch it up, sneering while he murmurs something under his breath to Aol. The toothless man brushes past him, wiping the back of his mouth with a hand, spitting on the ground at my feet on his approach.

"Wake up, kid." I whisper, wiggling my arm to nudge her. "Kid." She's limp. "Saedea?"

A pang of nausea waters my throat. She can't be dead. She'd been perfectly fine last night, despite the ugly swell of her cheek, the rattle of her lungs while she slept... did I miss something?

Aol shifts closer, seeing the flick of concern dotting my expression. He lifts her chin, her head lolling to the side, shoulders slumping over the second he releases his grip. Groaning, he kicks her leg a few times with a heavy boot, ignoring my pleas for him to stop. Then, he holds a dirty finger under her nose.

"Still alive." He chuckles, filling my entire being with disgust. "Looks like you are too. Unfortunate." Aol cracks his knuckles, stopping at the thumb that seems to be giving him some trouble. "How're the legs?"

That cocky tone. I would set him on fire right now if I were capable. "What's wrong with your face?" I match him, nearly spitting my words.

The dried clay no longer covers his burn marks. They ooze pale yellow, edged with reddened skin. *Does he recognize me as Burke had?*

Aol grabs me suddenly, lifting me by the armpits, throwing me violently against the tree. The back of my head cracks against the trunk. I can't fight back when I smell the rot on his breath, so I bite back the bile that burns my throat instead and hold my head high, ignoring the ever-present flush of paralysis coursing through my lower half. He watches the loosely tied rope fall to the ground.

"Just because *he* doesn't want to kill you, doesn't mean I won't."

I dare to laugh. "Wait your turn."

I hit the sand before splitting pain erupts across my cheek from the sting of his hand, swallowing the whimper that threatens to slip. His beady eyes burrow into me for too long before he whistles for the other two, a sharp note that drives the other's attention to him.

"Bring the camels this way! I am not carrying their dead weight to you!" Two droplets of spittle dust the tops of my hands.

Gunn and Burke stare at us in contemplation, eventually deciding not to fight him and drag the three, fully packed, protesting animals over, positioning them to be mounted. Burke drags Saedea's limp body to one of them and with Gunn's help, they place her in a slouch across the curve of the animal's neck. Aol jumps up behind her.

I make a poor attempt to move on my own, desperate to show them that I haven't been broken. They can clearly see right through me. "Don't touch me." I hiss when Burke places his hands around my waist, easily plucking me from the ground.

"What? Can't move?" He teases.

Collecting the rest of the saliva that's left in my nearly dry mouth, I forcibly eject it all, aiming for Burke's chin. I hit it dead center. The rust color drips from my target. He immediately backhands me with a reverberating smack. My neck cracks on impact; black waves dance around my vision in a horribly disorienting blur. I loll my head back up and stare him down, grinning while he wipes the glob from his face. Warmth coats my lips; I let the blood run.

"Oh, I am going to enjoy breaking a rebellious creature like you." His acrid breath is somehow worse than Aol's. "Do you have any idea what they do to girls who are deemed unsellable in the Underground? Because I do."

His tone sits wearily on my bones. "And I know exactly what I have to do to *make* you unsellable." Black eyes bury themselves in the confines of my chest.

Gunn groans. "Come on Burke, Qa'id will be pissed if –"

"Enough, Bonehead! That easterner is no Qa'id of mine." Burke's large fingers wrap themselves around the rope that ties my wrists. He yanks me up, uncaring how he's pulling me the short distance to the camel. "I can't stand when you two do that. What are you trying to prove? He isn't even around!"

A salty cloth is shoved between my lips before I'm hoisted onto the saddle. Copper rushes down the back of my throat.

"But you've called him that before."

The marked man places himself behind me and clicks his tongue. The camel obeys, finding balance as it rises. "Yeah, because I'm being sarcastic. Idiot."

I recoil at his closeness, leaning as far forward as the tight saddle will allow, having to continue to swallow to keep myself from getting sick as pain sears my spine in immediate, bright flashes.

"What do you *want* us to call him them, huh?" Gunn asks, pulling his camel alongside us. He gives me a gesture that forces a visual of my throat being cut.

"Traitor." Burke grumbles, almost silently enough not to be heard by his comrades, however, I catch it. Gunn does not, giving Burke an expressive sigh while his camel falls to the last in line.

"We used to be on the same side, you know!" He calls out words that are ignored.

Burke pulls ahead of everyone, provoking rumbling complaints from all three animals. I try to steal glances back to Saedea from time to time. She's still unconscious. Aol mentioned that she was still alive, however, I'm worried for how much longer that will remain true.

We cross the gate, heading back into the central area of the village, past the divot where Saedea tripped, where our fates were sealed. Blood still marks the sand there. It's fairly early enough in the morning, the sun begins to blister the air around us, bouncing light from the rusted panels of the silo ahead. There doesn't appear to be anyone awake yet. The street is clear. We turn before hitting the center; not even the aroma of oil and tobacco wafts throughout the expanse of it as it had yester-day. There's no indication that Aya is awake either. Only the sound of a rooster calling notes that the village hasn't been abandoned overnight.

I stare at the back enclosure of Harmon's, wishing desperately for the old woman to step outside. Would she try to help if she saw me? If she saw the state that I'm in? My mind blares the answer over and over again.

No.

She wouldn't intervene, and I wouldn't blame her. Not with three clansmen as our captors. Maybe she knows them; maybe her silent warning to get on their leader's good side truly was a warning to me because she knew the consequences of not doing so. Not like it matters; the sweaty fabric prevents me from calling out to her anyways. She'll never know we were here.

"This way." Burke orders, goading his camel to the right, passing a few more houses, then the forge. The blacksmith was so close. A bubble of regret pains my nerves when we clear his empty building too, then cross the village border, following a separate path for a few more meters. The plot of land we've reached contains a single, hurriedly built barn surrounded by an enormous span of short, open fencing. Half of the barn's roof is caved in; a mixed pile of stone and dried ash wood fragments line the side of a decaying wall. A broken hammer lays amongst a scattering of metal hinges, rusted and abandoned.

I shiver at the unwarranted relief I feel when their leader emerges from the shadows of the barn's doorless frame, resting a palm against the half-stained wall beside him. Another man moves alongside, shading his eyes from the heat. The long sleeves of his tunic rest just below his wrists, adorned in dark stone beads and iron cuffs that are heavily contrasted against his partner who wears no decoration except for that single, silver ring around his pointer finger.

I recognize the other instantly as the one from Aya's yesterday, still heavily armed, with the addition of a drawstring bow wrapped around his shoulder to pair with the arrows that ride his calf. The two share a blank regard, moving their attention to the five of us. The scarred one inspects me emotionlessly, averting his gaze to the man next to him.

"Get the horses."

My thoughts cease at the mention of the unattainable, unsure if I heard his words correctly. *How would they have –*

I've only heard of horses in the stories shared in my homeland. After the Seconds, Skeall's horse stock was completely lost to a disease that swept the lands, taking most of my people's livelihood. When I found myself in Isla, I heard that the same fate beheld this continent as well. Only a few rough sketches proved the fact that horses were still alive. The ones that were, however, were owned solely by the clans. The repeating question sets off alarms all around me.

Who do these men belong to?

Jax disappears into the dark enclosure again, the only sound breaking the air is the anxious shuffle of the camels as they wait for their next order. A few heartbeats pass, and Jax emerges from the frame with two bridles in hand. A pair of enormous beasts follow behind. They look nothing like the sketches I've seen. Suddenly, I believe briefly in the power of the Mystics, seeing as they were the ones in charge of creating these majestic animals. No wonder the clans are feared with these creatures at their disposal. No wonder there were wars over owning them.

"What's wrong with her?" Jax calls out, settling into the saddle of the gray beast. His partner copies, hoisting himself onto the large onyx one.

"Sleeping." Aol brushes Saedea's cheek, adjusting her to rest against his chest, trying to disguise the fact that she looks near to death. Her head bobs up and down a few times on its own before settling onto the cusp of her shoulder.

"I'm sure." Jax grumbles, observing her for too long. His attention gathers itself, landing on me. The quick glare at the leader is ignored.

"Let's go. I want to leave before the village wakes." The scarred one announces, leading us away from the farm.

We all fall into a line, heading surprisingly back towards the main road. Heading in the direction I wish I had gone before I ran into this group. We pass Harmon's for the second time.

Please, Aya, please see us.

Silence. My heart sinks.

But then, the moment we clear her bar, the sound of squeaky hinges makes their leader hold his fist up, forcing our caravan to stop. His awareness moves to the gate, I follow his eyeline and watch Aya latch the fence closed upon her exit. She wipes dirty hands on the front of her apron, shielding her brows with a palm to observe us all. I stare at her, wide-eyed, unable to speak, hoping, wishing, *praying*, that how I look – the position Saedea is in, will make her consider the situation that's spread out in front of her. Her chin lowers when her eyes meet mine.

"Aya." Their leader hops down, bowing at his waist.

"If you move a single muscle, I'll make you watch me kill that girl. As well as the old woman. I might even force you to help me." Burke whispers, shoving knobbed knuckles into the side of my ribs. I nod in silent understanding, knowing full well that he wouldn't bother to announce empty threats.

Aya glances at me again, clearing her throat. "Come inside fahr something tah eat. I was just about tah put on some stew. Rabbit. I know yah'd like it."

I hear the others grumble uncomfortably. The half-blind leader straightens, running a casual hand through thick hair. "We don't have time, Aya. Please, go back inside, I saw Rust's ox at Manari's."

His focus shifts, darting in my direction briefly while the woman rubs her hands nervously together, raising her brows in a way that's making me anxious too. I have to believe that he wouldn't do anything to hurt her if she tried to help me, but I can't say the same for the others. "I –" She starts.

The air turns thick, the leader seems to feel it too. He ushers her towards the gate, deft fingers unlatching the lock.

"This is not the way." Aya states, a stern wrinkle forming to the shape of her forehead.

"It's the way it has to be."

He mentions carefully, opening the door for her, then turns back to his horse. Jax throws her a respectful salute as they pass, but she isn't watching him. She's watching me. Her deep-set eyes bore into mine.

Burke kicks the sides of his camel, moving to pass her as well. She crosses her fingers, shaking it a few times, ticking her head to the front of the line in a suggestive way, towards the horses. I wish I knew what she was trying to tell me.

"What was that?" Burke accuses, snapping his fingers towards the old woman. "What did you signal?"

In one swift motion, he's off the camel, jumping from a height that only a man his stature could make look smooth, stomping towards her before she can close the gate. His height dwarfs her. I begin to rub my wrists together, wishing I was able to break free from the bindings that Burke secured.

"I saw that." He presses the palm of his hand into her chest. Just as I knew she would, she doesn't back down. If anything, she presses herself closer to match him, backing into the fence. "You think because you're Binehi that you can –"

"That's enough, Burke." The leader is beside him in seconds, rushing to Aya's side when the brute doesn't obey. "Get your hands off of her."

I notice that he doesn't make a move to pry Burke away, rather waits for him to back off on his own. The monster laughs, a bellow that echoes across the road, bouncing off the walls of the nearly empty houses surrounding us.

"What's the problem, *Qa'id?*" He teases, provoking him, pressing a curved hand into Aya's covered neck.

"Get back on your camel, Burke. I won't ask you again."

Each of the leader's words burn with authority, riding his tone unlike anything I've heard from him yet. Burke simply snickers, gripping Aya's neck harder. A shred of concern flashes beneath her hardened expression. When she doesn't give him the reaction he's most likely searching for, he finally releases his grip.

"A waste of my time."

Mockingly, he bows at the waist, spitting not beside his leader's feet, but Aya's. I watch the scarred man turn, chest heaving with cooled frustration, calmly placing a gentle touch on Aya's shoulder. She throws it off, anger lighting her face, pointing a steady finger towards Burke's back.

"One day Burke, you will learn to regret the harm you've caused."

I lock my jaw, wishing that she remained quiet as we all wait for the marked man's reaction. His fists tighten and release at his side, rage spewing in a burst of energy, shoulder straightening while he cracks his neck both ways before spinning back on his heels. Their Qa'id is too quick. One of his daggers is pressed into Burke's ribs immediately, not allowing him to take another step.

"You know what will happen. Let. It. Go."

I can tell Burke is at war with himself. I have to admit, it *is* intriguing to watch a grown man like him contemplate the consequences of his actions. His fingers are purple from squeezing his fists so firmly. The vein in his neck looks ready to pop.

"Let's move." Jax announce, impatiently. He scans the horizon ahead. "Wouldn't want any others to join in on all the fun." He taps his upper lip, an indication of the man I'm sure everyone but Saedea knows of.

Burke relinquishes a frustrated growl, throwing his hand down in Aya's direction. "You'll be seeing your husband soon, Binehi."

He offers a single, lasting curse before turning my way, pushing himself up in the saddle. I can sense the anger oozing from him, sticking like mud to my back. It appears the man with the daggers also has to calm Aya down, gently thumbing her neck before whispering a few words to her. She moves her hate-filled eyes to him, instantly soothing the fire inside them. Her chin dips in response, mouthing something back.

With that, the leader steps away, watching her carefully when she heads into the enclosure, latching the gate behind her. I can barely make out her hidden form between the slate. Then, the Qa'id swivels around, examining Burke. Examining me.

"She's the reason we have shine to sell. Understand?" He huffs. Burke shifts uncomfortably in his seat.

"Time to go." Jax shouts, strumming his fingers along the side of his horse's neck, waiting for his partner to resaddle.

I can't help but look back at Harmon's to see if Aya has chosen to keep watching us. A surge of relief courses through me when I know that she is. She has a certain strength about her that I recognize. How she could confront a man like Burke, without a flinch at his threat of her impending death is a testament to that. *Binehi.* Why did Burke make it seem like being so was an insult?

ELEVEN

ADESSA

"You must not let them see you. Remember the name. Lapis. Now, run."

The sun had already lowered itself, softly cresting the violet skyline by the time Saedea wakes up. It starts with a few tremors, barely noticeable. Shortly after, she slams herself upright from the scoop of the camel's neck, releasing a blood-scorching scream. Clearly unaware of where she is and what is currently happening to her. It turns everyone's attention, stopping the caravan in its tracks. Aol covers his palm over her mouth to stop the noise right as Burke pulls the animal alongside them. I try to lean towards her, to show her that I'm here. She clamps her teeth down around Aol's meaty fingers.

He shrieks, falling, throwing both Saedea and himself from the camel. Burke reaches to catch Aol but the bulky man slips from his grasp, landing below the girl with his hand still trapped between her teeth. Blood pours from her mouth. Her expression is wild.

"Get this thing off of me!" Aol wails, pressing himself on top of her, trapping her in the sand. Gunn reaches them first. Burke is unwilling to move, entertained by the scene below us despite my thrashing. The one with the limp wobbles, latching onto Saedea's hair. Burke eventually joins, bored, helping Aol pry his fingers from her jaw. The toothless man smashes his boot into the front of her face once he's free, a wet trail of blood pooling into the sand, down her bobbing chin. A mix of hers and his.

I continue screaming through my gag, fearful of Saedea's bloodshot eyes that roll into the back of her head. Her crumpled figure clings to life. Aol kicks again, yowling in pain, clutching his hand in a feeble attempt to stop the bleeding. The others are doing nothing to stop him from assaulting an already dying girl. It makes my stomach roar.

Stop them! Stop them! My mind screams. Torments.

Intense rage bubbles through my veins. I rock back and forth, ripping myself from the saddle. The impact of my fall sparks lightning throughout the length of my spine. I am barely able to lift my head through the sand that coats my eyelashes, but I hear someone dragging the girl away from me.

"That's enough!" In the distance, their Qa'id shouts, roughly dismounting. I can hardly hear any of their objections, the ringing in my ears is too intense. The binding around my wrists cut into me when I attempt to sit upright, a thick burn in its wake. I am desperate to push through my weaknesses.

My legs eventually curl to the side, my back straightening. I shake my head, blinking away the granules that blur my vision. Aol sends one last kick into Saedea's ribs by the time I'm upright. Jax violently pushes Aol away from her, bashing his head on the way down. Gunn carefully limps towards Saedea, checking her pulse. Burke seems all too distracted by the spread of blood, covering it in sand with the edge of his boot.

"*Malakiro!*" Jax seethes, stepping on Aol's neck. The rotten man releases a guttural sound, struggling to free himself.

"Don't you see what she did to my hand!" He spits out sand with his words, waving his injury around like some prize.

"Are you still unable to stand?" The steady voice behind me makes my heartbeat skip with terror. I've been focused all too much on the others; I didn't realize their leader had made his way to me. I tilt my head to meet him, squinting from the light that radiates his features. *Don't you dare pretend to look concerned.*

I wish this gag was free from my mouth. He matches my vengeful glare, the muscles on his neck are tense.

"I didn't realize how bad your injuries were." Crouching down, he wraps careful fingers around the base of my chin. His concerned expression roams over the swollen lump beneath my eye, the dried blood crusting the lower half of my face.

His other hand grazes the salty, wet cloth from my mouth. I tick my jaw from his fingers, working the muscles that have been stretched for an entire morning. The only muscle he moves is his throat, which bobs up and down, but no words come out. His hands remain firm after having moved to my shoulders.

"Yoon!" The richness in Jax's voice cuts through the air, interrupting our stare down. Jax now has Saedea cradled in his arms. I watch for any movements, squinting at the motion of her eyelids, the twitch of her mouth, surprisingly still alive. "We need to get her some help!"

Burke booms a retort against the idea. *I swear I'll rip out his heart.*

Jax shoots him a daggered look that matches my thoughts, setting the girl swiftly, carefully beside his horse. He relinquishes the drawstring from his shoulder, guiding an arrow to its dock. Burke, Aol and Gunn all raise their hands in defense.

"You all want to sell her, right?" He aims the tip at each one of them. "Don't think for one second that we didn't know that was your plan when you took them." He takes heavy strides, pushing the arrow into Aol's chest. "You all want silver, don't you? Since Yoon and I haven't provided you the cushy life that we never promised." He passes the threat to Burke.

"Need I remind you *all* that you are also named!" Moves it back to Aol. "If you think you'll be able to find a slave runner *before* someone recognizes us, then remember this one thing. She will not fill your pockets if she is beaten! And you'll make even less off a corpse!"

The man I've finally learned the name of, Yoon, rises, shifting a sturdy leg to my back, offering unwarranted support for me to rest against. I falter, craving relief. Still, I refuse to lean against him. Instead, I shovel my palms into the pockets of sand in front of me to help me balance.

"Yoon." Jax begs, turning our way.

"How do you suggest we help her?" Their leader shouts back. *He isn't against the idea?*

"Just leave her here!" Aol slurs. "We have the other one, we'll sell her! Won't make up for my stolen gems, but it's better than nothing!" I swallow hard at the mention of selling me, watching Jax shove him back to the ground, pointing his weapon to center Aol's forehead. "Don't you know how many women are left? Neither of them are disposable!"

His rhetoric frightens me. It seems like the words have a similar effect on the others as well, as if they are all aware of something I am not. Jax faces us again. "I met an elder in Teryal, buying supplies. A medicine man. He mentioned that he lives a bit further east from here, north of the Red Line. Said he'd sell us some tinctures if we happened along the way. We need to resupply, Yoon. We're out of healing clay. Thanks to Aol."

The blistered man gapes.

I make a mental note that Jax is the only one calling the man behind me by his actual name instead of Qa'id. Or nothing at all. Maybe Jax is also in charge of them?

But clans don't have more than one leader.

"Me? Thanks to that bitch over there!" Aol quips, throwing a fistful of sand at Jax.

Yoon sighs, motioning an agreement of some kind. Whatever it is, the others begrudgingly obey, glaring at each other. Jax continues threatening them with an arrow to the back as they mount their camels, all except for Burke. Only when the other two are all settled in does Jax return his arrow to its place on his calf, and moves the bow across his back to match his sword. He lifts the girl, cradling her along the saddle of his horse. For a split moment in time, I think I see her open her eyes and wink.

I can't trust my own vision right now, the black specks of pain weave too closely together.

"Allow me to help you stand." Yoon says softly as he bends down. I can't object quick enough, his hands are beneath my armpits. My feet dip numbly into the sand, knees wobbling. His hold is firm.

"Don't put me back on that damned camel." I object, hoarsely. I wish I hadn't. His chest heaves rigidly.

"I wish I didn't have to." He states blankly.

Burke stomps over to us before his words register. "Give her to me, I'll be sure this one doesn't cause any trouble." He growls.

Yoon's grip loosens after a long pause, replaced with rougher hands. I'm half-thrown onto the saddle, I don't have much time, or strength to scramble before the brute settles in. He positions me firmly between his arms. The fingers on Yoon's hand stretch at his sides, observing the interaction. He moves back to the front of the line.

"I'll kill you." I hiss, grateful that the gag is gone.

Burke whacks the base of my skull as soon as the words leave my lips. I wish I could fight back, I almost dare him to make good on his promise of making me *unsellable*, but my mind bleats in horror for me to stop myself.

Saedea. I can't risk any of their wrath, not when she's in a vulnerable state like this. The only thing that gives me relief is the fact that Jax has her on his horse now.

Aol pulls his camel alongside us, a bloodied hand wrapped deep in his sand scarf. A swell of pride can't help itself, tugging the corner of my mouth when I see the crimson that stains his lap. His pupils blaze once he notices the smile I'm not really trying to conceal.

"Think this is funny?"

I shrug. "I'm jealous actually. At least I know that my fire has left you scarred. That's enough for me." His realization widens.

There it is. Took him long enough.

I give him a wink. Burke grabs my chin, facing my head front. "Enough, Aol."

The toothless man attempts to object, brandishing the curved blade he has strapped to his back. All Burke does is kick the camel, prompting it to fall in line with Jax's horse. I'm grateful to be closer to Saedea.

Darde seems unyielding far now. So unobtainable. What I used to think would be the purpose of my life, has now become my nightmare. There is an empty silence soiling the landscape ahead, unbearable sorrow in my chest for the lack of time I'll be able to make up. So much hunger and disbelief lining the walls of my stomach.

I look to the sky above and see vultures circling overhead. I wonder if it's because of Saedea that they do so. Or if they've been sent by the Mystics, to initiate more bad omens. As if what I have been through already isn't enough.

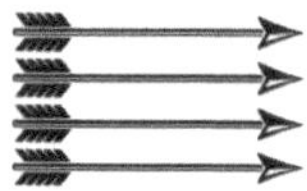

I'm only slightly consoled by the fact that we're at least still heading east. The sun is far behind us now, dipping lower and lower into the horizon, forcing a milky pink haze on the sand around us. Pockets of craters scattered across the landscape have made for a less-than-fragile ride. I've been keeping an eye on Saedea, who crests her head along Jax's collarbone. Still not waking, but at least I think I can see her breathing.

I assumed that this medicine man Jax had mentioned would have lived close by, if he had been discovered in Teryal, but we've been riding for a concerning amount of time. Surely, everyone else feels it too, shifting the occasional wayward glance between each other. They haven't stopped for anything, not even to eat, not even to water themselves or their animals. I wonder if they have any food amongst all those packs. "How much longer?" Gunn bays.

"There will be a sign!" A moment later, Jax points to the left.

Yoon directs his horse, leading the way. Buried in the sand, an ash tree is carved with the letter 'C.' Mounded sand dunes on either side loom overhead as our caravan moves past it, heading down the carved-out path. It's rowed with dried brush, buried in odd patterns alongside bright green cacti, spaced the same distance apart, lining the stretch of sand. The flowers on the cacti are blooming, which is strange for the season, especially after the area's drought.

Another curve follows a walkway of bundled almond trees, trees that I haven't seen since Farit, whose abnormally long leaves wave as we pass. I notice each one has ripe fruit bulging from the stems. The air immediately shifts. Burke tenses behind me, clearly feeling the same uncomfortable change in atmosphere the exact time that I do. Each animal slows their movement on their own, shaking their snouts with unrest the closer we get to the dip of a valley. There is only silence around us, not even the chattering of desert birds or the swish of the dusty wind. It seems the air itself doesn't wish to make noise.

A private limestone well is sat off to the right of our path. Within a few steps of that, a flat-top cobb hut is nestled among oversaturated date palms. The fruit it bears is thick and plump, so much so that I can see them easily from the top of the path. A fire burns in a swollen pit right outside the thatched door of the hut. The smoke coming from it is an impenetrable black. My nose is consumed by the smell of roasting herbs.

The clan moves from their mounts, directing their animals towards the shade of palms near a full water trough across from the well. There aren't any other animals on the property that I can see, so perhaps the trough is meant as a welcoming gesture for the medicine man's visitors. At least that's what I hope. The fact that he has his own well out here – *something isn't right.*

I ignore the bleating warning in my head, pressuring myself into gratitude. He's a healer. Someone whose sole purpose is to help people. He won't turn a blind eye to us when he understands that we are not willing companions to these men. He won't allow this to continue any further than it has.

Burke yanks me from the camel suddenly, dropping me to the ground without a second thought. "Stay put."

I wince against my bindings, rationalizing what to do, choosing to crawl to the edge of the well instead. His seething stare ignites.

"Burke." Yoon simply states, leading his horse to the trough after he warns his man not to go after me. I rest my back against the cool limestone well, scrutinizing the way Jax carries Saedea in his arms. Her head hangs unsupported while he bangs the bottom of the thatched door with the tip of his boot. A few agonizing seconds later, it opens, creating a space for him to duck under the frame, disappearing inside.

Something is not right.

Burke's fists clench then relax, impatience awaiting permission to strangle me. I shy away, knowing that there is a high chance he will act without it. Luckily, Aol calls out his name, forcing his blaring attention away from me, leaving air for me to breathe. I take in a heat-filled inhale, listening to water serenely slosh around the well. It envelops my entire being in an overwhelming thirst. I can tell the early signs of dehydration are creeping up on me, having felt it many times before in my life, so I'm aware of the consequences. The last thing that my poorly healing body needs is to be hindered any further.

So, I adjust myself, twisting on my hip, dragging my chest upwards across the rough stone. I press the front of my thighs against the lip of the well, using it as leverage to stay balanced. A rust-worn bucket hangs off-center above me. I gently press my folded knuckles along the ledge and stand on weak toes, still barely feeling the texture of the ground. Leaning forward, I gain enough height to be able to tip the edge of the bucket over with my mouth. I wish Burke had the decency to at least unbind my wrists, this wouldn't be half as difficult with them untied.

My teeth clack uncomfortably against the metal lip, warm water splashes the sides, rocking back and forth with my swaying. I tug hard-er, using the momentum to upturn the bucket entirely. A healthy dose of life-saving liquid dumps out from the vessel, wetting my face, and the front of my shirt, causing sloppy mud to seep around my toes. It tastes like the bucket. I swallow as much as I'm able to, then dip my chin down, holding the collar of my dirtied shirt in my mouth to suck the fabric dry. The essence of grime makes me squirm.

As I turn, hobbling into a seated position on the well, I don't avoid Aol and Burke's displeasure for me. I spit out the edge of the cloth in disgust for them, holding their stare, hoping that I look as intimidating as I think I do. Baring my teeth, Aol looks away first, but only because his attention has been turned to Jax. He steps out into view, empty-handed.

Yoon tilts his head downwards with a frown when his partner leans in to whisper something in his ear.

"We'll stay here for the night." Jax announces to the others.

The three mumble to themselves as they settle on their mats around the smokey firepit. It seems like they assumed they'd be staying here anyway, considering they already had the forethought to spread out the spaces where they'll sleep. I scan the area around them, hoping to catch another glimpse of my satchel, wondering how full it will be when I get it back. I'd love to know what they deemed worthy for themselves. It was in Gunn's saddlebag the last time I saw it. I mark the camel he's been riding – light brown, with a large brown patch painting its nose. The soft part of his right ear is halved.

A new voice draws my awareness back to the cobb hut instead of continuing my search. The deep, rattling sound that echoes from the pockets of his chest is an indicator of how many years lived. The Elder's face is smeared with reddish-brown clay, a shade lighter than the ashen skin beneath. It's a contrast to the simple canvas robes he wears. His bright, ivory hair is plated with yellow-gold bands hanging loosely past his waist.

The look of him immediately makes me feel nervous. It isn't the odd color of his painted skin, the strange, near-gray tattoos that etch every surface of visible skin, or his almost skeletal stature that unnerves me. No, it's his eyes. The whites are reddened, showcasing a pair of glassy, white irises; the wide-set pupils are cleaved. So divided that I can see the separation where I stand.

What are you?

The others shuffle nervously on their mats at the sight of him too. Yoon maintains a solid distance between himself and the Elder, carefully watching his every move. My heart sinks when he discreetly gestures for him to look my way. The Elder turns, offering a single nod. I grind my teeth, wishing the well would absorb me as this 'healer' approaches, robes fluttering with the unsteady sway of age. He rests his splintered pupils on my legs, then back up to meet my face. I stare blankly into the void of his expression.

"I am told that you cannot feel your legs." His voice is distant, like he speaks from a place that's much further from where we are standing. The beckoning sound flecks my skin in chills.

What are you? An echo harmonizes with the question, my voice alongside another's.

"Troubling." The Elder murmurs, blinking at my bound wrists. "May I?" He places his palms flat and openly spreads them out in front of me.

What are you? I – it – asks again.

The bindings fall to the sand, fraying threads slide out of the small cuts they've created around my wrists. He hadn't touched them. I stagger back in confusion, catching the ledge of the well with my butt. His palms reach for me again, waiting. Now intrigued by how he did that, I carefully place my palms along his. His skin feels like coarse sand, speckled in nearly black freckles, as fragile and weathered as I would have thought a man of his age's hands would be.

The moment his hands cover mine completely, a blast of energy bolts in every nerve my body has. I'm struck by a hot hammer; my mind washes, a blank canvas. Suddenly, nothing around me exists anymore. The grumblings of the camels are gone, the well behind me disappears, and the smell of the fire no longer lingers on my nose. The vast deserted landscape transforms into a place I've never seen before.

A beautiful glass ocean sparkles brilliantly in front of me. Indigo waves that foam as they rise and fall splash residual salt into the air. Barrels upon open barrels of what look to be ginger, cinnamon, cardamom pods, and spices I've never seen before fill the space ahead, nestled on top of clean, white sand. There are docks to the left, clear of people. In fact, I don't see a single soul *anywhere*. It's just me and the Elder, who positions himself in front of me. *Where am I?*

This looks nothing like the trading port in Isla, so it can't be my own memory. Am I dreaming? In the middle of the day? Attached against the main dock landing sits an enormous ship, no markings of the Tilidaan, or any other clan for that matter. Not a single flag flies across their sail. It's blank. The water beside the ship erupts with the blast of a raging ocean, raining warm droplets down around us. A mosaic beast emerges from the deep. The waves quickly become violent.

The creature bellows and sputters, rocking the giant ship, banging its wooden base along the dock rhythmically with the tides. The creature's body reflects beams of rainbows from the sun onto the shore around us, bright enough to make me blink against the light. I reactively shade my eyes, searching the top of the waves for the blur of a split tail. It doesn't resurface. I have half a mind to believe I was hallucinating the entire thing.

The Elder says nothing, he stands there solemnly watching, waiting. I don't speak a word to him either, in fear that if I do, all of this will go away. Even if it isn't peace that I feel, it's something else, something that I've never experienced before. Something that my soul recognizes, like it's been here before, but I have not.

It isn't until the ground begins to quiver, shaking the contents of the barrels out onto the clean sand, the sky above us swirling around in a green-gray haze, whipping salt-lined wind to bite at our skin, that I wish to leave this place.

Something isn't right. My voice yells at me to leave, that something horrible is going to happen if I stay.

The Elder doesn't move, the tattoos on his body *glow*, I can even see the light of them beneath his robes. I step back, away from the docks, nearly tripping over myself. The space transforms once more, blinking past us in a blur. I hear his hoarse voice speaking to me, all around me. *Now I can see you clearly.*

The words scratch at my eardrums, echoing through the corners of my mind.

This strange world shifts, whizzing past us in a blur that makes my ears ring, allowing me to catch glimpses of iron bars, a curved blade. Armor a deeper color of the ocean I'd seen only moments ago.

I've seen this. I've seen this armor, the blade. Where have I seen this before?

"Wait –" I start. "I don't want to go back." My body is being thrown into a desolate reality that I no longer care to be. "Please." Whatever I would face in this dreamlike state has to be better than what I'm currently facing with those men, right?

You cannot stay there. The Elder's voice answers me back.

The haze evaporates, bits of stormy gray swirl the Elder's pupils. I suck a heavy breath in, hitting my back against the curve of the well, shaking the blue from behind my eyes. I'm not sure how long we were in that vision, it didn't feel long enough. It doesn't seem like the others had noticed the world had changed around them. Both Jax and Yoon are busy tightening arrow points, completely unaffected. The other three lay back on their mats, relaxing around the spice-smoked fire.

"Where – what was that?" I'm desperate for an answer, fumbling my words. I almost forgot what my own voice sounded like when not distorted by the other. The Elder slowly releases his grasp on my hands, holding the crook of his arm to me.

"Come." That is all he says.

"No. Tell me what that was. What you did." My defiance goes unnoticed.

"It was not I who brought us there." His answer is simple, beckoning me to take his arm.

"You *were* there – wait, who brought us there?"

He blinks at me once. Twice. Raises a brow. "Follow me, child."

I stiffen, irritated by the lack of answers. He helps me take a step forward, only for me to falter against him. "I can't."

You are still not yet healed. It's his words, not mine that encompass me.

Another trip in the soft sand causes Yoon's immediate attention. I wince at the sight of him standing.

No, don't come over here. My words this time.

"Allow me, Chadron."

Yoon's frustratingly calm voice speaks up when he reaches the healer in a few strides, stepping alongside him. Before I can object, the old man unfurls himself from me, resting me against the well once more before giving a long, passing look between Yoon and myself. He hands me off as if I were the child he called me and trudges ahead, allowing space to lead us to the open doorway of the hut. Yoon offers me a new position, the crook of his own arm, but I slap it away and stumble forward. His hands are around me in less than a second.

"I don't want your help." I swallow dryly, squeezing the blurriness of uncomfortable agony from my expression.

Yoon's strong fingers tighten ever so slightly on my biceps.

"Fine."

The grip loosens, and I am filled with instant regret, feeling my legs buckle. I don't stop myself from leaning against him for unwanted support, if only to help level out my weight to balance on my own momentarily.

Mystics' around. My knees are too shaky. I groan, shuffling a half-step past him out of sheer defiance. Yoon matches my pace, repositioning himself at my side, wrapping a steady arm across my back and around my shoulder. At least he doesn't say anything about my dependance on his help right now.

"Mystics damn you." I glower, wishing I could crawl – if I didn't think it so demeaning. "I'm going to kill your man for –" My words trail off, knowing the mistake I might have just made.

"You would be doing me a favor." He responds, looking solely at the rough path in front of us. *What?*

He says nothing more in the short distance to the threshold of the hut. A bitter smell of burning sugar, paired with a tinge of acidic sour burrows into my nostrils. It's a smell my memory has encountered many times before in the opium dens of Farit. A smell that my stomach has always disagreed with. I swallow thickly. The pressure on my arms tells me Yoon has some associations with the smell as well.

The room inside is dark, with a single round window, if you could call it that, on the furthest right side of the wall. It's big enough to filter in a trickle of light, which casts the enclosed space in dark shadows. On the table below the window, sits disorganized jars and piles of parchment that topple the surface in a lopsided mess. A smoking pipe sits dead center, the acrid tinge filling the room, wafting from its tiny bowl.

To my left, two small cots are pushed against the cornered wall. Saedea's unmoving body is sprawled out on one, blanketed in a pile of dark furs. Above both beds hangs gnarled charms of bones and beads tipped with onyx feathers. Yoon leads me to the unoccupied cot and finally releases me. He clears his throat, burying his hands into his pockets, looking entirely uninterested as he takes in our surroundings. I choose to ignore how the shadows caress his golden skin.

"You may leave." Chadron speaks. Yoon doesn't respond. He casts a quick glance back to me, opening and closing his mouth, as if wishing to speak.

"All will be well, Qa'id." The Elder stands tall and places a firm hand on the leader's shoulder, giving a reassuring nod. Yoon straightens, squinting.

"We will be right outside." He mentions, pointing at the door.

"The fire will keep you and your men warm tonight."

Yoon taps his foot a few times before bowing, not to me, to Chadron; then he ducks under the frame and out of view. He closes the door with one last look around the room. The crunch of his footsteps walking away from the hut somehow makes me just as uneasy as I was when he was standing directly in front of me. I scoot back so my legs spread out on the bed, resting my back against the cooled mud wall. The healer breathes in, then out. In, then out. Then, he begins to chant.

He inhales the contents of his pipe, placing a jar that contains a soft, red powder in his hands. With deft fingers, he starts sprinkling the substance along the length of Saedea's body.

"What is that?" I question, fighting the sudden nausea that rises in my stomach from the combined smells of opium and whatever is in that jar. My hands rip at the jacket around me, peeling it from my sweat-soaked skin. Everything is too hot in this room. He continues dusting the powder over her, around her, a steady tap, tap, tap against the glass as he spills it among the furs.

"How will powder help her, exactly?" I don't mean to sound so demanding. "I knew a healer once. She never used anything like – that."

"Different techniques lead to different outcomes."

Another tap. I need to remain on his good side. I need him to keep these men from dragging us any further into the unknown, from at least taking Saedea. I'll go willingly if I have to, as long as that means the healer would allow her to stay here once we leave. I'm sure I'll find a way to escape them eventually, especially since I won't have to worry about her well-being in the process.

Besides, where I'm heading has no place for a girl like her. She won't be safe even if she's with me. Staying with the Elder will be her best chance at a new life, no matter how odd he seems. She won't be alone; it'll be what she wanted.

"How long until she wakes up?"

"That will depend on whether she wishes to or not." He brushes a sweaty strand of hair from her forehead.

"Those men out there are a part of one of the clans. I haven't figured out which one."

I leave the sentence open, hoping he has the answer for me. He doesn't.

"They've taken us against our will. You saw the bindings, how they beat us. The big one broke my back, they nearly killed *her*. They only brought us here so you could heal us. They'll sell us to slave runners once we leave."

Please, don't you understand that we are in danger.

"If you don't interfere, we'll die."

Chadron corks the jar. "They will not sell you." He pauses between chanting, keeping his back to me. "I cannot offer the help you seek."

"I'm not asking you to help me. I'm asking you to help *her.*"

I glare at the back of his braided head as he rubs a strange spiral into Saedea's forehead, matching the tattoo branded to his neck.

"I am merely a healer. How am I to be of any help?" The question is lined with retort. It confuses me to the core.

"You are not *merely a healer.*" I can hear anger rising in the hackles of my throat. I know he can hear the anger too. It pushes him to peer over his shoulder. His strange eyes blink. He was there in that same vision when his palms touched mine. He felt the same ocean breeze that caressed my face. I know he did. *It was not I who brought us there.*

"If you're not a healer, then at least you're still an Elder. You have an obligation to the Firsts. To keep our bloodlines intact. You *will* help her." I pause, hoping for a reaction. "Or I will end your life."

The threat doesn't appear to bother him in any way. He sways from the cot, heads to the table, searches among the mess. The clinking of glass between his fingers reveals another vial of powder, this time, black.

"Stubborn." He chides, repositioning himself between our two cots. "Strong-willed. Poisoned by hate." A sigh. "Why did I think this lifetime would be anything different from the last?"

My expression squeezes. "What –"

"I cannot help those who will only refuse to receive it." He shakes the contents of the vial into his palm and turns towards me. "And with one so firmly trapped. Refusing to know better." His tongue clicks. "Despite my previous warnings."

The echoing repeats the words of warning over and over again. I press my fingers to my ears in an attempt to make it stop. His pupils dilate, moving his attention to my hands.

"I've already intervened too much."

"What are you talking about?" I scoff.

"Your death. Your rebirth."

Rebirth?

That's what the monks preach. What Tirma – I shake my head. Perhaps this man is one of the Devout, a cultist. Maybe this is all for show. I've heard stories of things like this happening in Skeall, of how tales of the Mystics were transformed by believers who thought they could do good – for a price.

Same in Farit, the opium dens had the occasional 'seer' who simply made up their powers of sight, high off the effects of a certain plant from the east. Opium. That has to be what's happening. I'm being affected by the smoke. The vision, the voices, it all had to be a hallucination. A trick. Those men out there think this man is a healer. Albeit convincing, he's clearly a fake.

Very well, I can play along. Scammers are always satisfied with payment.

"Let's make a deal, you and I." I listen to the man resume his humming. "You help the girl, keep her here. In return, I will give you all the silver you need. I have a few coins in my pocket and I know where that clan is hiding more." A pause in his chant. "Do you want the camels too? I will help you capture them." I await the simple answer that greedy bargainers usually respond with. "I'm not sure about the horses, but if you have a weapon I might –"

"That is not the path."

He hisses, rubbing black powder around and around his palm with his crooked, branded finger. The lump at the back of my throat expands.

"What do you want then? What can I offer you to keep her here?" My breathing hitches, unwilling to part with the item I'm about to offer, but I might not have a choice in the matter. It heats around my thumb. "I'll give you this. It has to be worth something. I hear it's made of jade if that means anything to you."

I twist the circlet around my thumb anxiously, noticing the whites of his eyes brightening, flashing to the jade again. I don't want to give it up, but I will. For Saedea, I will.

"That is not yours to give." His tone shifts. Frustration flares across my cheeks.

What are you?

The question annoyingly thrums against my mind, pinching my gut.

"Then what is it that you *do* want?" There is a brief moment of empty silence before he finally speaks.

"You have already made a decision your other lives had not." Another lazy circle traces the heap in his palm. *Other lives? This man has lost his mind.*

"Humor me." I give in, not wanting to make him shut me out completely. Doing so would seal her fate indefinitely.

"Will you be seeking revenge this time as well?" The inquiry confuses me.

"I made a promise to myself to get to Darde a long time ago. Revenge is the only –"

The Elder shakes his head, humming along to a song that I don't recognize.

"Then you will die once more, Adessa."

I tense up, suddenly *very* aware of my surroundings.

"Where did you learn my name?"

The men don't know it, and Saedea had been carried here unconscious.

"You will not be allowed another opportunity." He continues. "One hundred times is one hundred times too many."

The words dry in my mouth. The air blisters around us, suffocating me. I feel the need to run, but conveniently, my legs still don't have enough feeling to even make the attempt.

"You must listen to me, child." He mouths the words, but the sound doesn't come from his lips, it's echoing in my head. It pairs with a deeper tone that continues to ask *what are you* over and over again.

The opium burns, more powerful, more intense. My eyelids are heavy, my head spins. My lungs are filling to capacity with smoke.

"You have been given a choice. One you must make rather quickly." The world swirls around me. I fall back on the furs. "This is not the way to remedy what your past has punished you for. Find him. *See* him."

"Who –" I can barely speak, hardly think. It's as if I'm underwater. My throat burns when I gasp for air. "I don't understand." There isn't a weapon in sight. I won't be able to help myself. "Please, I don't know what you mean."

This 'healer' holds his palm level to my face, and with a heavy rush from his lungs, the shadow of his breath glimmers with sparks of ebony powder. It reaches me, forcing me to unwillingly inhale. I can feel my body's untethered response. It buries me in haze, plummeting my mind into a terrifying darkness.

"I will show you."

TWELVE

ADESSA

"And what did you expect? That this time would be any different?"

The moon crests brightly at its peak, brimming the expanse of the sky overhead in a hazy glow. Its shadowed face etches the inside of the perfect sphere, growing heavier as my vision pans to the world beneath me. Tall trees, the trees of my homeland, surround the open field, nestled inside a forest of dark green, flushed with sharpened branches of thin blades.

The width of these pines makes them appear larger than any building I've seen on the desert lands I've grown so familiar with, but the ground they are standing upon is flat, dusted with white snow instead of golden sand. A small reminder that I am not where I am supposed to be. To make matters worse, I'm floating above the landscape, my limbs dangle weightlessly in the air above the trees.

A single shadow passes the moon to my right, the sky darkening with such intensity that even the stars appear to cower beneath it. I glance down again, catching a glimpse of a woman staggering forward as she approaches the open, inner circle. Her desert attire is out of place against the chill of the winter wind that roars around her, whipping soft curls that frame her face, biting into her skin like it were a fresh persimmon. I peel my sight away from the blood that trails down both her arms.

Do not look away. The Elder's voice whispers.

The woman tilts her chin upwards, glazed focus in those green eyes that match the forest around her. "That's – me." I hear myself choke on the words.

The moment they leave my tongue, I'm overwhelmed by the sensation of falling, snapping, whirling, plummeting to the earth. An all-consuming ice-cold fire burns throughout my entire being as I'm thrown back into my physical form. I suck in a disturbed breath, as if inhaling air for the very first time. My fingertips tingle, a sensation that finds its way creeping up the base of my neck.

Behind you.

The unsettling idea of being watched forces me to twist suddenly, facing the vast expanse of the darkened woods. I can hardly make out the outline of a person ahead of me. The moon brightens in turn, spilling light out over the landscape in response to knowing that I cannot see. My tongue refuses to move, wishing I could call out to the figure ahead. I'm frozen in place when I try to take a weakened step forward. I blame it on my bare feet in the ankle-deep snow that turns my toes numb.

I try to speak once more, putting pressure on my vocal cords with a soft touch to the throat. I immediately shiver when I watch the man stumble out of the shadows and reveal himself to me.

Yoon.

He looks different than when I saw him last. His hair is no longer tied back in that lazy way he wears it; instead, the tendrils fall far past his shoulders, longer than it has been, wet with snow and steam from the heat of his body. Liquid drips from the strands, hissing as tiny droplets hit the snowy ground below, loudly enough to hear it from where I stand. Maybe it's because the rest of this world is completely silent. Even the whipping winds have stilled.

Yoon's skin is pale under the cold gaze of the stars, no longer wrecked by the heat of the golden, desert sun. His blinded eye is no longer milky gray, the iris matches its twin in a dark shade of brown. The scar that once previously marked his face has also disappeared, as if it had never been there in the first place.

Yoon stands hunched at the shoulders, defeat written in the stance. The heavy rise and fall of his chest matches the crisp steam from his breath on the exhale. Another staggered step – my eyes wander down, utterly shocked by this leathered version of him. He lifts his head, and I soon know the reason why he looks the way he does. A large, open wound gapes his throat in a slice, coating his neck in blood. The thick substance drips down in wet clumps.

Red on white.

My lungs seize. The longer I stare, the more I'm able to examine the damage that's been caused. Crimson blossoms his bare chest, an open wound central to where his heart would be. My gaze roams further, noting that in his hand, he carries a loosely held broadsword. Nothing like the curved machete I've recently seen him touting. This blade is longer, with a hilt of iron, not gold, and a dark blue stone inset on the handle. He points the tip towards the snow. The gleam of steel is muted by more of the same blood that coats him.

Agony cleaves through me once I come back to my senses. I shudder, falling to my knees. The cold instantly freezes my clothing, seeping through to my skin.

What is this? I ask the void.

Do you still not see?

It answers back, following an unbearable pain that blows directly through my heart. A tang of copper crisps the dry winter air, tainting my tongue. I've never experienced pain like this, not even when I had felt like the arrows had killed me all those years ago. What I felt then was peace, disrupted by the horrible sense of waking up, of living once more. This is different. This is unyielding. My soul yearns for a release I know somehow will never come. My attention snaps back to Yoon.

Why do you not understand? It taunts me.

I am dying! I want to scream, but I can't. My fingers pull away from my throat, coated in scarlet. Ripe torture slices my neck, the sticky substance spills.

Red on white.

I now know why I wasn't able to speak.

Choking, I release my other hand from the handle of the ivory dagger I wasn't aware I'd been holding. It drops solidly into the blood spilled in front of me, its familiar moss inset, covered in my essence. Yoon's stare intensifies. Not with anger, but with – loss. Desperation. A wave of unsettled sadness covers my bones. Something deep within me wants to weep and I don't know why. It isn't from the physical pain; I can hardly feel it anymore. The world around me is turning numb. My bloodied fingertips reach for him.

He wobbles, falling to his knees, his focus becoming glazed and distant. I tremble when I hear hot blood gurgle from my open throat. Spitting, I watch Yoon collapse. The crimson spilling from his own neck is now unleashed like a broken dam. He holds a shaky palm out to me, fingertips reaching. I'm too far away.

Let me take his hand. Let me reach him. Please. My thoughts implode into rage.

Don't you care about what he's done? Why? Why? Why?

It's a new voice. A female voice. It doesn't belong to the Elder, it doesn't belong to me, but to someone – something else entirely. It scratches my core, screeching, mocking, over and over again.

What has he done? I plead.

His fault. His fault. She answers.

My body slumps, crashing into the deep cold, hearing Yoon's faraway cry. Darkness wraps me in an all-consuming blanket. Coating me in death.

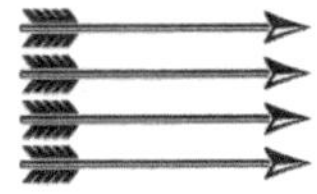

I wake with a jolt of intensity, my lungs threatening to burst. My hips spike into a seated position, forehead hitting the talisman of bone that dangles above the cot. I scan my surroundings with fierce defensiveness, skin glistening with sweat, hot-cold soaking the fur beneath me.

A few more steady breaths calm my heart rate, helping me grasp the fact that I am no longer in my nightmare. That it's sweat, not blood that my fingertips rub along my collarbone. That I am not in any pain. The quiet rustle of sleep draws my awareness to Saedea, who is resting in the cot where I left her, unbothered. To the dark room that looks nothing like a forest. I try to ground myself, gripping the fur as tight as I can to level out the drumming in my chest.

I'm in the hut. I repeat the mantra over and over in my mind until the subtle panic releases its torturous grip on my bones, allowing me to unfreeze my limbs. I circle my temples with calloused fingertips, wiggle my toes, I –

My toes! I can feel my toes!

My legs no longer throb with the dullness of paralysis. I lift my right foot and shake it gently, allowing the other to follow suit. The miserable numbness is gone. *Finally!*

My lower half swings over the side of the cot, testing the woven rug below. My feet are sturdy under my weight. *Yes!*

Balancing myself, I stand on limbs that no longer threaten to give out and start moving before my mind can catch up. I splay my hands out in front of me, feeling around to make sure that I don't bump into anything, or anyone in the darkness. I need to stay quiet, the Elder has to be sleeping around here somewhere, although I'm not quite sure where seeing as there are only two cots in his small hut.

Not to mention, there are five men sleeping outside the door who wouldn't hesitate to end my life if they caught me trying to escape, especially Burke. I'm sure the coin they assume they will get from selling me isn't worth the amount of trouble I've been putting them through. I'm not inclined to push my luck at the moment.

When I reach the thatched panel, I push it open slightly, revealing the stillness of the valley, dotted with stars. Tiny sparks crackle from the teepee of burning spice wood out front, cooling to soft embers when they hit the sand. I listen closely, hearing distant snoring, allowing me to locate the sleeping forms of the clan. Opportunity flushes my mind with concern.

Behind me, Saedea shifts herself into a new position. A tiny gurgle bubbles when she settles back into comfort, sinking into the itchy animal hides. A wary thought brushes past me. I can't leave her here. She's *alive*. No longer resembling a corpse. If she were dead, it would have been an easy decision.

If I escape alone, who knows if the Elder will allow them to take her regardless? He didn't seem very inclined to let her stay, to help either of us get away from them. If I leave, will she still be forced to follow? There's no guarantee, no vow of protection like I had been hoping for. I hate to admit that I just can't risk it.

Even since Tirma passed, I've only ever had to look out for myself. Why would I want to change that now? Why would any of my feelings differ after barely knowing this girl? My heart tears at me, coaxing resolve. Out here, Saedea will die without me. She may have done just fine in Er Rada, a community that she was familiar with. Seeing as she's barely survived the few days outside of her home, could I really leave her alone now?

I want to weep when my hold on the door falls to my side. Saedea's snoring evens out once more and I want to slam my stupid, fucking conscious into the same earthen wall my back begins sagging against. The decision I'm about to make will be a mistake, I know it. I haven't been making the best decisions since leaving Farit and the now, Mystics seem to be punishing me for it. I deserve this. I deserve it all.

It takes me a long moment, longer than I would like to admit, before I crack my now working spine into place, stretch out my legs one last time, and make my way back to the cot, wishing that sleep would take me. Wishing that my nightmares could kill me.

Knowing that they won't.

THIRTEEN

ADESSA

"It appears they are rising against us. We must do what we can to protect ourselves and follow suit. As the West has done."- ████████, *15 days before the Cull.*

No, no, no! Not again!

My thoughts bleat in justified terror, snapping myself upright, throwing out a fist.

Where am I? I can't afford to be caught off guard again.

Saedea dodges, her cheek nearly grazed by my knuckles. The tiniest smile tugs at the corners of her mouth as she watches me realize she's awake. That she's alive.

"You – you're okay?" I croak, latching onto her shoulders to examine her. She nods, water sparkling the whites of her eyes. She settles alongside me, searching for my own injuries as well. The sounds of the morning filter in from the door's open hut. I can hear the men packing up outside.

"How is that possible?" I ask, not to her, more to myself.

Her face is completely healed, not a single scratch on her. No remnants of the horrific bruising that swallowed her features last night. You'd never be able to tell she'd been beaten within an inch of her life.

She clasps her shawl tightly, pointing behind me, to Chadron, who sits with his back turned to us at the table by the window, scratching into wrinkled parchment with the inked stem of a vulture feather.

"I died. I think." She whispers with an unsettling shift, latching innocently to my arm. "And I had the strangest dream."

I pat the top of her head, moving to sit along the cot's edge, prying her from me. Away from the closeness. I don't want further proof that I've grown attached to her. That I made the active choice to stay for her own well-being rather than fleeing like I should have.

"I saw you die."

Her statement is an – unnerving one, to say the least, but I account for all of the stress her body has been put through. She couldn't possibly know of my own nightmare. Whatever Chadron put in that powder had to have caused our – dreams. They have no connection. It's stress.

That's all.

Saedea offers me a solemn grin, throwing her arm around my neck. "Jax said we'll be leaving soon."

I push her off at the words, and the gesture, forcing her at shoulder's length.

"*We* aren't leaving, Saedea. I need you to help me convince Chadron to let you stay." My rejection seems to *offend* her.

"But –"

"Are you really trying to argue with me? Saedea, we are their prisoners. Don't think for one second that finding a healer changed anything."

"But Jax –"

"He is one of *them*. The only reason why they needed to bring us here was because that one without teeth attacked you! He nearly killed you! You do understand that, right?"

She lowers her head.

"Have you considered for one moment that Jax would have done the same if it were him instead of Aol?"

Saedea straightens, offended once more. "He wouldn't. He saved me."

I suck in a troubled breath. "Saved you from his own men. His own clan. Look at the markings on those two, you saw them, didn't you? Which clan owns this territory, Saedea?" I force her to make eye contact with me. "You know who runs this territory. I know who runs this territory –"

"They are not Jidaani." She muses, a stern line between her brows.

"You don't know that for certain."

"I know that if they were, we wouldn't have been brought to a healer."

She replies, bored. Bored!

"Adessa, I really think that we should consider the fact that Jax and Yoon truly wanted to help. Like the stories Sev used to read me. There are heroes in those stories."

Stories?

"Your brother was wrong!" I try my best to keep my voice at a whisper. I try not to strike her with the sad reality that stories are not real, especially the ones that survived the Cull. The world before was filled with fantasies, unrealistic to anything we'll ever have the chance to experience. That's why it all ended the way that it did. Had the Elder wiped her senses clean like he did the blood from her skin?

"You were saved to be sold at a higher price, Saedea. You'd be a fool not to know that."

She lifts her chin, defiant. "The Elder doesn't want us to be here. I already asked."

Shit. I can understand Chadron rejecting me, especially since I haven't been respectful in my demands, but to reject Saedea –

The Elder ruffles the space around him impatiently, pausing his writing to fold one of the parchment sheets in his hands before setting it beside his inkwell. He twists in the wooden chair, those unsettling pupils sweeping over us, then towards the direction of the doorway. Jax appears in the frame less than a second later, arms relaxed at his sides. His body blocks the light from entering the space.

"Glad to see you're awake." His words are directed towards me.

"Sounds like you're packing up." He nods when I move to stand. "Chadron agreed –" I brush Saedea from me, the start of my lie shifting as the healer clears his throat.

"They will not require another night here."

Traitor. My sights snap to him. He merely blinks, resuming his work at his table.

"We are not going anywhere." I take a defiant step forward on strong legs. Jax notices, flourishing a cuffed hand towards the door.

"You've outdone yourself, Chadron. Thank you." He smiles. "Time to go."

Saedea confidently brushes past me, nearly skipping as she follows the heavily armed man outside like a stray that's been rescued. I pinch the bridge of my nose, no longer swollen, the cartilage healed. Everything is healed. When I rub my face, it feels clean of blood.

Chadron must have washed it while I slept. The idea makes my blood boil.

"What do you want from me. Hm? What will it take for you to help us?" I shout, grateful we're the only two left in the hut.

"You can walk again, can you not?" He replies, not lifting the ink from the paper in front of him.

I want to curse him, curse the Mystics, but the words melt on my tongue. He's right. Who knows how much longer, how much more painful the healing process would have been without his help. There's no doubt in my mind that Saedea would be dead without it, that I know for sure. If not from the injuries sustained, then at least from the infection that would follow.

Regardless of the anger I feel, there is also gratitude.

"That nightmare that I had. Did you send that to me?" Silence. I approach him, peering over his shoulder at his work. The jagged symbols match what's drawn on the open patches of his skin. They swirl and bleed into each other like paintings with a brushstroke. I shake my head, unwilling to understand him. I learned from Tirma that sometimes humans do – odd things. Perhaps this old man is like she - was. No point in arguing with someone who has lost their mind.

I take a solemn breath and turn toward the door.

"The fate that has befallen you one hundred times too many." He says, not looking up, shooting his arm up, grasping my wrist. A folded note is pressed into my palm, his fragile skin closes my fingers around it, keeping it safe. I'm held there, noticing a single worried wrinkle etching the line of his forehead.

"Cannot happen again." The air vibrates with uncertainty, echoing his voice.

"What do you mean?" I lean in, searching his face.

"Adessa!" Saedea. She calls for me from outside. *Why is she using my name!* I grimace, looking towards the door.

"The path will be shown, child. I will do what I can. The rest is up to you."

"Adessa!"

"Go." He releases his hold, leaving the note with me. I shove it into my pocket, unwilling to know what it says. Unwilling to let my confusion get the better of me. I give one last, empty look at the Elder's back, then step out into the daylight without another word.

Everyone besides Yoon and his horse, is lined up out front. The packs are evenly distributed between Gunn and Aol's camels, leaving only enough room for one rider each. Burke's camel is free of any gear. My belly clenches, knowing that I'll be riding with him again.

"Come on." Jax holds a hand out to Saedea, who takes it mindfully, allowing him to help her onto his horse. I suppose I should be relieved that she won't be riding with Aol, but whatever 'friendship' is forming between the two has me concerned. The toothless man spits at the ground when she passes him, his wrapped hand crusty with old blood, clearly not healed by Chadron.

Burke approaches me from the side, arms firm across his chest. A rope dangles between his fingers. He jerks his head over his shoulder, indicating the camel we'll be mounting. There's nothing else I can do but play along, seeing as I haven't formed any plan yet, and Saedea – well, I don't even know what she's thinking. I cross my wrists in front of me like the well-behaved prisoner I am. He yanks them behind my back instead, against my wishes, binding them together. I bite back the urge to smash my foot into his gut when he hoists me onto the saddle like a sack of rice.

We ride in silence for quite some time, the hut soon becoming a distant memory. The dunes, the date trees, the flowering cacti, the well filled with drinkable water - soon replaced with a barren landscape, stricken by drought. If I had my map, I would have marked Chadron's location. Not for myself, I don't plan on returning. Maybe it would give me some solace to know that someone else would find the information useful when I sell this piece of parchment for more silver.

The entire morning has passed when Jax whistles, waving his hand in the air. He halts the gray horse and the others follow suit, moaning at the sudden stop. I peer past all of them, watching Yoon ride towards us. Burke lines his camel with the other two, an annoyed growl leaving his chest at the sight of their leader approaching.

My own chest tightens for a different reason when the scarred man's gaze flicks over me in that odd way of his. I'm instantly thrown back into my nightmare. We'd both been covered in blood. We'd both been reaching for each other.

Red on white.

The pain of the memory sears my mind. I shake my head, attempting to clear the vision. He directs his attention to Jax while I immediately avert my sights to the sand.

"The Oasis is clear. We'll stop there to feed the animals."

"Hear that, Bonehead?" Aol calls out, laughing, a joke that none but himself and Gunn seem to get.

Yoon and Jax shoot a bemused look each other's way, guiding their horses to the front of the line. Not a single cloud in the sky today. The bleating sun rips across my skin without a break. Unfortunately for me,

I've forgotten my jacket at Chadron's. Now nothing can stop the sun and sand from terrorizing me. I shift uncomfortably in my seat.

"Quit moving." Burke grunts. I freeze, unwilling to entice a hit from him again, at least not this early in the day.

The distance covered comes and goes, and one agonizing afternoon later, we inch closer to what appears to be a human-made pool of water nestled between a grove of ash trees. A handful of sand-colored lizards dart past us, spooking the camels. I'd visited very few Oases in the past, similar to this one, near the Tracs. Another had been past Farit. That one was not so well off. Oases are unlike anything I'd seen in Skeall, where the resting huts along trails had been burnt down long before I was born.

On this continent, they had been built and maintained long before the Collapse, offering a means of water, food and shelter to those who desired refuge from the war. Nowadays, if they haven't been ransacked, Oases are shelters for those who are finding their way. At least I'm sure that's what everyone wants to believe. With clan control, they could be anything.

This Oasis looks like it hasn't had a visitor in some time. The abandoned shack that sits opposite the dirty, gray pool seems riddled with the markings of a dark past. A large metal box, picked apart for scraps, lies in a heap beside a doorless frame, the remains of a corpse piled on top of it. The dead date tree to the right is a good indication of how little this Oasis can provide. And the water past it looks like it should not be touched.

Burke leaves his camel, pulling him alongside a pile of sandstone that I assume once had been marked as a sign of welcome. His worn hands grab me, yanking me from the saddle. My heels dig into the sand, unwilling to be dragged like a worthless pack. Burke snarls at my disobedience, throwing me down into the hot sand. My skin blazes, patches of red burn at the rough contact. I move back on my hips, steaming, trying my best to remain calm. No one sees the mistreatment.

I glare at Yoon, who is too busy holding out a sugarcane stem for his horse to take. He smooths down its coarse hair before kneeling and investigating the murky water in front of him. Shaking his head to no one in particular, I sigh with grief for my once clean body. It had only been a few days.

Saedea runs to me, avoiding Burke, who heads towards the rest of the group with a grumpy huff. She grips my face gently in her hands, then takes a seat beside me. Her hands are free of any bindings, making me severely question her new role in this clan.

"Jax said I could do this." She whispers under her breath, untying the rope from my wrists. "Don't worry, he isn't going to let any of them hurt us." I don't pull away at the comment, allowing her to whip the last bit of binding onto the ground. I press carefully on the itchy sores.

"Your skin is turning red." She gingerly presses the new scars on my shoulder, the ones she created, curiosity lining her expression.

"I forgot my jacket."

She perks up, scanning the horses. "Maybe they have something for you."

"I don't want it." I grumble.

"Fine." She settles back, unwilling to argue. Good. She's beginning to understand me now.

"I like it here. I've never seen this much water in one place before." She mentions casually, then turns to look at me, wide-eyed.

"I thought you said you were from Damire." I grunt, picking at the hem on her brother's pants. Although I've never been, according to my map, Damire is tucked away near the ocean. Unless she lied. Her guarded expression tells me all I need to know. I wonder what else she's been lying about.

"Any word on where they're taking us? Since you seem to be *friends*?"

She winces at my words. "I'm sorry, Adessa."

I wish I had the nerve to ask her why she's apologizing. Maybe it's for everything. I would never be in this situation if it weren't for her, after all. Instead, we watch the gray horse jump away from a darting lizard. I need Saedea to trust *me*, not these men. Not Jax. I'd thought she'd already learned the harsh realities of life, what with having to survive on her own for however long she did. It appears loneliness has consumed her. Trusting the clan that holds her captive just so she can feel a sense of place in her world – that is something a weak-willed person would do. She rests her head on my blistered shoulder. I can't blame her, I just thought she was stronger. Yoon's voice interrupts the dull ringing in my ears, tearing my attention from Saedea's secrets.

"Here. Drink this." He says once he reaches us, offering his canteen.

He rubs at the stubble on his chin, dots of water bead his forehead, wet from the heat of the sun. I lift myself from the ground, brushing sand from my pants. Saedea tugs herself along with me, releasing my hand to bow. Yoon's expression sparks at the gesture. He seems uneasy, restless for whatever reason when he crosses his thick arms over his chest.

"Thank you for helping us." Saedea chirps. He sways uncomfortably, scanning my bare arms.

"Where's your jacket?"

"Gone." I say, smugly. He begins to unwrap the sand scarf from his neck. I hold my hand to stop him. "Don't even think about it."

Saedea slaps me playfully on the back, taking another drink from his canteen.

"Your skin is burning." He states plainly, holding the scarf to me. It smells like him.

Cinnamon. Clove. Blood.

"I don't care." I stare him down, waiting for him to take the hint. He eventually does, wrapping the scarf back where it belongs.

"At least drink something." It's Saedea this time. She offers me the metal canister. My parched throat begs, but I refuse. She sighs heavily, handing it back to Yoon. "Thank you for the water."

I glower when he reacts with a slight bow, reaching into his pocket to reveal a folded square cloth immediately after. The bright red fabric is adorned with threads of gold woven throughout. He unfolds it, offering a handful of dried jerky strips. *Meat.* My mouth waters, almost tasting the saltiness, the energy I'll receive after eating it. Two traitorous stomachs rumble instantly. Saedea suppresses her joy poorly once she hears my own grumbling insides. As if she needed the verification that even my stomach could betray me.

The last meal I'd eaten was the one Aya provided for me. The one this man paid for. I haven't been able to reach the saved corner of bread in my pocket with bound hands, completely forgetting about it up until now, so it's remained untouched. Two days without food. I've gone longer.

Yoon stretches the cloth out, beckoning Saedea to take it. She does, smacking her lips. He pockets the empty fabric afterward, watching her divide, and then hand me the four remaining strips. I shove the bundle next to the hardening pita.

"You're saving it?" A fleck of confusion rides Yoon's tone.

"To toss later." I snap.

I am starving, but regardless, I need to remain strong. Saedea, however, hungrily finishes her ration, licking each individual finger one by one. "Thank you." She says to him, a quiver in her voice. His cheek twitches, staring at me, waiting most likely to hear the matching words, some confirmation of his good deed. When I don't give him anything, he twists back toward his horse, shaking his head.

"Aren't you hungry?" Saedea questions, those hazel eyes of hers, wide with deceit. My gaze doesn't leave Yoon's back.

"I won't give him the satisfaction."

She tosses her hair over her shoulders, brushing out a section riddled with dried muck. "You'll only get weaker if you don't eat."

Brushing past me, she heads in the direction of the gray horse at the edge of the pool. Through rage-filled haze, I grimace at her willingness to join them. She lovingly pats the horse's neck with affection. The animal presses its large snout into her shoulder in equal tenderness.

Whose side is she on?

FOURTEEN

YOON

"Every initiate will be allowed one chance to prove their value to the clan. Through Hayga. Be not mistaken, a second opportunity will not be granted." *Fourth Law of the Jidaani. Written by our Third Zaiem. 3,580 T.A*

I hide my smile, watching her chew on the tough piece of jerky she eventually pulled from her pocket, scowling at it first before finally succumbing to the hunger I knew was threatening her. I had to stop myself from staring at the look of splendor that spread across her face with the first bite. She almost caught me. I make it a point to keep my head down, attempting to look distracted while she scans the Oasis, ensuring that no one sees her willingness to help herself.

Adessa.

That was the name Jax gave me. The one Saedea told him. I've decided not to give away the fact that I know it, at least for now; seeing as she doesn't seem inclined to give it willingly in the first place. She takes another bite. Time had passed so quickly the last few days; only this morning did I realize they hadn't eaten.

They both seem used to a life like that, one filled with an unknowing of when another meal would come, based on how well they've kept themselves composed amid starvation. It's a lifestyle that I have eventually gotten accustomed to again since leaving the clan. Jax too. The others, however, never appear to adapt well, even though it's been nearly a year. We were lucky we left Er Rada with enough meat to dry, otherwise I don't know what would have happened in Teryal. The small amount of food we try to always carry with us is never enough for them, which is why they've been reduced to petty theft, stealing from others no matter what my objections are. They don't have the same thoughts as I do now. In a world that suffers, I can no longer participate in making it worse.

My mind recalls Saedea's gratefulness when I handed her the jerky. Like she had given up the idea of eating entirely, only to be given the most valuable thing she'd ever held. Very different from the scrutinizing, almost accusatory look Adessa had worn both moments ago, and back at Aya's when I'd taken the opportunity to peer in through the barred window to ensure that Aya delivered the food well. Uncertainty had been written all over her face then also. *Is that when she last ate?*

That knowledge makes my throat tight. I should have let them go before we even left Teryal. If it weren't for Rust roaming around, I *would* have let them go. With us being directly on the Red Line now, doing so would be a sentence worse than death. When I tried to leave them with Chadron, nearly begged him for it in the dead of night, the old man flat out refused.

"They do not belong here." He said, pressing a bottle of healing tonic into my hands. *"Keep her close. There will be no end if she leaves."*

Can't say I wasn't confused at his meaning then, as I was scouting ahead, clearing the Oasis for our arrival. As I am now. I had, however, felt those words settle deeply in my bones. A knowing that I had felt long before he spoke them to me.

"Eyes the color of moss."

I lean back, picking at a cuticle, remembering my mother's tender voice, her absolute trust in the Mystics' guidance, even as we struggled to sleep with something as simple as a canopy over our heads.

"Find her. I've seen it, my son. Believe me. Believe him."

Her objective for me was clear, even though I could not fathom it at the time, and I had forgotten about it for longer than I'm willing to admit; until I saw Adessa at Aya's. It's all – horrible timing. For most of my life, my plans never involved finding *anyone*; besides the occasional bounty Tyg sent me out to find. And they never included being responsible for innocent lives. Now that I have an actual goal in mind, it makes my current situation much more difficult.

Keep her close.

I don't have a choice. Not like I was willing to go against the idea anyways. Besides, the others will retaliate if I let the two go, and Jax and I aren't planning on spilling their blood just yet. As much as I want to tell myself that I'm the one in charge, I know that isn't true. They call me their Qa'id ironically, a tone they would have never used if we hadn't left Grandia. I'll never understand why I gave in and allowed them to join Jax and me. It was messy, and confusing for all of us. I didn't regret it at the time. Now, it's a decision that haunts me. Especially since silver has become harder and harder to come by. We'd all been accustomed to the certain lifestyle our clan provided us, and I was only prepared to bring Jax to Mirit, not five people. Especially not seven.

Burke, Gunn and Aol have been adjusting poorly to these 'extreme hardships' as they so often put, taking every opportunity to make that fact known. Loudly. They didn't believe me when I told them that our shine transport and textile cargo would make up for all the riches lost in Farit, just like they didn't believe me when I told them that Jynn would offer amnesty.

That second part *could* turn out to be a lie. I mostly told it to keep them from letting scouts know where I was while we were hiding at the border of Farit, waiting for my distributor to negotiate his terms with the textiles. It cost me a sword to have them hauled to Teryal, seeing as our horses wouldn't be able to carry it all themselves, not with packs that already took up space on both saddles, forcing us all to walk.

I'm lucky that Aol didn't do anything but whine when he realized I'd stolen the rest of his gems in exchange for the camels. I couldn't fathom walking any further. What would they have done to me if they couldn't fathom it either? I provided potential wealth and security for them in Jynn, playing on their greed. On the fact that their reason for leaving Grandia was just as serious of an offense as mine was. Even though we all know it wasn't.

Jax never once questioned why we left. Never gave me any grief for asking him not to return to camp the night before.

"It's you and me."

He said it with fierce determination, knowing the consequences, understanding the fact that we had both built our entire lives around our clan and we were about to let it all crumble around us. The guilt always creeps up when I realize that in return for his loyalty, I continue to misguide him with my secrets. For a while, he knew exactly what the others knew. That Jynn would be our last stop. That Geal would grant us amnesty if he and I helped her reestablish the Red Line in her favor. Weeks ago, he figured out my plans in Darde, about how I was planning on leaving him in Jynn. We had learned a rumor of the riots in the City of the East from a Tilidaan traveler, one who had access to a Miritian cargo ship. Based on my reaction, Jax continued to prod me until I confessed.

"Geal might grant you a position. You should stay in Jynn."

"And miss crossing the Dying Sea? Do you know how pissed Tyg will be when he realizes we aren't on the continent anymore?"

"There will be no turning back."

"I'm with you, brother."

With that, he sealed his fate right alongside mine, never questioning why I wanted to go to Darde in the first place. I've chosen not to tell him, if only for the reason that I don't want the Mystics to overhear my plans. I can't help but wonder if the vow I made to myself all those years ago will remain true if I'm put in a position of choosing my own revenge or guaranteeing that Jax survives the crossing. In the deepest corner of my soul, I know the answer.

On the other hand, the additional obstacle of securing Adessa and Saedea's safety makes me very aware that I'm unsure of what to do.

Which is why I'm only focusing on Geal handling Burke for the moment. If all things go according to plan, I can sweeten the deal by handing over Aol and Gunn too. The girls will establish the beginnings of a new life in Jynn and my conscience will be clear. As long as they *stay* in Jynn. Otherwise, I could take them to Bine, where they would be welcomed a little easier, but in order to get them there, I'll have to ask for Geal's permission anyways. I'm running out of time with either option. I cannot delay my plans in Darde any longer than I already have.

The fact that we haven't been found yet surprises me, seeing as Tyg never denied his people a hunt. Perhaps he has bigger reasons not to engage us entirely. Perhaps he knows where we're heading anyway. That's why I can never find a reason to sleep more than a few hours here and there. My nightmares, both in the dream world and in reality, never grant me that peace.

I watch Adessa savor the final bite of her jerky, leaning back against a nearby ash tree, observing Hisan dip his snout against Tagan's. I find myself wishing to relax as well, if only for a moment, pressing against the outer wall of the shack. My eyelids weigh.

"Qa'id." Gunn wakes me from the haze I find myself in. I tilt towards him, noting a fresh layer of healing clay smeared on Aol's blisters from a few steps away.

"Me and Aol –"

Bonehead scowls in Adessa's direction. "We don't agree with them not being tied up. Her legs are working just fine now, so –" He begins rubbing his knee.

I almost laugh. We were once a part of the most feared clan on this and any other continent. I flick my attention back to the copper-haired girl, long enough for her eyes to wander back to mine.

"Scared she'll bring you down again?"

"No." Aol snorts, taking a step forward to match his comrade. They stand tall, their chests puffed up in prideful distortion.

"Then why do they need to be tied up?"

I direct my gaze to the ring around my finger, twisting it calmly, reminding them of their place. Both Aol and Gunn take note, mechanically. We all know that my former position now holds no weight.

"If they run, they could tell others about us. It could make its way to Grandia."

Gunn says in a quieter tone.

"They would never survive the desert long enough to tell anyone." I state plainly.

I don't believe my words to be wholly accurate, but what matters most is that I'm sure these two believe that the women wouldn't be capable of crossing the expanse by themselves.

"We would be fools to tempt them. They could take our silver, our weapons."

I pull myself together, considering my situation, of having to constantly play along to avoid conflict. The lesser evil would be dealing with the consequences of tying the women up again. Unfortunately for them, I need these men to trust me; at least for the time being. If they begin to believe that I have a conscience, I can only imagine what could happen. Going against the humanity I hope remains inside of me, I wag my silver-rimmed knuckle at him.

"Fine."

To my left, I see Aol's sly expression form out of the corner of my eye. I try my best to ignore how much it bothers me.

"Tell Burke to come speak with me first."

I suck my cheek as Gunn nods, spinning on his heels. He leans towards Aol, whispering something under his breath.

"Change that disgusting bandage, Aol." I interrupt. "I can smell it from here."

He waves me off, not allowing Gunn to finish what he was about to say and heads for Adessa. I watch Gunn run to the man I desperately want to be rid of, gleefully announcing the confirmed plans of securing Adessa and Saedea. Of my desire to speak with him.

I notice Jax trying to make eye contact with me as he does so, holding his palms out in confused defeat as Aol begins yanking rope from his camel. Shrugging, I avoid his glare. I know that he's taken a liking to the kid. I've chosen not to pry, the sadness in his expression when he looks at her from time to time tells me all that I need to know. She reminds him of his sister.

My attention flits to Burke, who begins heading in my direction, purposefully taking slow strides to make me wait. This Damirian is playing the long game, I can see it in the way that he carries himself. I wonder how long he plans on keeping up this ruse. If he'll ever give up. He has to know that Tyg will never allow him back. No matter what. It is – was – not our way. Handing him to Geal will be merciful compared to what would be done to him if he returned to Grandia.

I try my best to ignore Adessa, listening to the string of curses thrown in my direction when Aol ties thick bindings around her for the second time today. The girl wails in turn as Gunn does the same to her. My teeth can't help but grind into each other at the contrast of sounds. I have no choice but to distract myself with Burke, who finally stops at my feet, fists clenched to the side in irritation.

"Yeah." *Grumpy.*

"I need you to ride ahead." My order makes the over-muscled man frown.

"Why."

"Together, we won't reach Jynn for another week. If you ride alone, you'll arrive in three, maybe four sunrises. Which means we'll all be able to secure safe passage into the city rather than a convoy surprising them at the gates."

"What about my own safe passage." He crosses scarred arms across his chest.

"I'll send you with my insignia, they'll grant you amnesty."
He'll believe me. He has to.

He ticks his head. "How?" Genuine surprise.

"Believe it or not, Tyg relied on me for my access to Jynn. I know the Jiran."

Back to suspicion. "Ask for her when you arrive. Her Second might question you, but that's protocol. You understand. Offer the fabrics as a gesture of goodwill and give them all a bottle of shine."

No one really knows about the Jiran's Second, Ydir. Geal doesn't like to make it known she has an advisor. Especially one as – unwell – as he is, but Burke doesn't have to know that. I pick a loose thread from the hem of my shirt, unyielding.

Burke's expression flickers at the sudden change in our plans. He seems to be hesitating. "I refuse to send Aol. And you know I can't send Bonehead."

He rolls his eyes in disguised satisfaction, secretly praying on my nod to his ego.

"And how will the Jiran of Jynn accept me with only your insignia?"

"If she knows you're associated with me, and you tell her that I'm on my way, you'll be free to roam the city to wait for us. She's been waiting to meet with me for quite some time."

That isn't entirely *untrue.*

"She'll grant us passage because she wants to meet with you? For what?"

I refuse to tell him about our previous agreement of taking control of the territory for her. He already believes me to be the traitor that I am. It's better for me to play on his greed instead.

"I know of a considerable stash hidden in Mirit. The Jiran knows that I know it."

"Drowning in wealth." He repeats the lie I've told him. Then, "We're nearly in Bahani lands."

"Don't cross the bridge. Cross the narrow. They don't live that close to the Saddlebacks. Move along the mountain edge like we planned instead of going through Dahue, you'll be in Jynn in –"

"We're also near Kyr."

I shrug. "Leave early in the morning when they're all sleeping their liquor off."

I can see the wheels turning around in his head. He's always tried to be cunning but ended up becoming more of an order follower instead. Which must be why he feels his fall from grace harder than the others. This is his chance to outwit me. I wonder what he'll plan. I wonder what *I'll* plan.

"If you do this for me." I make it a point to sound honest. "I will split it. You can enjoy Jynn how it's meant to be enjoyed." His brows raise with intrigue.

I tuck away the dishonor in my chest. There is no gold.

At least none that Geal – or anyone - knows about. I feel a sense of relief when he nods in agreement.

"I'll leave before dawn."

I watch him turn, his steps sure and heavy with authority. The further he walks away, the stronger the knowing becomes that once he's gone, I'll start worrying about my status when we arrive in Jynn.

At least I won't have to worry about Adessa being killed for simply existing. That small comfort eases some of the tension, but it does nothing to quiet the fear that churns in my gut. No, above all else, her survival is a burden I can't escape, heavier than my own. And, unfortunately, that is what concerns me the most.

FIFTEEN

ADESSA

""THE WAY OF ELITE DIPLOMACY: NEVER LET YOUR ENEMY GAIN THE UPPER HAND." 'Even if the enemy might be your own people.'" – Writings of ███████ 2,200, T.B.

"You are such a bastard."

I spit as Aol shoves me down, wrestling my back to the base of the date tree. My head rams his against the bark during our struggle, but still, he's able to get my hands tied back around the trunk.

"Shut up." He moves to my feet, wrapping the scourging knot at the base of my calves with only a little trouble. I'm grateful my legs have feeling again. I kick at him once. Twice. He dodges each time, giving me a broad, gummy smile. "Won't fall for the same tricks Bonehead did."

Gunn throws Saedea beside me, grunting at the comment. She is also being tied up, a sad flicker dances along the lines of her face. I hide my joy. If only I could say, "See? These men are not your friends! I told you!" But I keep my mouth closed. No point in making our situation worse by insulting her ego.

Aol gives the end of my rope on final tug, then abruptly smacks Saedea across the face without warning. She cries out, hanging her head.

"You see what you did to my hand, you rabid dog?" Water droplets land on both of us as he spits, holding his injuries close to her nose. She winces. The side of his palm shows clear signs of infection. Puss soaks the already crusted fabric half-wrapped around his fingers. We both recoil at the sight, and smell of it.

"That'll kill you." I hiss through clenched teeth. Aol stands tall, matching my stance, then strikes me in the neck. The calloused fingers on his uninjured hand wrap around my throat, pulling me as close to him as the bindings will allow.

"Suppose I should kill you before it has a chance to then." Fingernails dig deeper, constricting my airways. I press against him, a fireless look in my eyes. Intimidation can be viewed as boredom if you will it strongly enough.

I refuse to let him affect me. Instead, I smile. One large enough to show teeth. Amused. Fearless. Sinister. At least, that's what I want him to think I am.

"You're rabid too. That's what you want, isn't it?" He sputters. I can hardly breathe at this point. My eyes water to the brink of tears spilling down my cheeks. There are two of him standing in front of me as I blink through the blur.

"Aol. Enough." Yoon calls out to him sternly but doesn't turn our way. He's too busy twirling one of his daggers around deft fingers, carefully watching Burke pack up one of the camels instead.

Aol groans, looking behind his shoulder a few times, finally releasing his hold on me. I am desperate to control my unsteady inhales. Luckily, he turns his attention back to Saedea so I can catch my breath. The girl beside me remains still as stone, occasionally whimpering. She gazes up at him, fear trembling her jaw.

"You rats are lucky." He throws a hand in the air, mimicking the motion of hitting Saedea again. She cowers beneath it.

"You won't get much for my corpse." Her voice wavers, but the words are clear.

The toothless man snarls, shaking his fist at her before stomping to his spot near the scrape pile. He kicks at it angrily, the screams of rust ring through the air until Jax forces him to stop. I tilt my head towards Saedea among the distractions, opening my mouth to speak words of comfort, but she beats me to it.

"Was that convincing?" She blinks away at what I've assumed were real tears. I try my best to wipe away the shock when she looks around, smirking. "What?" She bites her bottom lip. "I figured being a scared, helpless girl would work better than whatever *you're* trying to do."

I think back to the first day I encountered her. How weak-willed she appeared to me. Then she shot me.

"Have you been –" I keep my voice above a whisper. "Have you been *pretending* this entire time?"

She shrugs. "Mostly. I couldn't help myself when Aol's hand was over my mouth. I didn't expect him to beat me though." A sigh. "I came up with a plan."

What?

"The gray horse has warmed up to me, I think. We can use her to ride out of here."

I feel myself nodding in disbelief. "You've been coming up with a plan?"

"Duh. Your *strategy* wasn't working. My brother always told me to have three plans, just in case the first two options don't work out."

I don't know whether or not to feel betrayed – no, I feel proud. She's been so skilled at deceiving them, she's managed to make me believe that she was against me as well.

"I was weighing all of our options." I state, admitting to my lack of urgency.

"Yeah." She rolls her eyes, fixing her sight on Yoon. "Should we take their weapons or just make a run for it?"

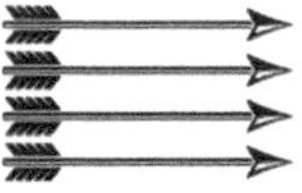

Saedea has produced many empty tears, from the moment they loaded us back onto the animals, to the moment the clan found a new place to camp. We rode for so long, the skin on my thighs roar with the ache of loose clothing rubbing against the leather saddle. My shoulders are taut and numb from my wrists being bound so tightly together behind my back, that my arms prickle with every movement. And the exhaustion; I can barely keep my eyelids open. I desperately cling to consciousness, maintaining focus on Saedea, who's been holding a quiet conversation with Jax for the last dip of the sun. I wonder what lies she's spewing.

By the time our caravan finally stops, my body is so terribly sore that the moment Burke dismounts at our next camp, a quiet notch in the hardened dune, I fall not so gracefully behind him. He doesn't make a move to help me up, not like I'd let him anyways. Aol walks past me, a mat underneath his armpit.

"Can't you untie these?" I moan, lifting my shoulders up while sand hits my face at the motion of Aol's sleeping pad being thrown on the ground. I spit out the granules, blinking. His response is a throaty snort; he moves the mat a distance away, to where the others are setting up theirs. Jax has a hole dug quickly, preparing to build a fire in that odd way of theirs. Gunn is busy transferring a few bottles of shine between two camels. The men exchange very few words with each other, methodically knowing their roles after having practiced them perhaps thousands of times.

Saedea pulls up alongside me, throwing me back into reality, her hands untied once more. I toss her a knowing look this time; all she does is wink.

"Jax told me that I remind him of his sister." She twirls an invisible thread around her finger with a dramatic flair.

"Hey!" Aol shouts in our direction. "Both of you!"

He waves for us to move toward him, toward the area that is await-ing us, with a rope thrown around the metal frames of debris beside their makeshift camp. We resist, unwilling.

"You said you wouldn't untie her!"

Aol throws an annoyed glare at Yoon, who sits back on one of the worn rugs, obsessively sharpening his already deathly sharp machete against a whetstone. With a crack of his knuckles, Aol half-jogs towards us, grabbing Saedea's arm first, then mine. I retaliate, grateful that he's used his infected hand to latch onto me. I twist away from his grasp, causing him to howl in pain and release Saedea. He lunges for me, bury-ing a fist into my stomach. I double over, sternum throbbing, the air leaving my lungs.

My scowl lands on the others, particularly Yoon, whose expression remains unimpressed. The cruel facade remains, save for the subtle twitch of his cheek. The tiniest flicker of fire in that working eye of his tells me all the confirmation I need. If Saedea can use Jax, I could use this one.

"Piece of –" I curse, spitting at Aol's feet, goading him. He lifts his hand to strike me before Jax crows.

"Just tie them up Aol, if that will make you leave them alone!" His command meets its mark. Aol holds a fist under my nose, huffing.

"Them!" I hear Saedea shout as Gunn drags her to the same pile of metal I've been taken to.

"I swear to the Mystics, I'll gut you." Aol is so close to me, I can see the weeping blisters on his cheek. He positions both hands against my throat.

"Aol!" Yoon stands, a hand on the hilt of the deadly blade in his palm.

"I don't know why they're protecting you." Aol hisses, throwing me into a rusted sheet of metal. "But they won't be around forever."

With a growl, he hoists me up by the shoulders, positioning me into a seated position. He wraps the rope around the chunk of debris, under and over the pipes that hang behind me. "There will be a moment when you are all alone. And I will revel in it."

The bindings are wrapped around my calves, tied in a way that feels unfamiliar. The complexity of it doesn't escape me.

"Tomorrow, you might not be so lucky. Right, Bonehead?"

Gunn, meanwhile, busies himself with tying a knot around Saedea's legs that's nothing like Aol's. He seems to give up tying it halfway through, glancing over at Aol's knot in defeat. When he stands, I can feel his eyes linger for a moment too long before he lets out a laugh – wild and frantic, the kind that claws at my ears. Aol smacks him on the back with camaraderie.

I don't care about their threats, I'm too distracted to focus on anything beyond the pressure of the tightened knot around me. The only relief I find is the sickly, nauseating smell of rot finally lifting as they grumble their way back to the circle. The others resume their idle tasks, their actions are mechanical, with no more words spoken between them.

I lean into Saedea, feeling her anxiously fidget.

"Tonight. We have to leave tonight."

Something tells me that Aol won't let us live for much longer. And I can't risk those consequences. She turns her head, giving me an almost unnoticeable nod.

"My satchel is with Gunn's camel. The one with the brown spot on its snout. Torn ear." I glance at the now steady fire below the surface of the sand. "We'll need my map. If it's still inside. I have the route to Mirit marked but not memorized." She continues to stretch her shoulders, giving small tugs that shake the debris behind us.

"Once they're asleep, we need to free ourselves from these bindings. Let's search for something sharp. There's a lot of metal pieces around here." I search the ground. Her head remains tilted in concentration, pretending not to listen. The men aren't paying any mind to us.

"Maybe I can –"

"Got it." She whispers triumphantly. My attention sparks back to her. Her hand, the one closest to me, is free from the rope. She grazes her fingertips against mine to let me know for sure. "Finally figured out how to get out of these things."

Another swell of surprise blooms within me. She's a smart kid, surviving on nothing but her instincts, trial, and error. She's kept herself alive because she had no other choice. I've only relied on the reckless knowledge that I cannot die – never genuinely thinking about the next step. I've thrown myself into danger, letting the risks wash over me, because for a long time, it didn't matter. I wasn't afraid of death. I welcomed it before I ever thought about revenge. That's another way where she and I are different.

I'm realizing that now, watching her navigate our situation with such grit, while I've only been stumbling through, caught up in my anger. I'm taking notes; quietly learning, even if I don't want to admit it.

"I think my brother would be proud of me." She says quietly, her words softly carrying a sense of comfort, like a reassurance she's giving herself as much as she's offering to me.

"I think so too." I reply, my voice steady and full of sincerity.

The words feel heavier than I expected, as if acknowledging her strength makes something shift between us. She smiles back, the expression fragile but real, as tears threaten at the corner of her eyes. There's a subtle nod as if accepting the truth, the weight of survival settling on her shoulders in quiet victory.

SIXTEEN

ADESSA

"I knew you were something special."

As the sky darkens, the soft hues of the sunset fades into the deepening blues and purples of night. It prompts me to begin noting where everyone is settling in. The camels are positioned to the right, a few steps from the fire, the sturdy boulders of hardened sand offering them a sparse but protective backdrop. The horses wander even further, their silhouettes barely visible in the fading light, grazing just beyond the reach of the camp's fire.

The vast and open desert stretches out before us, an unbroken expanse of sand and sky. The only signs of life are the seven of us – silent, isolated, as it has been since we left Chadron's. Not a single soul has been in sight since we began the journey. It's... strange. Quiet, unnerving even. I had expected more from this route, more of the danger I've been warned about.

Where are the caravans? The runners? The warring clans? Everyone in Farit had claimed this was a path steeped in risk, and yet, there's nothing – no signs of the chaos and conflict I had braced myself for. We've been heading in the same direction I had intended to take alone, with only the endless desert shifting around us. The emptiness, the silence, feels wrong. I have half a mind to shout my questions into the night, to demand answers from the others, to ask where the feared Red Line is. If we're even close to it.

But the words lodge in my throat, too heavy to speak. Instead, the only thing I can think about is my map. I desperately need it to tell me where I am, where we're headed, what I'm missing. If we're going to escape, it would be helpful to know how far down the route we are. It would have been nice if I had better tracking skills, some way to pinpoint our location without relying on my map. I try to remember which city is next in the territory, but I never memorized the line itself. Was it Idane? Or Dahue? The details slip through my mind like the sand between my toes.

I want to kick myself for being so ill-prepared. The map was supposed to be my lifeline, I assumed it would always be with me.

Hopefully Saedea has a better understanding of this place. She seems to know more than I give her credit for.

Ahead, the men look like they're all beginning to doze off. Aol and Gunn are already curled up in front of the slow-burning fire, the orange glow casting flickering shadows across their faces. Jax, still awake, lazily pokes at the embers, his movements slow and absent. Burke watches him with equal sleepiness riding along the expanse of his movements. Yoon has been drifting in and out of consciousness for a while, leaning against a pile of slanted supplies at the fire's edge. His head lolls forward every so often, only to snap back up again, barely holding onto wakefulness.

I wonder who is meant to be keeping watch. How they can all feel so comfortable sleeping. None of them seem the least bit concerned. The desert is vast and unforgiving, yet here they are, entirely at ease in the face of it. Why?

Jidaani. Jidaani.

Saedea too, has finally succumbed to sleep, her head resting gently on the peak of my shoulder. The loosened bindings make it possible for her, although the weight of her head against me is still a strange feeling. I can hear the soft rhythm of her snoring. Steady. Peaceful. It's probably for the best that she's able to sleep, given how much we've been through, how much ground we still have yet to cover. The thought of resting anywhere safe seems so out of reach; it feels like it'll be forever before we find an opportunity again. I can't shake the sense that we'll have to keep moving long before we're ever given a real chance to be at peace.

I hear Jax yawn loudly enough to grab my attention, the sound scraping through the stillness of the night. He stretches, throwing a half-hearted send off into the air to no one in particular, shifting down onto his mat, his breath coming in ragged bursts moments later. Aol has already erupted into his grueling snores. The others seem to be asleep as well.

I nudge Saedea with my shoulder once Yoon's chin dips for what I hope is the final time, his body slumping as he drifts deeper into sleep.

"Saedea." I whisper, barely above a breath. She stirs, her eyes flicking open, hazy from sleep. She shakes her head a few times, her movements slow and groggy, but soon, she's upright, slipping her hands free of the bindings with practiced ease. She makes easy work of the knot around her chest, then her legs. When she turns her attention to my bindings, it's as if she's already anticipated their complexity.

Once I'm free, I ready myself, quickly tossing the last of the bindings from me, my movements deliberate. She holds onto my arm tightly, helping me to my feet.

Then we both freeze. Aol shifts in his sleep, adjusting his position, followed by a few strained coughs into the empty air. His slumber resumes almost immediately, deep and undisturbed, the faint sound of his mouth-breathing filling the space once again.

I hold a finger to my lips, carefully pulling her into the shadows behind the crest of metal, gesturing towards the camels first, then shifting my hand to where the horses are being kept, the subtle movement sends a signal of urgency.

"See if you can get the gray one saddled." I whisper, my voice low. "I'll find my bag. If anything happens –" I pause, considering the weight of my orders. "Leave without me. Ride as far west as you can. Farit, if possible. There's a den there that –"

"What about east?" She interrupts, her voice tight with nerves.

I shake my head. "Going back would be better."

She looks at me with hardened eyes, a flicker of something sharp beneath the weariness. "There's nothing back there for me, Adessa."

The words hang in the air. I can see her more clearly, her face etched with a kind of war that has aged her far beyond the girl I once thought I pegged as weak. She's not just another mouth to feed, she's an equal. Much more capable of going where I am, possibly more than myself. Whether it be her parents, her brother, or herself, she's been taught well enough to stand on her own two feet. Now I know I cannot make the same mistake again.

I pause, feeling the weight of my decision before speaking, this time with resolution. "Fine. If anything happens, we fight back. And we ride east. Together."

Being recaptured by this clan is not an option. Not for either of us. Especially not for her. It would be a death sentence, plain and simple. I won't let that happen. The thought of it places a heavy pressure on my bones. She hesitates, searching my face as if trying to read through any cracks. I don't know if she sees the truth behind my fears; with one last glance over her shoulder, she takes off into the night, sprinting low along the edge of the camp's darkness.

I crouch low and make a break for the camels, my heart pounding as I push myself forward. I've never had firsthand experience with an animal this size, but over the last few days, I've kept a close watch on how their owners interact with them. At least I know how to greet them so they aren't spooked.

I spot Gunn's camel in the corner, its torn ear twitches when I hover my palm in front of its discolored nose, giving it space to inspect me. My pulse quickens when it recoils. I squeeze my eyes shut, expecting the damn thing to alert the others, but it doesn't. Instead, its warm snout presses gently into the cusp of my open hand. I whisper a quiet thanks, then move towards the saddlebag, pushing my racing thoughts aside. My breath steadies, helping me concentrate while I find the straps of my satchel and tug.

It's stuck.

I yank harder, my frustration growing. The camel shifts, forcing me to pause, to listen. Nothing.

I try again, one more tug, and the upper half of the bag loosens, just enough to give me hope, but then begins tearing at the hem.

Wasting too much time.

I shove my hand into the opening, my fingers scraping the inside of the bag.

Yes!

My palm wraps around the parchment map – thank the Mystics. I go in for a second time, fingers curling around the cool brass of my compass. A third search yields nothing more. They've taken my coins, the motte, even the bag of rice is gone.

Another throaty cough pierces the air opposite me, the lazy smacking of lips makes my heart stutter. A shuffle on the ragged mat follows and I freeze, breath caught in my chest. I crouch down, hiding behind the massive animals, my eyes darting around the camp. I can't raid the others for weapons. It's not worth the risk.

Another groan beckons me to my feet, slipping into the shadows. *Time to move.* I push myself to sprint for the horses, nearly stumbling as I navigate the darkness, almost colliding with the black horse in my confusion. Yoon's horse. He stomps his hooves angrily, the uncertainty clear, torn between warning his owner, or trampling me on his own. I back away to avoid a kick to the neck.

"Settle down, we're not taking you." I murmur, trying to soothe the animal.

The horse bristles, still uncertain, but as I move past it, all it does is nudge its nose into my back, a firm shove that forces me forward. Saedea is already busy trying to calm the other horse, her hand gently patting the neck of the animal, her movements careful and slow.

"Where's the saddle?"

"I can't find it."

I let my eyes adjust to the void, but the darkness is thick and I can't make out any of the riding gear. "I can't find the straps either. Should we have grabbed the rope?"

Who doesn't keep these things with their horses? Are they that confident in themselves – unless –

"We need to go without it." My heart pounds, the rhythm thrumming too loud in my head, panic bubbling up. "Do you think they overheard our plans?"

She looks at me, wild-eyed, a glint of fear flickering her gaze. "What should we do?"

"Get on." The words are sharp with urgency, cutting through the air. She nearly interjects, her fingers nervously scratching the underside of the gray horse's chin. The animal bobs its head up and down as I make my way between them, offering my joined hands to Saedea, lifting her onto the horse's bare back.

It whinnies, the sound piercing the night in warning. A chill runs up my spine, but I force myself to focus, craning my neck back towards the camp. The embers of the dying fire spark its final breath. I can see Yoon's shoulder twitching, his fingers flexing along his side, as if his sleeping form senses something is wrong. My stomach tightens.

I manage to half-pull myself up, and with Saedea's help and a not-so-gentle press on the horse's ribs with my foot, my fingers curl through its mane, knowing each second lost is a terrifying realization.

"Hold on tight."

Saedea copies my hand placement and I kick the horse's sturdy sides. The animal doesn't budge.

"Please, *please!*" I beg, kicking a little harder. The high-pitched whinny is much louder this time. She threatens to buck us from her back. The men have to be waking up by now.

"No! Please move!" I frantically lurch forward, goading the animal desperately.

"Jax is waking up." Saedea whispers, her arms trembling. I spin around, heart in my throat. Jax is slowly pushing himself to his feet, scratching his beaded scalp in that sleepy way of his. He'll be coming to check on his horse.

Shit, we're running out of time.

Saedea reaches out, her hand brushing the horse's head with a calming, gentle touch.

"Come on, Tagan, we really need your help. Take us somewhere safe. Please." Her soothing voice seems to calm the nervous animal.

"We don't have time for this, Saedea." I snap, grinding my teeth into my gums.

"Try to push her again, but softer. Two taps. That's what Jax does."

I grimace, frustration bubbling over, but force myself to try again. I tap her sides twice with my heels, gently. Tagan takes a single, hesitant step forward. My thighs instinctively squeeze, urging her to keep going, and she finally obeys, moving into a steady trot, carrying us further from our captors.

Behind us, I hear a sharp whistle pierce the air. The horse falters for a split second, but then bounces back into her pace when Saedea rubs the sides of her neck, whispering soft words of praise. Another whistle sounds, but to my surprise, Tagan ignores it completely, her focus remaining on the path ahead.

We need distance. They still have Yoon's horse. They have plenty of time to catch up. I tap my heels again, clicking my tongue the way I've heard the others do countless times before, and the horse surges forward into a full sprint. Saedea presses her back against my chest, and I thread my fingers through the horse's mane holding on with all of my strength, my heart hammering. We need to stay steady; we need to stay ahead.

We cling for dear life against the speed, knowing every second longer is a second closer to freedom.

SEVENTEEN

ADESSA

"Settlers from the sea have now made claim to the lands near the Tracs. Do not let their kind spread." – *3,600 T.A Message from newly established Grandia Roost* **#12**

Eternities stretch as we race across the desert. The sand beneath us stings my bare feet, a harsh reminder of our relentless speed. My muscles scream for release, the burn in my thighs threaten to give way at any moment. I grip the horse's stocky body with all my strength, refusing to give in – not yet. I'm all too aware of the consequences if I make her stop too early. The sky above offers no direction, no guidance to where we're headed. Not that I've had the luxury to even think about glancing at my map; my mind has been consumed with remaining anchored to Tagan, trusting this horse to carry us as far away from camp as possible.

We've been riding along what seems to be an endless riverbed, cracked and dry from drought, but it's hard to gauge its true extent or width in the dark. Tagan finally begins to slow, pulling us away from the harsh edge and into softer sand that gradually gives way to patches of cacti and the occasional palm. I feel Saedea's body shudder with relief, and I release the breath I hadn't realized I was holding.

"Thank you." She whispers, her voice soft, reverent.

I can't tell if she's speaking to the horse or the stars above, but either way, she gently pats the animal between the ears. I glance over my shoulder, scanning the voided horizon. It doesn't look like we've been followed. Honestly, I half expected at least one of them to show up by now. The night remains eerily still, as it has been the entire ride.

Why isn't there anyone out here?

"Look!" Saedea's voice snaps me out of my racing thoughts, pulling my attention ahead. There, in the distance, torchlights flicker against the harsh outline of what looks to be a wall, its silhouette cutting into the expanse. I take a brief moment to finally pull out my map, my fingers slightly trembling as I unfold it. I scan the Red Line, tracing the path to Mirit.

"Saedea, do you know anything about the Red Line?" It's a question that makes her straighten.

"I've heard about it."

"Do you know what it looks like?"

She shakes her head. "Not really. When I was little, my brother used to tell me that it was named that way because of all the blood that had been spilled. But it's hard to see red in the dark."

My finger adjusts, tracing the route that's marked on my map. I gaze up at the stars, searching for the one that points north.

"We're on it," I say quietly. "I think."

"We are?"

She doesn't see me nod, but I do. *Was the Red Line once a river?*

"Unless we got turned around. But it looks like we're still heading east. I'm so confused. Look." I hold the map out in front of Saedea so she can see it too.

"Is that Dahue?" She asks, pointing towards the walled city in the distance.

"I'm not sure. Do you remember seeing a bridge?"

"No."

My map doesn't show any other markings of a city, unless we went further south and this is Idane. But we'd only been riding throughout the night; the sunrise hasn't graced us yet, and the Saddleback mountain range would be visible. I squint, trying to make sense of the unfamiliar shapes ahead, a rush of unease floods my chest as uncertainty claws at me.

"I don't think the traveler marked this on my map." My voice drifts off as we edge closer to the warm lights ahead, the looming walls encasing the entrance of a barred city. Tagan continues pushing forward, seemingly determined to get us to the enormous gate that stands at the end of the hardened path, flanked by tall sandstone obelisks.

"I have no idea where we are." I fold the useless parchment, shoving it back into my pocket. Nervously fidgeting with the ring around my thumb. Saedea tilts her head in response, noticing the black and green striped flags at the same time I do. They hang loosely along the steel bars of the gate, reminding me of the merchant in Er Rada.

"Wait, those flags –" My question fades. "Do you think this is where the merchant is from?"

Saedea stiffens, her body shrinking back against my chest. "The Er Rada merchant." She mentions flatly.

"Do you remember his name?" Given how she seems to love learning them, I wouldn't be surprised if that's how she built rapport selling motte to him. "Maybe we can use it as leverage. Gain safe entry."

She jerks her head, eyes wide with panic. "No, no, no, we can't be here."

"What?" I exclaim. "Why not?"

Tagan's gait shifts, cautious, as though she recognizes this place, but perhaps not in the way I'd hoped. My grip on her mane loosens slightly, a wave of uneasy relief washing over me. I push it down, faltering hope residing against it. As exhausted as I am, as much as I crave rest, we aren't safe yet.

"Adessa, we really shouldn't be here." Saedea's tone quivers with doubt. The weight of my decisions presses down on me like a lead weight.

"We can't turn around. I don't know where we are, Saedea."

"Let's keep following the river. It has to lead us to the bridge."

"Stop!"

A booming voice cuts through the night, harsh and commanding. I barely register the two guards standing silently watching us by the barred gate until it's too late. My heart slams against my ribs, and the world seems to slow down as Tagan obeys the order, halting just before the end of the path.

The first guard, taller than the other, with wild, scraggly hair levels a rifle – *a rifle* – in his hands. My breath catches in my throat. The other guard holds his own similar weapon, his gloved hands trembling as he shakily trains the barrel on us.

Firearms.

The realization hits me like a punch to the gut. My bones grow cold.

"Hang on." The long-haired guard approaches us, too calm, too knowing. His eyes narrow as he studies us. It makes my skin crawl.

"I know this horse." His words are low, an ominous murmur. Something about it sends a sharp chill down my spine. Saedea latches onto my arm and squeezes tight.

The second guard raises his rifle, the metallic click of the barrel drawing my attention to him. "Doesn't it belong to –" He snaps his gloved fingers, eyes flicking to his partner.

The taller one's grin is far too wide, far too excited. He cocks his weapon too, in a slow, deliberate motion that I'm sure is meant to entice fear. My stomach turns to ice, and every muscle in my body screams at me to run. I don't even think as I slam my heels into Tagan's sides, desperate to force her to flee. *Please move! Move!*

But she doesn't. Her hooves remain solidly planted in the sand, still as stone as if the danger is lost on her. Saedea's voice breaks through my panic, her words laced with desperation.

"Please help us." The words crack with the edge of innocence; she slips into her well-rehearsed role. The air around us thickens, suffocating me. The guards pause, maybe this will work.

"What do you need help with, miss?" The shorter one asks, leaning in.

"We had to escape. We took the horse from our captors."

My breath halts as the tall one scratches his chin, lowering the gun only slightly.

"Who captured you?" *What a dumb question*, I want to say, but I remain silent, hoping that Saedea does as well. I nearly interrupt before she opens her mouth.

"Bounties."

My breath halts. The words fall into the night like a death sentence, the sharp realization of it all crashing around me. *Bounties?* My mind races, scrambling to make any sense of what came out of her mouth.

"Bounties? Saedea –" I whisper, pinching her.

"They told us they would sell us in the Underground."

The guards' expressions twist from bored indifference to a sudden, seething rage. It happens so fast that I can't process it. One moment, they're laughing at the idea of us escaping on a horse that they seem to know. The next, they're nearly snarling, eyes blazing with fury. My hand flies to her lips, clamping down to silence her, but the damage has already been done. The air has changed, thick with violence.

"Saedea!" I shout, wanting to shake her for what she's done.

"They'll come for us." She warns against my palm, determination in her stance.

"Bounties?" The first guard growls, like that of a predator. He steps forward, beady eyes bore into Saedea's with a feral intensity that makes my blood boil. He smells of sweat and dirt, of a life lived in shadows. I can feel malice radiating off of him. He shifts his rifle, sharpening his glare. "Is that so?"

"Ones that know of the Underground?" The second guard moves alongside Tagan, circling us. His face is now a mask of anger, his hands no longer shake with uncertainty. They've recognized the horse. They know exactly who it belongs to. I clench my fists, panic rising, our surroundings turning into a haze of regret.

His brow furrows, deep lines marking his stubbled face under the dim light of the torches. "How much are these bounties worth?"

The words fall like stones, heavy and final. I kick the horse again. She merely sways. The ground suddenly feels fragile, like it might crack open at any moment. I'm desperate to keep my hands steady, but they're trembling. The guards notice it, sizing us up, deciding how best to handle us.

They have rifles. They'll kill Saedea if we try to escape now.

"Ten thousand at least. Maybe more." Saedea's voice is thin as she pushes my hand off of her, urgency bleeding through every word. "If you help us, we can take you to them."

"Saedea, what are you talking about?" I tug hard on Tagan's mane, the coarse hair biting into my palms. The horse shuffles backward, but the long-haired guard is already there, blocking our escape.

"What makes you think we believe you?" His voice is cold, venomous, and the crack of his rifle slicing through the air sends a shockwave straight through my chest. Every muscle in my body tightens, a knot of dread building in my stomach. He forces Tagan closer to the looming gates, moving slowly, and deliberately, like a predator cornering its prey.

"What would bounties be doing this close to the Red Line?" The words hang in the thick desert air, sharp and accusing, making my skin prickle with the weight of their scrutiny. The guards' eyes lock onto us with a hunger that's impossible to ignore, as if they're waiting for the slightest sign of panic to prove us guilty.

"You seem to know this horse." *Saedea.*

My heart slams in my chest like a war drum, too loud, too fast. It feels as if my entire body has frozen in place, but beneath the frozen terror, the faintest tremor pulses through me. Saedea's grip tightens around my arm, her fingers digging into my skin, her body rigid. I can feel her pulse racing against mine, and in that instant, I know she's just as terrified as I am.

"They don't seem familiar with the desert. Maybe they're telling the truth." The tall guard speaks slowly, as if weighing his options, but there's still no doubt in my mind that we're on the verge of disaster.

"Maybe they've been sent to set us up." The other guard mutters, his voice dripping with suspicion, a cruel twist to his words.

Tagan's hooves strike the ground in a sharp, nervous stomp. She feels it too; the danger, the threat, the trap closing in on us. I can feel her restlessness grow beneath me, her muscles tightening, ready to bolt at any moment. And if she does... if we lose control of her, I know there won't be any getting away. My thoughts flash through the worst-case scenarios, each one darker than the last.

The first guard circles us slowly, his worn boots scraping the dirt beneath him.

"One of them –" His words freeze. "He an easterner?" He gestures to his right eye, a glint of malice in his stare. "Blind in this eye?"

My stomach twists in knots, a cold sweat breaking out across my skin. They know Yoon. They *know* him. The panic surges, hot and suffocating, and I can't get enough air into my lungs. My throat feels thick, dry. I can't speak. Saedea is still frozen, her hands lock onto me like a vice, her knuckles white with the force of her grip. I can hear her breathing, ragged and quick. I should've listened to her moments ago. I should've forced Tagan to turn back. Now, we're neck-deep in this mess and there's no way out.

The first guard's grin spreads slowly, terrifyingly, as he shares a glance with his partner. The exchange is subtle, but the deadly understanding between them is unmistakable.

"This isn't good." My voice cracks, raw with the weight of my fear. I wish I could take it back, but it's too late. The guard on the left is moving before I can even process the shift. His hand shoots out, fast, practiced. The rope hanging from the lowered flag is in his hand before I can react. He yanks it with a sickening precision, and in the next instant, it's looping over Tagan's neck. The knot tightens with a harsh snap, and I feel the horse flinch, her body jerking beneath me.

In a flash, she rears up, panicked, her hooves crashing upward in a violent frenzy. The world tilts as I'm thrown into the air, weightless for a split second, and then - *crack*. My body slams into the hard, unforgiving ground. The wind is knocked out of me, and my vision blurs with the impact.

I barely have time to gasp before Saedea tumbles after me, narrowly avoiding plummeting backward onto me when I roll to the side. The sound of Tagan's hooves pounding the ground fills my ears, the rope still tightening around her neck with every frantic movement. The guards' laughter, cold, mocking, cruel; it rings out like the death knell for any hope we had left.

They know they've got us. And they're enjoying every second of it.

I scramble on scuffed knees as the tall guard barrels towards us. I barely manage to push the girl out of his way, taking the brunt of his kick.

"Don't you dare move." He snarls, placing a heavy boot on my chest, pushing me back down as he points the weapon between my eyes. Maybe he believes that I won't fight back. I use that against him, grabbing onto his shin, yanking it back as hard as I can. The gun goes off when he falls, a blast of metal piercing an empty sky. I'm on him in seconds.

He tries to aim at me again, awkwardly setting the base against his shoulder. I readjust as well, hurling my fist directly into his jaw, throwing my arm back and repeating my violent onslaught again and again. Knuckles crack as they meet his nose. I can feel it crunch beneath them. Straddling his torso, I continue my furious attack. He is desperate to use his weapon as a bludgeon, whipping it around, but missing his mark each time as I dodge potential blows.

The skin on the back of my hands split against his face, leaving traces of my own blood mixed with his. It seems to last for an eternity. His eyes roll back into his head before rough hands grab beneath my armpits, throwing me off the freshly injured man. I buck, screaming.

"Saedea! Run!"

She scrambles to her feet, eyes trained on the badly beaten guard, then to the one holding me. "No!" She shouts back.

"Go!"

The man's injuries aren't enough to keep him from rising to his feet, cracking his neck and lunging. I toss my body out of the way, causing him to careen into his partner. They adjust faster than I do, gloved hands latch onto my legs, pulling me back. I claw at the ground. Another set of hands buries my shoulders into the worn path. My arms raise to protect my face while the vengeful guard swings. Vision blurs once he strikes my temple, his other hand squeezes my throat, forcing my breathing to release in strangled beats. Clouded dots dance across the sky above me.

No, no, don't pass out. Please don't pass out.

I buck, wedging my knee into the man's ribs while my other arm breaks free, searching behind me, tearing into the eyes of the guard who won't let me go. I'm able to kick the one on top away when he hears his partner scream, reactively covering his eyes too while I heave myself up. Both men curse, gripping their wounds. One wipes blood from his still shattered nose, he spits crimson onto the ground, blazing.

Saedea is nowhere to be seen. Good. The fear that she hadn't listened to me fades. Finally, for once, she has. My gaze fixes itself on Tagan. The horse thrashes, still tethered to the gate, fighting for her freedom. I can't waste any more time. I need to get her out of here. Now.

I break into a full sprint, each step sending a shockwave of pain into my feet. I'm almost there, just one more step. My body falters, screaming for a break, but the thought of leaving her behind – of outrunning these men on foot – propels me forward. I glance to my left, watching one of the guards moving with surprising speed, his heavy boots thumping along the path, mirroring my pace. He doesn't pull his weapon on me, doesn't even look my way.

Something's wrong.

My gut is screaming at me, an overwhelming roar that fills my ears, urging me to stop, to think, to reconsider everything about this plan of mine. It's a cold, vicious warning deep in my chest, and yet I ignore it. I push my body harder, the sweat running down my face, bleeding into the corners of my eyes. The horse is so close now – so close – but every instinct is telling me to turn back. But I can't leave her to their mercy. I won't.

The gate looms ahead, and I'm almost there. The sickening sense of unease won't leave me. It gnaws at me.

Something's wrong.

The guard at the far end slows his pace, his eyes tracking me, following my every move with a gaze that sends a rush of panic to flood my veins. He's not frantically trying to stop me. There's no urgency in his stance. Just waiting. Waiting for *something*. His partner watches from afar, just as detached, humored even. They aren't worried. And that makes the terror crawling up my spine all the more suffocating.

Something is wrong!

The warning comes again, more insistent, but I shove it down, pushing forward with reckless desperation. I reach out, fingers trembling as they close around the rough fibers of the rope. I need to get out of here. I need it so badly that the world is starting to blur around the edges, and all that matters is the taut, heavy rush of escape. My fingers bruise against the strain, but I don't care.

I've made mistakes before working on instinct alone. I know that. I *know* that I'm not thinking straight. I shift my body, pulling at the knot, but the moment I try to loosen it –

No!

Immediate, blinding pain sears the palm of my foot, ripping through my thighs in an explosion of agony so sharp, I can't even scream. My body freezes, paralyzed by the sheer shock of it. The rope slips through my fingers, my grip falters as everything goes white.

This was a mistake. This was a huge mistake.

I throw my head down, choking on a scream at the sight of jagged metal tearing through the top of my left foot. It's torn through skin, through muscle, *bone*. The blood sprays as a pulse of torment pumps into my spine. My body goes numb, as though it can no longer feel anything but the all-consuming agony that floods every nerve. A blank canvas of misery. Nothing else exists.

Going into shock. You're going into shock.

The words howl in my mind, sharp and panicked, but they're drowned out by relentless suffering.

Dizzy, I watch through cloudy eyes as the guard's hand leaves the side of the iron-wrought bars. His fingers move with cruel precision to press up on a hidden lever. The metal clicks, and I scream, the sound splitting my throat open, my lungs fighting for air. The row of spikes retract, but not before they gouge my foot entirely. I crumble to my knees, a wave of cold sweat flooding me as the world around me tilts. The red-hot burn of fear replaces the blood in my veins.

I hear the guards before I see them. They move on either side of me, their laughter mocking, distant. I barely feel them drag me from my place in the sand, over their camouflaged trap, their hands hauling me like I weigh nothing, like I *am* nothing. My body doesn't respond. I can't even fight them off. I black out just as we pass the torch-lit entrance, hearing my fate seal with a clank of iron.

EIGHTEEN

ADESSA

"Green, for the land that once was. Black, for the souls before us. Gold, to honor the status of our First Grandfathers in the Time Before." – Muhdam Manuscript, the Lords' Laws.

A block of cells surrounds me, and it appears that I'm in the last one.

Water. I need water.

I smack my cracked lips together, reaching for my waterskin – it's gone. Those bastard guards must have taken it. *No, no, no.*

Above me, the open sky spins, the stars a distant blur. A shadowed cloud drifts overhead, blocking the weak moonlight, confirming that it's still night.

How long have I been out?

The torchlights surrounding my iron cage offers just enough illumination against the void ahead, but I can hardly see beyond a few meters. I heard moaning earlier – distant, hollow, but neither of us has exchanged any words of greeting. I carefully nudge the swollen skin beneath my eye, the heat radiating from it like a burn. My neck is tight, the skin is stiff and puffy, a mess of bruises. I can't even *think* straight. I drag my hand up, feeling the split on my lip. Blood, thick and sour, coats my tongue.

The taste makes me gag. There's a fresh wound on my palm that wasn't there before, still raw, as if it had been created only moments ago.

I try to sit upright, but everything tilts to the right when I do. The agony tears through the seams of my composure when my foot – *my foot* – I feel the open wound as I move. It sears with dull throbbing. *What did they do to me?*

I try to gather my memories, the puzzle of waking up in here falling into place. I blink, trying to focus, noticing that the gouge has been pathetically wrapped with a sash, now soaked through. I want to scream. I want to *laugh*. Were they trying to stop the bleeding with *this?* It's almost as ridiculous as the fact that I'd fallen for their trap in the first place.

I press up again, feeling my ankle twist. The slit on both the top and bottom of my foot opens and closes with every adjustment, each pulse of pain making my bones shift beneath the muscle. "Fuck."

The fact that it had taken a healer to properly fix my broken spine overnight doesn't exactly inspire hope for this wound to heal on its own anytime soon. Not with shattered bones as tiny as the ones in my foot. My body really has been *perfect* at picking the worst moments to betray me.

"Did I wish for this curse to be lifted too soon or something?" I shout, the words splintering from me in a crazed laugh that bounces off the sandstone walls as I tear off a section of my shirt with sore teeth. I tenderly wrap it around my ankle, tying a tight knot to stop the pulse of blood. I won't be able to move if I'm drained of it.

"I didn't think anyone was actually listening when I said I wanted to die! You never listen otherwise!"

I'm unsure if death is finally now ready for me, or if it's just toying with me again. If it's real this time, it picked the wrong moment, because I am not ready for it anymore. At least, not right now.

The stench of rot hits me, drawing my attention to the corner of my cell. To the body slumped where the iron walls meet. Large flies buzz around a white head of hair. The skin sags, unclothed, lifeless. My stomach churns and I swallow to keep the bile down when I realize that who-ever this is – was – they're clearly dead.

That will not be me.

The sand is soft below my feet, the ground beneath it, wet. I glance at the base of the metal block surrounding me, searching for a way out. I could dig underneath, but that risks getting trapped between the bar and the ground if I don't have enough strength to pull myself up. I would suffocate. And then I'd be left at the mercy of the men who put me here. Left to rot like the body in the corner.

The hollow squares of soldered iron could be climbed, I suppose. My eyes flicker to the sandstone wall looming behind me, barely a jump-ing distance away. There's a dip a few inches from the top of the ledge - an outcropping. If I time it right, maybe, just maybe, I could leap from the top of the cage, grab the ledge, and haul myself over it. It's a fool's hope, but maybe that's the way out of here, out of the city, considering it seems like this entire area is boxed in by the obelisk barriers I saw from the outside.

The gouge in my foot throbs in protest at the mere thought. It shoots a bolt of pain up my leg, insistent. For a moment, I forget my plan, con-sumed by the pulsing regret. Then, the clinking sound of metal against metal grabs my attention. My head snaps to the right. The injured guard stands outside the bars. His nose is a twisted, purple mess, and his eyes gleam back as they fixate on me. He taps the edge of his torch against the bars, his lips pulling into a morose smile. He doesn't say a word. He only stares, beady eyes glinting in the pale, orange light at his side.

How long have you been standing there? I stare right back, pushing through the deep uncertainty saturating my gut. *Don't flinch. Don't let him see you cower.*

"Anyone come for her yet?"

His partner's raw voice speaks out along the tension, stepping from the shadows with deliberate swagger, rubbing the back of his head. A trail of dried blood caresses his cheek, staining the makeshift bandage that covers his damaged eye. I suppress my grin, my fingertips throbbing with the memory. *I hope you're never able to see again.*

"Why hasn't anyone come for you yet? The night's nearly ended." His directed words are sharp, taunting me. I don't blink. I don't break the stare. Instead, I sink deeper into silence.

"Damn them, I was really hoping one of them would show up by now." Frustration edges his tone in a whining way that makes my blood boil. This is a game for them.

The second guard spits to the side, irritation etching his features. "We have the horse. We'll at least get them to come for that. Who's watching it?"

"Amad." The man cracks his knuckles. "Told him not to tell Tyg about it just yet. I want first dibs. When I get my hands on that fucker –"

"Come on." His comrade interrupts with a soft shove, a too-friendly pat on the shoulder. "If he doesn't show by midday, I'll let you take out all that aggression on this one right before the gathering. As a treat for waiting."

The comment makes my skin crawl with disgust, fire licking the bottom of my feet with the need to flee. At least they haven't mentioned Saedea being used for their trap as well. That must mean she got away.

Their laughter echoes down the corridor; a high-pitched wail marks their exit when one of the prisoners beyond the torchlights begs them for mercy. I hear a blast from their gun, a sharp crack of light blurring the edge of my vision.

The laughter dies, then there's silence.

"Mystics above, this place gives me the creeps."

That's the last I hear of them as the flame from their torch flickers through the archway, slowly fading into darkness. Mystics' around. I have to get out of here.

Do I have anything to pick the lock?

My mind is frantic, scraping together possibilities that don't involve me scaling the cell. I search my pockets – nothing. A map. A compass. Loose coins. The crusty pita, now a rock – hardened from the dry, desert air. I try to bite into it and nearly crack my teeth against its surface. Cursing, I launch the damn thing across the cell, the hollow clang of it ricocheting off the iron rings against the silence.

This is the only moment I will regret burning the sour fruit jerky. I would have eaten all of it if I knew I would very quickly be depleted of everything. I stuff the few items I have left back into my pockets, my hand brushing against the parchment note – the one from Chadron. My heart skips. I yank it out, unfolding the crinkled paper with shaking hands, squinting in the near-complete darkness to read it. The curved letters blur, then jump out at me, forming a single word.

FINALITY.

I want to spit. *Finality?*

His cryptic, maddening word twists in my chest, a rush of boiling anger rising like ichor. What was the purpose of writing that to me? A single word on a blank page, scribbled by a man who – who – didn't help me. All of that knowledge – a man who was hallucinating on opium and forced me to participate in whatever crazed visions he wanted me to experience. I would have never been put in this damned cage if it weren't for his selfish decision!

Finality. As if everything, every bit of pain and struggle could be wrapped up in that single, meaningless word. I try to fight the urge to tear the note to shreds, but as soon as my fingertips graze the edge, the paper sparks. It sears against me, too hot in my hands, like it's alive. My heart races as it catches a blue flame, dissolving into the sand when I toss it from me. *What in the Abyss –*

My breath catches. I watch the tinted smoke twist into the air, drifting in front of me. It floats towards the dead body in the corner. The horror sinks in and I suddenly wonder if I've already lost too much blood. If this is some kind of trick. The smoke wraps around the corpse, encompassing its entirety.

It's trying to tell you something.

My voice is a whisper in my skull, echoing off the stone walls of the cage. I force myself to stand, and adjust my weight to my right foot, using the iron behind me for balance. I don't know how I'll be able to get across the expanse without help, so I go the long way, latching onto the metal with each swollen step. Somehow, I manage to hobble over to the body, shoving the hem of my shirt over my nose – not because of the smoke now swirling around me, but because of the stench.

The body reeks, a foul, putrid scent; terribly decomposed, but I can tell that she was once a woman. "What did you do to end up in here?" I whisper, more to myself than to her – not that I think she can hear me. There's nothing left of her to give me an answer of who she was. No clothes, no jewelry, nothing to suggest the bare traces of her life, which means she can't offer me anything sharp to pick the lock with.

I hesitate, then force myself to look away. I am not going to desecrate her. I am far above using a bone as a splintered tool to pick my way out of here. My stomach churns at the mere thought of it. The Mystics would surely curse me further, if they ever saw it happen. The priests in Skeall once called them benevolent creatures, but I've always disagreed, playing along with Tirma's words of fear and obedience. Never theirs.

Best not to do anything disrespectful to their dead and tempt them to turn their backs on me further, whether they truly still exist or not. I begin moving away from the corpse but freeze when I notice the blue-flamed smoke contract, narrowing until it locks onto the woman's leg. On sagging, bloodless skin, an invisible edge slices through, painstakingly carving out a word.

CLIMB.

I stumble back, my heart hammering against my ribs. A spear of smoke shoots past me, darting up and over the top of the cage, heading straight for the dip I'd been considering.

No, this can't be real.

My head spins. I'm definitely hallucinating. I look away, knowing this is the only chance I may have to get out of here. The sky above is softening – early morning haze creeping in at the edge, the faintest hint of dawn. It's almost here. I don't have much time. If I wait too long, I might not get another shot.

With a sigh mixed with more concern than anything else, I turn back to the etched word.

"You want me to climb that?" My voice sounds like it doesn't belong to me. I'm clearly delirious. The smoke doesn't answer back, obviously. I blink a few times, forcing my focus, the blueish tint finally disappearing altogether, leaving nothing but a faint image of where it wants me to go. One thing is clear, I can't just sit around waiting for the guards to realize that Yoon and the others won't be coming for me.

Why would they? Maybe they'll come for the horse. I hope, I *hope* they'll come for her. She doesn't deserve whatever hell they're putting her through just because she led us to the wrong place. But me? I am far less important to them, so I'm the only one that can fend for myself.

And so, I'll have to pretend that the pain doesn't exist, that the gap-ing hold in my foot doesn't burn with every shift of my muscle. I'll have to ignore the fact that it will make this climb unbearable.

NINETEEN

YOON

"Akhal-Teke will be rewarded alongside their riders. Matching brands and one full week to revel in their victory will be awarded to all participants. As is the game of war. As is our way." – Eighth Law of the Jidaani, etched in stone by Relik, the First Zaiem. 3,500 T.A

The first pale light of dawn breaks across the horizon, spilling weakly over the endless stretch of sand. It does little to ease the gnawing tension that coils in my chest, an unease that settles deeper with each step. I've finally tracked the women to Kyr.

Tagan's prints still faintly dip the sand, leading straight towards the Blood Market's gates. This wretched city. The one I swore I would never step in again. I knew the risks when I chose the Red Line as our path, but I had hoped the distance would be enough. The bounties on our heads, all of the people who would be willing to sell us out – it's all a part of the danger of being here, but it's also the route I know best. The truest route to Mirit. One that I could follow blindfolded if I had to.

Kyr, however, was never supposed to be a part of the journey. Although it sits just to the north of the Red Line, I never planned to ride anywhere near it. The city's walls keep its people in place, they rarely ever wander outside the gates. I thought we could stay far enough away to avoid it altogether, considering merchants rarely use the trade route anymore. Fate, it seems, has other plans. A tangled mess of my own making.

"They could have at least *tried* to cover their tracks."

Hisan grunts in agreement, watching me idly kick sand around, covering our prints and theirs in a futile attempt to avoid unwanted attention. The weight of what we've stumbled upon is unbearable.

"Just had to be Kyr, huh?" I ask my horse, who dips his head tenderly in response to our unspoken understanding. Poor Tagan. She must have thought this city was their best hope, that it would be the safest option while she awaited us to catch up. She had no way of knowing how badly things had soured, how fractured our relationship with Kyr had become. How it all changed so quickly.

Can't say I blame her, it would have been a great plan, considering the last time she and Jax were here, we'd all been on better terms, if you could call it that. At least there wasn't a reason for her to feel unsettled as Hisan feels now.

My palm traces the outside of my neck in frustration, hair strands briefly catching the cooled silver around my finger. The ring, once a symbol of something I held dear, now feels like an anchor, dragging me down with its burden. A thousand unspoken promises press against me, suffocating my lungs with each breath. A constant reminder of who I was, of the mistakes that have led me here.

A traitor doesn't deserve such a gift.

Yet, even now, I can't bring myself to remove it. Perhaps I'm holding onto the fact that it can serve as a tether to the person I once thought I was, the person who I never desire to be again.

Hisan nudges my shoulder, his warm snout grounding me, snapping me back into the present, to the mess I've let unfold. I took too long to get here. If Jax hadn't decided to leave without me – taking one of the camels, knowing full well the consequences of leaving with Hisan – I might have caught up to him sooner. Maybe I could have prevented them from reaching Kyr. Damn myself for allowing myself a whisper of rest after the relentless nights of being without any.

We'd been so careful. I'd overheard their talks of escape and dis-missed them completely. Even Jax noticed that Saedea had slipped her bindings and knew that the temptation might arise. We assumed hiding the riding gear would be enough to deter them. I never imagined they would be reckless enough to leave – especially not in this territory. And yet, here I stand, the consequences bearing down on me as sturdy as the looming walls ahead. Planning to enter a city I swore - how did they even know how to ride a horse anyways?

I should have known better. The moment I realized they were gone, it hit me with the force of a blow. I had failed them. I'd underestimated them. I wish I could beg the Mystics to allow us to start over. For us to have met in Teryal once more. For me to approach Adessa at Aya's with more solidity instead of – Mystics' around, what would have changed if I had helped her myself instead of relying on Aya's good intentions? The regrets are unsurmountable. My only hope is that it's not too late to make things right, though deep down, I know I might not deserve to.

"Head to Jynn. Burke knows who to meet with. We'll catch up in a few days."

My orders felt hollow as I hurried to saddle Hisan, waking Burke, Aol and Gunn up in the process. I didn't have time to think of a new plan for them. I'd offered Burke up as the sacrifice, and now I'm giving Geal all three. At the same time. There might not be a bargaining chip anymore; I have no idea what I'll do when I finally reach Jynn, what will await me. If they'll conspire against me completely. I feel like I'll be trying to rearrange pieces in a game that's already been lost. At least I left before I could hear the three complain about having only two camels to ride on. I at least managed to catch up to Jax earlier, matching his camel's pace so we could continue to track them together. We hadn't mentioned our regrets to each other, the silence in knowing had already been enough.

For us both. There was no mistake that they were heading to Kyr once we noticed their direction changed, heading north.

Jax had left my side moments ago, leading his camel over the jagged rock formation that marks the dried stream to the left, tucking Tagan's saddle carefully behind it. We both decided it would be best to find our own ways into the city, his scowl a clear indication that he resented the fact that his horse was more than likely being used as bait. I agreed with him – the last thing we need is to get caught together, although Jax and I have never been the type to leave the other behind. We never have. We certainly won't start now.

Hisan shuffles nervously, sensing the tension. I reach over and pat his neck, offering what little comfort I can. He nudges me again, so I oblige, letting him finish the last of the sugarcane in my pack. I'll need to get more soon before he realizes there's nothing left.

"Ah, it's alright, Hisan," I murmur softly, checking to make sure my weapons are securely in place. "I won't make you go near it." Hisan pushes me gently with his snout. "Just listen for me."

He bobs his head and trots off, back toward the direction we came. As long as he's far enough from the city border and close to the camel, I'll be satisfied. Not that it matters all that much if we don't bring the other animal along. After all, it was Aol's stolen gems that paid for it. I doubt I'll hear his complaints if Geal remains on my side. No time to dwell on it.

The moment Hisan disappears beyond the rocks, I start moving, my feet quiet against the hot sand. Low and fast, I cover the lower half of my face with the sand scarf around my neck, grateful that my clothes blend with the surroundings, offering me some semblance of camou-flage. Maintaining a wide berth from the path, I dip behind the arches of brick and the date trees surrounding the city's outer garden. The one once designed to lure in travelers. They used to make the outside look welcoming on purpose, but it's always been a façade.

Finally, I reach the sandstone and peek around the corner, squinting at the two posted guards who kick a ball back and forth, passing the time. This could very well be a trap. For me, or anyone really, an invitation to enter a city that's guarded by those who are indifferent enough not to care. These are Blood Market Muhdams we're talking about, some of the most spiteful creatures on this continent. Deceitful to their very core. Thriving on the misery of those unlucky enough to cross their paths. Traders, wanderers, anyone who might be foolish enough to get too close. To them, entry is nothing but trespassing. Cockroaches caught in a spider's web. That's Kyr.

I scan the ground behind the men. I've heard whispers about new traps being set up since their barricades were breached not that long ago. Smart, I suppose, for someone trying to maintain a ruse with guards who clearly can't be bothered. The trap is an extra cushion to continue their dealings inside.

The traps are always hidden well – right there. I spot the Muhdam flags hanging right above a small metal lever near the gate, about waist-high. It's subtle, almost invisible to any unsuspecting traveler who wouldn't notice if a guard were to press down on it. That's their real weapon, not the rifles they wave around, those things are practically useless. They're only for show, intimidation. A treasure from the past that they once traded with in order to keep the peace, but generations have lost the knowledge on how to maintain them properly.

As opulent as the Muhdams believe themselves to be, they'd never waste time or coin attempting to trade for bullets that are impossible to find and recreating them is nearly unheard of. Even if they were able to manage to collect bullets to load their showpieces, these so-called 'guards' wouldn't be able to hit the broadside of a barn, much less a target anyway.

They're the sons of wealthy lords and merchants, spoiled and aimless second and third-born boys, who have nothing better to do than stir up trouble. They're collateral – bait for whatever might wander too close, just so their fathers can boast about their family's fake prowess; while their mothers busy themselves with worshipping their actual heirs and daughters, ensuring their idle wealth stays intact in a land that is hardly livable.

A smear of fresh blood in the sand near the threshold of the gate catches my eye. Someone must have triggered the trap recently. I glance back at the two boys standing guard – they look unscathed. There could have been a shift change earlier this morning.

I don't believe the women would've crossed into Kyr without putting up a fight. And I doubt they were welcomed with open arms. Riding late into the night on a horse that I'm certain was recognized wouldn't have helped their case. They would have been immediately associated with Jax, and in turn, associated with me. Which would have sealed their fate before they even attempted to gain entry.

In Kyr, pretty, non-Muhdam women don't last long in a city like this. They're brought to one of two places. I have little doubt about which category Adessa and Saedea would fall into. In a way, being used as bait is their best option – and my best option to be able to find them. They're most likely locked up in the Muhdam's miserable excuse for a prison. At least, that's the only place I'm willing to entertain. The other, far darker possibility is that they're being shuttled into the Underground – a place where I would never find them, not unless the auction was in full swing. The thought of them, of *her*, down there is unbearable. I can't let it happen.

I instinctively check my daggers one last time to confirm they're with me before peering around the corner once more. Facing the guards head-on, in broad daylight *is* tempting – entertaining even. But I am not here for a fight. Jax must have felt the same, considering he didn't bother with engaging them either. I bet he's already scaled one of the outer walls, searching for a more discreet way in. Luckily for me, I know one that doesn't involve climbing.

Keeping close to the sandstone, I make my way around back, past the staged date trees, under the leaves of large palms made of realistic fabrics, making a turn around the corner, free of guards and sprint parallel with the wall until I reach the center of what I know to be one of two main storage quarters. My fingers find the smooth stone, tracing the outline of the fake panel I painted to match the tanned, slightly orange exterior. The wood panel shifts, revealing the hidden entrance I've used thousands of times. I push aside the matching plank that covers the inside of the textile room, remembering how long it took for me to dig into the sandstone all those years ago. The entrance I had once relied on to smuggle hundreds of Jynn's supplies to the Underground under the noses of the merchant Lords.

After the Cull, Kyr wasted no time making its mark on the continent. With trade being the lifeblood of survival, the city quickly rose to dominate the market as the epicenter of merchantry. The Blood Market. Run by the wealthy Muhdams who are rumored to have been favored by the Elites in the Time Before, it became the beating heart of a sprawling network that stretched from the southern slave runners to the farthest reaches of Bahani territory in the east. And with such power, came opportunity – one that the Jidaani didn't hesitate to sink their claws into. They offered protection, while the Muhdams granted them full access into their Blood Market.

Relik, First Zaiem of the Jidaani, forged a new path that would secure the dominance of both tribes over the entire continent's trade. He expanded their main route, using existing lines the Eiltes once used, pushing it all the way to Grandia, positioning it closer to the ancestral lands of the Jidaani. In doing so, he not only solidified his clan's influence, but also conspired with the Muhdams in the creation of their Underground – allowing only those who contribute to it, gain access to it. Eventually, the Nevadem slave runners were allowed to create their own system within the depths, free from the constraints of other territory powers, unleashing a new fear into a world destroyed by the Cull.

Unfortunately for both sides, Tyg ascended to power generations later, and with his rise, everything shifted. He named the route the Red Line, forcing all trade to pass through that single, loosely controlled route instead of the open paths that had once crisscrossed the lands. It was his way of asserting complete control, ensuring that more Jidaani were free from the burden of security duty and could focus on expanding the territory by any means necessary. In doing so, he destabilized everything. The remaining routes became unpredictable, the Red Line became overpopulated. Revolt began to simmer.

Both the Muhdams and the Bahani, both incredibly reliant on trade, were plunged into turmoil. Clan wars broke out. What was once a secure, reliable route turned wild, untamed, soaked in the blood of countless lives. It was as though Tyg had planned for chaos, the very name of the Red Line echoing his cruel foresight. Merchants became fearful of trading outside their own territories. The Muhdams sealed themselves off, trading only with their own, barricading their city completely.

That's when I stepped in.

It took time – far longer than I care to admit – and a great deal of convincing, making me never want to have to negotiate terms again. But eventually, Zahre, former Lord of Kyr, bent the knee to Tyg. He agreed to allow me to restore the Blood Market to its former glory, allowing the Red Line to function properly once more. Tyg was given most of the credit, as is – was – our way, but I didn't mind at the time.

Merchants began to use the trading routes again. Fabrics, spices, and even gold became a vital source of revenue for both clans. But above all, shine. The missing piece to all the trading in the past. It was an instant success. With it, I established a network of suppliers that stretched from Mirit to Ferack, even as far as Isla. My success only fueled Tyg's envy, a fire that burned brighter with each passing year. In my early days with the Jidaani, I had been nothing. It wasn't long before I rose through the ranks, securing the position of a router, which led to the network that allowed me to gain swift recognition, until I had eventually made it near the top and rose as Tyg's second. It was a title that I never thought I would hold, one that *no one* thought I would hold. It was one I reveled in at the time, drinking deeply from the power it afforded me. Until it no longer offered me peace.

Harmon had become my primary supplier of *pure* shine. He had perfected the method to make it authentic, the only one to do it within the territory. With the steady stream of silver we brought in, he and Aya managed to leave their failing farm behind, focusing instead on their secret distillery. They had crafted the bar to hide the operation in Teryal from men like Rust, who had been selling a poisonous imitation of shine on the route. For nearly a decade, Aya and Harmon kept the Muhdams well supplied, thriving under the radar, and my protection. That is, until Harmon's death. The crumbling start of my own carefully built life.

Aya however, agreed to honor our arrangement even after his death, even after I ran. She remained loyal to me, not the Jidaani. She once told me that I must have been a son to them in another lifetime, because they had no children of their own in this one. She owed me everything, including her life – not just for helping them escape the hardships of a drought-ridden farm, but for something much deeper, something unspoken.

At least Aya doesn't blame me for his death like I do. I carry that burden with me every day. She claims it eases her heart to look at me without anger, even though I desperately wish she would.

Rust was the one who killed Harmon. There wasn't any reason for anyone else in Teryal or the surrounding villages to do so. His illicit trade had been ruined by Harmon's refusal to back down, especially in the later years, creating dissent in Teryal. It forced Rust to deal with the slave runners just to get by. I wish I would have ended him at Aya's when I had the chance. It's not like I plan to return to the continent after I cross anyway.

I lift my gaze to the towering ceiling above me, the weight of the memories sinking in, reminding me of what I had to do to get here. Everything that I've sacrificed echoes in the linings of Zahre's reformed market. It was, after all, his intention that had forced me to build the hidden entrance in the first place.

Once I stepped into the Underground, the temptation for more was inevitable. It's the only place outside of Isla where the rarest goods trade hands – Ferackian gems, blasting powder from Mydiza, salts from the Dying Sea, blessed by the creature said to dwell beneath the waves. These were items that people from all over the continent dreamt about, but were never able to get unless they went through one of my merchants. All beneath Zahre's Blood Market, all mine to command.

I risked Tyg's wrath every day by not telling him that I was also dealing in the Underground. He had been satisfied with what I had been bringing in already, so I didn't find it necessary to let him know I was obtaining so much more. Once Jax joined the operation, it blossomed into something far more lucrative than we could ever imagine, dwarfing our clan's stipend entirely. We'd been keeping most of the gold and silver made from the secret profits all to ourselves, gradually storing them in a hovel in Mirit.

My long-term plans now depend on that stash.

Our Zaiem, in all his pride, never caught on to the fact that we were basically stealing from him. That made it all the sweeter. He was happy, we were happy, and we flourished for quite some time. Even Zahre stopped asking questions, filling his pockets with equal greed. Then, came Zahre's son, my former partner on the inside, Saram. He thought betraying me to his uncle, Rahish would grant him certainty as heir to his line. That fool. I'd always known better than to trust the lords themselves, the so-called guardians of the Blood Market's integrity. I had only trusted the outliers who worked beneath their feet. What I failed to see was that Rahish, not Zahre, was the true master. His control extended far deeper than I realized at the time, and I'd made the fatal mistake of underestimating him.

In hindsight, I know it wasn't bad luck alone. It wasn't merely a Lord's brother-in-law making a power play. No, it was my refusal to share the wealth – my failure to give them a cut – that turned everyone against me. I was too proud, too arrogant, and in the end, it was my greed that set the stage to piss everyone off.

The traitor, of course, had been acting with hopes of securing his position in Rahish's vision of overthrowing his sister's husband. As a bastard son by marriage, he needed to claw his way to respect. He was an untitled heir; Zahre didn't have sons of his own – he was rumored to be incapable. Who could blame him for wanting more in a world where a title meant everything? I can't say I would've done it in the same way he had, but then again, power is all-consuming. He knew Rahish saw Zahre as an obstacle; the Lord of Kyr never stood a chance. And neither did I.

I was arrested in the early hours of dawn, precious stones lining the canvas of my textile pack, ready for the auction that always took place every fourth morning. The taste of tobacco still clinging to my lungs, the warmth of chai settling in my belly. The irony of it all was that I'd been standing beside the same traitorous bastard who cursed my name to his uncle the night before. He lingered longer than usual in our conversation that day, his words unusually drawn out, which now I see was his means of distraction, while we waited for the blooders to open the stairway. Guards swarmed, tearing my bag apart, revealing the gems I had been planning to auction, but not portion out for a cut.

That's when I knew that he had betrayed me. The large bag of coins pressed into his hand had been a dead giveaway, but it was the scream that followed – the kind of sound you can't unhear – that confirmed my suspicions that he had been working alone. In the end, even the most justified men can betray, yet loathe the betrayer. Once trust is shattered, there's no point in keeping anyone around who will only stand to be in the way. They severed the hand that held the bag of silver with a dull blade and threw him and myself in their prison.

Saram's life didn't last much longer after that. At least it was only a few days of torture, of begging for mercy, of crying out for his uncle – they forced him to spill everything he knew. The names of everyone I had ever been known to deal with inside and outside the walls of Kyr. Unfortunately for him, most of those names belonged to his own friends.

I know all of this, because I had no choice but to overhear their interrogations. I was kept locked in the opposite corner of our shared cell; all while being tortured in a similarly unpleasant manner at the opposite end of the cage for the four days he remained barely alive. The only difference was that I didn't break.

Words were never exchanged between us during that time – mainly because his tongue had been carved out on the second day – but the glares he threw my way spoke volumes. I knew then that he'd cling to a grudge for the remainder of his life, and the next, regardless of the fact that he brought it all on himself. In the end, it was his own uncle who snapped his neck, locking eyes with me as he did so. A gesture to say, 'you will be next.'

Fortune favored me that day, deciding that one death was enough, that it would be a waste of time to try to kill me, which created the opening that I needed. I slipped from the ropes that bound me, using the fractured finger bone of my dear traitorous friend to pick the bolted lock during guard change later that night. I even took the time to bury Saram's body loosely beneath the sand, a small gesture of the respect I held for his mother. I knew she played no role in my betrayal.

I shift the panels back into place, sealing the entrance to my hidden tunnel, pulling myself fully into the center of the textile room. It looks nearly empty now, nothing left but the echoes of goods that had once filled it to the brim. The grandeur has faded – my absence has clearly taken a toll. No wonder we didn't cross paths with any merchants. The trade routes seem to be dying once again.

I wonder if it's because of Rahish. Zahre was as benevolent as a Muhdam Lord was capable of being. He indulged in the trade but he also made sure it was somewhat fair. Perhaps his successor has maintained other plans for the city of Kyr. There's also the fact that Tyg had gone on a *slight* rampage when I returned to Grandia, covered in old blood from wounds long healed, with only deepened scars to show as proof. Fresh brandings on my chest, marking me as a traitor to the Muhdams – ironically placed alongside the faded divot that once marked the class branding that I'd worn as a child.

I was wary when Tyg returned from his spree, wondering if he learned the reason why they branded me. He seemed blissfully unaware, taking days to rest from his rage and coming out of it with compassion for what I had been through. I'd been awarded another mark, alongside

Jax, who helped our Zaiem with his revenge spree without question. Tyg had been fiercely holding on to his trust in me, his Second. I realized that he had been more loyal to me than I ever had been to him. I often wonder if he ever found out. If he's added it to the long list of why I should be hunted and brought back to him to face the consequences of my leaving.

The quarter is eerily still. The sun has already begun to crest the purple-hazed sky, but not a single bird is singing in the streets. I at least expected a servant or a router to cross my path by now. The silence is unnerving. I make my way toward the main archway, noting the shacks ahead, now adorned with sun-faded tapestries that I –

No.

I hurry to the other side of them, jaw-dropping at the view of large, obsidian triangles woven into the fabric. Jidaani markings. Those *definitely* weren't here before. The Muhdams have tribe markings of their own: green and black with gold thread. Same as the ones hanging outside their gate – a symbol of their fragility, masked by the flaunt of their wealth. But these – these are Jidaani flags. Strange. Even if my former clan backs the Red Line, seeing the familiar symbols in a place dominated solely by Muhdams feels – wrong. I can only assume that more than just the emptiness of the storage room has changed.

The question now is: why would Tyg lay claim to Kyr? The Jidaani are not traders by blood, we – *they* – run the largest territory on the continent. Uncontrolled, untethered, feared, yet constantly constrained by the contracts signed by the remaining clans. Contracts that prevent more clan wars to break out. Geal is supposed to be the one to break the agreement first – that's the plan. But now, with Jidaani flags flying here, I have to wonder if Tyg has begun his quest to take the Bahani as his own. The thought of my former Zaiem running rampant through Kyr sends a chill down my spine. It makes me realize that I no longer have the ability to know what's on his mind.

I slip into one of the alcoves to the left and wait, pressing deeper into the shadows, feeling a subtle relief at the faint signs of life around me.

Pots clatter, a dog barks in the distance, the smell of a first meal wafts through the air. This part of Kyr is waking up, reminding me that I need to be quick. I have to remember where the prison is.

The irony of the Muhdams lies in their prisons. Built in a city where so many already belong to a hellish fate of their own making, they've created something much worse to hold those who the lords no longer want roaming their streets. Their prison is also meant for outsiders who won't sell in the Underground, allowing the merchant sons to redirect their sick desires rather than taking it out on the residents who actually belong here. They're no different than the rulers who became our Firsts after the Cull. No different from their predecessors in the Time Before.

I glance up and down the empty street, then, relying on instinct alone, I sprint across the path, hiding under another building's shadow. A harsh, smoke-filled cough latches onto my attention to the open door-way – to the circle of men gathered around a crude metal table inside the room. Each one is armed to the teeth, coins and marbles scatter the aluminum surface in a heap of greed. One man slaps another on the back, laughing maniacally as he swallows the silver pieces with pock-marked arms, a surge of envy glimmering the expression of his companions.

I exhale slowly, creeping along the splintered wall, rounding the corner. Above me, more Jidaani propaganda flutters in the breeze. The familiar herb-scented fabrics hang like ghosts in the air. *Have they been trading with Mydiza?* The thought passes quickly. *Prison... prison...*

If I remember correctly, it's near the western quarter. I adjust my steps, moving carefully on swift feet until I reach the halfway point. To my right, the bleating of caged sheep signals the entrance to the Blood Market. But where there once stood a Grand Bazaar, filled with every basic necessity one could want, thick with smoke from packed pipes, and the soft strains of a consort's song carried along by a buzuq – now it's all gone. It's all been replaced by canvas war tents. The Zaeim's symbol marks the largest tent of them all. The sight sinks like a stone in my gut.

Jax has to be around here somewhere, that nosy man wouldn't miss a chance to investigate the changes in Kyr before rescuing Tagan. I search the surrounding area, my eyes darting towards three, unveiled women, chattering softly as they float past my hiding spot behind the fence. Their shawls are pristine, adorned with sparkling woven gems marking their high ranks. They wear cloth shoes, meant only for cherished feet, and each cradles a sleeping baby in her arms. Muhdam wives. I don't see any guards following them. If their husbands were still alive, these women wouldn't dare step outside without security.

Something isn't right.

I slip further behind the shadows of half-empty ash barrels, the stench of rotting fruit wine thick in my nostrils. The damp wood seeps its sourness into the air but I don't dare recoil from it. A horse whinnies in the distance, a sharp, startled sound that makes my pulse quicken with memory. My gaze snaps back to the stables.

Seven Akhal-Teke cut through the fenced-in training ground, their golden coats slick with sweat, hooves striking the hardened earth in ear splitting rhythm. Each movement is fluid, powerful, just as they were taught from birth. My stomach coils tight as I watch the man standing in the foreground, barking clipped commands at the trainer. His voice, harsh as the crack of lightning, hasn't changed. Not like I expected it to. Neither has his stance, rigid with expectation, his hands clasped behind his back like a king surveying his ownership.

I should hate him. I do hate him. And yet, beneath the fury, lies something else – something that claws at the edges of my resolve. A longing, bitter and sharp as the whip slicing through the air. My desire to never cross his path again upends every reaction I thought I would have if I ever did. This man shaped who I became. Who I am desperate to free myself from now, still trapped beneath the shadow of who I've wanted to be. He's the reminder of why I can't look at myself without feeling emptiness – and rage.

My old Zaiem.

TWENTY

YOON

"Do you remember the forest? Where you were born, my son? Do you remember the soft moss that grew on the trees? The way you felt when your small fingers brushed against it? Hold onto that, my son. Never let that peace leave you. One day, you will be there again."

He's soon flanked by his two assassins, Tero and Ren, armed with the matching blades awarded to them years ago, strapped tight to their biceps. The emerald stone insets glint against their iron hilts like the eyes of twin serpents, unblinking, watchful. I press myself lower, adjusting my sand scarf, the rough edge of the barrel biting into my shoulder as the three men turn. My breath stills.

They don't look in my direction. Instead, their attention shifts to the women crossing the courtyard, their conversation momentarily forgotten. Tyg snaps his fingers in silent command. He doesn't need words – his men move without hesitation. Tero and Ren fall into step behind him, their forms slipping behind the frame of the Zaiem's tent. The fabric sways gently in their wake. I don't move. Not yet.

"You saw them too, right? It isn't my imagination playing tricks on me?"

A risky voice whispers behind me, nearly threatening our cover. My pulse spikes as I spin, my body tense and ready, only to find Jax crouched behind a stack of boxes less than an arm's length away.

"You idiot." I exhale, my voice a sharp whisper. "You nearly gave me a heart attack."

Jax grins, barely containing his laugh, and for a fleeting moment, it's the same as it's always been. That brief, reckless amusement in the face of everything that could go wrong. Coping the way we always have, balancing on the edge of life or death.

But it doesn't hold the same resonance that it once had. I know he feels the change as well. His smile fades only slightly as he shifts closer.

"Found Tagan, she's with the Akhal-Teke." A pause, his tone dipping lower. "They've abandoned the bazaar. I wonder what the Underground looks like now if Rahish's precious market is gone."

The words sit heavily between us. Suffocating. The bazaar's fate is an unanswered question that hangs in the air like the distant scent of fire burning. The uncertainty claws at my bones. My friend clears his throat. "You find the girls yet?"

I shake my head, holding my breath as Tero and Ren step out from under the tent's opening. They don't move; they're clearly waiting for their leader. Time breezes by all too slowly, until Tyg finally emerges, a fresh mark etched into his rich, brown skin, above the matching others. Six in total now.

"Looks like he just promoted himself." The weight of Jax's words holds a grip on my spine. Our tattoos are a permanent reminder of our rank within the clan. A tradition that Tyg himself created – to set us apart, to define us as Jidaani. Triangular in shape, a nod to the great pyramids that once stood on his ancestral lands, long before the First Grandfathers were brought into the world in the Time After.

Each mark is earned. A demonstration of loyalty, a reward for service to Tyg, to the clan, a rise in position. None of them come easy to obtain. Tyg has ruled as Zaiem for nearly four decades – the longest in Jidaani history – and yet he only now bears his sixth. I have never met a Jidaani with more than four.

Jax and I earned our third together after the falling out with Kyr. We should have had a week to celebrate the victory. Release from our duties, freedom to travel within the territory, anything a person could ever want, everything I *had* wanted once. Instead, we became traitors.

Those who fall from rank, rarely live to talk about it – unless they run. We still have our marks – but only because we haven't been caught yet.

"I'll head for the cages," I say steadily, but my thoughts are already ahead of me, mapping the quickest path through the camp. I'll have to cut through the cluster of tents to get to the prison.

"I'll grab Tagan. Where should we meet?"

I shake my head, knowing what he wants to hear, advising against it.

"Head to Jynn. The others are on their way, I need you to try to undo the damage they're going to cause. I'll catch up once I get Adessa."

His eyes glint with both curiosity and understanding. "Saedea too."

I nod in return. Jax throws me a lazy salute, and the curve of his lip tilts to the side.

"I'll leave you the camel. See you in Jynn." He gives me a wink. "Don't die."

With that, he leaves, slipping through the fence and under the canopy toward the side of the stables. I don't watch for long. Jax knows how to stay unseen, it's what we've trained our entire lives for. Speed is what matters now. Tagan might be safe with the Akhal-Teke for now, but that doesn't mean they'll show Jax the same respect.

They are trained as fiercely as those who are permitted to ride them and rewarded in the same way. Their prowess is represented with brandings of their own, etched on their golden coats. Tyg's own stallion, The Akhali, had five brands burned into his golden coat the last time I saw him. His latest had been earned after trampling a half-dozen Nevadem scouts to death, without his rider to guide him. Watching armored soldiers be crushed under hooves like wheat beneath a millstone is a humbling sight to see. One I hope never to see again. If The Akhali is caged with the others, there's no telling what he could do if he sees Jax.

The moment my gaze leaves Jax's back, it lands on a free path between the camp. Tyg's sights are on the pens. Tero and Ren are focused on prying the crates that are stacked along the Zaiem's tent open. I don't hesitate. I sprint low, skimming the opposite edge of the tents, slipping under lines of damp clothes, still heavy with water. The scent of raw incense thickens, blending with the sharp tang of cooking oil. The haze of morning heat presses in.

I weave between abandoned storefronts that give way to newly restored cobb houses, their walls still dark from the night's chill. The muffled voices of residents rising from their breakfast tables sends a shiver of urgency through me. I hasten my footing, knowing the prison is not much further, I can see the archway that opens to the inside ahead. It's a shade darker than the rest of the sandstone. A Muhdam tradition – one I used to admire before having experienced it myself. Each time a prisoner is added, the blood from their palm stains the sandstone. A blood-smeared offering, a gift to the Mystics, meant to keep their favor upon a city that reeks of desperation. Mystics love blood, or so the Muhdams have told me. I wonder where my own handprint is on the arch.

The absence of guards outside the cell block makes me question if I'm in the right place. Not a single soul is standing watch, no laughter, no idle chatter. The silence seems deliberate.

What kind of trap have they set for me?

I slip quietly inside, facing the beginning of the cluster. The smell of death and rot clings to my nose, like molten metal lining a furnace. It's a stark contrast to the patchouli-dipped air outside.

The first cage holds the shrunken body of an older man. His limbs are missing, his body is collapsed inward. I can't tell if he's breathing or not. Next to him, another body, facedown, his tangled hair soaked in a pool of dried blood. His chest rises and falls in drowned breaths between the sad murmurings of a soul who has lost his sanity long ago. I hope for his own sake that death won't be far behind.

I hurry to the next block; a stack of stained barrels lay against the opposite side of the middle cages. The smell of this wretched prison seems the most prominent here. I shudder to think what, or who, might be inside those drums. The last cage comes into view among the still-lit torches. From this distance, it appears mostly empty. Unfortunate, for my hopes. I really needed the women to be here.

"Adessa?"

I keep my voice barely above a whisper, yet it echoes throughout the stone corridor, swallowed whole by the void. Nothing. The memory of being trapped in this very cage brushes my skin in an unwanted embrace. I can picture myself hanging by the neck for the second time in my life, my toes just barely touching the sandy ground, desperate to find support. Rahish thought of making a wasted example of me. It was a viewing for no one but him and his guards to see. I toss my head around to clear the image from my mind.

The final cell rests at a dead end, pressed into the outer wall like a forgotten thought. A place meant for those who are not meant to leave. Then, I see it. A body, slumped in the corner.

"Adessa?"

The word barely escapes before rot clogs my throat. My stomach clenches when I lean closer. The corpse is twisted, crumpled inward at the torso, skin stretched over taut bones, gray and waxy. Her hair – what's left of it – is too brittle and sun-bleached to be anywhere near the color of copper. Blood has dried in jagged streaks over her ruined body, seeping into the dirt like ink spilled on parchment.

Relief flickers through me for only a moment – this isn't Adessa. The feeling is short-lived. The prison is empty. That can't be right. They had to have been brought here. They should still *be* here if they were. Unless...

My pulse hammers as my mind tries to piece together the cracks. She couldn't already be traded; it hadn't even been a day. Unless they were never meant to be traded at all. Maybe they were never bait. Tagan would have been enough to lure Jax, that part made sense. But Tyg –

He wasn't worried. He wasn't scrambling, wasn't searching for anything. He was celebrating himself. There aren't any Jidaani crawling around the prison, there aren't even guards. An uneasy feeling glazes over me in a sweat.

Does he already know?

My fingers curl into fists as the possibility settles like lead in my gut. Tyg has never been above taking unwilling women for himself. Some of us had tried to protest, but only in whispers, fearing it would be useless against the weight of his wrath.

Is she in his tent?

If he's aware that Tagan is here, he would know the women were here too. And if he knows that – he knows I'm here. My body locks into place. He knew I would come. He knows how foolish I am, as Jax is with his horse, regardless of the Ramouz nearly bleeding on every surface of the city. This could very well be so much worse than a simple Muhdam trap.

I try to convince the panic in my mind that it isn't what it seems. If he knew we were here, the entirety of Kyr would be on lockdown. It's been two hundred and ninety-eight days since I ran. Tyg would not be acting so casually. If there's one thing I know about my former Zaiem, it's that patience has never been his virtue.

I exhale, tilting my head back, groaning at the possible complications that this rescue might have caused, letting my gaze drift upward in frustration. Only to catch something – strange – along the wall behind the iron bars. Inconsistencies. Markings, leading all the way down into the sand. And at the base, half-buried between a gap that is wide enough for someone to slip through, something glints in the weak light.

I press into the narrow space and pluck it from the ground, turning it over in my hands. It's bronze, with a damaged hinge. A flick of my thumb pops the latch, revealing a small compass inside. The faded gold arrow stutters before settling backward – pointing behind me. I look to the sky again, watching a cloud pass. North isn't that way.

I have half a mind to toss the broken thing aside, until I notice the jagged, faint whisper of an engraving on the lid. Squinting, I'm able to make out a single letter. An *A*.

That can't be a coincidence.

My finger traces it briefly, eyes following the length of the cell to my left, catching more discarded items in the sand. Coins. I pick up three, rolling them between my fingers. My memory unfurls to the moment Aya paid Adessa for spilling my shine. *She was here.*

A breath I hadn't realized I was holding slips out. Relief, edged with a sharper, colder thought. She *was* here. She's not anymore. A few steps further, the sand dips, darkened with bits of crimson. My gaze follows the rivets along the wall; the markings I'd seen on the other side now look like claw marks, scratches from fingertips slipping down the wall. A ledge, right near the top levels with the cell's lip across from it. Blood stains the rock in splattered streaks, a rusted red-orange that drags down-ward. I turn and notice the same wet, sticky substance covering part of the opposite iron bar across from it. I don't need to touch it to know what it is. My brain scrambles to connect the dots.

Did she climb the cage? And then try to – jump?

Ahead, a trail of tracks curves around the corner, erratic, stopping at the dead end before veering left along the length of the wall, towards an archway that leads to the street.

Step. Shuffle. Step. Shuffle.

I toe a crusted strap of linen that lies inside the exit's frame with the tip of my boot. Torn, bloodstained. It reminds me of the state Adessa's feet were in. The image swarms my vision – raw, blistered, bare. She hadn't been wearing shoes. If she had stepped on the trap outside the gate, if that spike had gone through her foot –

I swallow hard. How much blood has she already lost?

The tracks falter at the exit, doubling back before breaking towards the opposite end of the street. My breath slows as I peer around the corner. A Muhdam guard stands at his post, idly kicking loose rocks along the wall. He doesn't look alarmed, he's clearly unaware that she's escaped. He must be here as a deterrent, hopefully for the Jidaani, to distract them from entering the prison. The thought gives me an odd flit of relief. The Muhdams don't seem to want their new occupants to know what they were trying to hide inside yet. That means Tyg hasn't sent out a hunt. Not yet. And that works in my favor.

The Muhdam's back is turned with methodical boredom, so I seize the moment and break out into a sprint, sliding into the shadowed barrier of the alley across from the prison, clearing the gate and landing silently on the other side. The trail of footprints resumes around the corner. Instinct drives me to smooth over the tracks with handfuls of sand. A small, habitual act I have embraced my whole life. No point in being followed.

Then, hushed voices drift in from an open doorway in the dirt alleyway. I press myself against the cobb, almost ignoring the murmurings of the fragmented conversation until the words of Darde catch my attention.

"...making everyone on edge. I'm thinking of joining them in Darde before –"

"Don't you dare say what I think you're going to say. Tyg would *never* allow –" A torn voice responds, one that I instantly recognize.

"Achk, what's he's going to do, Lee? He's damned near lost his mind anyways." A palm slams onto the hard surface of a table, rattling whatever scattered items are on top.

"He will *kill* you. But not before he makes an example of you. Need I remind you of what we witnessed with Pyro?" A pause. "Besides, do you really think that after Qui Mehrijaan he'll allow *anyone* to leave without his consent? He'd send Ren after you in a heartbeat." The ensuing silence is bone-chilling.

So, the news in Darde has spread this far too. So much for bribing the wanderer to keep the secret between us, that rat. Frustration knots at the base of my jaw. Tyg will piece things together. He'll realize where I'm headed soon enough, it's only a matter of time.

"He ordered us to leave for the Sunce tonight, remember? Az is scouting ahead with the others anyway. I can slip away easily. If you two join me, we could be halfway to Mydiza before he even notices we're gone. We'd be –"

"Enough! Stop spewing this traitorous nonsense, Sadirh! You are lucky it's just us two listening!"

Sadirh?

The name echoes as a third man snickers, quieting when Lee continues, his tone scathing. "You don't have a lick of sense, do you? Don't you know *why* Az was sent there in the first place?" He exhales a breathy sigh that betrays his reluctance to share secrets. "It was to scout the temple. I know you both have heard the rumors, so don't play dumb. Do you know why *we* are being sent to follow?" He seems to wait for a response that never comes.

"To make sure the newbie completes his task. To make sure this new 'King' of theirs bends his knee to Tyg like the last one did." His voice turns icy. "Our Zaiem has eyes and ears all over this Mystic-be-damned continent, do you really think betraying your duties will serve you well? Especially now?"

"Well, yes, if we leave before he finds out what we're doing. If Az fails, Tyg will be distracted with handling that problem. You can take us to Mydiza, Lee. In order for this to go smoothly, we need you in on it too."

I edge past the side window, visualizing myself inside that room, a ghost of the past. Once having similar conversations of rebellion in secret and opposing against it all. I'd once been in Lee's position, fiercely defending my Zaeim from the musings of those who didn't feel the need to fear him like they should have. Look at me now.

I wish I could stay longer to listen, to learn more about what Lee has to say about the Sunce temple, about Tyg, even if only to relive my glory days. But I can't risk wasting any more precious time. Someone may have already found Adessa – or worse, she could be dying out in the street from blood loss. The thought sends a fresh wave of urgency rippling through me.

I tuck their conversation into the folds of my mind, determined to relay every bitter detail to Jax later. He'll appreciate the irony of it all.

Adessa's bloody footprints reappear as I round the corner of the same house the men are in. The prints are uneven, dragging in places, smudged in others, as if she barely had the strength to keep moving. Ahead, streaks of crimson mark the wooden railing of the staircase, but the trail doesn't continue upward. Instead, a dark smear stains the rough edge of a crate on the last step, as if she collapsed against it before forcing herself forward. She can't possibly still be upright at this point.

I press my lips together and rub the blood from the railing with the outside edge of my tunic, attempting to clear any evidence of her before one of my former Jidaani walks out of that house and finds it curious enough to follow her tracks. Gritting my teeth, I shift the crate just enough to turn the stain away from view. It's not perfect, but it will have to do.

Continuing on, I weave around a weathered wooden fence, my gaze sweeping the ground. More thick blood streaks the railing here too, droplets spattering – everywhere. That, I cover with sand and pause my tracking near the corner of a small shack. I let my eyes wander, flicking upwards to an enormous silken Muhdam flag draping over the roof. Considering the circumstances, the sight of it offers a surprising bit of welcomed comfort. Her footprints seem to end here.

I close my eyes, trying to listen clearly. Silence guides me in solemn instruction when I hear soft sniffles, barely audible through the thin walls. The tiniest of groans pressures me to step toward the slightly ajar window and peer inside.

Adessa.

TWENTY-ONE

ADESSA

"And so, all at once, the banks of the Halitia set the stage for their fates. Newly bonded in prophecy by the Mystic who would one day try to save them. The one who had originally crafted their downfall in the hopes of maintaining balance." - Unknown Devout, 3,800 T.A

I make it halfway up the cage before my foot slips on my own blood, slick against the iron bars. My stomach lurches as I barely manage to steady myself, my fingers cramping under the strain. I want to give up so desperately – but I know that I can't. It isn't like I really have a choice. Tears well in my eyes, mixing with the cloudy black dots swimming across my vision. I'm horribly close to losing consciousness, I can feel it creeping up on me. I'd prefer it to happen on the *other* side of the cell. I can't go through all this work only to end up back in the same place. If I fall, I don't know if I'll have the strength to try again.

My toes wedge between the square gaps, making it incredibly difficult to want to remain upright. My arms tremble, my fingers are beginning to cramp as they hold the majority of my weight. I feel so weak.

I lift myself higher, clenching my jaw hard enough to taste blood. Every inch upward burns, making my skin slick with sweat, making it harder to hold onto the narrow bars. My injured hand finally finds the edge of the cage, and I choke out a laugh, barely managing to pull myself up and over. Hooking my legs around the top bar, I cling desperately for balance.

Then, my heart nearly bursts. *No. No, no, no.*

The gap is too wide.

From the ground, it seemed so much closer. I was being unreasonable. I hadn't accounted for the exhaustion, the way my body would barely respond by the time I reached the top. The actual distance of the gap. The realization of relying on false hope sinks in like ice in my veins. I allowed hallucinations to convince me of this, didn't I? My vision warps as I stare at how far away the ground is.

Climb.

Yeah right. *Mystics, what is wrong with me?*

I wobble; the drip, drip, drip of my blood smacking rusted metal snaps me into action. I can either pass out now, fall and break my neck; or jump and have a glimmer of a chance to escape. Or break my neck. Climbing down can't be an option, the spikes lining the outside of the bars would make it too challenging to maneuver blindly.

Wasting time.

The backs of my thighs scrape against the corrosion, pinching the fabric of my pants. I steady myself, digging in my heels, splaying my hands out. My lungs expand, retract, expand, mustering up the courage that I need. I focus on my target, push off, and leap. For a split second, I'm weightless.

Then, I slam into the sandstone wall.

The impact rattles me as my fingers frantically find the dip. I latch on, my nails pushing into my cuticles. My knees throb from the impact. I hang there for a moment, testing the crumbling ledge, straining. My arms shake violently, fear chills my throat in a panic – I can't pull myself up.

My right hand slips, the force causing my body to shift and swing to the left, smashing into the rock. My other hand loses its grip immediately after. A strangled whimper escapes me as I plummet. *No. No!*

I claw at the crumbling stone, desperation driving my fingers deep, but it does nothing to slow my fall. In a final, reckless effort, I push off and twist mid-air, hurling myself toward the metal cage. The impact is brutal – my body slams against the bars with a sickening crack. The force whips me upward, my hand snagging on rusted metal, reopening the slow-healing wound on my palm. Blood slicks my grip, but I cling tighter. Jagged spikes rip through my tunic, biting into flesh. Gravity yanks me downward once more, my chest crashing against the iron. Somehow, I've managed to hold on.

The world around me grinds to a halt. My mind struggles to catch up, piecing together the brutal luck that spared me. The fact that I didn't knock myself out on impact, the fact that my body hadn't been ripped to shreds on the way down. My grip fails moments later, and I plummet the last quarter. Unfortunately, it's my injured foot that takes the brunt of the landing. A ragged wail claws at my throat, but I bite it back, driving a bloody fist into my mouth. My body folds in on itself as I dry heave against the cage. Specks of orange and red spray the granules from my empty stomach.

I sit motionless, silent in my suffering, rage searing through the pain. When the worst of it passes, I scan my surroundings, attempting to rise. To my left, the wall corners sharply beyond the cages, revealing another opening – one that had been hidden from my view in the cage by a stack of barrels. Opposite the archway that I assume the guards dragged me through. Since I wasn't conscious when they brought me here, I can't be sure which way is the safest option, if there is one.

But the choice of going through that particular arch, the one that I can finally see amidst the morning light, smeared in dark, rust-colored streaks that stretch in the shape of hundreds if not thousands of palm prints – it makes my stomach churn. I glance at the gash in my palm, knowing deep down that I had played a part in painting the frame.

Opposite it is then.

Using the cell bars for support, I hoist myself up all the way and stumble along the sand. The same iron that caged me, holds me as my wish for freedom looms ahead. Each step is fresh agony. When I reach the corner, I press myself against the wall and peek around. Across an unpaved street, cobb houses huddle in the shadows of large posts that fly flags different than those hanging outside the gates. A series of black triangles woven throughout flutters against the fabric, reminding me of Burke and Aol's tattoos. I don't like what that could mean.

What's worse is there are no guards. At least none that I can see. No one but the birds watch from their perch on the thatched roofing across from me. I look to the sky, soft purples and pinks brighten at the edges in warning.

"If he doesn't show by midday –" The guard's voice hollows my mind.

The air reeks of burning sugar. Glassware clinks in the distance, making me painfully aware of how little time I have – how quickly the city will wake, how soon the guards will return to make good on their promise. My stomach rumbles again, in such a nauseating way that it forces me to retch off to the side a second time.

I can't afford to be lost and disoriented in this unknown city. Bleeding, starving, vulnerable. I need a plan. My only option seems to be following the towering outer wall, hoping it leads me back to the desert, to freedom. But that seems so out of reach now. Following it directly could leave me exposed. My head spins.

I need to find somewhere to hide. I need to gather my thoughts. I can't always work based on my delusional instincts; they clearly haven't done much good for me this far. Glancing back, I curse under my breath. A crimson trail follows me, seeping from the soaked cloth around my foot. Muttering, I tear another strip from my stolen shirt, discarding the soggy bandage. Using the archway for balance, I clumsily wrap my wound. It will have to do for now. The bleeding seems like it's slowing, but the bone is healing too sluggishly for my liking.

You're wasting time.

Shuddering, I press a hand to my hollow gut and scan the street again. If I get caught, I'll have no choice but to fight. I don't know if I'm ready for that.

Then, run!

I exhale sharply and launch myself across the street, slamming into the low, wooden gate opposite me. My fingers grasp at the stacked crates for balance as I shake the doors, realizing the gate is locked. I don't think, I don't feel; I act, throwing myself over the frame, heaving my body up and over, and landing with a thump on the other side.

I wish I could lay there, writhing in pain, but I can't afford that luxury. Someone could have seen me. Using the crates beside me for help, I stand, stretching out my sore back with a grunt. My hand throbs. That too, is leaving tracks behind, but I'm too out in the open to get it under control.

I hear voices in the alley beside me, women singing songs for the rise of their household. I need to hide. The set of stairs to my left could be a promising escape. I lunge for the railing, hauling myself up – only to hear louder voices behind the closed door.

Shit! Mystics, help me!

I double back, panicked. A bird cries, calling out ahead, forcing my attention. The largest raven in a flock of sparrows has left its perch, leading my vision to a lone shack nestled between the buildings ahead. It beckons me with a familiar flag, seemingly the lesser possible evils.

Green and black blur as the sting of my wounds drains the water from my eyes. I don't want to stand anymore. I make a break for the tiny building. No voices, no signs of movement. The door is unlatched in invitation.

Gripping onto the last bit of hope I have left, I slip inside.

TWENTY-TWO

YOON

"Eyes the color of moss. That's what They told me. Why aren't you listening?"

Her back is turned, but I'd know it's her anywhere. That hair – too bright, too familiar – burned into my memory like an ember that refuses to fade. The same shade as the King Vipers my father once was sworn to protect, before he was thrown into the pit with them. The same as the fire my mother fed to keep us warm beneath the citadel after we had been thrown out onto the streets. The same as the massive, gleaming gates that led us to our fate in Geming. I'd recognize Adessa's copper hair anywhere.

"Damnit."

She curses under her breath, wincing as she prods the blood-soaked fabric wrapped around her foot. It smears the ashen planks she sits on, a stark reminder of what she's been through. I shake away my small flicker of relief, replaced by concern.

She's alive. She's *alone*.

There's no sign of Saedea. *Shit.* I don't want to admit that I know where to start looking, but after all this time, I just wish I didn't have to.

Adessa reties a knot above her ankle, her fingers twitching. I want to call out to her, tell her that she's safe now, but I don't. Not with my former clan holed up in a shack barely a building away. I can't risk unwanted attention if she screams.

"What in the Abyss are you doing, Adessa?" She whispers to herself, groaning as she pushes up on one leg. Blood drips from her hand too.

She really did escape the prison.

For some reason, I hoped, irrationally, that she never went through it in the first place, even though I know that being imprisoned was probably the best thing that could've happened in her situation. I flex my fingers over my own palm as I crouch lower, the sound of Jidaani pounding their fists in motivation, echoing across the alley. They're preparing themselves for something. Adessa seems to hear it too. She shifts, listening carefully, fear etching her wide eyes.

The door of the shack opens moments later. I watch, frustration twisting my gut as Adessa stumbles out into the morning light, half-hopping down the steps before breaking into a limping sprint toward the end of the alley. My breath tightens. *Slow down.*

My gaze locks onto her back, tracking her every move as I mirror her steps from a safe distance. I don't know how she'll react if she sees me, and now isn't the time to find out. She abruptly stops to catch her breath, pressing her back against a paint-peeled panel. Drying pots hang from a line above her head, the swollen water droplets hiss when they reach the hot sand. Someone could step out to retrieve them at any moment.

I tuck myself along the fenceline, hearing the beats of heavy footsteps. The clink of metal. Coming from the direction of the shack.

"Come on, come on, why aren't you moving?" I murmur, my pulse throbbing in my veins. I shift my sights anxiously toward the path. Finally, *finally,* Adessa hears them too. Without hesitation, she bolts across the path, without caring to check to see if it's clear. I grit my teeth, sliding into the corner of the last building in the row and chase after her, relieved that the street is still empty. A stroke of luck.

That soon runs out. She trips. She uses her shoulder to break the fall, a strangled noise gurgles loudly in her throat, raw with pain. I'm too far away to help her. Thankfully, she scrambles back, dragging herself frantically towards another wood-slatted house. She hides behind the dried bush that's been planted for show. I scout the area around us, scanning for an escape. There – a storage hut to the right. It looks unused, unassuming. I pray to the Mystics that she's able to see it too.

Angry voices cut through the corridor, forcing me to find a hiding spot out of view of the road.

"I told you! He hasn't shown up yet!"

Stay right where you are, Adessa.

"Well, what about the horse then? Can you explain to me why it's *missing?* When was the last time you checked to see if she was still there?"

"Amad was called to the center, so I told Yar to keep watch on the stables. But he's afraid of the Akhal-Teke!" A reverberating slap bounces off the walls. It seems like they're still around the corner. "We couldn't miss the meeting! You know that damned Jidaani –" I hear him spit. "Doesn't like it when we're absent!"

They're all too close. And the bloodstains in the sand will lead them straight to us. My heart pounds.

No time.

I launch myself towards Adessa, moving with a hasty attempt to cover her tracks as I go, clamping my hand around her mouth to prevent her from screaming, then hurriedly drag her backward.

We hit the slatted door of the hut. My fingers fumble desperately for the handle as she thrashes against me, unknowing that I'm *saving* her.

Please be empty. Please be empty.

We tumble inside, crashing over the threshold when the door gives in. Air wrenches my lungs when Adessa lands bluntly on my chest, but I force myself to tighten my hold on her and slam the door shut with the heel of my boot.

TWENTY-THREE

ADESSA

"One hundred times too many."

The fury that ruptures through me is thick as wool, suffocating, blinding – I see nothing but red. A calloused palm scrapes against my cracked lips, an arm clamps too tightly around my waist. I burst with fight, twisting with every ounce of strength I have left, and throw my fist back. A grunt vibrates against my ear when I connect with the solid body beneath me. But the hands don't release their grasp, if anything, the grip constricts *more*, pressing me flush against his chest.

"Stop fighting me!" The voice, low and rough, and achingly familiar – rasps against my hair. I freeze. His breath is warm and uneven as he loosens his hold ever so slightly. Pressing into a seated position, he pulls me along the grain of his body, maintaining a firm hand on my belly while I helplessly kick at the floor, attempting to summon strength out of nothing.

The thickly accented voices outside carry around the corner of the hut I now find myself in. They pass the closed door, pausing briefly at the stoop. I squeeze my eyes shut along his exhale, feeling every muscle behind me braced in the quiet tension of survival. I should pull away, but my silence means so much more for the sake of my life. There's a high chance that I've led these men straight to me with the blood trail outside, I can't draw any more attention. I look at my bloody foot. It's soaked. The floorboards are riddled with fresh marks.

My heart nearly stops when they continue to argue with each other, cornering the small room, mixing words that I understand with a dialect that I don't. Beyond the cracked glass of the window behind us, boots scuff the ground. They're too close. I shift my body and feel his fingers flex against my stomach, anchoring me.

"Well they can't be here for much longer, I heard –"

"Quiet your voice."

It's followed by the language I don't understand. I make out the words, *Mahudami* being used multiple times and store it in the confines of my mind for later. I feel the chest against my back heave, as though he's trying to contain a laugh. It nearly slips as he quickly scoots us against the wall, under the pane and out of view, hiding us from the possibility of curious eyes. My ankle rolls while doing so, and I bite back the urge to clamp my teeth down around his palm. I dig my torn fingernails into his forearm to satisfy my misery instead.

He grates, squeezing his muscles. "Adessa."

My name is a whisper on his tongue. It's steady, and infuriatingly calm. It even has the gall to sound *annoyed*. I barely have time to process the fact that whoever's holding me knows my name when someone places a hand on the window above us. My pulse slams into my throat, my breath catching so violently I swear I can feel my ribs strain. Maybe it's from fear, perhaps it's from the fact that I can now smell the spices that cling to his skin.

Yoon.

The fingers at the window twitch, a frustrated grunt follows. The heat radiating from Yoon is unbearable, his grip keeping me firm and unmoving, and I hate the way my skin burns from the sensation. My hands move to tear his palm from my mouth, but he remains still as stone. His breath ghosts against my temple, measured and controlled. I know he's listening, waiting – just as I am.

"Achk. It's empty." Someone outside says, as though he's been peering in through the window. Shouting echoes from somewhere distant, and soon enough, that drives the others away from the glass. Their voices taper off into the alley, unknowing of the pair hiding right under them. Thank the Mystics.

It's only then that the calloused hand hesitates slightly, releasing its cover to silence me. My lungs fill with the stale air of an unused, dusty room. Yoon copies me with his own relief-filled breath. I'm not sure if it's him or I who pushes away first, but I use the moment to scramble toward the center of the hut, ignoring the way my limbs shake.

Yoon is right there with me, his steps slow and cautious. He doesn't touch me, but he doesn't have to – I can feel his presence, his half-blind gaze trailing me, mapping every inch of me. I force my chin up, my expression locked onto something cold and unreadable, even as the shame of my own weakness gnaws at my ribs. I hate this. I hate how exposed I feel. I hate that it's *him* who sees me like this.

"Surprise." He chuckles soundlessly, rubbing the center of his chest, irony gracing his lips. *Surprise?*

I don't answer. Only shove myself farther away, gripping the uneven planks for balance as I push to my feet. Yoon steps alongside me immediately, his eyes flicking over my tangled hair, the state of my torn shirt, the wound on my palm, until he lands on the loose wrappings that are holding the gash on my foot together. His jaw ticks.

"You climbed the cage." It isn't a question. His pupil sparkles. "Not bad. Pretty brave thing to do." *How could he possibly know what I've done.*

"Didn't kill anyone on your way out, right? That would raise an alarm, and I'm not really keen on drawing more attention to ourselves at the moment." His voice is edged with something almost teasing, far too casual for the weight of the words leaving his mouth. He says it with a rough-edged smile, as if he's making idle conversation rather than ad-dressing the fact that he *found me – bleeding* – in the middle of an alley. In the middle of a barred city. After I stole a horse to *escape* him.

I glare at him, eyeing the waterskin he now holds out to me. "You must be thirsty."

I let my needs win over my pride, taking a very long swallow of the cool, crisp water, and for a few blessed seconds, the world blurs. My problems minimize for only the time it takes for the liquid to travel into my belly. He urges me to drink more, pressing the opening closer to my lips when I try to hand it back to him. Annoyingly, I obey.

"There wasn't anyone *for* me to kill." I finally say between swallows, the euphoria of satiating my throat comes to an end with a backhand swipe to my chin.

"Interesting." Yoon scratches his neck, not hiding the fact that he's scrutinizing the state that I'm in.

I scowl and scan *him* with equal curiosity. There's a splatter of red-brown pigment near the hem of his tunic, but his unsullied machete is still strapped across his back. The twin blades remain freshly polished at his sides. The blood doesn't seem to belong to him. He's here, entirely unharmed, not even a scratch to show whatever trouble he must have gone through to find me. That makes me squint.

"How did you find me?" The distrust on my face is undeniable. He notices. Of course, he notices. Yoon rolls his eyes.

"Well, you aren't exactly good at covering your tracks." He gestures to the stain on his shirt, as if I'm supposed to know what that means. I frown.

"Oh, does this belong to you?" His fingers disappear into his pocket, only to re-emerge with something in his palm. My compass. A slow, awful realization slithers through me. I resist the urge to pat myself down, to check for the rest of my things. If I lost my map too – my thumb absently rubs the circlet around my finger that surprisingly, gratefully, has managed to stay on through everything. I snatch my belonging from his waiting palm.

"It doesn't work." He bemoans, brushing his hands along his tunic like he's wiping me off of him.

I snap the latch open, ignoring him. "It does when it wants to."

The golden arrow spins, dancing around and around between the worn letters NESW, until it suddenly stops – dead still, pointing to the direction in front of me. I glance up to find Yoon watching, curiosity deepening his brows. He turns slightly, thumbing over his shoulder.

"*That* is not north."

The certainty in his tone makes me bristle, but I don't admit to him that he's right. I don't care to. My fingertips graze the worn engraving along the brass lid, the markings that I watched Tirma carve with the sharp tip of an arrowhead, one that had been buried in my stomach when she found me long ago.

"*Do not lose this. It will show you. You will see.*"

That's what she told me when she pressed the gift into my palm. She'd said it with that faraway look in her eyes, as if someone had whispered the words to her first.

"*It wasn't me, it was the Mystics.*"

She always claimed that she was merely a vessel, that the terrible things she'd done, the things that made the villagers in Skeall pity her, were not her own doing. And they believed her. They were *terrified* of her. But instead of killing her, of angering the Mystics further with her death, they cast her out, condemning her to the caves.

"*I didn't do it. They made me.*"

Over and over, she had repeated those maddening words; after every test to break my abilities, wondering if I could heal from anything.

"*The Mystics did it.*"

Those words are ingrained in every scar I own. The compass feels too heavy in my hand, pressing down on me with something much more burdensome than brass. I've never truly used it to find my way, mainly because it doesn't point anywhere consistently. I've primarily relied on the stars, as my father taught me. Or the rare kindness of a passerby when I'm left with no other choice. This bronze and broken thing... I hate the fact that it's become the most treasured thing in my life. And I nearly lost it. Again.

"Where's the kid?"

Yoon's question cuts me out of my old guilt, directing me into a new one entirely. I shrug, feigning indifference, but dread coils my gut. I hope I was enough of a distraction for Saedea to slip away before I was beaten unconscious. If she's smart, which I've learned she is, she'll have started back to Er Rada. At least, that's what I want to believe.

Deep down, I know she's doing the complete opposite. Believing in a promise that I wasn't even sure I could keep when I said it. I desperately hope that she's at least out of sight. If she's left for Mirit, I hope for her sake that the stories of benevolent Mystics are real.

"I was just about to catch up with her." It's not entirely a lie.

"Was she in the prison with you?"

"No."

"Is she in the city?"

I really hope not. Dread overtakes the guilt I feel. I shake my head, wishing it to be true.

"How did you find me?" I ask again, evading the uncertainty I feel. *Saedea said you were a bounty. She said that to the guards. She knew you would come.*

"How were you planning on getting out of here?" He counters, ignoring my question again.

"I was following the wall."

"The wall?"

His razor-sharp stare cuts through the stifling air between us, slicing straight through my feeble attempt at nonchalance. He rakes a hand through his dirt-matted hair, the strands sticking together in sweat-drenched clumps. Then, as if he's trying to ground himself, he presses his fingers down the side of his neck, rubbing slow circles against skin streaked with grime.

"Was that from the trap outside?" His chin jerks towards my foot, gaze locking onto the soaked wrappings with that haunted, unreadable expression of his. I give him a single, short nod and shift uncomfortably, using a worn plank to elevate my injured foot slightly.

"I'm fine." I say, though I wince when I say it. "It truly isn't that bad."

It's a lie. We both know it. I make the mistake of looking down. The amount of blood I've lost should have killed me by now. Lucky me.

Yoon exhales sharply, a quiet scoff disguised as a breath. "Isn't that bad?"

His fingers graze my elbow. I make sure to pull away, stumbling into the corner. He doesn't move closer, but he doesn't step away either.

"I'm surprised you're even alive. I thought I would be searching for your corpse based on the amount of blood I've already seen leading me to you."

Thick liquid pulses from the wrappings in response, as if agreeing with his statement. I clench my fists. First, a broken spine. Now this. The Elder had accelerated the healing process last time, masking what my body would have eventually done on its own. But this? This is different. Yoon is going to start asking questions, as any normal person would. And I can't give him any answers. All I can do is hide the fact that eventually, it will heal completely. Hopefully I'll be rid of him before I'm threatened to give away any part of my secret, to avoid the many consequences that could stem from it.

A woman who heals from *anything?* That's not a miracle; that's not a gift. It's a commodity. One that could be bargained for a *very* high price, if the buyer was cruel enough. Tirma never let me forget that.

"Are you injured anywhere else?"

The tenderness in his tone stiffens my spine, scraping against everything I want to believe about him. It brings me back to the day at Aya's, when he was kind. I replace those memories with purpose, latching onto everything that has happened since, allowing my feelings to turn back to hatred. Whatever warmth I thought I saw in him was nothing but a trick.

And yet, my cheeks burn anyway. I'll blame it on the beating the guards gave me last night. The swelling feels like it's gone down significantly, but I'm almost positive it doesn't look ideal. Hence the strained look on Yoon's face every time he meets my stare.

"I said I'm fine."

I ignore the stiffness in my movements, willing myself to sway towards the door. My mind already traces the path I've set for myself. Turn right, follow the sandstone wall, pray to the Mystics that there's a break in it. I don't care why Yoon is here. I don't need, nor do I want his help. Unless, of course, he's here to drag me back to his men.

That would be another fight entirely.

He latches onto my arm, stopping me. "Adessa."

"Stop it, you bastard." I hiss, loathing the sound of my name on his tongue, the ease with which he wields it. Like he has any right to it. He doesn't flinch when I spit venom lined words his way. Instead, he unspools a strip of linen from his pouch, tearing it with his teeth before mindfully wrapping it around the deepened cut on my palm. The gesture catches me entirely off guard. That's what I'll blame for not immediately pulling away sooner.

"We'll clean this up later, but for now –"

I yank my arm back. The soft fabric sticks, the sudden movement tearing at the wound, sending fresh pain to lance my arm. I bite my tongue in frustration. Yoon curses under his breath and wrenches my wrist forward again.

"You're bleeding all over the damned place! Let me wrap it!"

His grip is firm while he wrestles with the corners, tucking them securely. For the past few days, all I've known is the bite of rope around my wrists. And now? A gently tied bandage to stop the bleeding. The irritation I feel, burns. The second he lets go, I snatch my hand back, cradling it to my chest.

"Leave me alone!" The room tilts. "Are you really that stupid not to realize that I was running away from *you*? Why would you – why did you come here?" I steady the quivering of my body, the crack in my voice.

"I wasn't given much of a choice." He groans, crossing his arms.

"Why? Because of the horse? Can't you see that she isn't in here with me?" I throw my arms out, displaying the darkened room around us.

"No." Is all he mutters, the tone flat. I waver, feeling a dip of dizziness. Of heat.

"Because you're so desperate for money that you –" I can't finish my sentence.

The fear threads too deeply, lacing itself into my veins. *He's going to try to take me back. Back to Burke.* My thoughts slowly shape themselves into a reality that would suit his narrative.

Yoon scoffs, but it isn't the tired, frustrating exhale I expect. It sounds amused. "Jax already found Tagan."

My spine locks. Jax is in the city? If he's here, the others must be too. And if they weren't planning to kill me before, they definitely will want to now.

I barely register the rest of what Yoon says. "And no, the others may have been able to prove things differently to you, but I'm not in the market to sell people. Let alone an innocent person like you."

I *should* focus on his words. On the fact that he wrongfully called me innocent. But all I can think about is the fact that they're here. Don't they have anything better to do? Anywhere else to be?

"I'm not as innocent as you think." I snap, standing straighter, refusing to let myself be backed into a corner. Yoon laughs, but there's no humor in it. No mockery.

"Your dog already told me that I'm not worth the scraps they would get for me anyways, just so you're aware. I'm not worth any of this trouble. If it's revenge you came all this way for, then fine. Kill me now then. Don't bother wrapping –"

"Did you know you were heading straight for an outpost?" His words cut through my confused fury. My mouth opens and closes. My mind claws for a defense, but I have none.

"The outer wall was –" I search for something to say in my denial.

"There are outposts lined on each of the corners, and at least two on each of the sides. You were almost in direct line of one."

Whoever was guarding that post would have easily seen me from that vantage point. That would have been a dire mistake. I wouldn't have made it out of the city at all. Every ounce of energy I've scraped together would have been *useless.* Mystics' around, I hate him even more for being right.

"I can help you out of here." His voice is calm, confident. He takes a step closer, holding out his hand. "But you need to give up on the idea that it's for the wrong reasons."

His stare burns for a few seconds too long. He must see the fire dancing in my eyes because he softly adds, "I've made far too many mistakes. Allow me to correct them."

He bends his arm slightly, offering the crook of his elbow. The gesture is almost gentle, but I can see tension in his neck, reluctance in his jaw. I shouldn't trust him. Whatever guilt he *thinks* he feels has to be a lie.

"So you believe that I'm better off following you into the unknown –"

"As opposed to doing so perfectly on your own?" His retort is a blade, twisting deep into my self-doubts.

My fingers tap along the splintered wall. His eyes track the movement, like I might bolt at any moment.

"How do you know a way out? You're familiar with this city?"
It could be another trap, for all I know. He could be leading me back into the nightmare I barely escaped. Maybe he's working with the guards. My mind flickers to the markings on the flags. The ones marking the skin of his men. I scrutinize him again, wishing more of his skin was visible, if only to catch markings of his own that would tie him to my suspicions. What mistakes is he willing to own up to? Why would he want to correct them anyways?

Maybe he does feel guilty for the girl he'd fed. The one he stood by and watched get dragged across the desert.

"Allow me to show you."

I want to say no. I can almost feel those two letters, bitter on my tongue. My chances of getting out of here alone shrink with time. I can't run. I was barely able to make it *here*. I don't know if I'll be able to hide long enough for my body to heal, not with guards lingering around everywhere. They're bound to notice that I'm no longer in their prison.

I need another option. If anything, Yoon could hold value in being a shield for the time being. A distraction in case we get caught.

"They were using your horse as bait. Shouldn't you be helping your friend instead?"

"I'm aware of what they were trying to do. And I'm not worried about Jax's ability to get them both out safely." He sighs, shoulders dipping. "Look, if you want to do this alone, on that –" He gestures at my foot, voice dry. "By all means, be my guest. But I have no doubt in my mind that you're a smart woman. And I know for a fact that your best chance of getting out of here, would be to accept my offer to help you."

I sneer at his confidence. "So you can sell me off to the –"

"Can you really think of only that? Can't you at least wait until I prove you wrong before assuming the worst of me?"

"You already have." I say coldly. "By tying me up and dragging me for days against my will."

That makes him flinch. He stumbles back. only slightly. Finally, I've struck a nerve.

"All I want is to make up for what I've done."

There's a steadfastness in his tone that makes me wish I truly hated him. I focus on the arm he holds out for me once more. *Use him.* He seems willing enough. If he knows that this is a trap for him, he won't want to be caught either. And if it's a trap that *he* himself is setting, well, every choice comes with risk. I'll take advantage of his own desire for self-preservation and ditch him once I'm free. Or, I'll end him.

"Okay." My fingers twitch at my sides. "But if I get even the slightest hint that you're lying –"

"You'll gut me." His stare cleaves into mine. "I would expect nothing less."

I feel his arm tense when my raw and blistered fingers lock through the crook of his elbow.

"Stay beside me." He orders.

I will. For now.

I give him a nod, a tucked away frown hidden in the corners of my mouth when he moves us towards the door. He cracks it open slightly, then without warning, I feel myself yanked over the threshold. I stumble when he hurries us down the two steps, catches me when my toes scrape the splintered wood. He moves us past the row of buildings to our left, down another alley. His posture is alert, constantly moving his gaze from side to side, up and under, scanning every shadow.

The towering peaks of canvas tents come into view not that long after. Smoke curls lazily above spit-roasted meat, thick with the scent of rendered fat dripping onto open flames. A massive carved table sprawls out around Baobab's trunk, a feast laid out in obscene abundance on top.

My belly can't help but betray me for the hundredth time today. The smell – rich, greasy, intoxicating – hits me like a stone. I squeeze my eyes shut, willing away the nausea as we duck beneath a fence. We hide directly behind another slated table, this one filled with skewered meats, crusty bread, glistening fruit. Untouched piles of food. Goblets scatter the surface alongside the meal, spilling dark wine that drips onto the ground. I've never seen such a display of carelessness. Not even in Isla. How many people are starving out here in the desert? While the people of this city get the option to let food rot? To be picked on by birds and flies?

As if in retaliation, my hand unconsciously reaches for one of the persimmons nestled along a platter near the top of the fence. It's plump and gleaming, just begging to be taken. *I only want one –*

Yoon grabs my wrist instantly before I can snatch it up. A muscle feathers along his cheek as he shakes his head, motioning towards three armed men at the far end of the table. Brass goblets in hand, their expressions teeter with boredom. Their uniforms match the ones who dragged me through the gate. So do their weapons. Rifles sling lazily across their backs. I was so consumed by hunger, by rebellion, that I hadn't even seen them. Another careless mistake.

I wish I knew where I was. My map is quite old, out-dated in every way that counts, but I thought it was reliable. The fact that this city wasn't even on it couldn't have been by accident. I should have listened to Saedea.

Yoon pulls me right along, forcing us low as we weave through stacks of heavy supply crates pressed against boarded up storefronts. This must have once been a marketplace. Now it serves a different purpose. I catch sight of the contents inside one of those crates. Pellets. Similar to the ones I dug out of my shoulder. Another box sits beside it, this one filled with copper wires attached to palm-sized black boxes.

I don't get a chance to examine it further; Yoon tugs me away. We halt near the edge of the barrier where the largest tent in the circle looms. The emblem that's painted on sends a chill down my spine. A large, upside-down triangle, with a 'Z' in the center in a mazed pattern. Past that, a sharp whistle, followed by a sound I've grown familiar with. One that sets my nerves aflame.

Horses.

I dart an uneasy glance at Yoon, questioning – everything. He meets it with a warning look, pressing a finger to his lips. Then, he tilts his attention towards the main tent. I sink lower, watching as two men step out from beneath a heavy canvas flap. They're built like stone. Bare-chested, corded with muscle and brutal efficiency. No rifles, only a simple blade strapped to their bicep, one for each. One half has his head shaved, the other mirrors the opposite side with his own bareness. Twins? They can't be the same kind of guards that wander this city.

They're not merchants either. At least, not the kind I'm used to – not the kind Saedea seemed to be frightened of when we first came upon this place. The tattoos on their skin confirm it. Heavily pigmented triangles. Four each. *They belong to a clan.*

Yoon shifts beside me, fidgeting with the sand at his feet. The look on his face is one filled with – malice. His eyes sweep the area, as if he's hunting someone. I try to match him, to see if I can find what he's looking for, but the longer we linger, the closer we are to getting caught. My pulse ticks faster. I hesitate, tapping him on the shoulder, redirecting his attention with a crease of my forehead. He blows out an uneasy breath, then wordlessly guides me backward, slipping us behind another row of clay-walled huts. My injuries throb with the need for relief.

"Yoon." I say his name carefully, out loud, I believe for the first time. He stops dead in his tracks, slowly bringing his eyes up to match mine. I direct my gaze downwards immediately, making a pointed look towards my foot. I hate that I need to say it. Hate the growing certainty that I can't keep up.

He bobs his head knowingly at my silent admission but still urges us against the brick at the sound of women's voices drifting from an open window above. Fresh desert air fills their homes, carrying the scent of bread baking out onto the streets. The same air that scrapes raw against my lungs, tight with dehydration.

"It won't be much longer." He whispers in my ear, waiting for my response. I huff silently to myself. *I can make it longer. I have to.*

We slip between a tangle of tapestries, thick with the syrupy aroma of incense. Yoon lets me use him as a crutch as we half-run into another tented space, similar to the last, although much less populated. Barrels line the stone walls of the surrounding buildings, obscuring a patchwork of bounties. Each one is slashed through with runny black ink. Looks to me like a wall of trophies.

Saedea's warning echoes in my head. *Bounties.*

"Who were those men back there?" I question, trying to scan the faces of the bounties within eyesight.

"No one important." He catches me searching them, clipping his response as he waits until a resident finishes shaking a rug of dust from her window, disappearing inside before he pulls me down a narrow alley, darkened by woven blankets stretched overhead. We turn the corner.

"It seemed like you recognized them."

He shrugs, guiding me toward the left side of the passage. "Why do you say that?"

"Just a feeling." I study his expression, searching for a tell. He offers nothing. "They weren't like the other guards."

He glances back briefly, an eyebrow twitching.

"Do you think they're bounty hunters?" I press. It would make sense, considering the circumstances. *"Ten thousand at least. Maybe more."*

Yoon snorts.

"Jidaani?" I'm baiting him, desperate to make a connection, wondering if he'll give me the clues I need. Maybe revealing himself to be involved in a clan like *that* – it would make leaving the safety net he provides that much easier once he helps me escape.

He doesn't hesitate with his response. "Do you really think I'd be helping you if I knew Jidaani were here?" *Interesting.*

"So you know the rumors?"

He laughs a silent laugh, showing his teeth. "Everyone on the continent does."

Then, he turns, pushing us against a wall, listening to the sounds of the road on our left. The deeper we go, the more deserted the paths become. This one is no different. When he drags us out onto the alley, I notice that all of the buildings seem to be abandoned.

"Where are we heading exactly?"

"The storage quarters." Yoon's voice levels. "I'll leave you there."

My heart skips. He notices. "It won't be long. You need to rest for a moment. And I need something from their market."

I arch a brow. "You're risking being seen to – what – buy –"

"I never said *I* would buy anything." He retorts. "It won't be a risk if you agree to wait."

I stop walking, forcing him to halt. "Do you think I'm stupid?" I can't allow him to leave me alone. Not here. He watches me, his expression unreadable. His fingers skim the rough stubble on his jaw. "You can barely walk."

"I'm not letting you out of my sight."

My teeth clench, the ache in my foot is secondary to the distrust tightening between us.

Yoon exhales sharply. "Fine." His words are taut with stress. "But we'll need to be *extremely* careful."

"As if we didn't need to be before." A hollow laugh escapes from me, more out of exhaustion than amusement.

"You won't be laughing when you see where I'm about to take you." A fresh wave of hesitation grips me. "You're trying to scare me, aren't you?"

He doesn't answer, instead, he grabs another swath of linen from his pouch.

"Are you sure you're –" He peeks behind me. I follow his gaze, my stomach twisting at the sight. Footprints of blood trail our path like breadcrumbs. "If you're worried that I'll leave you behind if you change your mind and want to wait, I promise you, I won't."

I shake my head firmly. He sighs, dropping to a knee. Without warning, he grips my calf, lifting my injured foot. I wobble, instinctively bracing against his shoulders.

His touch is quick, efficient, as he wraps fresh linen over old. I pray to the Mystics the bleeding stops soon. He's going to start asking questions I know I shouldn't answer.

"At least no one will question it."

The casual way he says it unsettles me more than the blood itself. He was careful before, obsessed with covering our tracks. That can only mean one thing – blood is common where we're going. And that does nothing to calm my nerves.

TWENTY-FOUR

YOON

"As stated in The Rights of All Integrity, the continent shall be divided by the three surviving tribes. Jidaani. Bahani. Nevadems. They are responsible for dividing the territories. Each will be responsible for their own inhabitants, unlike the One United In the Time Before."– Excerpt from the journal of the First Grandfather, The Benevolent Hitan. 3,499 T.A

It isn't until we move under a looming archway, its entrance still lit by hazy lanterns, the air humming with trade, thick with spice, that I regret bringing her here. I should have been firmer. But the thought of leaving her hidden in the textile room, no matter how safe it could be, didn't sit right in my bones.

The area ahead of us is bustling and dense. Women and children weave through the expanse, their laughter bright against the sound of merchants calling out their wares in rhythmic chants. I knew the Muhdams wouldn't let go of their precious Blood Market, even after witnessing the abandoned bazaar. But the fact that it's been moved to the entrance of the Underground sends a ripple of unease through me.

I push it down. We're only here for one thing.

The shadows conceal us as I assess our situation. "Stay right here."

Her fingers catch mine before I can slip away, a silent protest.

"I need something to cover your hair." The words do little to reassure her.

I pull away before she can stop me again. Keeping low, I edge toward a break in the wall, where a barrel of backstock sits within reach, filled with bundles of fabric meant for Muhdam wives. When the merchant selling them is distracted, I pluck one from the barrel, quickly returning to Adessa's side.

"You have blood on your shirt." She whispers, pointing out the obvious splatter of *her* blood on my tunic.

"No one will care." I answer back, lifting my sand scarf around the lower half of my face, then up and over, covering my blind eye. It's not like I can see out of it anyway.

"Keep your head down." I say gently, wrapping the adorned red scarf up and around her head, then her neck, in the style I've seen the women here do. She lifts her chin as I do so, not seeming to be entirely fond of the closeness. "And whatever you do, don't speak. Your accent will give us away." That initiates a glare.

"This scarf smells." She protests. I take one end of it and wrap it around the lower half of her face in response, tucking in the edge.

"I said don't talk."

My fingertips rest lightly on her shoulder, joining the crowd of Muhdams entering through the archway of their market. Their unworthy wealth drips from them, forcing me to swallow. There was a time when I wished my caste had been different, like theirs. Like those in Darde who know nothing of struggle in a time where that's all there is to be had. Now, watching these lords, their wives and children strolling without any time constraints, silken robes rippling with each step, gold-threaded turbans gleaming in the sun. Their hands, heavy with rings, gesturing lazily as they speak to one another. It's like stepping into a reality that I'm no longer familiar with. That I never want to be again.

No guards, no weapons. No hunger.

Opulence and greed, all in one place. The contrast is sickening.

Adessa must feel it too; her eyes are wide with judgment, hobbling slowly but with the crowd, matching their leisurely pace. I steer us to the right, pressing her against a column as I scan the first merchant's table. Bundles of roots, herbs and vegetables spill across the worn cloth – exactly what I'm looking for.

Without a word, I gesture to the bundle of sugarcane. The merchant's gaze flickers between me and Adessa. His brow lifts in curiosity, lingering on her as she keeps her head lowered, just as I ordered. Even with her face partially hidden, I know those green eyes might draw attention. I only hope it doesn't bring the wrong kind.

I slide three coins from my pocket, letting the metal catch the light. A silent transaction the merchant is all too willing to complete. I can't afford to be recognized here. I know all too well what could happen if I am. At least Adessa's presence might help. In the past, I was always seen alone, or with Jax. And I was never this covered. So far, no lingering stares, no murmured names. Still, I don't want to risk it. I shift towards her, placing my body between her and the crowd, shielding us both as I shove the sugarcane into my pack.

"Sugarcane?" Her quiet voice sharpens, edged with disbelief. I press a finger to my lips in warning. She stiffens, brows pulling tight into the irritated expression I've already grown familiar with.

"You try dealing with an angry Hisan." I murmur close to her ear, my smirk deepening. "Thanks for buying."

The confused expression she wears now makes me want to stay locked in her gaze forever. Even here. Even in the middle of the Blood Market.

Then, a voice shatters the hum of the bazaar.

"Make way for the Nevadems!"

A ripple moves through the crowd. Muhdams mutter to each other in hushed nerves, their annoyance cut through by another sharp command. "Move!"

The sea of bodies part, revealing two older women leading the charge. Their brown robes hang loose around them, their sun-worn faces smeared with dried clay to protect against the brutal heat. Their gray hair, wound tight into bundles, is decorated with thin beads of ivory. I tuck close to Adessa, pulling her deeper into the shadows of the pillar, careful not to jostle the merchant next to us. Thankfully, he's too distracted, a worried gaze locks onto the scene unfolding around us.

"Damn Rahish." He says in Mahudami, shrugging in my direction. "Forcing our market to the gates of the Abyss." He clicks his tongue, busying himself with his organized mess.

I can feel my nerves pulse. If the slave runners are here, that means that the auction must be in full swing. *Shit.* I'm now all too aware of the lack of guard presence. They must all be dining with Tyg, unconcerned about the auction even though they should be here. Adessa attempts to peek over my shoulder, I try to shield her, but she pushes away, gripping my arm for balance before quickly letting go – realizing what I hoped she wouldn't. What I myself had hoped to avoid.

Two lines of withered women, children, and men move in a slow, shackled procession. Iron clasps bite into their wrists, their ankles, their necks, chaining them together like cattle. A display of Nevadem power. A reminder of who is free – and who is not. It should be only midday at best. Why would slave runners make their appearance in broad daylight? When I was here last, they would only come in the dark of night. Never in the presence of the Muhdam lords, especially not their families. That's why the auction started in the morning. Only the strongest of their haul lived long enough to see each daybreak, that's what strengthened their price.

Things have changed in Kyr. Now I wonder even more to what extent.

I scan the faces among them. I know Adessa is doing the same, balancing on her good foot, searching for Saedea. I don't want to let her know that if she had been picked up in or out of Kyr, she'd already *be* in the Underground if someone meant to sell her. It seems like her relief sways when she notices Saedea isn't with the bound.

But that feeling vanishes just as quickly – replaced by something far worse.

Adessa reacts at the same time as I do, though hers is laced with curiosity, mine is brimming with shock. Most of these captives have been taken from the usual places, villages on the brink, but three of them –

"Bahani." I whisper.

The merchant next to us repeats the word, eyes darting nervously. I join him, checking if others are coming to the same realization – or if I've lost my mind entirely. This can't possibly be real.

The truth spreads through the crowd like a cold, blistering wind. Everyone in the market watches the three figures in the back of the line. Their hands are bound into fists, wrapped tightly in sap cloth. Red-rimmed eyes flicker, scanning their surroundings as if they're absent-mindedly hunting, their bodies staggering forward in a lifeless march.

Bahani. Bahani.

Even in their exhaustion, the other captives shy away from them, putting as much distance between themselves and the three as their bindings will allow. Their masters, armed with spears, move with false confidence, raising their weapons in show. But I can see it. Even they are afraid of bringing Bahani here. Even if it's only three of them.

Most of the crowd stumbles back, knocking over crates and baskets in their rush to get away. Shop owners yank their curtains down, shielding their inventory from whatever is about to unfold. A child wails, high and piercing. Panic takes hold. The mob surges toward the exit. Lords dig their way out of the center, abandoning their traded items. We hear the cries of worried children, their mothers embracing them along the presumed safety of the wall while waiting for a path to clear.

"Shit." I tighten my grip on Adessa.

"What's happening?" She squirms, letting out a pained noise. I immediately withdraw in apology, not realizing how firmly I was holding her.

We watch in rigid silence as the slave runners march their emotionless captives to the front of the Underground entrance. I don't want us to be a part of the few stragglers that remain, watching from the edges of the chaos, unwilling to stand in the way. The Nevadems push past the auction overseer, forcing their way into the tunnel. He doesn't protest, he doesn't stop them.

"I'll explain later." My words are rushed.

"Why is everyone so – scared?" She presses.

The sugarcane merchant throws his own curtain down, clearing his table quickly, throwing it all into baskets. I know she won't let us leave here without some kind of answer.

"Everyone's afraid of the slave runners." I state plainly, wishing I never brought her here.

"What's down there?" She points to the tunnel.

I sigh, moving us past the table. "The Underground." I regret my words when she pauses.

"Saedea could be down there."

Turning, I shake my head, trying to convince her that it's not a possibility, even though I am not at liberty to guarantee it. "No, Adessa. She's not."

"How do you know?" She pulls back.

There's too much chaos around us to make anyone pay attention to our conversation, thank the Mystics. I open my mouth, trying to think of a lie. When I can't, I feel her fingers leave mine.

"Get back here!" I yell, watching her stumble through the wave that is busy swarming the exit. I chase after her, reaching her before she can get any closer to the hollow entrance. She pushes me off of her again.

"I am not leaving her behind! I have to see for myself!"

"Do you want to leave this city or not?" I question, guarding her with my back from wandering eyes. The crowd is beginning to diminish. I have to make a decision.

"*Your* men threatened to sell us to the Underground. If she's down there –" Her eyes glaze. It seems like she's making a decision as well. Repressed cries from the tunnel strengthen my desire not to step anywhere near the stairs.

"Adessa, we can't." I give her a dire, pleading look.

Bahani.

Does Tyg know? Does Geal? None of this will be worth it if we cannot find a way out of Kyr. The new bazaar no longer feels like a market, it feels like a snare tightening around us.

"Leave without me then. I'll find her myself." She tries to throw me off of her, but I remain firmly at her side.

We're running out of time. I can't drag her out of here, Muhdam lords would never treat women that way, it would cause too much attention. And I know for a fact that she would scream in protest. If we went down – I scan the entrance. The overseer is gone, more than likely preparing himself to begin the auction. I look to the sky, a desperate plea, squeezing my eyes shut.

"Do not leave my side."

That is all I say. I take her hand in mine, leading her to the edge of the stairs. To the wailing. To the smell. To the absolute.

TWENTY-FIVE

ADESSA

"Do not underestimate what the Bahani have become."

The lanterns flicker, their sickly glow casting long, relentless shadows against the damp walls of the stairwell. The deeper they descend, the stench intensifies – a mix of sweat and decay, lined with something sweet, like rotting fruit. Beneath the hum of murmured deals and shuffling feet, there is the ever-present sound of distant weeping, a constant reminder of what lies ahead. Yoon keeps me close to his back, refusing to let go of my fingers, as if he's afraid I'll bolt.

Each step creaks beneath our weight, the oppressive heat thickens, as if the very air is protesting us being here. I hold onto my resolve, reminding myself that Saedea *could* be down here, dreading that she might be, hoping that she isn't. I don't want to spend much time in whatever is happening only a few steps away.

At the base of the stairs, Yoon moves me in front of him. I can feel his breathing, slow and constrained against my back as the Underground spreads out before us like a disease. A vast cavern of filth, where fortunes are traded in whispers and lives are measured in silver. Are the rumors of the Blood Market being mistaken for *this?*

Smoke chokes the ceiling, curling from oil-drenched torches mounted high on the stone wall. Cages line the perimeter; crude iron bars and hefty chains keep their captives confined. A lesser version of the prison I had escaped from last night. Some sit in silence, eyes dull with resignation. Others, mostly the younger ones, press against the bars, their gazes darting wildly, searching for an escape they won't find.

Carts of – bodies rest beside the cages. My body hums with unease as I notice slashes that mirror my own curious wound, all on their own palms as well. They've been stripped bare, nothing but a cloth covering the top of the pile. I hold my stomach, forcing myself to look away before my nausea gets the best of me.

You don't belong here. The voice in my head confirms what I already know. At this moment, I wish I would have listened to Yoon. Saedea's face doesn't belong to anyone behind the bars. What if I've led us into a nightmare for nothing?

The floor is slick, the air heavy with the scent of damp stone and unwashed bodies. Somewhere deep within, the sound of chains clinking together echoes in ominous rhythm, setting a pace for the suffering that thrives here.

"The auction." Yoon whispers against the thin fabric of my scarf.

I follow his gaze to a raised platform at the center of the chaos, a makeshift stage of worn wood and rusted metal, its platform designed for a showcase. Torches bracket the frame, flickering across the hunched figures waiting their turn to be sold. Below, cloaked bidders stand in ranked lines, their faces hidden behind elaborate masks carved from bone and gold.

"Those are the lords' assistants." Yoon's voice interrupts the heavy pounding in my heart. The cloaked figures all wear different colors, perhaps that's what separates them from each other. Each holds parchment in their hands.

Yoon directs us towards the shadow of a storage crate stacked high with grains and dried fish, close enough to watch, far enough to go unnoticed.

"We will begin!"

A man dressed entirely in gold silk exclaims at the very top of the platform. He gestures his hand amongst the people below, like a god beckoning his flock. Beside him stands a woman, decorated in ornate beads and gemstones that stack around her neck and wrists. She beams, presenting the line of slaves beside her. I squint, scanning each of their faces. No sign of Saedea.

I shift uncomfortably in place. Yoon rests a gentle hand on my shoulder that I wish I could brush away. I hate the fact that it comforts me.

A boy, no older than the age I once was when I left Skeall, is pushed forward first, his small hands are clenched into fists but his expression remains emotionless. The bidding starts low, but rises fast, the parchment in the assistants' hands raises and lowers as the price increases.

"Sold!" The auctioneer booms.

The boy trembles as he is led off the stage, vanishing into the sea of bodies. His fate has been sealed without even a chance for resistance. I glance back at the stairwell. Leaving without knowing where Saedea is shouldn't be an option, but neither is getting caught in a place like this.

She got away. She had to. I distracted the guards long enough, she's heading to Mirit.

My mind soothes the possibility of the lie I'm telling myself.

A ripple moves through the crowd, the two older women, spears in tow, emerge from the shadows, heading for the stage stairs. Their ragged garments tell of the journey they've made to get here, their sunken eyes gleam with a knowing cruelty. They lead their line of lifeless captives onto the platform, waiting for the man in gold to finish his next bid. His gnarled finger gestures for them to approach when another withered child is taken away, wailing.

The crowd hushes instantly. The entirety of the Underground quiets at the new offerings being presented. Even the jeweled woman drops her unsettling smile, glancing at the golden clothed man beside her with a worried etch between her brows. The eerie stillness makes my body want to flee immediately. I can sense it in Yoon too. He stands rigid, alert. He pulls me deeper into the shadows.

The auctioneer clears his throat. "Tonight, we have a very special bid for the lords who are brave enough to participate."

A murmur spreads through the masked bidders. A single raised hand silences them.

"The Nevadems offer three Bahani." His lips curl into an unnatural grin, revealing teeth that are too perfect, too white against his ashen skin. His voice slithers over the bidders like an unseen hand pressing against their throats. The sounds they make in return are guttural – not from fear, but from envy.

"Truly a rarity. Our Lord Rahish shall be praised."

He waves the women forward. They busy themselves with unlatching the last three captives in their line, the ones with cloth-bound hands and red-rimmed eyes. The others back away immediately, causing the tied line to stumble and fall onto the stage.

"Saedea isn't here." Yoon says, leaning close.

I feel myself nodding in return. I know what he wants. He wants to leave. And I do as well, but curiosity is getting the best of me. I want to know why everyone seems on edge. The air is thick with anticipation.

"Our first offering will start at two thousand."

Gasps. Parchment flutters as assistants snap their bids high into the air.

"Let's go." Yoon's grip tightens around my wrist. I let him pull me back, but regret begins to gnaw at me.

"Four thousand!"

The bidding continues. No one seems to pay attention to the two of us sneaking back to the base of the stairs.

"Five thousand!"

Then, a shift. A turn of a head. Yoon stiffens. Across the way, on the very last step, stands a man dressed in simple robes, with stacks of small barrels in his arms. His eyes lock onto the scarred man behind me. Recognition seems to flash between the two of them. For a single breath, neither move. Then, the man's lips begin to part, drawing in air, as if to make our presence known to those around us.

Yoon reacts instantly, the auctioneer's booming voice distracting the rest of the crowd as he yanks us towards a maze of crates and cages to the right. The thumping of footsteps follow behind us, I peek around the see the simply dressed man drop his barrels and run in our direction. Yoon shoves a wooden cart into his path. It crashes onto its side, spilling its contents – jugs of oil and cloth – across the floor, the sharp crack of breaking pottery punctuating the growing commotion.

I stumble, my injured foot catching on the uneven ground. Yoon steadies me, eyes darting for an exit – there – beyond the next row of cages, a small tunnel, barely more than a crack in the rock. The shadows thicken, a possible escape beckoning us closer.

"Go!"

He hisses, shoving me forward right as the first shout rings out behind us. I look back, watching some outliers in the crowd turn their heads in curiosity, some annoyed, some amused. On the platform, the older women watch with unreadable expressions, their lips curling at the edges, as if happy to witness the chaos unraveling. I gasp when Yoon pushes me into the tunnel first, plunging me into complete darkness. The Underground stretches behind us like a closing mouth, sealing away the world we've escaped, only to find ourselves in one that could be much worse.

"There are stairs ahead, watch your footing." His voice soothes the ringing in my ears.

"I can't see anything." I swallow, carefully moving my feet in a way that won't hurt too badly if I misstep. Then, I feel the base of a step.

"Count to twenty." He says behind me. Distant shouting echoes in the corridor.

I take the first step. "One."

Second step. "Two."

"Three. Keep going."

It feels like an eternity by the time I reach number twenty. My hands splay out, feeling around us. My fingers graze the solid wood in front of me.

"There's a latch. To the left."

I feel him shift against me, reaching. A clicking sound shoves the door open. The darkness no longer caresses us. The smell no longer clogs my throat. Blinding sunlight floods in.

TWENTY-SIX

ADESSA

"Four arrows. Four arrows. And that horrid bird."

We're... back. The exit – the one I left not long ago – looms ahead. Fear coils around my throat, cold claws pressing into my skin. The hidden tunnel led us up here, right? Not Yoon. But he – *no, no, no. He's taking me back?* Dizziness washes over me, spiraling too fast to catch. Betrayal sharpens, lodging itself into every one of my wounds. The edges of my vision blur with red lines, pulling me into a reality I honestly didn't expect. My feet catch the sand as I twist, my hand jerking against his grip. He shoves the wooden door closed behind him, not noticing, not caring for my reaction to the prison entrance ahead.

He was working with them. He only agreed to take me to the Underground because he knew it would lead us back here. The guards knew I had escaped, that's why no one was watching me, why it was so easy for him to find me. Why isn't anyone following us now? My thoughts screech. I try desperately to cling to the facts against them.

There weren't any guards in the bazaar, there weren't any in the Underground. No one stopped the stampede of people after the slaves were brought in. The guards who captured me were waiting for *him.*

They were baiting him; they expected him to walk straight into their hands. They were *confused* as to why their trap hadn't worked. I have been watching him the entire time. If he had tipped anyone off, I would have seen it.

My mind fractures into warring pieces, thoughts unraveling. The war tents – I saw his reaction to those men. Aol and Burke have the same symbols tattooed on their skin. Yoon *knew* them. He knows exactly where to go in this city. He's been desperate to gain my trust. He knew about the secret tunnel. He knew how many stairs to climb.

Yoon tightens his grip, dragging me forward. He's a traitor. To whom, I don't know.

"I'm not going back there." My breath comes in panicked beats. My head is spinning. I yank my hand harder, anger flooding my veins, clawing at his hand to release me. Sweat slicks our grasp.

"What are you doing?" He double-takes, confusion etching his face. "We need –"

He strains his muscles, trying to contain me. I persist, struggling to free myself.

"Adessa!"

"No!" The word hisses through my clenched teeth, a whisper only because I know the attention that shouting could bring. We just escaped the Underground filled with the worst kind of people. With slave runners. I've never seen one before today – let alone *two*. And the red-eyed ones, Bahani... where am I?

The ringing in my ears fades, drowned out by his voice.

"Adessa!" He tugs. "Please, you can trust me!"

His hands grasps my shoulders, shaking me, urging me into the archway, but I throw him off, nearly forcing us to topple over. I have half a mind to tear into his only working eye, to blind him entirely. I urge myself against it, that would only make more noise, cause me more problems. The guards could easily be waiting for us inside those prison walls. Waiting for him to lure me back before they make their move.

"Listen to me."

His words barely cut through the storm raging in my head. He's able to wrestle me against the sandstone, pinning me in his strong arms. He brings his knee up to my side, holding me center. I thrash, but it's no use. He's too strong. I'm too weak. I'm no match.

I'm cornered.

"You went in the wrong direction, remember? You were heading for an outpost!"

His voice is tight. I can tell he's desperate to keep quiet. But he doesn't stop himself from explaining, he keeps pushing. "The prison cuts off the two districts between the storage quarter and the Underground. *That* is where we came from." He points behind us. "*This* is where we need to go."

The voice in my head screeches, high and relentless, a cruel echo of Tirma's madness. It's *laughing* at me, mocking me, shoving me deeper into the frenzied pounding of my veins. *Liar. Liar. Liar!*

"Please listen to me."

I stare into him, wishing I could see through his lies. But I can't.

Thump. Thump. Thump.

Instead, I choose to fight. I lunge. My knee flies up – he dodges it, catching my arms before I can strike again.

"Adessa, you don't need to be afraid of me!" The words crash into my resolve.

I force down a shaky breath, and tear away from the chaos I'm creating in my head. I match the frustrated look on his face with my own, swallowing dryly.

"I. Am. Not. Afraid. Of. You." Venom laces every syllable. But doubt gnaws at my certainty.

When I escaped the cage, I believed I'd been going the right way. However, that was purely on a hunch – a desperate gamble. I could have been wrong. I probably *was* wrong. Yoon knows this city. He moved through its maze, like he's walked it a hundred times. It's a fact that finds itself lodged in my gut. Why can't I seem to trust him?

I've never trusted him, although Saedea seemed to think he was deserving of it. He loosened our ropes without question, he gave us jerky to eat. Water to drink. He had taken Saedea and I to Chadron's, despite the other's wishes. He waited for us to heal. Did he do it all for Jax? Or to make sure we were healthy enough to sell?

The blood in the archway – the streaks smeared inside the prison – the wounds on the palms of the dead –

As if he can hear the questions screaming in my head, he answers the one that blares the loudest.

"They keep the cages tucked away from the main sector. That's why it's over here." His voice remains even, measured. "Can't torture people in a district where the wealthiest lords live. It's bad for business. That's why there's a tunnel that leads here. Can't be parading corpses through the streets. Only the blooders know about it."

The amount of terror that seeps into those words – I have to force it down.

"I need you to believe me."

Why, why, why?

"They haven't followed us yet. Probably because of the auction. But they will. We need to keep moving."

My sights land on his machete, hanging within reach. To the daggers at his sides that might be easier to grab.

"If there is *any* sign that you're betraying me –" I let the unfinished threat linger, watching the way his lips twitch into something that looks too much like a smile.

I want to spit.

His fingers give me an odd, reassuring squeeze. The gesture unsettles me more than if he had yanked me through the archway outright. I glance at his weapons again. When I finally meet his gaze, a strange flicker of emotion dances across his mouth. As if he can hear my consuming thoughts, the murderous ones, the ones dripping with hate.

But instead of forcing me through the passageway, he waits.

Waits until my nails loosen from his skin, the ones that have been digging mercilessly into him, leaving open indents of anger and fear.

Waits until the pulse of my panic dulls, my breathing slows.

He waits until it appears enough to him that I've reclaimed a thread of sanity.

And I wait too, eyes locked on him as he reaches into his bag. He holds the item up to me, with a steadfastness that makes my heart numb.

A persimmon.

I stare at it, cold suspicion leaking through my glare. "What is that?" I ask, warily.

His voice is rough when he responds. "A promise."

He tucks the stolen fruit back into his bag, and my mouth waters at the hope of being able to taste it.

"I will never let them put you back in those cages."

His differing pupils bore into me, the weight of his words pressing against my ribs. The words do little to console me, yet he adds, "I promise – you'll eat this once we make it out of here alive."

And for one, stupid, fleeting moment, I believe him.

He can see it on my face too, I just know it, because his own features soften instantly. With a wink, he reaches for my fingertips, and for some inexplicable reason, I let him pull me back through the prison without a word. We sneak along the corridor I had left only this morning, tucking close between the rusted bars and high sandstone that had proven impossible for me to climb. Voices echo in the open space ahead, but neither of us turn back. I have no choice but to trust that I'm making the right decision.

A sudden burst of rage-laced slander forces us to duck behind the stack of rotting barrels in the center. I wrinkle my nose as the scent hits – a scent I've grown familiar with in this city. Rancid, cloying, something half-decayed and souring in the heat spills out of the oozing tops. I crin-kle my nose when I peer over the wood, but recoil instantly, knocking back into Yoon's chest. He steadies me as I mouth a silent curse.

The two guards who locked me in here are pacing near the entrance, shouting at each other a distance away from our hiding spot. One gestures wildly at the empty cage. The one that I was supposed to be in.

"How was I –"

A sharp *smack* at the base of his skull cuts him off.

"You are an absolute *waste* of the Utar line! I thought you said Shehid was going to be watching the prison!"

"He was! He must have been called for entrance duty! I don't know the rotation! I've only been assigned to this post for a few weeks!" The second guard waves a gloved finger, jabbing it into his partner's chest. "Don't you *dare* blame this on me. You said we'd check back after the gathering. It wasn't *my* decision to drink with the others!"

"Oh, don't try to convince the dead of your innocence. They can't hear you."

"Maybe she got out on her own?" Another crack of skin hitting skin.

"She was nearly dead already, you moron! How could she possibly have escaped without his help? He was here!"

"But the cage is still locked!"

Yoon catches my eyes, raising an amused brow as the voices fade into the background. It's unsettling how entertained he looks.

"You've made some enemies here." He muses, tilting his head slightly. Then, he traces a slow circle around his face with his palm. "You do that to them too?"

I don't answer. I'm too busy questioning him – questioning the ease with which he moves through this nightmare of a situation. The way he seemed utterly unbothered by my silent accusations of his involvement only moments ago, all made worse by the admiration flickering behind his gaze of what *I* did to these two.

He gestures towards the bloody archway with a careless thumb. One of the guards, the one with the broken nose, rubs at his chest where the other had shoved him. He spits a yellow-hued glob onto the ground.

"Stay here." Yoon releases his grip on my hand. I didn't even realize he'd still been holding it. "Wait for my signal. Unless –"

He lifts the brow over his milky eye. I don't move, don't answer. I think I'm in shock. Does he plan on taking down both of them? They still have their rifles – if they see him first... I swallow. *If they kill him, I'll be alone here. Again.*

The guards' argument escalates.

"What did you call me?" The long-haired one spits something vile in their dialect, it sounds too harsh to be anything nice.

"I swear, I'll tell Agai about this! You are *so* lucky you're my cousin, otherwise Rahish would know exactly how you're treating a member of the Gid!"

The other curses, then slams into the cage with a dull clang, sending a cloud of dust to swirl around them. Yoon taps my knee once. Then, he's gone.

He moves like water, flowing through the gap in the central cell, his steps too light to stir the sand. The guards don't notice him. They're too busy tearing into each other. I curl my fingers over the sticky rim of the barrel, my breath tight in my lungs. I don't know if I should prepare to run or to fight. He could signal me any second.

Or he could die. And then what will I do?

One second ticks. Yoon unclips a dagger from his belt.

Another second. He tosses it into the air, catches it in a seamless arc, all while breaking into a full sprint.

Another. He vanishes into the swirling dust – and buries the blade deep into the long-haired guard's neck.

One. More. Second. I gasp as blood sprays, too easily, drenching Yoon and the surviving cousin. It spatters the arch, joining the layers already painted there, by my hand, by others before me, by Mystics know how many more.

A strangled cry escapes the second guard's throat.

Then, time stops altogether. Yoon rips the blade from the freshly dead's neck, the sickening sound of tearing flesh thickens the air. He pulls his sand scarf away from his face, letting it fall loosely around his neck. The guard's eyes widen.

"It can't be –"

The words die with him. Yoon's second slash is precise and merciless. The guard crumples on top of his cousin, their bodies folding into one another. They didn't even have time to reach for their weapons. I don't think they even had time to realize what was happening to them.

Time starts again when I look up hesitantly, to find Yoon casually smearing the thick, dark blood from his face with the back of his hand. More heaviness drips from the strands of hair clinging to his cheeks, sliding down his chin. He flicks the mess away with a shake of his head, then looks at me as if nothing at all has happened.

"Mystics around." I murmur, the words slipping from my tongue before I can think to stop them.

He casually, *casually*, flicks his head in the direction he wants me to follow. A shiver laces my spine. This man, who just killed two trained guards in the span of a single breath – is far too calm. The survivor in me wants to be impressed.

But I am not. I am terrified.

Jidaani. Jidaani.

The name pounds in my skull, a whispered warning at the back of my mind. I know of no other clan with a more brutal, ruthless reputation than the Jidaani. If Yoon belongs to them – if he *is* one of them – then I have just invited something far more dangerous into my world than I ever intended.

He beckons me again. Would it be so wrong to run?

My body tenses, weighing the thought, but I know the answer. He would chase after me. He would catch me. I have no choice.

I push to my feet, staggering along the inner wall as quickly as my injury will allow. When I reach the bodies, I hesitate. Their mixed blood pools, blending with the orange-hued sand, spreading around them in slow-moving tendrils. I can't see their faces, which maybe I'm grateful for. Still, I spit onto the ground that surrounds them, cursing them for the Mystics to see. I'm all too aware of the role I've played in their deaths. My escape had determined their fate, even if I hadn't known it at the time.

Yoon waits for me at the far end of the alcove, a step past the marked arch. His hand reaches for me, but I shove past him. I don't want to touch the palm stains on the walls. Don't want the warmth of his skin pressing into mine. The air is heavily laced with the scent of iron, clinging to the back of my throat, mixing with the sweat crawling down my spine.

Behind me, he follows, his presence burning hotter than the sun beating down. He peers out onto the street ahead with a borderline, crazed smile, speckled with the blood of the guards.

He's insane.

The thought rattles through me as I tug my scarf free, loosening it around my neck in an attempt to cool myself down.

"We're nearly there." He's breathless. As if the weight of what happened hadn't touched him at all. His bone-colored pants stain darker as he wipes his blade clean, sheathing it back into his belt with simple efficiency. The corridor gives way to the empty road, the sun now high in the stark blue sky. Sweat beads my temples, pooling into the hollow spaces of my collarbones. My leg now throbs, paired with an unbearable numbness. I can feel my body shifting, forcing itself to heal. I am desperate to cling to consciousness because of the heat, the sheer agony of it all. I can't afford to pass out now.

Yoon leads me forward, and for the first time, I begin to hope that he was actually telling me the truth. That he wasn't leading me deeper into something worse. Because ahead, towering and real, the outer wall stands firm. A sign of freedom. Lining its base are numerous inner rooms, some with doors, most without. Signs in what I can only imagine are written in this city's language, are scratched out above each doorway, barely hanging onto their nails. Crates covered in faded flags of green and black sit in uneven stacks, empty barrels are overturned, leaking the remainder of sugar wine out onto the ground, allowing the flies to feast.

Above us, a lone vulture takes off from the ledge, wings casting shad-ows over the sandstone. It circles lazily, a hungry search writing into the angles of its body. *It smells death.* Luckily, fresh corpses wait for it not far behind us. The sight of the bird is another reminder of how close we are to the outside of this city. The stretch of desert has to be within reach. The only thing between it and us, is this wall.

The area is quiet and unassuming, yet Yoon hurries us along. We round the next corner too fast, maybe because of the excited pace I set. Maybe his. Maybe because my body has chosen the worst possible moment to start healing and right now, it's fairly fragile. My leg slips, bends at a wrong angle. Pain explodes as I crumble to my knees. My breath snags, choking against the immense pain of my clumsiness. The cracked bone brims with a rusty ache as it begins to bind itself back together. The raw muscle will be next and oh, it's familiar but that doesn't make it hurt any less.

Yoon drops to my level immediately as water wells the pockets of my eyes. His hands settle above the peaks of my shoulders, his expression dimming, etched not with frustration, but something much worse. Concern.

I flinch. I'd rather it be anything but that.
"Take a moment. We don't have much further to go." He dips his head. "Just a bit longer?"

I swallow hard, curling forward to press my palm against my wrapped foot, attempting to center the pain. I shake my head, too stubborn to say the words that I have little left to give.

"Okay. I can carry –"
Something behind me makes his spine straighten immediately. His head perks up, on high alert at the sound of footsteps exiting one of the rooms, past where we've come from.

"What's this now?" A gruff voice bellows.

My vision locks onto the man in front of me, watching his features ignite with recognition. The muscles in his neck twitch when he swal-lows, preparing. Slowly, he releases a hand from me to reach for the ominous weapon strapped across his back. It rings through the air when he slides it free from the clip.

"It can't be. Is that who I think it is?" A laugh – low and savoring – follows. "How am I to be so lucky? And today of all days!"

The stranger's glee is unsettling, and the look on Yoon's face confirms what I already suspect. This is no friend. The tips of his fingers brush along my arm. He leans so close into me that the blood-dried strands of his hair prickle my cheek.

"There's a hollow panel in the back of the room behind me. It leads outside. I'll distract this one while you find it."

His tone is brimming with – what, amusement? Is he enjoying this? I barely nod when he flicks his head towards the doorless frame at his back, rising to his feet. He cracks his knuckles, then his neck. A predator readying himself.

"Oh, Tyg will be pleased to hear you found your way back."

The name sends ice through my spine. I know it. I've heard it from the mouths of the guards. That recognition fuels me. I scramble onto my knees, ignoring the fire in my leg, throwing myself into the chilled dirt-floored room Yoon had motioned for me to go. It's nearly empty. Rows of textiles loom against the far wall, stacked dangerously high, their fabrics reeking of dye and dust.

Trailing me, is Yoon. He draws the stranger's attention, luring him away from the path. It makes sense, keeping prying eyes from us, but it crushes me in a rising wave of panic. I immediately begin searching for the hollow panel he was talking about, kicking up dust in the process.

"It is good to see you again, Agai." Yoon taunts him. That name... Agai. That was the man the guard had threatened the other with. "Although I was made to believe that Tyg demoted you months ago."

I slap my hands against the soft stone, searching.

A bark of laughter echoes. "Ha! Quite the opposite actually." The man savors his next words. "My title is now –" He pauses, relishing the moment. "Head executioner."

Where in the Abyss is this panel?

"It's somewhere towards the lanterns. More to your right." It takes me a second to realize that Yoon is directing me.

Lanterns? What lan –

My knee collides with something sharp. A row of unlit metal domes, the height of my thighs are propped against the corner. My fingers rake the wall until it raps against something hollow. There is a subtle difference beneath my knuckles. The panel is nearly invisible, the same dusty hue as the rest of the wall.

I dig my nails into the edge, straining every muscle as I haul the plank up and over. It lands at my side with a dull thud. A narrow opening reveals itself ahead, its twin panel blocking the view of what I hope is the desert.

"Who would have guessed your name would be at the top of my list now?" Agai's tone darkens, his amusement shifts into something more hateful. "Don't want the hunters to have all the fun."

The predatory sound that rises from Yoon's throat forces me to make the mistake of glancing back.

Agai is a *giant*. His enormous frame fills nearly the entire storage room, blocking the doorway's light. No wonder the space feels so suffocating.

And he's unarmed. The lords of the bazaar seemed to wield power instead of needing to arm themselves, but everyone else in this city had something on them. Rifles slung across their backs, knives and machetes along various parts of their bodies.

But Agai doesn't seem to be in need of weapons. Not when his fists are the size of my head.

"Back to old habits, I see?" The oversized man spews a hateful glare my way. "Or is she a feeble attempt at a peace offering? We don't seem to be in short supply of that, the lords want to make sure he's satiated. But maybe Tyg will allow for one more."

A primal growl rumbles from Yoon's chest as the giant's eyes roam the length of my body.

"If Tyg doesn't want her, maybe he'd be kind enough to give her to me."

I swallow the stickiness in my throat, squeezing into the space between the tunnel and use the rest of my fleeting energy to push the other panel to the ground.

"Let's hurry this up. I'm late for the celebration. Killed a pig for it." Agai's voice slithers after me. Blinding sunlight erupts when I pull myself into the open air, collapsing to my knees. The desert.

A snarl, followed by a sharp, wet smacking sound echoes through the passage. Steel ripping through flesh, the sounds of a struggle, is enough to force me to my feet. Splintered wood scratches at my busted palms, urging me to hurry. The desert stretches ahead emptily, no sign of a road. The outer gardens peek around the corner, meaning I must be at the back of the city. A single outpost juts from the wall, but there's no movement. No sign of a guard. I silently beg whoever could be listening for it to remain that way.

Gripping the barricade, I move my body forward. At my back, I hear a deep moan of concern before it's soon cut very short. A revolting gurgle follows, thick and final. I bury the begging that's wishing for me to know of Yoon's well-being. Bury the crazed fear that I could have just left Saedea to fend for herself. I urge myself to run, but something inside me won't move. A thread yanks sternly in my chest, a screeching demand that I stop. That I wait.

No!

I nearly collapse at the overwhelming feeling, forcing me to grip my chest. I push through the pull, shove the guilt down. I have to find Yoon's horse. He had to have ridden here on it. If I can reach it, I won't have to walk. I can get to Mirit. Maybe I'd find Saedea along the way. *She isn't in this city. She can't be in this city. She got away.*

Moments tick. The only sound is the rough grate of my breathing before I hear steady shuffling directly over my shoulder. Panicked, I spin around to see Yoon pulling himself from the hole in the wall. He hops off of the panel, taking the time to carefully adjust it back into place.

Then, slow as death, he straightens, his fiery eyes locking onto mine.

Blood soaks the length of his body, darkening the sand around him as it drips from the clothing it clings to. I stagger back, hitting the ground at the sight, wishing I'd managed to create more distance.

Red on white. *No, no, no.*

He's at my side in a matter of seconds.

"Were you not going to wait for me?" A humored grin dusts his lips when he doesn't receive an answer. He steps in front of me, offering his hand. Blood paints his arm. With what I know to be what's left of the giant. I waver at the smell, willing myself up on my own. My legs nearly give out before I can straddle the wall for balance. His fingers close around my elbow, steadying me against the warm barricade. I try to glaze my expression, keeping myself from scanning the rest of his body.

I can't explain why I care whether or not his blood is mixed alongside the giant's. Whether or not his throat has been sliced open like it had been in my nightmare. My own neck aches in response, a phantom gnawing I refuse to acknowledge. I suck my teeth, shoving the worry down, willing myself detached. Unafraid.

"The blood isn't mine." He lowers his head slightly, as if offering comfort.

I catch myself feeling *relieved.* My fingers pinch my forearm, punishing the reaction. I force a dry laugh.

"I wouldn't care if it was."

He squints. *Liar.* He doesn't have to say it. It's written all over his face. Probably all over mine too. I dig my sore nails into the stone. One step. Then another.

"Is that right?" The cockiness boils my blood.

I ball my fists, intent on leaving. Alone. He only matches me, repositioning his hand at my side in that infuriating, calculating way.

I hate him!

A wave of chaos erupts from inside the city walls. He tucks his fingers under his tongue and whistles a deliberate series of notes.

"Sounds like they found some bodies."

The wailing continues. It sounds like an instrument of some kind. A horn, like the ones used on Isla to announce the arrival of a boat. I can't remember what Arthur used to call them.

It won't take them long to discover the hidden panels. If Yoon at least put the other one back to cover the inside, maybe it'll buy us some time.

"What are we waiting for then?" My voice shakes.

"I thought you wanted to leave without me." He raises a brow.

"I do." I glare, hoping it pierces him. "Why aren't *you* leaving?"

"Gotta wait for Hisan." Yoon says casually, watching me the way he's done countless times before.

"But we need to move." The panic makes my words slip. Another alerting sound of the horn bellows, this time closer to where we are. I look up. The outpost is still unguarded.

"We?" He chuckles. "Hm. Must have already found his head." He thumbs over his shoulder.

I gape at him as he crosses his arms, standing there like we have all the time in the world. Like we aren't moments from being caught. My stomach knots.

I can't go back to that prison. I refuse.

"Must have wandered further than I thought he would." He cracks a whistle again, calling out his horse's name. I am distraught.

"Will you be heading east?"

His attention turns back to me. I could use him. I could use him to find Saedea.

"Why? Want to come?" He leans in, brushing his hand against the sandstone near my head. When I don't answer, "Idane. That's where I'll take you. It's on my way anyways. It'll be a safe haven until that foot heals."

Idane?

The steady beat of hooves joins the sounds of scrambling, reminding me just how close they are to finding that panel. They wouldn't let their executioner's killer go free. Dust sputters as the horse with discolored hooves appears, charging towards us.

"Ah, there he is." The stallion stops firmly at Yoon's side. "Get on." His command is sharp, one that in any other moment, I'd be foolish not to obey.

"No." The two letters escape before I even process it, surprising myself.

His eyes brighten. "Not sure if you're aware, but those men back there aren't going to thank me for killing Agai."

"I need – I need your word." My voice trembles. I won't be left behind in Idane. I don't know anything about that place. If he's already heading east, I could use him to get much farther. Maybe even as far as the ports.

"Here!" A shout pierces the air. "Look what I found!"

"Found the panel."

Yoon says, tapping his fingers impatiently against his arm. If there was ever a wrong time for me to be asking – no, demanding – something from him, it's now. But this is my only leverage. His time. I'm gambling on the fact that he'll agree to my terms, if only to keep himself alive from whoever's coming out of that wall. I'm relying on the hope that he doesn't plan on leaving me to the mercy of the guards. Not after what he went through to get us out.

My heart pounds ferociously in my chest, drowning out the distant wail of the horns. The faint sound of an explosion in the distance. Yoon remains unfazed, *annoyed* if anything. He stares at me with a challenge in his gaze, like he's indifferent to the time it's taking me to pick this fight. The horse doesn't share his calm demeanor. It snorts, pushing its snout into Yoon's shoulder, sensing the tension.

"My word on what, exactly?"

I stare him down, carefully taking time with the answer.

"We really don't have time for this, Adessa. There's somewhere I need to be." Clearly the trouble we're about to find ourselves in very soon doesn't have a place in his concerns.

"You're going to Darde, right?"

"No, I'm –" He falters, thrown off by my words. "What? How did you know that?" His face tightens, betraying him. A flicker of discomfort flashes at the ticking of his cheek.

"Before you and your men made me a prisoner, I heard you and Jax talk about it."

He raises a palm, jaw open, trying to interject, but I barrel on. I'm not oblivious to the unorganized chaos unfolding behind him. They've found the panel. They've breached the other side. I can see the beginnings of a hand creeping out of the narrow passage as the plank falls.

"Agree to take me with you. As far as you can. Not Idane." His stare burns. "Mirit. If Darde is your destination, then –"

I hesitate, unsure if I'd be willing to go that far with him. At this point, it's purely about self-preservation.

"Why in the world would you want to go to Darde?"

"I should be asking *you* that." I squint, meeting him with equal suspicion.

"I have my reasons."

"As do I."

"Oh?" His working pupil sparks with curiosity, then softens as he drums his fingers against the wall in thought. I need a weapon – something to make this all more convincing. I'm running out of time. And patience. I lunge for his dagger.

He moves too fast, like he was anticipating it. My fingers only graze the edge of his blood-soaked shirt when he dodges, a wild look flashing across his face.

"Do you mean to threaten me? *Now?* After all I've done to save you?"

A slow, taunting grin stretches across his lips, aching at my raw confidence. Who am I to confront a person like him?

Past him, a shout erupts, motioning for more to come out of the wall, pointing in our direction. They're so close. The horse whinnies, shifting restlessly, warning us that time is up.

"And with no fear in your eyes." Yoon's voice dips into something darker. "Get on the horse, Adessa."

"Not until you agree."

"And if I refuse?"

I take a step back, but he moves with me, pressing me between the wall and his agitated horse. His demeanor only fuels my recklessness. Irrationality grips me; I dip under his arm, stumbling forward, half rotating to latch onto the machete on his back.

It doesn't unclip as easily as I expected.

He releases the heaviest sigh before swinging around to grab me. I push away, but not fast enough. His arms lock across my back, dipping me, sweeping my legs out from under me. I twist, swinging my fist up, colliding with his jaw. Pain bursts across my knuckles, reopening split skin while he wrestles me into the air.

Grunting, he throws me haphazardly onto the saddle as though I weigh nothing more than one of his packs. I barely have time to grasp the horse's mane before I'm jostled forward, my stomach slamming against the saddle horn.

I lash out, aiming a kick at Yoon, hoping to at least use it as a distraction to take the horse for myself. Another bitter failure. Yoon vaults onto the horse, seats himself behind me, his grip firm as he rights my body into position, forcing me flush against his chest. I can't object fast enough, he snaps the reins. The horse explodes into motion.

It rips into a full gallop. I twist, shooting Yoon a glare over my shoulder, but my attention jerks towards those behind us. The mob gives chase. Their shouts, raw with anger, tear through the air. Luckily, they are no match for the horse's speed.

They won't catch up to us, but that doesn't stop them from trying to kill us from a distance. A gunshot rides the howling winds. The bullet whizzes past my eat. Another flies dangerously close to the horse's side. Yoon shouts something in a language foreign to me while Hisan dodges a third shot. Strong fingers wrap around my chin, forcing my head forward.

I react instinctively against his touch, a touch that reminds me of my lack of control. I throw my head back. A solid *crunch* sounds as I slam into his face. He barely flinches. Only a hard swallow betrays the fact that I hurt him at all. His grip remains firm, his focus unwavering as another flash of metal slices past us.

"That's what I get for not leaving you back there with them?" He shouts as we clear the open desert, heading down into a valley of empty white sky.

"If that was your plan, you would never have hunted me down in the first place." I force the words out, willing them to be true. "Empty threats don't scare me."

His chest puffs up in response. "I would never have had to *hunt you down* if you hadn't stolen Tagan. For that reason alone, I should've left –"

"I never asked for your help. Why waste –?"

"I never said it was a waste of my time."

I scoff, fighting the urge to look back at him. "What do you want me to do, grovel? Oh, thank you for tying me up and dragging me across the desert! If it weren't for you, I would have never ended up there."

His knuckles are nearly white against the reigns.

"If it weren't for me –" His voice trails off, all ease and arrogance once more. "I'll accept your apology at any time. I'll even be generous and count this as only the *second* time you've needed my help. Though, if I weren't so kind, my hand would already be full of favors."

He lifts two fingers past my eyeline. "I'm sure I'll run out of fingers to count on by the time we reach Idane."

"The only way you'll run out of fingers is if I cut them off myself!" I snap, daring a glance at him. Blood seeps from his nose. *Did I break something when I hit him?*

He snickers, but his smile turns slightly into a frown as he studies me. "With what?"

His daggers are right beside you. Show him that you are not someone to taunt.

As much as I hate to admit it, I need him. At least long enough to get me closer to Mirit. Just a little longer.

"I would have found a way out without your help."

"I never said you weren't capable, only that *I* was the reason you succeeded."

I roll my eyes, smacking his still-upheld fingers away. My pride refuses to entertain the possibility that he might be right. That without him, my chances of escaping the city itself would have been much slimmer. Maybe I would have seen the Underground alone, for reasons against my own wishes. A shudder runs through me. I remember the empty, hollowed look each person had. From the sellers, to the ones being sold, to those merely watching. That place didn't seem real.

The wind howls between us, stealing our argument as Hisan surges forward. The horse glides across the sand with such grace, barely skimming the surface. I never thought anything on this earth could move so fast.

After a long silence, I can't help but mutter hateful words to the man who seems to be rescuing me again.

"I'm sure Aol will be pleased to know I'm worth much more than he thought, considering all the effort you've put in to keep me around."

The horse slows to a steady pace. The wind no longer whips at my face, the danger at our backs is far gone, and that of all things is the first thing I choose to say.

"You still think that's the goal? Saving you, just to *sell* you?

His tone is different. No longer cocky. It sounds almost – hurt. I shrug it off, knowing the lies people tell when they want something, how easily they weave them beneath the guise of friendship.

"Where are you taking me?" I ask, hoping his answer is a different one.

"I told you, Idane."

"If you leave me there, I'll tell everyone who listens where you're heading." I know he belongs to something bigger. From the way he acts, from the bounty Saedea mentioned – he's worth something.

His reply is immediate. "And I'll tell the Muhdams exactly where to find *you*."

I sit up a little straighter. I wasn't expecting a response like that. Without another word, Yoon pulls Hisan to a complete stop and swings himself off the saddle.

We're out in the open, why is he being this reckless?

Maybe I've pushed him too far.

TWENTY-SEVEN

ADESSA

"The coalition will never allow for our future's world to not remember. Good luck." – Last surviving General of the UF. T.B. Unknown.

He must mean to tie me up. Bind my mouth shut to keep me from talking, like his men were fond of doing. I brace myself to fight him off. But Yoon's eyes aren't on me. They're on my foot. The wrapping is soaked through once more, tiny droplets of blood fall from the fabric into the sand. Leaving tracks.

That should be my biggest concern, blood loss. It isn't. I know I won't bleed out. If that were possible, death would have already taken me. Am I weak? Yes. Dying? No. But that isn't what unsettles me. It's the way Yoon is watching the blood drip. He's scrutinizing it, and his curiosity about it all is obvious.

He scans the empty expanse. "I need to rewrap this."

I tense at the idea, uncertain about what he'll find underneath the bloodied cloth, what stage of healing will we see? I nearly refuse. Until he pulls the persimmon from his pack, holding it out to me as though it were the most precious gift in the world. I gently take it, treating it like it's a figment of my imagination. It isn't until I notice a puncture in the skin, a bead of juice slipping free, that I realize the fruit is actually real.

"As promised."

Thump thump. Thump thump.

He busies himself with his pack, pulling out a roll of fresh cloth and a small glass vial. I press the persimmon to my lips, letting its sweet, tart nectar coat the crease of my mouth. It keeps me grounded, keeps my focus off the tugging of dried blood while he peels away the two layers of bandages. Keeps my stomach from flipping at the smell. My teeth sink into the fruit just as liquid fire spills across my wound. My skin *steams*.

I bite back a sharp inhale, eyes flicking to Yoon as he presses a clean cloth to the injury, absorbing the sting along with old and new blood. He works quickly, hands sure and steady, winding fresh wraps around my foot, gentle and tight all at the same time while I chew. I swallow thickly, the pulp of persimmon lodging comfortably in my belly.

When was the last time I've tasted something so sweet?

Sadly, before I know it, I'm down to the final bite. I meant to savor it. Really, I did. But I couldn't help myself. Juice coats my fingers and I chase every last drop, licking each one greedily, as if I could summon another fruit from the sky. As if I could convince the Mystics to give me one more taste of something this good. I frown, already knowing that I'll probably never get the chance again.

I hear Yoon clear his throat, drawing my gaze downward – to the pair of white canvas shoes in his hand.

"Swiped these at the bazaar." He says smugly.

Thump thump. Thump thump.

My chest tightens. My fingers twitch with the urge to wipe the blood that stains his cheek.

"I'm not sure how comfortable they'll be, but anything is better than that." He stretches the center of the shoes out, sizing them up with my feet. "How could you have gone – what?" He asks, lolling his head to the side when he pauses his work to glance up at me. Whatever expression

I'm wearing must have given something away. I smooth it into indifference, giving a short nod as I wipe my sticky fingers against my pants.

He chuffs at the lack of gratitude, taking one foot, placing it into the mouth of the shoe. Then follows with the wrapped one, tucking the cloth inside so it stays secure. The fabric is soft. Too soft. Not the kind of shoe made for someone who needs to work hard or walk often. I shift my toes, getting used to the unfamiliar feeling of them being encased.

"Why are you helping me." It isn't a question.

"Burying you would take too much time."

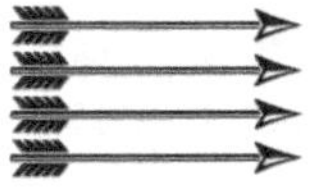

There's a river. A *river*!

It's shallow, but the water is running from somewhere – *to* something. Somehow, this wide, beautiful ribbon of life has survived the drought that's swallowed most of the continent.

"How is this even possible?" I hear myself ask, curling my fingers back when I stop myself from brushing the top of the soft current. I almost don't trust that it's safe to be near it.

Yoon doesn't share my awe, he acts like it's nothing new, like he's known it to always be here. He wades into the water without hesitation, water lapping up to his calves, just below his knees. His steps send soft, rhythmic splashes across the surface, gentle enough to nearly lull my exhaustion to sleep.

I kneel beside the water, trailing a fingertip along the surface, resisting the desperate urge to wash away the grime clinging to my skin. The last time I cleaned myself, it led me to make more mistakes than I'd made in years. Superstition demands that I punish myself instead. I watch Yoon attempt to scrub the remnants of blood from his hair and skin, wringing out the edge of his shirt. It does little to clear the stains. Another swath of muddy crimson dirties the surrounding water, deepening with the color of the sunset to our left.

"Here."

I barely have time to react before a soaked rag flies toward me. I smack it away in disgust. Bloody water sprays, spattering the ground, but I scramble back in just in time. My spine scrapes against the rough stone of a crumbling column, one of the many ruins surrounding us – remnants of a tower maybe. Destroyed, but not entirely, more than likely shattered in the Cull's wake.

Yoon smooths his hair back, waiting for the current to allow the rag to reach him with an open hand. He wrings it out in front of him.

"It might feel nice to get that blood off."

Sitting in this filth will remind me not to make any more mistakes. I can deal with it. At least I'm not as coated as he is.

"When are we leaving?"

We had stopped here not too long ago, but with the sun already setting, I'm impatient to continue moving. As far as I know, he hasn't lied. We're still heading east, considering the way the sun dips into the horizon. One day closer to Mirit.

"In the morning."

"What?" My back stings as I jolt upright. "Why?" I've wasted enough days already.

"I don't wish to ride past sunset." He answers back, tugging at his shirt, wiping lazy circles into the cloth with the rag, which is doing nothing to clean it. It only spreads the dried blood into a matching, milky pink that dirties the water with another squeeze.

"That's the dumbest thing I've ever heard."

I grab a piece of rubble and toss it into the stream, aiming for him. He steps aside unhurriedly before it can hit him, watching the uneven ripples spread across the water. I can't stand the smirk he wears. He must think I missed him on purpose.

I play off the annoyance flitting between us by pulling out my map instead, resting tenderly along the column. My knowledge of the sky only yields to the stars, and since it isn't dark enough for them yet, as of right now, I don't have a clue as to where we might be.

My sights wander back to Yoon, who is busy frowning at his clothes, inspecting them with that useless rag. Maybe I can coax some information out of him. He *wants* to help me, doesn't he? Said so himself. I can swallow my pride and play along for now.

I furrow my brow, scrunch my nose, add a troubled squint to my hardened green eyes, all while tilting the parchment from side to side. From the corner of my vision, I catch Yoon watching me, hesitating.

Come on, fall for it.

He wades out of the water, and just when I think he's about to approach, he turns and leans against a shattered column of his own. The one directly across from me. Once he settles in, he crosses his arms, offering me nothing.

Fine.

Changing tactics, I pretend he doesn't exist. *Forget him.* My fingertips trace the map, searching for any mention of the barred city. As expected, there's nothing. In fact, there isn't a single indication that *anything* is between Er Rada and Mirit, which are both clearly marked in the traveler's hand. I see Idane, Dahue and Jynn to the east, but there's nothing in between. At least the Red Line is shown, but how accurate is that anyway?

I walk my fingers a few steps west, from Jynn. To get to where I am now, from Er Rada, took three days – or was it four? Five? Am I losing track of time? I've never traveled by horse before, so my distance is very skewed. Three days on foot would place me – here. I circle an invisible area with my nail. But now that means –

"Kyr isn't on there, is it?" Yoon finally gives in, clearing his throat. "How much did you pay for that thing?"

"I didn't."

Not with money, anyway.

Seizing the opportunity, I push further. "Why have I heard that name before?" The distant memory feels much further from me now.

"Everyone has." He says with a shrug. "It holds the Blood Market."

His answer blurs while I continue searching my mind for the memory that mentions the name of Kyr. I tap a finger against my solid chin, picturing the harem in Isla.

Yana. Yana of Kyr. That's it. Isla's Matron. I'm unsure if it was her real name or not, or just her stage name, fashioning her title around the legend of her homeland. The Tilidaan paid fortunes just to be near her, to hear stories that made their own conquests seem insignificant. I always thought her tales were nothing more than a grand performance – a means to fill her pockets, a way to remind Arthur that she was worth the trouble of keeping around.

The Tilidaan adored her more than anything. She never broke character, never slipped. She had a way of weaving drama into every retelling of her escape, spinning it into something richer each time. Since experiencing a taste of the city of Kyr myself, maybe she wasn't making any of it up like I'd thought. I didn't know she had been talking about the Blood Market – or the Underground, that entire time.

I close my eyes, hearing her voice for the first time in a lifetime.

"Greedy, lust-filled bastards. They only care about one thing. Well, perhaps two. Luxury. And blood."

She would always say that right before unsheathing her gold-tipped dagger, the one she claimed to have stolen from one of the lords.

A city once made from gold, with walls as high as dunes. The Mystics smile upon these people, or so they say."

The Tilidaan never believed in the Mystics. That part always earned sneers from the crowd, and Yana would pause, letting the weight of her words settle like sand in a storm.

"The people continued to offer them blood, to quench their thirst. They believed the Mystics wanted more. More. More."

The regulars of the harem would pound their fists against the tables. The newcomers, starry-eyed and entranced, would always lean in, hungry for more.

That was usually when Arthur would find me, hiding amongst the crowd. He'd drag me back to the kitchen, out of sight. He never wanted me near the patrons. As I got older, I often forgot to thank him for that.

I always used to wonder why she ran away. Exchanging a city of gold for one overrun by pirates who were not accepted as an official clan by the rest of the world. Leaving behind the walled fortress to live each day not knowing if it would be your last. Now I know why. I saw what that city had to offer. I should have made the connection to Kyr earlier. Saedea did. And I didn't listen.

"How many days to the port?" I ask, seizing the rare moment of conversation. Anything to keep me from seething at the apparent warning signs I willingly ignored.

"Days?" Yoon barks out a laugh. "A week at least."

A week? On foot, maybe, but on horseback? That can't be right. I glare at the parchment.

"The distance between Teryal and here is longer than –"

"We'll have to take the long way around."

"Why? There's a bridge. Why would it take so long." I place my finger on the river, the one we *have* to be on right now. There's a bridge connecting this side to the next. Dahue follows.

"We can't cross it." Yoon says, picking at a cuticle.

"Why not?"

"It isn't shown on your map?" He asks, shifting in his seat. He takes the time to uncuff the bottom of his pants, then makes his way over to me. "Going straight through Bahani lands would be *suicide.*"

I press the parchment to my chest, unwilling to show him. He sighs, taking a seat next to me.

"Look." He pulls the map from my resisting hands, spreading it out in front. "Bahani territory has been pushed back, it now starts on this side of the river." He points to the right, pushing Kyr and Idane out of the lines that mark the boundary. "This is where Kyr is."

I scratch the area with my nail. It's not like I plan on returning to the continent after I leave it, but it's reassuring to know that the mark is there. Just in case.

"And here –" He circles the Saddleback Mountains. "Is where we need to go in order for us to arrive in Jynn undetected. Without protection, the route to Mirit could be nearly impossible. That's why getting to the ports will take a while. It's not an easy route."

"What do you mean, *we*. I thought you said you were taking me to Idane." I scowl, searching the Red Line again to distract myself.

He shrugs, ignoring me. "How old is that map anyway?"

I swallow my tongue, not wanting to share how old it really is. Or how I got it. His grating laugh cuts into me.

"You were out here, *alone*, with a map that hasn't been updated since The *Reversal*? Do you have a death wish or something?"

"The Reversal?" I regret asking the second the words leave my mouth.

He throws a hand up, beckoning the sky. I knew, of course, that the continent had changed. I'd been warned about it when I left Isla. I expected obstacles. I knew that things might not be correct. I had been younger when I met the trader outside of Isla. He told me that it was accurate. I remained firm that the Red Line would take me where I needed to go, as long as I followed it east. I didn't really care to know the bound-ary lines, anything outside of Farit was owned by the Jidaani anyways. I didn't think the Bahani would be a problem too.

Turns out, I was wrong.

My mind visualizes the stories I've heard of Mirit. My final stop before leaving this Mystics' forsaken continent. I have to get there. I chant my plan in my mind, calming myself with words of restless peace.

Strike a deal, secure passage.

There's a Mydizian captain who can be bartered with. At least, that's what Arthur advised – begrudgingly after he found out that I planned to leave Isla. He said the captain transported opium from the Dabieshan Mountains and might be willing to trade me for a ride across the sea, if

I can convince him properly. And by convince, Arthur meant offering something of value. Yoon's daggers could work. They look ornate, expensive, fit for a captain.

"How do you not know of The Reversal?" He shakes out water from his hair, speaking lightly, despite the weight of his question. "Where are you from?"

"I'm not interested in small talk." I snap. Venom laces my tongue. My fingertip could nearly burn a hole through the parchment by the way it's pressing against it. Kyr. That damned horse. Why did it bring us there? I don't want to think about how far away from him and his useless questions I would be if that stupid horse didn't lead us to Kyr. The bridge was *right there.*

I feel Yoon's stare burning into me when I fold the map into a square and shove it into my pocket. He huffs. "Clearly not from here."

"That isn't any of your business."

"I'm only wondering how a foreigner could possibly have the guts to wander the desert by herself. No weapons. No real map. On foot. It's honestly the biggest question I've had since we met."

If I could roll my eyes any harder, I'd go blind. "You don't seem to fit in either, *easterner.*" I use the word I've heard used to describe him over the last few days. I have to flip this conversation around before he starts prying too deep. "If you aren't from here either, how would *you* know where we're going?"

I haven't seen him pull out a map of his own for the entirety of the ride. Not in the days he forced me along with their caravan, not even when we had to change course – more than a few times, to avoid the earth-caving craters that had been there since the time of the Collapse. The continent is riddled with them. Another damning reminder of what the Elites had done in the Time Before.

Yoon snickers, swiping sand from his palms. He's still much too close to me. I wish he'd stayed on the opposite side. My chest tightens at his nearness, and I hate myself all the more for it.

"Don't you think I'd be well aware of where I was leading us?" He nods towards my pocket. "I just described the entire eastern half of this continent to you."

I scoff. "You could be lying."

"Yes." He leans closer, resting his forearms on his knees. "But I'm not."

A groan slips when I adjust my body to get away from him, regretting it immediately when concern floods the space between us. His posture changes. Worry replaces the usual sharp edge in his stance.

"Has the bleeding stopped?" Without a second thought, he crouches in front of my feet. I pull my foot back, hiding it from his view.

"Mystics' around, can you leave me alone? It's fine."

It certainly doesn't feel fine, but I can't have him realizing the impossible truth that the bone has already healed. I felt it while we were riding. The muscle is already in the process of stitching back together, the sensation of it doing so brings a numbing agony, yet somehow there's comfort in knowing my body isn't willing to give up completely.

"We need to clean it again. Infection still lives in the desert." Yoon's determined gaze makes me snort.

Infection has never been a concern of mine. I've watched it take people year after year in my village. Sometimes it couldn't be helped. Same could be said in Isla as well, seeing as the Tilidaan didn't take care of themselves. There weren't healers, they believed only the strongest survived. Disease was known to run rampant. One of the main reasons for death in Isla was due to infection, not the actual fights that created the wound in the first place.

Although still part of the Tillidaan territory, Farit had healers who were trained to at least stabilize those who *could* be saved. Still, I never needed any of their treatments, no matter how adamant some tried to be. Once my wounds healed, they just – healed. That's why I always hid them. Tirma's warnings never left me, always lurking in the corners of my mind, prevalent in every pocket of my worries of being found out. Again, I can't tell Yoon that. He cannot know.

Instead of waiting for my answer, he sifts through one of the buttoned pockets of his bag. A familiar vial appears in the sand beside me – liquid fire. It reminds me of Chadron. Then, a with a sharp whistle, he calls for his horse, which meets him halfway.

It isn't long before he's back, a roll of linen in his hand, and even less time before he's kneeling in front of me again, this time with a needle and thread between his fingers.

"Absolutely not." I wince, covering my foot with my hands. "That isn't necessary."

"Unlikely. Let me see."

He tugs at my shoe. I don't fight him, partially because I know struggling will send another spike of pain up my leg, and partly because I know he won't stop until he gets his way. I close my eyes at the agony that rubs against my wound as he gently pulls the soft canvas away.

"Hold still."

He has the audacity to sound *annoyed!*

I glare at him, ready to snap, willing to fight him – and nearly faint at the sight before me. His clothes are *soaked*. Not tinged with the milky pink of water-thinned blood. He's drenched in deep, fresh crimson. It coats his cheek. His neck. Every inch of skin is now swallowed up in a color that I've now come to strongly associate – with him.

TWENTY-EIGHT

ADESSA

"A command, wrapped in fear."

I can almost feel the blade slice across my neck.

The hole in my chest.

Cold snow on my eyelashes. Fingertips frozen.

Breathe. A voice screams inside my head. *Remember.* It doesn't belong to me.

Feverish. That's how I feel. It hits all at once, sudden and crushing, the weight of my heart heaves at the idea of this being true. Of this ever becoming a possibility. I feel *loss.* I feel *grief.*

Why, why, why? More shouting. More feelings I don't understand.

"Hey."

My throat tightens. Yoon's lips are moving. He reaches for me, like I *mean* something to him. A snap of fingers – silver flashes in my vision. Yoon circles his hand in front of my face. I bat it away. His touch –

"Adessa?"

His question is so distant, like I'm hearing him through water. The whites of his teeth are brightened by the crimson on his lips. The vision won't leave. It won't *leave.*

Breathe.

Is that my mother's voice? She used that tone when I was only a handful of years old, when she used to soothe me the moment my panic attacks swallowed me whole. In a way Tirma never did. In a way she was never capable of.

You are not in your nightmare.

I picture my mother's arms around me. The warmth of them. Mystics, why did I have to choose to disobey my father that day? Why did they have to take *everything* from me?

"Adessa." Yoon's voice again.

I slam back into my body, blinking rapidly through blurry tears at the concern worn into his expression

"What just happened?"

I could mistake that tone for accusation but choose to breathe through the lingering ghosts in my mind, focusing on clearing them away.

"Nothing." I manage, lifting my chin. He rubs his teeth against his bottom lip, as if trying to decide whether or not to push further.

"Blood loss finally getting to you?" The brief smirk falls. "Are you dizzy?"

He's talking to me too – gently.

"Just leave me alone." I sputter, rubbing my arms absently, squeezing my chest. Almost wishing it *was* real. Because if it was, then at least I wouldn't wonder if I'm beginning to slip into the same madness that ate at Tirma.

"Take this."

He leans forward, unclipping the waterskin from his belt, quickly refilling it with the river at our side. Then, from his pocket, he pulls out the sturdy decorated cloth I remember holding dried meat. The dull ache of hunger resides just below the numbness I feel when I see the jerky nestled inside it. The persimmon from earlier hadn't sustained me in any way, it only allotted me a brief moment of happiness.

Yoon sets the cloth in the sand and offers me the open waterskin first. I take it without a word, grateful for the slightly warm, mineral swallow that coats the back of my throat. Meanwhile, his rough fingers work at slipping off my shoe, then he moves to the wrappings, peeling away the sticky layers of dried blood and cloth. He tosses the ruined fabric aside. I find myself unwilling to look at anything but the sky, which begins clearing into a dark shade of purple. Yoon's not-so-subtle reaction tells me that my injury may look worse than it actually feels.

He's wondering how I'm not dead yet.

The waterskin is lifted from my hands. He uses it to pour a thin stream of water over my wound, washing away dirt and blood. Doing so allows me to inspect it with him. The bleeding has slowed to a soft ooze, but the gash is deep. Nauseatingly deep. Yoon tilts his head in judgment, his hand hovering near my leg, hesitating.

Can he see the muscle healing beneath?

If he does, he gives no sign of it, simply unscrewing the cap of the vial and lifting it to my eyeline. It's not the same liquid he used last time; this one is thick, black. It runs down the sides of the glass like syrup.

"Apparently this is supposed to help things heal."

I wrinkle my nose as the smell reaches me. It's sickly sweet. I've heard oleander is sweet. Lots of poisons smell sweeter than one would expect from something that can end your life.

"I'm not supposed to – drink that, right?"

Yoon studies the vial with mild confusion. "I would hope not. Although Chadron –"

"Chadron?" My pulse stumbles.

"You've lost a lot of blood. He said to use this wisely, I think this is one of those times." He holds the vial above the wound. "Are you sure you don't feel dizzy?"

"I already told you I'm fine!"

The way he's taking care of me – like I'm fragile, like I *need* him- makes my stomach turn far worse than any dizziness ever could. I force myself to toughen up, to breathe through it. He shifts to the pad of jerky beside me.

"You should eat something before I stitch you up."

The borrowed clothes hang loose around me, reminding me of the hollowing skin and weakened bones buried inside them. The last thing I will ever give him is the satisfaction of knowing he's right. Starvation has been my reality for a long time now, I can last a while longer. If only out of spite.

"No."

"Suit yourself."

"And I don't need you to stitch me up."

"And I don't want to be the one to tell you what happens if we don't take care of this tonight."

This irritating man. He's doing what he thinks is best, I shouldn't fault him for it. What any normal person would do when faced with an injury like this. I should be grateful that he isn't suspicious yet. That his curiosity hasn't gotten the best of him.

Without warning, Yoon tips the vial forward. A thick, syrupy stream glazes the top of my wound. I flinch, bracing for a sting that never comes. Instead, warmth blooms, soothing my skin in an outward wave. The uncomfortable misery is replaced with cooling relief. The muscle underneath is no longer throbbing with the untamed pang of healing. I can't feel a thing actually. It's euphoric.

"You couldn't have just listened to me." Yoon mutters under his breath as he threads the thin needle. For a moment, I think I imagined the words. Until the overwhelming calm is overtaken by a sharp lick of fury.

"What is that supposed to mean exactly?"

He loops a knot at the end of the thin fibers, dips the needle into the vial, and hovers it over the top of the gash.

"Why didn't you go to the blacksmith?"

The needle pierces my skin, cutting through my thoughts. I wait for the pain. It doesn't come. Maybe it's the tonic working, maybe I'm in shock. When I open my eyes, Yoon is watching me, waiting, testing.

When he seems satisfied by my lack of agony, he tugs the thread through. The eerie pull of skin being woven together without pain forces a phantom twitching sensation up my calf, sending nausea to curl in my gut. I briefly do wish I'd eaten first.

"Did Aya not suggest it?"

"She did." I grumble, finding my voice.

"Then why –" Peering up, I glower at the look he gives. He shakes his head, returning to his work. "The girl."

Calloused fingers loop another knot.

"She wasn't with you at Aya's though. Had you been looking for her? Is that why you didn't find meeting with me important?" He pauses, searching for some kind of connection.

I offer him nothing.

"I would never have allowed this to happen if –"

"If what?"

"If you had just met me at the blacksmith's."

"So you could force me into paying back a favor for a meal I didn't ask for?"

"Force you?" He huffs, loud enough to make a statement. "I didn't expect you to pay me. You looked like you were starving!"

Discolored eyes bore into me now, just as heavily as they had back at the bar days ago.

"I waited there so I could help you. Rust was out hunting, he already had eyes on you... and when you didn't show –" His fingers reach for my chin, but he pulls back instantly, as if touching me would scald him.

"I assumed the worst. So I went back to Aya's and she told me she saw you turn in the *opposite* direction. I went back to camp to try to catch up with you." Another loop. "I found out they had your friend at the same time I realized they had *you*."

"Liar." The letters are cold on my tongue, drawn out, punctuated with hate.

"I didn't have any part in taking her." He looks at me like I've just spat in his face. Like I'm wrong for even suggesting the idea.

"But you did play a huge role in taking us *both*, didn't you?" I sigh, wishing I could give up on this conversation. "Why would you have wanted to help me in the first place? Hm?"

I want to hear his excuses. It will help me hate him more.

"How would going to the blacksmith's change anything? How would any of this be different?"

I push myself to stand, forgetting the thread is still attached to my foot. Yoon tugs it carefully, slicing it free with his blade. He shoves me back down. Then, he not-so-gently yanks my toes up to keep me in place, stretching my heel back into his lap. He pours a little more of the tonic onto the underside of my foot. I feel it rush down my ankle, burning along the way.

"I don't know." His tone sounds uncertain. "Maybe you would have had something to protect yourself with. Maybe you would have agreed to come with me if I had a chance to know where you were heading. Maybe I could have handled things differently if we arrived together. Maybe we wouldn't be in this situation at all."

For a single, fleeting moment, I question everything I've believed about him. I restrain myself from making it known.

"You honestly believe that I held you captive, *willingly?*"

"Yes."

Baffled. That's the only way to describe the expression he wears. His jaw closes slowly, widening into a grin. "Oh, you are a pain."

I can't tell if it's an endearment, or some kind of insult. The tone he uses, the one where the words coat his tongue like honey, make me think it's the former. I hate that he isn't treating me the way I expected a brute like him to. I hate that I feel anything other than sheer annoyance towards him.

"Stop." I jerk back, forcing him not to complete the stitch. "What do you want from me? In return for all this *help*. Just tell me, and maybe we can come to an understanding."

He rocks back, sitting on his heels. "Nothing."

"Liar."

I bundle my fists into the sand, wishing I could go back to the days when I aimlessly wandered Isla, despite the Tilidaan. When revenge only lived in the darkest corners of my mind, never clawing its way to the surface. When I began to believe that I had a home somewhere not buried in snow. Not abandoned and oh so lonely.

"It isn't normal to not require something in return." I murmur, the weight of those words pressing down on me. On both of us.

He leans back slightly, brows drawn tight, questions lining every crease of his face.

"If you had no motive, you could have let us go the moment you saw us. The moment you recognized me, the girl you apparently wanted to help. But you chose not to." I harden myself further. "We were almost free and you told them to take us back. That doesn't sound like someone who's –"

"You're right."

The needle pinches my skin again, distracting both of us with his resumed work. His steady hand crosses the thread over the wound, knots it, repeats.

"But I wasn't left with many options. You made the mistake of leaving Gunn alive."

A regret I've already made peace with.

"Then you pissed off Burke almost immediately after he caught you."

His fingers swipe strands of fallen hair out of his eyes.

"Taking out Gunn was taken as a challenge. Against you. And let's not forget, you were the one who cooked half of Aol's face the night before. They were already holding a grudge against a woman who looked like you, even if they didn't recognize you right away."

Burke did.

"How did you –"

"Didn't take me long to figure it out. I knew it the moment I saw you searching for something. Then I saw Gunn catch you watching him too. When he shoved the satchel back in his saddlebag, the one they "happened across" at an abandoned camp, I made the connection that it had to belong to you."

"Some of my things were missing from it."

"There was more stuff in there?"

He cuts the last bit of thread, tying a knot to secure the end. My attention moves to the neat, precise lines closing the wound at the top and bottom of my foot. I wonder how many times he's done this in his life to be able to be so precise.

"Yes, I'm missing –" I stop myself. I only wonder who has the motte now. I don't care about the rice. It's not like it matter anyways.

"So what you're saying is, you tied us up and dragged us along because you didn't have a choice?" I don't believe a single word that comes out of his mouth.

"Can you imagine what men like that would do if I had released the woman who threatened their *pride*? They would have forgiven me, eventually, for letting Saedea go. Especially since I was expecting to make up for all of the silver they so desperately thought they needed. But I would never have been forgiven for letting *you* go. If it weren't for that healer – Burke paralyzed you because you inconvenienced him. Imagine what he would have done to *me*."

A snip of his tongue follows. "And once he was done peeling the skin from my body, he would have done so much worse to you. Then they would have sold you to the first runner they came across. You'd get a first look at the Underground, without me, and you wouldn't have been able to get out. That, I can promise."

"You're dramatic." I say, albeit knowing that he has to be telling *some* truth. "Afraid of your own men?" I challenge him instead. "I watched you kill three guards in Kyr without a glimmer of hesitation."

He laughs, almost cocky.

"Aren't you their Qa'id?" Sure they muttered complaints whenever they could, but they followed his orders all the same.

Yoon doesn't give anything away. He reaches for the spool of clean linen.

"I barely know them. Besides Jax." His response is measured. "They've been trailing along ever since Jax and I met them a few months ago. Said they were runaways. I thought I'd help them out. They like to *pretend* that I'm in charge so they don't have to plan anything for themselves."

That doesn't make sense. They moved together too well. They knew their roles like they'd practiced it thousands of times.

"What do you mean you barely know them? They *knew* you. The men in the city did too. They were all after *you*. And the flags in Kyr had the same symbols as Aol and Burke."

He hesitates but then nods.

"So they're all from the same clan? The clan that was in Kyr?"

"Maybe. I never asked."

"If you were traveling together, wouldn't that mean *you* are from that clan as well?"

"Not necessarily." *This infuriating man!*

"But how –"

"Look, I know you aren't from here." He interrupts with a raised palm. "So I know you might not understand how the territories are split. But even you should know that when a city is barred and guarded, that means *stay away.* "

The hair on my neck rises with anger.

"Allowing yourself to be put in such a dangerous situation –"

"Allowing?" I spit. "That horse led us there."

I can tell by the smug look on his face that he's baiting me. He has to be. This has to be some kind of distraction.

"*You* were the one who forced us to make that decision! If you actually wanted to help, you could have left us with Chadron, but you chose not to!"

"I tried!"

Thankfully, my stitched wound doesn't weep while he wraps it. My body can't afford to lose any more blood. Yoon reaches for my hand next, shoving the bandages aside. His grip is firm. Too solid for me to pull away in time.

Oh no.

I see a flicker of interest dancing across his features. The cut is healed. Newly pink skin lines its edges, fresh and tender. Maybe he'll think it was only superficial. He doesn't know how deep the blade had cut. Maybe he won't question it.

"How is this –"

"What do you mean, you tried?"

I cut in, desperate to distract him. His expression shifts. Whatever curiosity was there slips behind something unreadable. He releases my hand, cracks his neck, and stands.

"The Elder told me no."

Silence settles between us, syrupy and dark like the tonic numbing my foot. Above, pinprick stars begin to appear, popping up one by one. I search the sky, looking for the familiar cluster that has been guiding me since I left Skeall. If I can find it, I'll know we're still heading in the right direction. That I'm not being lied to. I am so tired of feeling this way. I hate that I have no other choice.

Yoon finally settles into the sand a short distance away, leaning against the crooked stone.

"Up there, to the left." He points.

"What?"

"Are you looking for the hourglass?"

My heart stumbles over what he just said to me. How could he possibly know that's the group of stars I follow. Is he really able to read me that well?

"I follow it too. When I need to go east."

The bundle of stars blink down at me. A comfort to know I'm on the right path. I was told of them by the traveler, perhaps that's what a lot of people use to find their way. I try to swallow the odd thoughts I'm having.

"What clan does Kyr belong to? The ones who use the triangle markings? Or the ones that use the green and black flags."

He doesn't answer.

"Your men are from Kyr, which means the ones who own the city must be the same who wear that symbol."

"Burke and the others are not Muhdam."

"The merchant had a green and black flag. And had bounties on his caravan. Posted just like they were in Kyr. He must be Muhdam then. But you're saying your men come from Kyr? But they aren't Muhdam?"

A small chuckle escapes his throat, but he covers it with a cough.

There were two different clans there. His men are different. He is different.

I wait in his silence.

"Fine don't answer." I huff. "Are you a bounty?"

I shove the panic away, not allowing it to drag me under. I have to trust what he said – that he wouldn't have come for me if he knew Jidaani were in the city. But something is lurking beneath his covered responses.

The man across from me shifts. He looks far too comfortable, too natural out here in the desert. "I hope not."

"How did the executioner know you then?"

"Agai?"

It's almost too frustrating to see how unbothered he is by my prodding.

"Him and I go way back." Yoon closes his eyes and keeps them closed.

When the silence lingers further, I latch onto a bit more confidence. He isn't holding me captive, at least I don't think he is. I'm free to leave if I want to. I'll continue prying. He has to slip eventually.

"How did *any* of them know who you were?" Nothing. "Don't you want me to trust you?" The worst he can do is continue to ignore me.

"I thought you weren't interested in small talk." *Now he brings that up.* "Believe it or not, I know a lot of people. From everywhere. All over the continent. I've been here most of my life. That's what happens when you enjoy trading. So if you're trying to connect anything, don't bother. It's pointless."

A retort. But I hear the way his breath shifts – heavy, uneven. He's fidgeting too, a sign of unopened truth. I almost don't continue prodding him. Almost.

"You aren't a trader." I nearly choke on the words. "What clan do you belong to?"

He clears his throat, as if he'd been waiting for me to ask.

"You know what, Adessa? I'm afraid that if I tell you, you won't be begging me to take you to the port anymore. And you'd be wandering Bahani lands without a clue as to why their boundary lines shrank."

Fear prickles my spine. I scan the darkened landscape, suddenly feeling like an absolute fool for trusting this man for all the wrong reasons. Selfish reasons. Now I sit here, without a weapon, with no means of protecting myself. With someone who is *much* more than he says he is. Yoon lets sand slip lazily through the break in his fingers. Making himself look like he has all the time in the world. As if this conversation means nothing to him.

"Is that enough for you to stop asking me these questions?"

"Wouldn't it be smarter to gain my trust by answering them?" I counter.

I can almost *hear* his smirk lift. "I don't see how that would work in my favor. So no."

Oh, how I loathe him.

"You must be so excited to be rid of me then! Makes me wonder why you made us stop riding, why you've decided to draw out your time with me!"

"I needed to tend to your foot." He stretches out, deepening his comfortability against the stone. "Besides, if they're looking for us, we're safer in the cover of night. And I don't want to be found. Hisan and I know these lands better than they do. The Muhdams never come this far."

"And what about the *other* ones in the city?"

"Well, I hope the Mystics favor you more than they do me."

I wish I could strangle him!

"What if I don't want to stay and wait until you deem it worthy to travel again?"

Yoon doesn't even open his eyes. "Well then don't stay. The desert is yours."

He palms his hand outward in an easy, dismissive gesture. I follow the motion, letting my gaze sweep the endless stretch of sand and consider my options.

He doesn't owe me an explanation as to who he is, I'm already aware of the accidental danger I've put myself in for being associated with him. If he wants to keep the clan he belongs to a secret, then so be it. At least I'm not the only one hiding something. I just need to use him, like a shield. If he's being hunted, self-preservation will win over anything else. And if we *do* get caught, well, perhaps he could be a bartering chip. Or he'd be a distraction. What did Saedea say her brother told her? Always have three backup plans. Maybe I should start living by that mantra.

"What's stopping me from taking your horse?"

"Don't forget some sugarcane." His chin tilts down, slumber latching on, beckoning me to follow suit. I blink at his confidence.

"You aren't concerned that I could kill you in your sleep? I'd take all of your weapons. Everything you own."

"I'd be dead anyways." He breathes a laugh. "Besides, you wouldn't dare."

"You don't believe I would?"

He shrugs, like the thought is mildly entertaining. "That was actually an invitation to try."

His flecked tone sends an unwelcome caress along my neck. I shake it off.

"I just threatened you, and now you plan to sleep?"

He doesn't flinch.

"You haven't tied me up either."

A lazy grin sparks when his eyes lock with mine once more. I can see the whites of his teeth against the reflection of the moon on the river. The glimmer of humor spreads. It makes me want to skin him alive.

"I think you're smart enough not to announce your plans outright again. At least smart enough to have learned from your mistakes."

So, he had overheard us before we took Jax's horse. That's why all of their equipment had been tucked away, making everything more difficult for us. It was meant to stop us from trying. But how did he hear us? I was sure we were out of earshot. I grit my teeth.

"Despite what you may think, you're not my prisoner, Adessa. I'm not baiting you. You're free to go as you please."

He folds his arms behind his head. "Kill me if you can. Take Hisan. I can't stop you. All I can say is... good luck."

There isn't any freedom in my choice though, not really. No matter if I'm his captive again or not. And he knows it. He's arrogant enough to believe I won't be able to overpower him. Arrogant enough to know that I'll choose my own self-preservation by sticking around too. I hate that he's right.

"Be warned though," he adds. "If you do manage to kill me, you'd be stranded out here. Alone. With a very angry horse. He may even try to avenge me. I trained him myself."

The desert air grows colder. I wish there was something to start a fire with. I have half a mind to ask him to do so, but there would be nothing nearby to feed the flames.

"If you still wish to leave, Darde is that way."

He flicks his dismissive fingers towards the opposite side of the river.

"However, given the circumstances, it isn't just me they'll be hunting. You more than likely have been added to their list. And your decades-old map isn't going to get you very far."

I remain silent, unsettled by a realization I can't quite place. For the first time in a long while, I wonder if another person might not be as against me as I've always assumed. Even though he's disguising it by being cocky. I don't know how to take it. I've never been more aware of my own distrust than I am right now. And I wonder when that started.

"Darde." I roll the name around my mouth.

"That is where you're heading, right?"

"Yes. Same as you."

"Same as me." He repeats, almost like he's testing me. "When I take you to Idane, you can do whatever you want when I leave." The faint amusement etched in the idea is something I choose to ignore. "Just re-member, there are slave runners close by. And don't forget the Red Line, it might have seemed abandoned the closer we were to Teryal, but it's a different story on the opposite side of that river. So I don't suggest you cross it. Idane is a decent place. Not many people there anymore. The plague almost drove them into extinction a few decades back. But other than that, you should be perfectly safe."

What is he doing? Trying to deter me from leaving wherever he plans on dropping me off? Or warning me against staying there? I have no knowledge of any of these new places, including the only port I'm aiming for, and no updated map. I have to convince him to let me come along. Kyr might not have been the worst thing I've run into yet.

"I'm not going to Idane."

"We'll see." He grunts.

I dig my fingers into the ground, frustration curling my hands into fists.

"Get some sleep. You need the rest."

I grimace, searching for a reason why I didn't choose to learn more about the continent when I had the chance. Why had I been relying on the sole fact that I simply can't die? What in the Abyss is wrong with me?

He notices me nervously picking at the canvas shoe, unwilling to shut my eyes.

"Why do you want to go to Darde, anyways? What have you heard?" He unclips his machete, to make way for him to lie on his back. A bold move.

"I have my reasons." I snap. Too quickly. I adjust my posture. My tone. I need him to be on my side. The more I resist his help, the less likely he'll be willing to continue offering it.

"You know," he muses. "Trusting each other is a two-sided coin."

He's right. If I expect him to answer my questions, I'll have to answer some of his. We can't keep circling each other in this endless, frustrating game if my goal is to make him give in and agree to take me further, at least to Mirit. I can handle the rest.

"My family is gone." I hesitate, picking my words carefully. "I have nothing left. And I hate this desert."

It's not entirely untrue, but the meaning behind my desires is a lie. He must know it too, because he laughs at the thought. At me. I feign innocence, shifting the attention away from myself. "Why are *you* heading there?"

"I'm after someone."

I have to admit, I'm surprised by his abrupt honesty. I refrain from telling him that we have similar goals in mind.

"And Darde is the furthest you'll go?"

"Is there anywhere further?"

I wouldn't know. To be quite honest, I don't even know how far in the city is on the next continent. I was hoping I'd be lucky enough to purchase a map at the docks, or at least in Mydiza.

"Does that mean you've already secured transport across the sea?"

Nothing.

"You *are* going through to Mydiza, aren't you?"

I hadn't been told there was any other option. Does he know an easier way to cross the Dying Sea? A way that doesn't involve bribing a captain? A way that wouldn't force me to smuggle myself on board, or barter with something far more valuable than what I'd be willing to offer?

"I suppose there isn't another option." My heart sinks. "Tell me, Adessa. Do you really hate the desert that much? Enough to cross the world by yourself?"

Thump thump.

"Not exactly." I swallow.

He waits, patiently. Expecting more. I know that once I start, I won't be able to take my words back, so I make sure I'm careful not to say too much.

"I'm after someone too."

If I can give up one, single secret, it may be easier to keep the others.

"I've been traveling from the Far North since I was small."

"Alone?" He's much too quiet. I don't look up.

"Yes." I sigh. "Once, I thought I had a home here. Isla was my home. But I was very, very wrong that it would be like that forever. And that reminded me that I have larger priorities in this life. Which is why I'm here. *Alone.* Why I can't wait any longer to get to Mirit. Why I can't –"

"Who are you after?" He doesn't accuse me of withholding any of this from him, like I kind of expected him to. His tone is attached with something that feels much more than curiosity. It sounds pained.

"The man who..."

The memories tear through my defenses, raw and unrelenting. The day I swore I would forget, desperate to keep it buried. It tries to surge to the surface regardless, but I force it back down. I've already succumbed to weakness too many times since Er Rada. The shame licks my cheek, reddening it with heat.

"Never mind. You know –"

"I'll take you."

The air shifts. As if some invisible weight has lifted between us. Did my vulnerability actually work?

"To Jynn, at least. It's close enough to the dock. There will be people there who might be able to help you find a way across, if that's still what you'll want."

"Jynn." I echo. "Is that where you're meeting the others?" Burke and the rest of them must be heading there too. "Once Burke sees me, he'll kill me."

"He won't." His voice remains firm. "I'll guarantee your safety."

I squint. "How?"

"I just –" He tapers off slightly. "I know their leader. I'll make sure you're protected." A pause. "I may even be able to pay for your transport to Mirit myself, if you're willing to wait."

I thought he didn't have any money, which is why the others wanted to sell us in the first place. Is the shine really worth *that* much?

"Why the change of heart?"

His sarcasm returns, lacing me with annoyance. "So I can sleep at night knowing you aren't rotting away in another trap."

"I wouldn't have been rotting away if it weren't for you!"

So, we're back to this argument. Good. Seeing his gentler side makes me nervous.

"I didn't put you in Kyr. That was your own doing. I tried to stop you, but you're too stubborn for your own good."

I roll my neck, fighting the ever-present urge to blind him completely. I'm getting what I want, aren't I? He agreed to take me further.

"Why did they recognize that horse, anyways? Why use me as bait?"

"So many questions when you really should be getting more sleep. Jynn is far from here. We have plenty of time to talk about it later."

Yes, and I have so many more that you haven't answered yet. I glare at him, hoping he sees it under the cover of night.

"You never really did answer how you were able to find me so fast. If you're taking me to Jynn, and you say I'm not your prisoner anymore, I want to know what kind of person I have the pleasure of traveling with."

Once again, I believe I've pried a bit too much. His silence makes me slowly begin to think that he won't respond at all. Until he does.

"Jax and I once wanted a foothold in Kyr. Years ago. We meant to further our... trade. So we dealt with the Blood Market because it was easy. I needed a way into the city without being obvious, which is why I knew where the panels were in the storage quarter. I put them there. I know the city well because I spent years using the Muhdams to my advantage." I can feel his stare back on me.

"Besides, you made it too easy. You have to realize anyone with eyes could have found you. And I only have the one."

His teasing makes my neck stiff. I reach for the waterskin he left at my side, taking another long drink to cool my rage down.

"They recognized Tagan because Jax helped me from time to time. They knew she was associated with me. And when they saw you riding her, they assumed you were connected. So, unfortunately, you became collateral damage for their trap. They aren't too smart, the Muhdams. Especially the guards. They must have believed you were important to me and ran with it."

I frown. "They turned on you, because you had been using them?" I think I'm beginning to understand some of the dynamics. "They must really want you dead, considering they set two separate traps."

A low, humorless, "Yeah."

Can't say I'm shocked by the pride. The way he looks, the ways he kills, the way he knew his way around Kyr – his confidence. Mystics' around, he decided to buy his horse sugarcane in the middle of the Blood Market. He willingly took me into the Underground. He never thought the trap was a problem. He'd been wandering around the city looking for me with no care in the world. Because he knew he could get out. And yet, he claims all of this knowledge was because of trade. I don't believe that. Traders can't possibly contain the kind of skills Yoon has shown me in the past few days, can they?

The giant's words come back to me. How he eyed me. Like I was some kind of reward.

"What did you trade? Women?"

Yoon recoils like I've struck him. "Never."

The answer is swift, clipped with disgust. "Gems. Silks for the lords' wives, ivory if I could ever get my hands on it. Shine. Opium, when I was able. But never, ever people. Especially not women. Or children for that matter. Just because I was there doesn't mean I ever agreed with what went on in the Underground."

The strangled statement repeats the firm belief that he's against the idea of slave trading. Even if he played along while his men tied us up against our will. Maybe guilt had kept him from crossing certain lines, but that doesn't mean that he's innocent.

"I made a few too many enemies because of my – beliefs." A smack to his thigh. "But thanks to you, I'm not the only one with enemies in Kyr now."

"They don't *know* who I am."

"You kind of stand out. I wonder if you'll have a bounty soon enough."

"Then we'll match."

"I'm not on one."

"Then why did they want you dead so badly if not to claim a reward?"

I feel a little uncertain about continuing. This is the longest conversation we've had. I assumed he was a man of few words. Turns out, I was wrong. For some reason, I need answers. I need his honesty, to convince myself that my fears hold no weight.

"Maybe I'm not as well liked as I thought."

It's edged with something bitter. Something I recognize. I don't belong here. I hadn't belonged on Isla either. Perhaps he feels the same way.

"It wasn't smart of me to deal in Kyr anyway. They're actually quite horrible." A yawn lengthens his sentence. "I wouldn't recommend working with them for as long as I did."

As expected, he plays off something that should be serious with something light.

"You really should get some sleep. I can tell you're exhausted. And we have a long ride tomorrow. If you still wish to come with me."

"I'm still deciding."

He sighs. "Well, if you do end up leaving, at least take this with you."

The clink of a glass bottle lands near my swollen toes, followed by a roll of bandages.

"And take the jerky with you too. It'll keep death at bay while you wait for me to come find you again."

Back to being an ass.

"You know, I've survived perfectly fine without all of this *help*. Thanks." I grind my nails into my thighs.

"You certainly have. And Mystics' around, I'm still trying to figure out how."

He can't be serious!

"Asshole. To say all this when I could easily slit your throat." His even breathing answers back, clearly unbothered about my potential threat. Frustration coils in my gut.

Without another sound, I grab the ornate bandana of jerky and fling it into the river. I might not have much control over my life right now, but I can at least deny him the satisfaction of his so-called generosity. He probably has more in his pack anyway.

I'll eat tomorrow.

TWENTY-NINE

YOON

"String the boy up high. Let his bones be picked clean. He'll be a warning for all to see."

Bodies surround me.

The stink of blood clings to the sky like sap from the tall pines of Ashwau.

A voice – one I know well – calls out my name. My mother.

In these nightmares, I know she's always just beyond reach. I've heard her cries thousands of times before but am never able to see her face. Never able to find where her wails are coming from. The truth is, I've long forgotten what she looks like, and the affliction of that reality is a heavy reminder. One that haunts me even when I sleep.

As always, gnarled, sinewy hands shoot up from beneath the sunken soil, clawing at my limbs, dragging me under. Their grip is unyielding, forcing me into the darkening earth alongside the hundreds of corpses piled above it. I am made to watch as birds of all kinds descend, picking at the dead, at their glazed and lifeless eyes, rotting lips, swollen tongues, before I transform into one of the birds myself.

It's always a raven.

The Mystics favor their ravens.

The dream shifts, as it always does, and I see through the bird's eyes, scavenging the nearest body. I peck at the man's face, my vision blurring, but I always swear that I knew him once. It's a familiarity that has unsettled me each time I have this dream, but I can't seem to remember who he was.

My mother's screams pierce the air the moment I ascend. Flames rise, licking at the clouds, consuming the landscape in a feeble attempt to erase the slaughter below. My blood thickens with something akin to rage, an anger as wild as the fire. I know what comes next. I always know. But I still resist, I'm still unwilling to see it, especially now. Luckily, it seems I don't have to tonight.

My dream warps as I'm thrown back into my physical body, the sound of heavy hooves from the west waking me, jarring my mind back into my sweat-covered reality. I squint against the darkness, scanning my surroundings. Hisan is gone. That is not ideal.

I squeeze my eyes shut, relying on my hearing, listening closely to the steady beat of hooves along the sand, hating the fact that I know all too well which animals the sound belongs to. I wish I could deny that they're anywhere near us. Hopefully, they'll change directions and head north like I've been banking on. They said they were heading to the Sunce. They shouldn't be this far east. We were supposed to feel safe enough by the river to get some much deserved rest. I don't know the next time we'll be able to once we cross.

Adessa sleeps soundly across from me, curled against the stone, her form nearly blending into the pale sand. Still, I find myself crawling over to her, instinctively positioning myself between her and the open expanse to camouflage her further when I hear the riders stop. The heat from her body seeps into the space between us. Is the tonic working?

"We've been riding for too long. Let's go back." A voice grumbles, low and booming. I peer out from our hiding place, barely making out the outline of two horses in the dim light. My stomach plummets, even though I knew deep down that it was them when I woke up.

Akhal-Teke.

The last breed.

Owned solely by my former clan.

They are no longer confined within the walls of Kyr, which means Jidaani are roaming freely near the Bahani's river. And that is very, very bad.

When Tyg first seized control of the clan, before I was even old enough to beg on the streets of Geming, he enacted a continent-wide search for every one of the sought-after horses. The Jidaani once had sole ownership of the breed since the Firsts, and the other clans respected that for a time, until laws weren't followed and the respect was no longer upheld. Tyg disagreed with that. It was his first act as Zaiem. To collect each Akhal-Teke that had been stolen from their lands a few Zaiems prior, no matter how many died in the process, or how much chaos was caused from doing so.

His insatiable hunger for control started his legend. And it wasn't only the Bahani who loathed him for it, it was every clan from Grandia to Ferack, Farit to even as far as Majinka. They all cursed his name. So he simply took most of them out.

That was also his first great mistake. He made enemies too quickly, allowed peace to fall apart. Hundreds of horses were captured. More than half of them died by the time they reached Grandia. The Bahani and Nevadems broke their siege against each other, not out of peace, but to try – and fail – to reclaim the golden horses for themselves. Their failed attempts only fueled an uncontrollable territory war.

Resentment festered, so much so that even the rest of the Jidaani were becoming unsettled. That's when Tyg began rewarding his clan with symbols of rank, to twist their minds further, to make it known to the rest of the continent that the Jidaani were no longer here to maintain peace. They were here to take. Tyg began awarding the horses as well. They were bred to hold no fear. They were bred for war. And back then, I wanted one more than anything.

The rarity of being rewarded with an Akhal-Teke of your own was enough to do whatever it took to earn one. There were only a few dozen left after all. I reveled in that motivation for a very long time. I held title after title, gained wealth, and power. I was given everything – except for the one thing I wanted most. Tyg knew it. He used that to his advantage.

But that was before I met Hisan.

The only foal to survive crossing the Dying Sea from a Mydiza cargo transport. He wasn't Akhal-Teke, he was something smaller, a foreign transplant on an unfamiliar continent. Like I had been.

I'd been hunting down my opium dealer in Mirit, chasing the costly mistake of trusting a captain with a larger shipment than usual and paying him handsomely in advance. Only to hear he vanished with my silver. And my product. My search led me to the far side of the docks, where I found a scrawny horse tied down in an empty stable. The sole survivor in a stock of twenty. Deemed diseased. Unsellable. Left alone to die. I felt an instant connection.

So, instead of tracking down the bastard who stole from me, I decided to sneak the foal out of his mold-soaked grave and brought him all the way back to Grandia. It took half a month to get there. Each day brought more fear that I would have to watch the poor thing die. By the Mystics' grace, he lived long enough to earn a name.

And I never dreamed of owning an Akhal-Teke again.

No wonder Hisan wandered off. He must have run the second he heard his former clan approaching. I don't blame him. As fearless as he is, he knows he doesn't compare to the breed's unnatural ruthlessness. That kind of killer instinct isn't born. It's beaten in, generation after generation. Fear is the Jidaani's greatest weapon when it comes to training, and I've never allowed him to know that kind of treatment.

Still, he could have at least warned me before taking off.

The sound of splashing echoes ahead. The men are in the river. They're searching it. Why? I exhale, wishing we had crossed it and just continued moving.

"Rahish said he was heading in this direction." Two voices carry over the stones. My spine aches at the mention of that name. Rahish is still alive. Tyg is in Kyr. They are in the same city – together.

"Tyg is only giving us until tomorrow night to get to the temple. We need to get back to camp." A breathy sigh. "He's probably long gone by now; you know Yoon is smarter than to stick around when he knows he's being hunted. He wouldn't have lasted this long otherwise." Another pause. "And I don't trust Sadirh with her for much longer."

Lee. I'd recognize that voice anywhere. Unnaturally throaty from all the honeyweed he smokes, carrying the slightest Mydizian trill. The man beside him says nothing, but I hear my old mentor answer a silent question.

"I know. Trust me, I know. But did Agai really deserve a better death than the one he got?" A hearty chuckle follows.

I feel no guilt for killing that would-be executioner. The only regret I have, if I can even call it that, is that his death confirmed my presence. I had been too cocky both inside and outside Kyr, waiting for Adessa to make up her mind when I should have just grabbed her and dealt with the consequences. Of course they knew I was there.

Tyg would have known right away after seeing Agai. A man his size would be impossible for someone to take down, unless that person knew certain techniques. Techniques that Tyg himself had once beaten into me to master a long time ago.

I shift to the problem at hand. At the mention of Sadirh.

Sadirh had been given a nickname early on. They called him The Crazed. I can only assume he's still living up to it. I thought it was a joke until I saw what he could do. He joined the clan only a few months prior to me – fleeing, and received his first mark in his second week. One of the first few to ever achieve that. Central to his forehead, that's where he chose to place it. Most likely meant to deter others from staring at his disfigured mouth.

I like to think it was to harden his false sense of entitlement. He's not someone I want to cross paths with. None of them are, really. But if Sadirh has been left to watch someone at their camp, it means he isn't defecting anymore – at least not yet. It makes me rethink the conversation I overheard earlier. They're bringing someone with them to the Sunce. An offering maybe?

Lee used to lead one of the more powerful branches of the clan before he retired from the outer flanks, what is he doing leading a scouting group to the temple? And who is this third man who's with them? I resist the urge to peek over the rubble. The desire to keep Adessa safe outweighs my curiosity.

"She will be fine. We have to keep her alive."

The hoarse whisper is nearly lost beneath the rush of water. It's too quiet to place. The only reason why I hear it at all is because they've finally stopped walking.

"No, I don't trust him. He wants to leave, remember? We need to return."

With a loud splash, the two depart, hoisting themselves on their beasts. Hooves pound against wet dirt as they head back the way they came. I can breathe again.

I glance at Adessa. She hasn't stirred. I press the back of my knuckles to her forehead, half-worried that she's no longer breathing. Just because I've managed never to succumb to infection, doesn't negate the fact that there's still a risk for her. She twitches in her sleep, seemingly gripped by her own dreams like I had been. But she isn't feverish. Maybe the tonic really is working.

I make a quick gesture of respect towards the sky, sending thanks to Chadron and wonder if I should wake her. Then, I see Hisan's silhouette in the distance.

"There you are."

Standing, I brush sand from my knees and slide my machete back into place. Hisan pads closer, pressing his muzzle against my palm, tilting his body towards the path the others took. I lift a finger to my lips, then point to Adessa. There's no need to wake her, not when this is the first real sleep she's had in days.

"I know you won't like what I'm thinking. But I'm curious."

Hisan grunts, shifting impatiently. He already knows what I'm planning.

I wrestle with the beige wool blanket on his saddle that had been given to me once in Dahue and drape it over Adessa. She stirs, but only to pull the fabric tighter over her shoulder. Hisan shakes his head as I mount him. I pat the space between his ears.

"Might as well keep her hidden, right?"

I linger for a moment, watching her, never entirely sure of any decisions I make.

Then, with a quiet click of my tongue, I accept that I won't be gone long. That she'll be okay.

THIRTY

YOON

"You will bleed for us."

Their tracks are too easy to follow.

Large hoofprints disrupt the riverbed's delicate curves, sending tiny sand peaks to spill into the water, making me stumble a bit when I leave Hisan's saddle to investigate. The tracks beckon me up a small dune, where the water cuts through and then down to the left into the valley below. A single tent peaks over the crest.

"Shit."

I glance back at Hisan, knowing full well that turning around would be the wiser choice. Sadly, I've already made up my mind. I need to know who their third is, and I need to know who they're dragging to the temple. I wave Hisan back. He whinnies at me, what I can only assume is his way of cursing me, knowing what I'm about to do. I motion for him to stay within whistle range, then lower to my knees, sliding carefully down the dune.

There isn't much cover. Only sparse cacti and the shadows cast by the stars. My camouflaged clothes are stained in blood. I know I stick out among the pale sand. I have to move quickly. I keep low, crawling at an angle toward their camp. As I close in, the quiet musings of

Jidaani float around me, beckoning me closer. I crouch behind a cluster of brush, scanning the small area. Two figures sit near a shallow fire pit, tossing in shavings of dry brush to keep the embers alive. The tent they've pitched doesn't look like it would hold all three of them. I know for a fact that Lee prefers sleeping out in the open anyways. The large obsidian Ramouz has been painted proudly on the back of the canvas.

Why are they heading to the Sunce?

Tyg never wanted war with them, he wanted their allegiance. And the King gave it to him willingly, as long as the Jidaani left his people alone. Tyg allowed it, mostly because the Sunce unsettled him. Who wouldn't be affected by a tribe like that?

Tyg has always been greedy, always vengeful, but outright war would cost him too much. The Jidaani were a First Clan. That meant something. It meant we – they – won every fight before it began. The Jidaani reputation alone was enough to keep the peace. Not out of respect, but out of fear. Tyg was a legend. Worshipped like the Mystics themselves.

For the last year, I thought I had been leading us away from that familiar danger. The Jidaani rarely went east. The Bahani had a reputation too, which did a good job at keeping the clan away. But it appears we've been on the same path all along. I'm honestly surprised I hadn't run into one of them sooner. Hopefully they don't have the nerve to cross the river yet. Jax probably crossed already. He knows not to take the bridge, so if we leave in the morning, we might be able to catch up to him.

From the corner of my eye, I catch something dark fluttering in the breeze. A strip of fabric, caught on the stake securing the bottom of the tent. I inch closer, watching the two by the fire, reaching blindly until my fingertips brush against it. Silk.

It's the girl's shawl. Embroidered with colorful flowers decorating the hem. I remember noticing the details back at Chadron's, wondering who Saedea might be since her shawl wasn't something you would find in the middle of the desert. My nails brush over a crusted patch. Blood. It's dried and flaking. I curse under my breath, rubbing it between my fingers.

Shoving the shawl into my pack, I flatten against the sand, concealed by the shadow of the tent. I'm close enough to hear soft cries coming from inside. Saedea has to be in there. Poor girl can't seem to catch a break. How did she get caught?

I sink lower, nearly on my belly as I duck around to the opposite side, peering around the curve. My hand instinctively moves to my dagger, but I don't unclip it yet. If I were alone, I'd leave confronting them to fate, trust my luck. But Adessa isn't far enough away. I can't risk getting caught right now.

Lee may be a washed-up soldier, his gut hanging over his belt, his spark for fighting etched in the leathery corners of his skin, but he's still a four-marked man. He belonged to one of the highest ranks awarded. Tyg respected him like his own brother. Killing *him* would have immediate consequences.

Sadirh's death though? I wouldn't lose sleep over it, nor would the rest of them. Unless his bloodlust has miraculously changed. It wasn't fear that others felt when he was around, it was more unease than anything. He's dangerous, especially if he gets to his bow. And then this mystery man, whoever he is... I have a few names floating around in my head as to who it might be, each one worse than the last.

Not to mention the horses. Monsters trained for war. Too smart for anyone's own good. The last thing I want is to be trampled by one of them.

The fabric of the tent rustles, pulling me from my restlessness. Someone steps out. I crane my neck, watching a thin, heavily veined man groan as he stretches his arms up, wandering a few steps towards the river's off-shoot. I press deeper into the brush.

His hair is mussed, covering much of that veiny sweat-slicked back, sparsely covered in pock marks from a disease that destroyed his home-land when he was a child. A story he rarely told. He was never one to boast about surviving the plague. Three gleaming marks on his bicep confirm my horror.

Neem.

Oh no.

My lunges squeeze, holding in air that I refuse to release while he unbuttons his pants and pisses into the sand. He hocks and spits into the wet patch, then wipes his mouth with his knuckles, frowning at his missing fingers.

The fingers I took from him. Rage coils when he turns towards the fire, scratching absentmindedly at the stubble on his cheek.

What in the Abyss is he doing here? I thought Tyg sent him to Majinka.

Sadirh's laugh directs me back to the present.

"That didn't take very long."

Neem kicks sand at him, spraying the fire, and them, with pellets. Sadirh is on his feet in an instant, blade drawn.

"That's enough, you two." Lee bellows, picking his teeth with a pinky nail.

My heart pounds as Neem dips his hands into the water, running damp fingers through his scraggly hair. Inside the tent, I hear Saedea shuffle.

This is impossible. I'm being stupid.

I'm insane to think I could help her. Not with Neem here. Not alone.

I start backing away, but then Neem stands. Something wet and crumpled dangles from his hand. He twists, silver teeth glinting.

"Lee."

The other two look at him, their expressions slowly brightening as Neem unfolds *my* bandana. He shakes it out and walks towards them, holding it out like a prize.

Shit. Shit. Shit.

"He is here."

The words slither from Neem's mouth right as I lurch to my feet.

No, no, no!

I bolt. Water splashes as my former trainee flies towards the center of the circle, collecting his weapons with a giddy, soul-ripping laugh. I whistle for Hisan, hearing the roars of tied up Akhal-Teke respond instead. They strain against their tethers. Tethers made of chains because they would break anything weaker than steel. I'm grateful for the fact that Lee decided to keep them tied.

The dune slips beneath my feet as I claw my way up, glancing over my shoulder to see chaos unfold. Lee struggles to untangle the horses, Sadirh kicks sand over their fire, plunging them entirely into darkness. I'm lucky Neem hasn't caught up to me yet, but he will.

I whistle again, crossing the mound. Hisan barrels towards me at full force, no doubt readying himself for whatever trouble I've trapped us in. I leap onto the saddle, ensuring all my weapons are in place. We take off right as I hear the spinning whorl of Neem's scythe.

"Go, Hisan!" I shout.

He rears, launching into a sprint.

A metallic shriek pierces the air, almost forcing me out of my seat. The sharp edge of Neem's blade rips open the side of my arm instead as it passes. I duck, knowing what's to come, barely dodging the Deathbringer's curve as it spins back around, aiming for me, recalling itself to its owner. Neem screams my name. He's faster than he was years ago. More confident. Stronger.

Hisan pushes himself, his controlled breathing is steady, every movement is calculated. We've trained countless times for moments like this. He knows we need to get back to Adessa. That we need to cross the river. My incredible horse glides across the sand, a bullet compared to the speed of the Akhal-Teke, who are weighed down with packed muscle. The first traces of abandoned stone rise ahead.

"Adessa!" I shout, flying from the saddle. She hasn't moved. She's still lying where I left her.

"Adessa!"

I toss my hand over her mouth, not wanting to give away our position if she screams. I block her instinctive punch with my other hand.

"Yoon?"

Her voice is groggy, muffled by my palm. Her eyes widen with alarm. Even though she quickly realizes that it's me, instead of relief, she chooses to fight. She struggles against me, trying to pry my hand from her. I remain strong, leaning in until my lips barely brush her ear.

"We need to move, now."

She stills instantly, allowing me to pull her onto her knees. She scans me quickly, squinting at the gash along my bicep. Her eyes dart up and down my body, as if afraid to find more wounds.

Why does she look at me like that?

I move to help her to her feet.

No.

The ground vibrates. The beat of hooves crashes through the quiet, too close. Too soon. Hisan snorts in warning, ready to bolt.

"Fuck, how did they get here so fast?"

"Yoon!" Lee calls out, gravel-thick and commanding. I peer over the stones. He's a hulking shadow against the pale morning light, weapon drawn, scanning the ruins. It's too late.

"Yoon!"

I yank Adessa further into the rubble, motioning for Hisan to leave us. He stomps his hooves, eyes flashing in protest, snorting at the golden warhorses that are not too far away. Thankfully, he takes off, unwilling to stand off against them. Slowly, I unclip my machete and hand it to the woman beside me. Then I draw my daggers, knuckles whitening around the bone hilts. My heart is racing, covering the sound of Lee's feet crunching the wet riverbed.

Where are the other two?

"What do we do?" Adessa whispers, her voice barely trembling. I wish I had an answer for her. I really wish I did. The truth knots in my gut. Neem and Sadirh wouldn't leave Lee alone. They're circling, waiting where I can't see them.

"I only wish to talk!" My former mentor shouts into the night.

I keep us hidden, weighing the consequences. If I kill Lee, Tyg will send everyone after me. *Everyone.* He hasn't done so yet, which is why

I've been able to get as far as I have. But if he sends *everyone*, I really don't know how I could evade death if my body were scattered along the desert. How would something like that even work?

I glance towards Hisan's tracks. His outline lingers on the ridge. There's still a chance Adessa can get away.

"Go to Hisan." I whisper. Her brows scrunch together, questioning my intentions. "Please."

A sharp inhale. She clenches the machete.

"Yoon! Come on, it's me!" Lee calls again. Baiting me. I peer over the ruins to see him scanning the space in front of him. The grip on his mace is relaxed, but I know better.

Then, a whisper of movement. Not Lee. It's too light. Too quick.

Neem.

He streaks across the ruins like a phantom, silent as a shadow. A tornado of death. He hurls himself at us. I shove Adessa aside right as Neem lunges. The Deathbringer is now attached to his back, he's chosen to fight with his clawed blades instead, slashing towards my throat. I barely get my daggers up in time. Sparks flash in the haze.

Neem grins, silver teeth flashing as he presses forward. I can feel the force of him, the raw strength that rides his strikes.

"Get to Hisan!" I roar, having difficulty finding my footing with the next swipe. The tip of one claw rips into my cheek.

"Go!" My order remains firm, longing for the hope that she actually listens to me.

THIRTY-ONE

ADESSA

"The Jidaani do not defend."

The tips of Yoon's daggers slice through the wiry creature on top of him, each movement deliberate. Concise. Yoon struggles to gain control, but the other man is too fluid, his body twists and shifts like a snake, never allowing Yoon the satisfaction of a full strike. I hurry to my feet. Now would be the perfect time to listen to him. To do exactly what he says. Hisan is *right* there, and now I finally have a weapon. This is the chance I've been waiting for.

"Ah, you found the Muhdam's bait!"

The heavier man by the river grins, his broad shoulders shaking with laughter, twirls his weapon – a mace – in slow, taunting circles. The whistling sound it produces makes it sound like the steel is screaming. The wind cuts into the silent night, surrounding itself in only that horrible noise. It prompts the snake to twist mid-fight, his slitted eyes locking onto me. A mistake.

Yoon takes advantage of the distraction. His dagger flashes, a quick, clean slice crosses the man's side. But he doesn't falter. He doesn't even flinch.

Did he even feel that?

The wiry man's fingers, tipped with gleaming metal talons, slash across Yoon's chest. The sickening sound of flesh splitting open is followed by a strangled, breathless curse. Yoon stumbles, gripping his chest, lifting his knees between them. He manages to kick the stranger off. The attacker hisses, pressing a thumb against the stretched gash along his ribs, smearing the blood along his bottom lip with slow, humored ease, allowing me to see that on that very hand, he only has his thumb and forefinger intact.

Yoon hurries to his feet, pressing on the claw marks torn into his chest, watching in horror when the skinny one quickly loses interest in him and begins running towards *me*. The maced man rushes forward, seizing the moment. He lunges and drives his fist into the back of Yoon's neck. Yoon drops to one knee with a choked sound. My breath catches in my throat.

I tear my gaze away, panicked. The snake is closing the distance. I raise my arm and hurl the machete.

It misses.

The blade clatters uselessly against stone. My attacker stops. His spine arches, body curling inward to let out a breathy, sadistic laugh. Then, he bends down, picks up the machete with his ruined hand, turns it over –

And tosses it back.

He's taunting you. Don't let him see you waver.

I've faced men like him before. Men who crave fear, who feed off of hesitation. But there's something very off about this one. Can't say I've ever confronted someone like him in my life. He hangs his arms loosely at his sides, his silver teeth gleaming as he gestures toward the fallen weapon.

"Pick it up." He looks delighted. He's absolutely toying with me.

"Don't!" I hear Yoon beg, muscling his own attacker. His opponent roars, swinging his screaming mace around and around into the air above his head.

"Yoon!" My cries are a desperate warning, to force Yoon to focus. Thankfully, he rolls out of the way in time, missing the blunted edge as it cracks against a pillar instead of him. Dust and debris explode, clouding the air.

The mace is already swinging again, gaining more traction. And this time, it connects. The crunch of bone doesn't go unnoticed when he lands a blow to Yoon's temple. He staggers, his body swaying. For a horrifying moment, I hold my breath, believing that he's dead, that he couldn't possibly survive an injury like that. Instead, I watch Yoon circle his head as he rises, grabbing for the assailant's shins. He forces the man to buckle backward as blood pours down the side of his face.

He's alive, but for how much longer?

"Come on." The skinny one purrs, almost as serpentine as his features. "Pick it up." The light catches his sharpened teeth. "Show me your value."

The handle is now too heavy in my hands. I see my fingertips tremble and hope that he doesn't. My body betrays me, the weight of the machete is suddenly foreign, belonging to someone else. Like I shouldn't be holding it at all. A crawl of terror climbs the back of my neck.

Show me your value.

The words bring an unwelcome knowing of my place in this world. An understanding that I've tried to be blind to, refusing to care. Either way, I still won't accept it. Another grunt sounds as Yoon crushes his boot into his opponent's nose. He's gained the upper hand.

"Where is Sadirh, Lee?" He demands, spitting blood from his mouth, his voice raw.

The man – Lee – sputters below him. In such a way that makes me all too aware that they know each other. He rubs the side of his head when he sits up, holding his palms up and out.

"Mystics' around, how can you be so *stupid*?" Lee tugs the red bandana from a watery pocket, the same one that I threw into the river before falling asleep. He tosses it back to Yoon. "You led us right to you!"

Yoon tilts a glance back to me as he catches it, with an unreadable expression, a soft heave of his chest.

"Ignore them."

The man with the missing fingers growls, snapping my attention back to my own threat. I hold the weapon out, the tip pointing towards him. He watches me with amusement. He hasn't moved while I've been distracted. He's been waiting patiently. If I wasn't so terrified, I would laugh at the blunt arrogance.

I'll use his cockiness to my advantage. He doesn't expect me to attack I surge forward.

The machete slices downward, carving into the edge of his tattooed arm. It catches on his bone. I can feel it when it slides inwards. I didn't go deep enough. I yank the blade free with a hard tug and fall back from the exertion.

His pupils flicker wildly between the wound and me, a breathless laugh catching in his throat. He didn't expect me to actually be capable of hurting him. I also didn't expect this reaction.

Blood spills freely, trailing down his forearm in gushes, dripping with a hiss into the sand. He stretches his shoulders and smiles at the wound.

"Good spot for it."

He cracks his neck. "I am going to enjoy you." His slithering tongue licks his lips, taking a single step in my direction.

A roar breaks our staring match. Yoon.

He and Lee are still locked in combat, but something has shifted. There's a hesitation in Yoon's stance, his daggers are tilted downward, his body coiling like he's fighting something more than the man below him. A moment of hesitation is all it takes. Lee strikes before Yoon does, spinning him onto his back.

"Hold it up again." The snake's voice is closer now.

"Leave her alone, Neem!"

Yoon shouts amongst the struggle, all too distracted with his own fight but not enough to know what's happening with mine. He's thrown backwards with a powerful kick to the stomach, sent sprawling into the wet sand at the edge of the river. The horses stomp violently at his closeness, their golden eyes flashing.

Neem takes another step, smearing the blood playfully down the length of his arm. He circles the deep, vertical gash I left behind.

"Try it again. I dare you."

I know better. I know that this is what he wants. But I raise the weapon anyway.

A steady beat of footsteps running over the pillar to our left breaks the tension between us. Yoon barrels into Neem's side, knocking him to the ground. Yoon grapples him, pinning his legs beneath his own.

Lee heaves himself up on straining knees, unable to catch up. He watches me from a distance as I point the tip of the machete in his direction. He raises his palms in defense, a show that doesn't seem very fitting for his type. Not with a mace like *that* in his hands. I don't trust it.

Yoon and Neem rip at each other's throats in a deadly rhythm, their movements controlled, almost like a dance. An onslaught of perfectly timed dodges and counters, as if they know each other's favorite moves. Like they've fought with each other before.

Until it no longer looks like a game.

Yoon drives his dagger into Neem's upper thigh, using the pain as a distraction to pry Neem's claws from the cuffed bracelet around his wrist, yanking it free and flinging it to the side. Neem snarls and rolls away, but the blade embedded in his muscle only buries itself deeper. Yoon is forced to release the handle but offers Neem no time to recover.

He spins, throwing his full weight into another attack. Neem seemed to anticipate it though, catching the tip in his full-fingered hand before it can carve into his throat. Then, with a vicious snarl, he slams his forehead upward, cracking Yoon's face, throwing him into a pile of broken rubble.

Neem grips the dagger in his leg. Yoon pushes himself up the moment Neem rips the blade out of his muscle and whips around.

I gasp when Neem plunges the entirety of the weapon into the back of Yoon's shoulder without hesitation, enough to make the half-blind man stagger forward, cursing. He twists with the strike, using the momentum to grab Neem by the neck with his injured arm. He shoves the snake to the ground, the impact kicking up spirals of sand. Yoon braces his knee against Neem's injured ribs, pressing the tip of his second dagger against the soft flesh of Neem's throat.

"Yoon!" I scream, noticing Neem try to pry the massive scythe from his back.

"Yoon! Stop!" The man I've been preventing from intervening bellows, matching my own concern, huffing to climb over the pillar at my side.

Yoon hesitates. *Why is he hesitating?*

Emotion flickers across his face. He's between decisions, when there should only be one made. One, singular swipe of his blade could end it all.

But he doesn't do it. He smashes his fist into Neem's temple instead. The man cries out, lunging for Yoon's throat, but Yoon shoves him back, staggering to his feet.

I finally grasp onto the courage I'd been feeling run its course and step between them, hovering the blade inches from the space between Neem's eyes. Yoon repositions himself at my side.

The bone dagger moves against his muscle with solidity. It's completely embedded into the back of his shoulder, the tip peeks through the loose fabric of his bloodstained shirt. Bright red drips from his fingertips, soaking the cuff of his sleeve. And yet, his expression remains cold, locked onto Neem with unreadable intent, not at all looking like someone who should be riddled with pain.

Neem watches us both, holding his bleeding wounds like they are nothing more than an inconvenience. "Interesting." Is all he says.

Yoon gestures for me to hand his machete back to him. Fat chance.

"Adessa." He murmurs, waving his fingers at my side. Again, I refuse. Yoon exhales harshly, his patience clearly thinning. Instead of grabbing it right from me like I expected him to, he throws his fingers up, whistling as loud as he can. It's a piercing, layered sound, different from the times I've heard it before. At first, I expect Hisan, but the answering call does not come from the desert.

It comes from the river. The two golden horses explode into motion, kicking up wet rock and sand as they charge toward us with blinding speed. Before I can react, Yoon latches onto my wrist. My grip loosens in my shock, and he takes advantage, prying the machete from my palm in one smooth motion. In an instant, he clips it to his back and yanks me backwards, maneuvering us over the broken stone remains, pushing us towards the river. Neem and Lee barely manage to avoid their own incoming horses, commanding them to stop charging, and failing. One of the beasts rams into Neem at full force, sending him flying.

But instead of fleeing, as any terrified animal would, the horse veers. Its muscles gleam, its hooves tear through the sand as it sprints – parallel to us.

"This way!" Yoon shouts, pulling me to the left along the bank. The wide river doesn't seem to be like something he wants to cross yet. His grip is ironclad, a lifeline dragging me forward even as my limbs scream in protest. My foot lands wrong – pain flares hot and immediate through my ankle, nearly making me collapse. But Yoon is there, a steady guide. Behind us, water erupts, hooves slamming into the shallows with terrifying force.

"They're going to get away!" I hear Neem screech somewhere off in the distance.

"Control your fucking horse, Neem!" Lee shouts back.

We tear past a jagged rock barrier, the pounding of hooves relentless. I risk a glance over my shoulder, breath catching at the sight of the monstrous stallion leaping across the slick, embedded rocks we'd just passed, its eyes locked onto us with a hunger that can't be natural.

Yoon hesitates. "Fuck." He snarls, throwing us fully into the middle of the river. The jagged ground is rough against my shoes, I can only imagine what it would feel like if Yoon hadn't given them to me.

The current pushes and pulls us, but Yoon is there helping me to stay balanced. He pushes us harder, each step draining. The horse stomps its feet.

"Trakal! Don't you dare!" Lee commands, his words punctuating our surroundings. For a moment, I think we'll be alright. The horse is listening to his master.

The second we step on the other side of the bank, my gut flips. Yoon whirls his head back.

"No."

The horse places a hoof in the water, then another, until it's fully emerged into the river.

"Trakal!"

Lee is ignored. The horse gains steady movement. Yoon groans.

"The valley." His chin bobs towards the dip. It doesn't look very much like a valley to me from this angle, more so a cliff. He hurries us to the edge. The horse has made it to the other side, shaking the water from his coat. He surges forward, shaking the ground beneath his hooves.

Yoon doesn't hesitate. In one brutal motion, he shoves me down. I hit the bottom of the ravine, hard, and he follows as the horse's snapping teeth tear through the air where we'd been standing. Yoon crashes beside me into a thick grove of cactus brush. He's immediately on his feet, baring his teeth while he slides his machete free from its clip.

The horse skids to a stop, unwilling to make the leap down to us, stomping its hooves in agitation. It paces, unsettled, tossing its head back as if something ahead is repelling it.

"Come on." Yoon extends his hand without looking, inviting me to take it. This time, I do, willingly. When he grips my waist and helps me to my feet, I force myself not to put too much weight against his injured arm. The horse flares its nostrils when Yoon leads me down the valley. The fact that the beast is unwilling to follow sends a different kind of fear through me. It's not like the drop was far enough to intimidate a creature like that.

What's stopping it?

Yoon whistles for his horse, the tune familiar this time. His eyes flick over the empty horizon, scanning, searching, then without another word, he pulls me into an outcropping of ash trees. "We can't let them see us." He whispers.

The moment we're hidden from the view of the small cliff, he presses me tight against the rough bark, his arms caging me, one hand curled protectively along the hilt of his blade. His breath is warm and ragged against my temple, his heartbeat a rapid drum against my ribs. The scent of sweat, blood and earth mixes, enough to make me dizzy. I shift, attempting to create some space, but he holds firm, listening.

I strain to hear what he does, some whisper of movement, some clue that they've followed. The valley is eerily silent.

"Your injuries will slow you down!" Neem's voice rings out, his frustration as harsh as the whistling sound his scythe makes as it spins.

"They can't cross." Yoon murmurs against my hair.

I don't understand. Why wouldn't they be able to?

"You know you aren't safe there either!" Neem laughs, slicing his weapon through the air in warning. But even with the threat thick between us, they don't cross, just like Yoon said. Lee and Neem both stand in a line at the edge of the valley, alongside a very unsettled horse that's at least twice the size of Hisan.

"Don't you think of it, Neem! You know what will happen!" Lee warns, his tone taut with something much more than anger.

I tilt my head up, searching Yoon's expression. He leans his head back, forehead slick with sweat. I can't tell the damage to his temple; there's too much blood. It creeps into his blinded eye, watering in tear tracks down his cheek.

The snake cackles. "You know you aren't allowed in there!"

"Let it go. You're losing too much blood."

"I want to send his head back!" Neem hisses.

"We cannot risk it!" A pause. "Oh, don't look at me like that."

Yoon doesn't move. I feel his muscles tighten where he's still bracing me.

"You know what he's capable of. We would never catch up!"

"We almost did!" Neem snorts.

"Listen to me, listen to me! We'll send word back. We have to follow our own orders!" Lee spits. "It is out of our hands!"

Neem curses, spitting loudly into the valley.

Their departure is marked by the pounding of hooves that sound further and further away. We hear the distant splashing of water. They must have crossed the river. Yoon waits. And waits. For what feels like an eternity.

Finally, he releases me from him, falling to his knees. He shudders, hanging his head low. I step away from the tree, trying to give him some air, to cleanse myself from the heaviness of it all.

"You were going to take Neem on all by yourself." Something like a laugh scrapes its way up his throat.

Defensive, I plant my hands on my hips. "So?" I try to play off the terror still clawing at my insides.

Show me your value.

Neem's words echo, an ugly reminder of what he thought of me.

Another ragged breath. Yoon shifts, attempting to stand. Instinctively, I reach for him. I don't know why. I immediately regret it when his gaze sweeps mine. He clears his throat, wiping his dew-beaded forehead. Thankfully, it's still fairly dark outside. Hopefully he can't see the concern written all over my face.

"What did you mean when you said they couldn't cross?"

I'm distracting myself from the blatant energy that consumes me with his look. The tear I feel in my chest at the sight of the dagger in his arm, the torn, bloody shirt. His gouged temple.

He doesn't answer. Instead, he smiles faintly. Avoiding my question, he latches onto the handle of the lodged dagger and rips it free in one swift motion before I can even think to stop him.

"What in the Abyss are you doing!?"

Unbothered, he meticulously wipes both sides of the blade clean with the bottom corner of his already soaked shirt, then clips it in the empty spot along his hip. Blood spills in thick pulses, spreading across the length of his back. Dripping past his naked fingers. A deepening pool of burgundy forms in the pockets of sand at his side. I nearly pass out.

I find myself frantically tearing the scarf from my neck, kneeling be-side him, looping it up and around his shoulder, tightening it as fast as I can to prevent him from bleeding out. It's going to be useless. There's too much blood. But I have to do something, anything to stop it from flowing.

"Do you have a death wish or something? Why would you do that?" I try to suppress the panic, the sheer anger that he would do some-thing so stupid! He needs a healer. Now. And there isn't one. I'll be left alone out here, in a territory that even those terrifying mem were unwilling to cross into. Does that mean something worse is out here?

"Where – where is the t-tonic?" I stammer, looping the fabric around and around, tying it off with more force than I intend. He grunts.

"I'll be fine." The words slur at the edges. He uses his uninjured arm to quickly dig a shallow hole in the sand, then another, a few marks behind it. He glances up at the tree above us, pointing to the gnarled, low hanging branches.

"We need kindling."

"You mean to start a fire? Now?"

"Don't really have much of a choice." He pauses, watching my features twist. "They're gone. They won't waste time waiting for us."

I hesitate. Not because I don't believe him, but because there are a hundred questions burning on my tongue. *They knew you.* I swallow them down, knowing now isn't the time. Every second he loses blood, the closer I am to being stranded out here by myself. I don't even know where Hisan went. So, I grab one of the branches, using my weight to snap the brittle arms free. I crack a few over my knee and toss them to him.

He shoves them into the larger hole, then pulls flint-stone from his pocket, followed by a rough-edged piece of steel and a scrap of charred leather.

"You're going to bleed out."

"I will if you keep wishing for it."

His mouth quirks in dry humor, his brows dotted with the kind of resilience only someone who's endured agony a hundred times over can wear with familiarity.

My vision wavers. I don't know why I feel so weak at the thought of him... dying.

There's too much blood! I can't stop it! I think that's my own voice throwing the words at me over and over.

"Adessa?"

The tone snaps me from my trance, from seeing images of his un-moving body trapped beneath me, images that I don't recognize but somehow know –

"Adessa." He repeats, softer this time.

I blink hard, forcing my vision to clear, and meet his gaze. Brighter now. The weight pressing my lungs loosens slightly.

"This is nothing. Okay?" He traces his finger on my knuckles. When did my hand start to hold his? "Can you light this?"

Resting his injured arm along his thigh, he hands me the flint and steel. For a moment, that sarcastic mask he always wears slips, revealing the flicker of vulnerability lurking underneath. The guarded pain he keeps so well hidden. It startles me. I stare into his blinded eye, realizing just how similar we may be, hiding the full breadth of our nightmares behind a steady shield.

I say nothing, striking the steel against the flint. Sparks dance to-wards the leather square. I strike again until one catches, curling into a tiny, delicate flame. I blow gently along its edge before tucking it into the pit. Smoke rises, but not in a way that would give our location away. The second hole, dug right behind the first, feeds the fire a steady current of air, keeping the flames hot, but the smoke contained.

It's the kind of fire I watched them all build as Saedea and I were their captives. It's not a fire meant for warmth. I wish I had known this technique earlier. It would have helped in the times I didn't want others to find my camp. Which was always. Maybe it would have prevented me from being discovered outside of Er Rada.

Yoon peels the blood-soaked shirt from his body, up and over his head. The claw marks scream, bleeding into the angles of his stomach. I resist the urge to scan the rest of him. He straightens, placing the machete's blade into the fire. The steel rests directly on top. We watch the metal heat. Seconds stretch agonizingly slowly while we both wait for the inevitable. He's planning to seal his wound.

Without warning, and seemingly without a second thought, Yoon grips the hilt, closes his eyes and presses the hot steel against the front of his shoulder, over the three-finger wide slit. His skin hisses, burning on contact.

I recoil, the sour scent of charred flesh and metallic air floats around us like ichor. Yoon growls through gritted teeth, his body rigid with pain. When he finally peels the blade away, a thin layer of skin comes with it. He exhales slowly, eyes half-lidded, placing the blade back into the flames.

Yoon matches my stricken stare. I allow myself to inspect what had been left behind. It appears to be completely sealed. The skin now turning a bright pink, preparing to blister. A new pain in its place. I track the rest of his skin, his neck, his chest. There are plenty of other scars running down his body, old injuries. Blood covers a lot of the expanse, but I can still see many raised scars building from his collarbone, down his sides, parts of his arms.

There aren't any of the markings I'm looking for though.

Not wanting to make it seem like I'm examining him, I absentmindedly add more wood to the fire, watching the embers pop and glow. Yoon reaches for the handle once more, lifting his good arm up, repositioning it over the torn flesh on his back. I see his throat work around a loud swallow while he blindly angles the hot steel.

I stop him before I realize what I'm doing. My hands cradle his elbow.

"I'll do it."

He releases a sigh of relief. The machete is in my hands before I can second-guess myself. I place it back into the fire to reheat, using the moment to avoid his stare.

I adjust my posture.

Yoon braces, his hands buried in the ground.

I hover the hot metal above the wound. Steady my stance. My free hand grips his bicep, anchoring us to each other.

"Don't tell me wh –"

His words die in his throat when I press the red-hot blade against his open wound, listening to it hiss, trying not to purge the contents of my empty stomach from the sight and smell. Yoon trembles, fisting the sand around him, but makes no sound. I hold firm, counting to five – just as he had – then peel the blade away. Cooked skin clings to the steel.

"I have to admit." He grits through his teeth when I finally release my hold on his arm. He leans his head back against the tree. "I half expected you to stab me with that."

I hand back the machete on my own accord.

"Trust me, I thought about it." I reply meekly, crouching in front of him.

"Thank you." He gives me a lopsided grin. "For not turning on me."

Vulnerability seeps into the wound that has been throbbing in my chest since I met him. I lift a single finger in response, mimicking the teasing game he'd played with me as we were escaping Kyr.

Yoon lets out a breath of laughter, his smile widening while he smacks my hands away. "So, she *does* have a sense of humor."

I suppress my own smile, refusing to let him see the – security I'm feeling. It's stupid, reckless. He could be dead within days, depending on how his injuries choose to heal. It's best not to feel this way. Still, I can't help but be grateful.

I didn't turn on him. And he hasn't turned on me either.

Then, my gaze catches the burst of blood on his temple, and whatever warmth I felt vanishes. I frown. He's lost too much blood. I push the half-empty waterskin into his hands, urging him to drink.

"It's best we save it."

"We can refill it; the river isn't too far away."

All he does is hum, closing his eyes. The wounds on his chest ooze. They look deep.

"I – I don't have the tonic."

He left it with me before I fell asleep. Which means it's across the river.

"Do you need it?"

I nearly choke on his words.

"You do."

A scoff. The fire crackles softly, shifting in the silence around us. Its embers dim, pulsing, like a dying heartbeat. The smoke begins to thin out, whispering into the empty air. Something about the stillness around us feels *wrong*.

Yoon leans forward, clipping his weapon back into place, grunting when he stands. I watch him from my kneeling position on the ground. He kicks sand over the flames, smothering them with practiced ease. "That was exciting." He dusts his hands off.

"Exci- " I would scream if not for the finger Yoon suddenly presses to my lips when I stand along with him.

"Just because *they* couldn't cross doesn't mean *we* could either."

What could he possibly mean by that?

Suddenly, everything doesn't feel safe. There's too much emptiness, too much – death – around us. The plants have no life. There's no movement. The wind doesn't even make a sound. I nod silently, wondering where we are. The river is *right there*, why is this land not fertile? I swallow hard and out of habit, twist my ring.

The ring.

It's... gone.

"No, no, no!" I drop to the ground with a frantic whisper, sifting desperately through the sand. "Where is it?"

"What?" Yoon leans forward, barely able to mask the pain as he does so. "Your ring?"

I ignore him, my fingers clawing through the earth. It had survived *everything*. The fights, the falls, the blood – and now, it's gone.

The machete.

I must have lost it when I threw that damned machete.

"Is it important to you?"

The question makes me frown. At him. At myself. I've already deemed the stupid thing important. So much so that I'm allowing panic to crawl into my bones. It doesn't feel logical. I didn't feel like this when I lost my compass. Why am I so upset over losing something that was never mine to begin with?

Yoon watches me closely, my lack of response giving him enough of an answer.

"Well, let's go back and look for it."

"It'll be impossible to find. We'll waste too much time." The sand, the attack, it would be buried deep by now.

"There's no use in not trying. We have to find Hisan anyways."

The wet, blistering mess on his shoulder is another reason to go back. For the tonic. *That's* why we should turn around. Not for a silly circle of jade.

"Come on, we shouldn't stay here any longer."

"Why couldn't those men cross?" I ask, navigating around the dead cactus as Yoon scans the slope ahead. We'll have to climb it if we want to get to the river. I don't know how he'll manage in the state he's in.

"Technically no one from the outside is *really* allowed in Bahani lands anymore."

"They knew you, Yoon."

What clan do you belong to?

"Everyone knows me, remember?"

I search his naked back, only seeing old scars and blood. Still, not the markings that I'm looking for. I decide to pry more. Wondering if he'll tell me the truth.

"They had the same markings. The ones Aol and Burke have."

He stops, tilting his chin towards me, opening his mouth, ready to spew another lie about who he is, but instead, he wraps his hands around my shoulders.

I push against him.

"Interesting." He murmurs, eyes wide. That motivates me to match his stare, twisting around to face the area we just walked away from.

There's a raven. Perched on the branch of the dead ash tree. Its claws click along the wood, the nub of the branch I tore off for the fire. Its body twitches, jerky movements as its line of sight follows us.

"That's odd." Yoon states, striding towards it. I fall into a step beside him, peering up.

"There's something in its beak." Whatever it is, glints as the raven squawks, bobbing its head up and down.

Your palms.

A cold sensation prickles my spine alongside a voice in my mind that doesn't belong to me. I think I've heard this voice before, but it's too warped to place. Is it the raven who's speaking to me? I look up as it sears its beady gaze into me.

Open them.

I don't think. I obey.

Fingers unfurl, palms facing upward, opening to the bird. It hops at the very end of the branch, dropping something small and hard into my waiting hand. I stare, stunned.

"That's impossible."

The jade ring glows dully in the moonlight. My grip tightens around it, making sure it's real. I glance up, pulse hammering. The raven watches, dark eyes blinking once. Twice. Its chattering call shivers through me, and somehow the meaning presses into my skull.

Do not lose it again.

My body drops.

"Adessa!" I hear Yoon call out, fading with the light. Swirls of darkness consume me, dragging me into the unknown.

THIRTY-TWO

ADESSA

"In the Time Before, the Mystics were believed to be good. Who can blame them now for their retaliation?" – Excerpt from *The Script*, The Hidra, creation unknown.

Adessa.

The silken hum of my name, no louder than a breath of wind, calls out to me.

Adessa.

The brightness sears through my closed lids, dragging me unwillingly into consciousness. I open my eyes.

Snow.

Blinding, endless white stretches in every direction. A ridge looms above me, crowned in ice. The wind howls mercilessly. The stolen wardrobe of a brother long gone still clings to my starving body. It does nothing against the cold. The impossible cold.

I shudder, smoky breath pluming into the frozen air.

I was in the desert. I was just in the desert.

Adessa.

The voice – a woman's voice – fills the entire sky. It's honey-sweet, caressing my skin tenderly, but the underlying tone does nothing to warm me. I resist feeling comforted by it. The humming that accompanies my name carries itself along the breeze, crafted by it.

I hurry to my feet, scanning the landscape, searching for the owner of the voice, for anything to make sense.

I know this place. The Far North looms in terrible familiarity. The jagged peaks, the cavernous mouths of tunnels that stand ominously behind the frozen fishing lake that I now stand on. I know this place.

I lived here once. I suffered here. I survived here.

Adessa.

"What!" The scream rips from me, raw and pleading.

Good. You're awake.

Lightning scars the mountainside, echoing off its face, rolling thunder through my bones, vibrating through my feet. The ice shifts below me.

"T-Tirma?"

I see her. She's standing across from me, on the other side of the frozen lake, motionless. *What is she doing?*

Her gray hair whips around her face, hiding her features, but I know it's her. I wave my hands, frantically trying to get her attention.

"Tirma!"

She doesn't look at me. She's looking up. The sky twists above her, swirling clouds thick with something I can't name. The wind carries whispers – no, hymns. I soon realize that she's the one who's chanting them. She raises her hands to the sky like I've seen her do countless times. She's dressed in her prayer robes. The ones she only wore when she sought counsel from the Mystics. Her skinning knife is at her side. She –

"No!" I plead, tears burning my eyes. "Tirma!"

I watch in abject horror as my friend, my poor, confused friend, slices her wrists, offering her blood to the sky. It spills down the length of her arms in dark, gleaming rivets, soaking into the pristine white of her robes.

Her head tilts back, her lips part. The sky answers.

The ice beneath me wails, the crack splitting into the lake, racing toward me at unnatural speed.

"This isn't real!" I sob, staggering back, the harsh storm biting into my exposed skin. It freezes my tears.

Are you sure?

I tear my eyes from the woman who I no longer recognize and break out into a sprint. Not towards her. I wouldn't be able to reach her in time anyway. She collapses into the snow with another crack of lightning.

My canvas shoes slip against the frozen water, making it all the more difficult to gain traction. I don't have time to take them off. The icy ridge begins to collapse, chunks of mountain crash into the lake, forcing more breaks to splinter in my direction.

The ground beneath my feet buckles, the world tilts violently.

My feet leave the solid ground.

And then, I'm falling.

I scream as I plummet, clawing at the ice, catching the edge of a newly formed crevice at the last moment. My body swings over the abyss, feet kicking against empty air. The void below is waiting for me.

I dangle there, tightening my hold, nails digging into the ice until they splinter. Until I feel them break. The pain is distant, drowned out by methodical footsteps crunching against the snow. For a moment, my desperate, twisted prayers hope that it's Tirma, alive and well.

"Help me!" I beg, frozen fingers losing feeling against the ice. I can't lift myself up over the ledge, my arms are far too weak.

Are you serious?

Squinting, I watch in terror as the tips of claws stretch overhead. They connect to veiny human hands. Their sinewy fingers end in jagged talons, latching onto the backs of my wrists.

What is this?

The creature asks, the words repeating on the surface of the abyss below me over and over again until the sound makes me sick.

"No!" I thrash, the claws tighten, they swipe at my thumb, tearing skin as they try to pry my ring from me.

This is MINE.

The deafening screech is nearly too much to bear. I pull and pull, agony bursting as the claws leave deep, bloody lines in my hands. My free hand grips the edge but my strength is failing. I can't hold on.

"This is not real!" I whimper, watching the talons feel around for me again. The creature above laughs, no longer rosined with honey. It's laughing at me. One by one, its talons find me again. They begin peeling my fingers from the only surface that's keeping me from falling into the void.

This is not real! It mimics, fake-weeping, taunting.

Fear glides across me the moment I realize the last of my fingers is being ripped away from the ledge. I plummet. The fall is endless. Filled with that of my nightmares.

Of Tirma.

Of my parents.

Of the Lapis.

Of revenge.

My back collides with the ground. The impact jars me, knocking the air from my lungs. Something soft has broken my fall. It isn't ice. In fact, there is no ice. There is no snow. Above me, the Far North has disappeared. I'm no longer inside the crevice, but the chill hasn't left my bones.

My vision alters, the gray sky overhead darkening, the sun covered with a putrid smoke that seizes the air entirely. I blink at my surroundings, my hand searching for any clue as to what I landed on. I'm in an open field. I rise into a seated position.

Corpses. I'm surrounded by bodies. A field of them. Hundreds of them, scattered across the landscape.

My hand pats loosely at the solid object beneath me with a new kind of unease. It's clear what I've landed on. I graze metal, leather, flesh. I close my eyes, unwilling to see who it belongs to and scramble to stand, feet slipping, sinking into the dead. A sharp pain in my stomach jars me when I step onto something hard. A head. The sickening crunch makes me gag.

"Where –" My words splinter into choking horror.

The air is thick with the stench of burning, the sky suffocated by black. Red-hot fire crawls hungrily along the edges of a battlefield, devouring everything in its wake. I have never seen anything as terrible as this.

Overhead, birds screech, watching me with beady black eyes as they wheel through ash and dust. I twist and follow where they're heading – it must be towards safety –

I stop in my tracks, wincing. Feeling emotions that can't possibly wholly be my own. I want to become one of the bodies beneath my feet. I want to die. I want him to die. The anger, the sadness, is almost too much to carry.

"No. It's not you. It can't be you. This isn't real." My words are strangled as I take in the figure ahead of me.

Yoon.

He stands among the corpses, unmoving. Dressed in black leather armor from head to toe, a uniform, it seems. Not his sand-colored attire that I'm so used to seeing him wear. The outfit is fitted closely to him, with open sleeves that show clear, unmarked skin beneath. A golden scarf is fashioned in a band around his head, stark against his hair, now cropped short.

In this dream world, he has both of his eyes intact, as he did in my last nightmare. The sight unsettles me, but not nearly as much as the blade in his hand. I recognize it. A broadsword. An iron hilt with a dark blue stone centering it. An image of death paints my mind. The blade ominously drips crimson onto the lifeless bodies below, as though he alone is responsible for this massacre.

I don't dare call out to him. If anything, I crouch lower, trying to blend in. He is too busy scanning the landscape with something dangerously close to satisfaction. Victory paints his expression. And when he finally turns his gaze to me – he looks through me.

Time stops.

He takes my standstill as an opportunity, raising his blade like a trained assassin. He rushes for me. I barely drop in time, the edge missing me by mere inches. But he wasn't aiming for me.

A wet, gurgling sound chokes behind me.

I turn just in time to watch a man collapse, a man whose face flickers in and out of my memory like an illusion within this nightmare. Yoon's blade has torn his throat open. A river of blood rushes forth, spilling over the mound of bodies, pooling in the crevices of rocks disguised as human heads.

Above us, the birds swoop, their black wings blot the sky, circling around and around like omens. Yoon gazes up at them, as if something inside him is trying to wake.

Then, his gaze finally locks onto mine.

Is there recognition there?

"Yoon." I speak his name quietly, unsure of myself.

The sky crackles with an energy that buzzes all around us. It's so hard to swallow. It's so hard to keep myself from crumbling to my knees. Is it because of my fear?

Yoon tilts his head, expressionless. A warning pulses through me – sharp and shrill like the laughter of the birds overhead. I reach for the nearest weapon, wrenching it from the person who had it last. I lift it high, steadying my grip.

If I have to kill him, I will.

The moment never comes. I'm too late.

Yoon's sword carves through me before I even have the chance to defend myself. I crumple to the ground, shocked, open-mouthed, attempting to speak but blood fills my throat, drowning me out.

Yoon watches my life begin to drain.

"Yoon."

He can't hear me. I know he can't. His brows furrow, suddenly questioning. The sword in his hand drops. I watch as he falls to his knees, his own neck splitting open with an invisible blade.

The circle of birds breaks apart. I can see them clearly now. They're not just any group of birds, they're ravens. Their bodies plummet like falling stars, joining me in a death that feels inevitable, unworthy, deserved.

The last thing I see is Yoon reaching for me.

THIRTY-THREE

ADESSA

"Do not be afraid of death. Be afraid of repeating."

"Adessa!"

My name. I'm so *tired* of hearing my name.

The ghost of torment splinters me in half, like the blade that went through my chest. I can't allow myself to open my eyes. I can't trust that I'm back in my body.

All I feel is agony. An old wound festering somewhere deep inside me. I don't recognize it. Heartbreak. Betrayal. Relief. My body shakes, sobbing with a grief that doesn't feel like mine, yet I know it belongs to me.

Large hands tighten around me. Claws dig in – I rear back, fighting against the creature holding onto me. It shouts at me. It uses my name again. I kick at it, desperate to be released, hearing a grunt follow when my foot hits its mark. My eyelids flutter open. Bright morning sunlight seeps in through the mouth of a cave.

The Far North.

No, no, no! My voice is my own. I wait for a haunting echo that never comes.

My fingers scramble to feel the bodies beneath me, but I find nothing but a scratchy, worn mat. I could almost convince myself I'm still lying in the ice and snow, if not for the rough stone surrounding me. Or the grit of sand clinging to my sweat-drenched skin. And the canvas shoes that feel too tight, too warm on my feet.

"You nearly broke my ribs!"

The voice isn't syrupy sweet. It isn't filled with an anger that makes my spine grow cold. A small laugh follows; light, amused. I blink, clearing my head. There's only one person in the world who would find a situation like this funny. Wherever I am, Yoon is here with me.

Not the one who didn't recognize me. Not the one who has killed me twice now in my dreams. I sit up, my heart racing as I watch him rub his side with a sneaky grin.

"I couldn't wake you."

I do my best to ignore the concern in his mellow tone. Anxiously feeling for the jade around my thumb. It's there. The claws weren't successful in taking it. Yoon crawls closer to me, apparently deeming it safe to do so.

"One hell of a nightmare."

I flinch at his words, shaking my fear of dream-him away. I've never truly been *afraid* of this man. Not even when I witnessed him killing others with ease, not even when he refuses not to share his secrets. He has a right to them, as I do with mine.

He retracts the hand he probably meant to hold out in comfort, and busies himself with unclipping his waterskin instead. He holds it out to me. I don't take it. I'm too distracted by the fire at the mouth of the cave. The smoke smells different, herbal. It reminds me of Chadron.

"Where are we?" My voice sounds strange to me, unfamiliar. It weighs thousands on my tongue. "How long was I out?"

Long enough for him to drag me here. Long enough for the morning to come.

"Not too long." He sighs, rubbing the back of his neck, looking so... lost. "I wasn't sure what else to do. I had to find somewhere to hide us while I waited for you to wake up."

I rub my hands against my arms, still feeling the chill of my homeland kiss the bare skin. My fingertips are numb, as though they actually had been clinging to ice.

"Why does the fire smell like that?"

I point to the bundle of herbs roasting in the flames. It isn't the buried fire that he favors. This one looks like it was built in a hurry.

"Oh." He waves his fingers towards it. "Wishful thinking."

"What do you mean by that?"

"Only that –" He pauses, stumbling as if he's trying to find something that fits. "I thought it would help wake you. I have nightmares too."

What is he trying to do? Relate to me? Of course a man like him is haunted by nightmares. I can only imagine they're a result of all the horrible things he's done in the name of his 'trade.'

"Usually the same one on repeat. I see it all as a raven though, which helps me realize it's not –" He casts a sideways glance towards me. "What?"

I must look stunned.

"A raven?"

"Yeah. Why?" *Is he serious?*

"Don't you think it's strange that a *raven* just so happened to give me back my missing ring?" *Does he not grasp how strange that coincidence is?*

"I don't see the connection you're trying to make. There are a lot of ravens on these lands. The Bahani own them." He leans in, pupil narrowing. "We're in their territory."

"Yes, but –" I stop myself.

"Maybe the raven knew it was important to you." His voice softens with the slightest hint of fondness for the idea. "They're much smarter than we've been led to believe." He straightens, his gaze flickering to my face. "Why do you look upset?"

"It's – nothing." I stammer, shying back into the cool, stone wall. We're at the same distance we had been when he killed me.

"It's not nothing. I couldn't wake you up. I thought you were dying from all the noise you were making."

I can feel my bones aching under the weight of the words I've been holding back.

"I – I was." I don't stop the silent sob that racks my insides.

"What?"

"I –"

Maybe it's because of my survival instincts, maybe it's because I've been so alone. For so long. Whatever the reason is, I feel like I need to tell him. I have to let this fear out.

"I was back in my homeland. Skeall. It's very far from here." I pause. "I saw –"

I can't bring myself to say Tirma's name, refusing the knowledge that she was even there. That she sacrificed herself.

She sacrificed herself.

"There was a storm, the ice cracked and I fell through the ground."

The reality threatens tears. I hold them in. Yoon shifts closer to me. His presence doesn't repel me like it should. Clove and cinnamon ride the edge of the herbs roasting out front.

"I don't know where I landed. Somewhere I've never been before. And – surrounded by bodies. There were birds circling above. Like the one on the ash tree. I think they were trying to get my attention."

I swallow loudly, watching Yoon's face. The color seems to drain from his cheeks. His expression turns blank, gaze fixed on me.

"And then I was –" The words are sticky in my throat. I desperately want to find the right way to say it, but I don't know how. "In my night-mare, you were there. You –"

"I, what?" He asks gently, clearly noticing my wet eyes, lifting his hand but resisting the urge to brush the sweat-lined hair from my face.

"You killed me."

He recoils instantly, as if I've just burned him. His warmth slowly fades.

"This isn't the first time I've dreamt of something like this. It's happened once before. In Chadron's hut."

"I –" He stands abruptly, moving to the opposite side of the cave. Away from me. I rub my eyes with the back of my hand, suddenly feeling exposed. Unwelcome.

"It was only a nightmare."

"Only a nightmare." I repeat his words, trying to convince myself too. Wishing I could forget it and knowing I can't. I can tell he's trying to level his breathing.

"The Mystics will grant you visions. One day, you will see."

I should have listened better; I should have paid attention to what Tirma would tell me. She would ramble on and on for days on end. I would try so hard to shut her out, to stop her from prophesizing my life. Her words creep back slowly, a fresh wound of memories spilling into my mind. Although it's still unwanted, perhaps now more than ever, I should try to understand.

"Dreams are not just dreams. Nightmares are real."

"Adessa." He says my name carefully, forcing me to look back to him. He says nothing more, only holds his head in his hand, a pained look writing his features. It's almost like he said my name not to speak to me, but to himself.

I push myself up and inch towards him, wondering if his injuries are causing him the agony I see in his expression. "Are you alright?" I ask, taking another step.

"Yes." He finally says, wavering only slightly. I wish there was something I could say to erase that distraught look he wears. It's an emotion I'm not used to seeing on him. My sight wanders to his temple. A normal person couldn't handle a blow like that to the head. He must really be struggling.

"Did you grab the tonic? Did you go back to the river?"

"No."

Why not?

"Don't you have that other vial with you? The one you used after we left Kyr?" That one was different. Maybe it was only meant to manage pain, but that's exactly what he needs right now. His pack is on the ground beside me, within an arm's length. I want to show him that I won't hold the dream version of him over his head. That I'll do what I can to help him, like he's done for me.

Trusting each other is a two-sided coin.

I have to keep him alive. I have to convince him to bring me along with him to Mirit. That's the only way things will work in my favor. I'll be one step closer to Darde. And for that, I'll do anything.

He snaps himself out of whatever trance has a hold over him when I make a move for his bag.

"Don't worry about –"

My hand skims the mouth of the pack, feeling something soft inside. Silk? Fingers clench as I pull the fabric free. An embroidered scarf spills into my lap.

It's... a scarf. *Her* scarf. The one that I had prayed – no, begged – to see wrapped around the head of the girl I still hope is alive. Yoon has it.

"This is Saedea's." My body sways. "Where did you find this?"

She had been wearing it the last time I saw her. Does that mean Yoon's known her fate this entire time? We looked for her in the Underground, did he know that she wouldn't be there? Is that why –

I spin around to face him, clutching the fabric like it's the only thing tethering me to reality. "Please tell me you weren't hiding this from me."

I take a trembling step toward him. Not one filled with fear. One that's filled entirely with rage. "How long have you had this?"

He doesn't move. He watches me like I'll set him on fire any moment. Like I will be his end. Good. He should be worried.

"I didn't want to –"

"Didn't want to, what? Tell me that you knew where she was? Did you do something to her?"

The trust, the fragile, painstakingly built trust that I had been trying to form with this man completely washes itself away in the blink of an eye.

His promise to take me to Jynn. Was it meant to be a distraction? Was that all a lie too?

"You acted like you actually wanted to –" I let out a bitter, humorless laugh, my thoughts tearing me to shreds. "Mystics' around, you really made me believe –"

The sadness turns to anger so quickly, my vision blurs with it.

"Adessa." He says, very calmly, still unmoving from his position against the cavern wall. His hands are raised as if I'm a bull ready to charge.

"Don't you dare use my name!" My voice cracks, fueling the fire burning bright within me. "Where is she? Where is Saedea?"

"Please! They will hear you!"

His voice breaks too, raw with something that almost sounds like despair. The words hit me. I blink, my pulse pounding between my ears. *They?*

Where are we? Where has he taken me? I take a half-step back, my grip tightening around the scarf. "Another trap, huh?"

"No!"

I don't believe him. Not anymore.

"Is she dead? Did you kill her? Sell her?"

"How could you accuse me of that?" He drops to his knees, painfully stabbing my heart with his desperation. "I know you're angry with me, but please, you have to be quiet."

"You're just trying to keep me from ripping you apart."

"No. I'm trying to keep you alive."

JJ Laflin

THIRTY-FOUR

YOON

"Ashwau will burn for this."

I've made a mistake.

A huge mistake.

The fire in her tear-filled eyes tells me as much. She doesn't understand. How could she? I didn't have time to tell her I found Saedea; we were too busy being attacked. And after – well, I suppose I should have mentioned seeing her, but I didn't want to change the growing dynamic between us. It was selfish of me to do so.

She didn't leave.

She even made a joke about not turning against me. For one single, blaring moment, I was entirely present. I saw the trust she had given me. It was a gift. One I hadn't realized I'd been longing for.

The look she gives me now expands the hole in my heart. I can't ignore the intense disappointment I feel in myself for allowing this to happen. When she collapsed earlier, the only thing I could think about was her safety. We'd just crossed into Bahani lands. And we were nowhere near the safety of the Saddlebacks at the time. We were too exposed. I had no choice. But I couldn't get us away as quickly as I wanted. The ring had been lying in the dirt beside her. Something told me that I couldn't let her lose it a second time. It seemed to be important to her, and the raven seemed to think so too.

I will never forget the myths of the ravens. Stories that kept me awake as a boy, training to be stronger than I should ever have had to be. The Bahani revered them, believing they held the essence of the Mystics. That they were something to be feared. Something to be praised.

So, with that superstition lining my thoughts, I picked the jade ring from the ground, intending to pocket it for safekeeping. I didn't know it wouldn't allow me to release it. Not until it was satisfied with what it would show me.

The vision she described moments ago – I saw the same one. She experienced the same nightmare I have always been poisoned with, only this time, *she* was inside it. And I – who had never been wholly myself in these dreams, was the one to kill her. I watched myself strike her. I watched her body fall to the corpse-riddled ground.

I was *conscious*. I was in my physical body. Trapped. Unable to stop myself from my own actions, even though on the inside, I was *dying*. I was screaming, pleading with whoever would be listening, for my hands to drop the sword. But they didn't hear me. They didn't help. It wasn't *me* who cut through her. It wasn't me who made her bleed. But yet, in a terrible, horrible way, it was. And I couldn't do anything but watch.

When she fell, I felt my own chest rip open. An invisible wound bursting with the regret of conjuring up something so unimaginable. Guilt pouring from my eyes for what I had done to this woman. Death spilling from my neck. It all felt so real. I could hear my mother shouting, as she did in each one of my nightmares. I smelt the fire that had been burning everything around us to ash. And that raven – that damned bird – landed on Adessa's unmoving body, fixated on me with its vexing glare, inspecting me as I fell to my knees.

Roaring with hatred that I'd felt for myself, confusion for why the dream I've dreamt hundreds of times suddenly twisted itself into my worst nightmare. Emotions I haven't felt in a very long time drowned out everything around me. I've never dreamt of my own death before. Never believed it would ever be possible. And now, I can't stop thinking about it. I can't help but know what will now lead me to my death. It will be her.

When she confessed that I was the one who caused her nightmares to end in death, I finally realized that I've been riding solely on the fact that I need to keep her alive. Even if my physical body refuses to fail in this life, if she ever died... I can't stop thinking about what would happen to my own reality. Now that I have found her, it isn't a life that I would want to be a part of without her.

When I woke up, it was still dark. I didn't know how long the vision had lasted; didn't know how long we'd been left exposed. She was still unconscious. I searched desperately for a sign that she was still breathing, hoping that my nightmare wasn't true. The raven hadn't left us. It clicked its head towards Adessa, directing my attention to the ring. It was wrapped around her thumb, as though it had always been there.

Thankfully, Hisan had been willing to cross the river on his own, finding us in the valley, knowing we needed to leave. Half-filled with shock, the other with sickening worry, I watched the raven screech at me to move. It flew from the ground, heading in a direction that I didn't want to go. I wanted to cross to the other side of the river, head further south, cross when the mountains were more in view. But no, the raven continued to make noise until I gave in. Who was I to deny the warnings of a Bahani superstition? I couldn't test our fates in a moment like that.

So, I obeyed, draping Adessa over Hisan's saddle, allowing the bird to guide us deeper into the edge of the Dead Lands than I was mentally prepared to go. Adessa refused to wake when I moved her into the cave, believing that even though we weren't completely immersed in the mountains, we were at least within that realm. Believing that the raven knew where it was taking us, that it would be somewhere safe. I built the fire all too quickly, threw the protective herbs I'd bought long ago into the flames to keep the Bahani away. An old wives' tale perhaps, but I wasn't in the mood to gamble.

She'd been shivering too violently. I wondered for hours if it was because of a fever. Maybe I messed up her stitches, maybe infection was going to take her from me. And then she was screaming. Her dreams were tormenting her and I had to listen in agonizing silence, knowing that *they could hear us.*

The reality of it all crashed around me at the sound of her rage when she found Saedea's scarf. Not only had I betrayed her in my vision, in her own nightmare, but I had in real life as well. I've been betraying her with my secrets this entire time and it's finally catching up to me.

But what am I supposed to do?

If I tell her everything, there won't be room for even a flicker of trust. Not that there is now. But if I tell her what I know she wants to hear, if I say the words without a chance to explain myself, explain that I no longer wish to be that person – I'll lose everything.

If I tell her about my plans in Darde – I'll lose everything.

Maybe I was never meant to gain her trust. No version of this ends with her looking at me the way I wish she would.

And that's why I've chosen to lie.

Her gaze flicks to my blades. She's thinking about killing me. I don't blame her. I have half a mind to let her try. But I know that when she realizes she can't it'll only terrify her more. And then how could I ever bring her back?

"Where is she? I know you know where she is." She repeats, this time, as a whisper, heading my warnings. "Do not lie to me, Yoon." Emerald blazes into me.

"They're heading north."

"North?" She stiffens. "What do you mean, *they?*

I swallow, catching my bearings.

"Answer me, Yoon or I swear I will find a way to kill you!"

I can't avoid her questions for much longer. If they haven't heard us already, they surely have now. We'll be trapped in here if they find us, and I can't drag her out of this cave without giving her a good reason to follow me. If I break what little hope remains, she'll never believe my intentions again.

Keep her close.

Chadron's warning rings in my head, but it doesn't matter. If she finds out what I am – if she realizes I'm Jidaari... keeping her close will be impossible. Lucky for me, she hasn't seen my markings, she hasn't been able to confirm her theories yet. I can use that in my favor.

"Those men. The ones who came after us. They have her."

She leans in, listening intently with her arms crossed.

"While you were asleep, I heard them searching the river. I assumed they came from Kyr, maybe one of the lords told them the direction we were headed in. Thankfully, they didn't look very hard, so they didn't see us while you were asleep. When they gave up, they went back to their camp. I followed them because I thought I'd be able to take them out quietly, so no one would bother us while we crossed, just in case."

She tilts her head. "Then why did you lead them right to us?"

I know she's wondering why I didn't end up killing them, she's seen my abilities. I'm sure she realized Neem and Lee had markings as well, I know that she's connecting those pieces together. It will all lead to me eventually. Regardless of my dishonest answers.

"It was an accident." I grit out. My thoughts are scrambled, I can barely keep the lies straight.

"So what happened then, when you got to their camp?" She lifts the scarf, the fabric trembling in her grasp.

"I found that. I knew it belonged to Saedea." I don't let my gaze wander from hers. "I found Saedea too."

I try to take a step forward, but she bares her teeth.

"She's alive. I heard her in their tent."

Adessa doesn't blink. Doesn't breathe.

Please believe me. I'm telling you the truth.

"I wanted to do something. I really did. But then Neem found my bandana in the river, and I knew I only had seconds to run. I couldn't take them on all at once."

I wince, my temple throbbing as the hole begins to heal. I'm thankful I've replaced my blood-stained shirt with a new one from Hisan's saddlebag, otherwise she would see that my chest wound is healing too. My shoulder, however, might need more time. The nausea returns, a dizziness I haven't felt in a while grows as my skin warms.

"Please believe me when I say that I was going to tell you. I just –"

"You said north. How do you know where they're going?"

I can't help but glow at how steadfast she is, regardless of if it's bad for me or not. No wonder she's gotten this far across the continent on her own. And to come all the way from the Far North too. I wonder what motivated her to do so. I have to reel myself back. I won't be able to find out anything about her if she isn't around to tell me herself.

"Because you helped them take her and now you regret it?"

Her voice is laced with betrayal. The weight of it presses against my chest. I can't help but feel saddened by the fact that she thinks I would do something like that. The accusation stings more than I expected.

"No, of course not." I meet her glare, willing her to believe me. I need her to believe me. "In Kyr, when I was looking for you, I overheard a conversation involving the temple. That's how I know where they're going."

She squints. "And how do *they* know *you*?"

Lie, you need to lie.

"I've traded with them before. That's how I know about Kyr, that's how I know about the market there, and that's how they know about me."

She doesn't believe me. I see it in the way her face drops, in the way she looks at my daggers again. "And this temple, is north."

"Yes. There's only one temple on the continent, and that's in Sunce territory. Which is north of here."

"Of course you know where it is." The bitterness in her tone is a blade, sliding clean between my ribs. I let it pass through me. "Let me guess, you traded with them before too."

"I've actually never been there." *Mystics' around, I can't stop myself from spewing more lies.* "I only know its location. All merchants do. To avoid it. They formed after the Cull but were never granted -"

I stop myself. She doesn't care about any of this. I'm only filling the space, trying to fix something that cannot be fixed with words that mean nothing.

"Why would they be bringing her there?"

She has to already know the answer to that. The reason why anyone would meet a fate like being taken against their will in this unforgiving world.

"Maybe she's meant to be a gift. Just in case they need one. Please lower your voice."

"Just in case, what?"

Was that movement behind us?

I look to the back of the cave. I searched some parts of it before settling down to wait for Adessa to wake, but the tunnel systems in the Barrens are legendary. I couldn't possibly search each one. Still, Bahani don't usually wander this close to the mountain...

"Yoon."

I nod, clearing my throat, redirecting my attention to the problem I've created.

"I heard them mention something about a new King, back in Kyr. They were going there to negotiate with him." *Still, not entirely a lie.* "Saedea might be used as a way for them to convince him to agree in their favor. It happens all the time in these areas."

"You sure know a lot about their plans."

There it is again. The accusation. The knowing. Maybe she's never believed a word I've said to her. I was a fool to think the warmth she had shown me meant anything.

"What will this new King do with her?" She loops Saedea's shawl around her neck, tying a loose knot, a determined glaze in her expression.

"Nothing. I'll stop them."

The words leave my mouth before I have a chance to process them. I bite my tongue, wishing I could take them back. But then, she seems to relax a bit. It's very subtle, but her shoulders don't seem so rigid, her brows rest instead of raise... it wasn't a part of my plans to go after Saedea. Maybe, in a way, that's why I wanted to keep the knowledge of her shawl a secret.

But now, I have no other choice. The only problem is that I'm running on borrowed time. With Burke, Aol and Gunn on their way to Jynn, I can only hope that Jax isn't too far behind. At least he'll be able to buy us some time. Going to the Sunce will add at least two extra days of riding. I'll deal with the consequences later.

"You'll stop them." She snorts, pulling out her map. "Here. Show me where this Sunce temple is."

I stiffen, knowing her intentions. She plans to go after her. All of my wishes to keep Adessa safe, vanish right in front of me. She's too stubborn to understand how bringing her along would be a bad idea. But there's nowhere safe for her to wait until I'm able to bring Saedea back. She'll put up a fight if I try to force her somewhere else. She'll run if I leave her in Idane. She'll have to come with me.

"Adessa –" Still, it doesn't stop me from trying to convince her otherwise.

"Show me where it is."

The parchment slams into my chest. I hesitate, but there's no way out of this.

"Here."

I point to an area across from The Barrens, opposite the river.

"It's somewhere around here. Ad –"

She glares at me. For using her name in the way that I do. I stop myself, swallowing the instinct to plead. If I push too hard, she'll run.

"You have to understand how dangerous this will be. Neem –"

"The one with the scythe." She states it like a fact, brushing ash along the area I showed her.

I nod. "Yes. And the other one, Lee. There's a third, but he must have stayed back with Saedea when they attacked us." I pause. "You've seen what those two are capable of, his skills are very much the same. They nicknamed him The Crazed, if that gives you any –"

"Mystics' around! Just admit it!"

She furrows her brow, rolling the map up, tapping it against her palm.

"They are not traders. *You* are not a trader!'

The words land harder than they should. Why did I have to continue explaining?

I don't want to tell her. I can't.

THIRTY-FIVE

ADESSA

"Even the greatest of leaders can make the poorest decisions."

"I *was*, but -"

The man standing before me shifts his gaze to the ground. Yoon, the one who I'd seen slit two men's throats with ease, who took down a giant without breaking a sweat and then laughed about it afterward. The one who is standing right in front of me with a hole in the side of his head, who acted like sealing his shoulder shut was merely an inconvenience because doing so left us out in the open. The one who says he isn't a bounty, that he doesn't belong to a clan. Yet everything points to that being a lie. Is he finally going to admit that he's been lying?

"I was also more than that. Much more."

"Was?" I repeat, interested in his use of the past tense.

"Yes."

His sights are back on me. Burning me. I wish I could read the look on his face. Neem. Lee. Their fighting styles, like they've fought many times in their lives. How Lee spoke to him. How Yoon *listened*.

He – is – them.

Jidaani. Jidaani. The name blares in alarm.

"Show me your markings." I let the words tumble from my lips one by one. "I know you have them. The others do."

Jidaani. Jidaani.

That's what he is. I need to hear him say it. I don't know why, maybe it will make me feel better. It won't make me trust him; it will actually do the opposite. But I'd rather face the truth than be fed another dishonest word, another excuse meant to soften the weight of what he's done in the name of a clan.

He doesn't answer. He seems to be listening keenly to something at the back of the cave. Turned away from me. Ignoring me again.

Fine. I'll force him to confess.

I pinch myself to be brave, wrist snapping forward. Straight for the machete at his back. I've watched him unclip it enough times to know how it works. I learned it for a moment like this. A single latch on the left side, near the base of his neck. Pull upward, release the blade. The golden handle is between my fingers in seconds.

That gets his attention.

A glimmer of curiosity flickers across his face. Or is it fear?

He reacts fast. Way too fast. He twists his torso before I can drive the blade into him. The machete's tip slams into stone instead. The force jerks me backward. He takes advantage of it, wrestling me to the ground. I'm not strong enough to fight against him when he shoves the weapon aside, kicking it out of reach when I lunge for it again.

"What are you trying to accomplish?" His fingers hold my wrists together. "Fighting me isn't going to..."

His voice tapers off. We both freeze, hearing the sound of scraping coming from the back of the cave.

"Shit."

Yoon moves first, latching onto my waist, plucking me from the dirt and heaving me up over his shoulder in a way no man in his condition should be capable of doing. I flail, but his grip is unbreakable. He snatches his bag from the ground and runs for the entrance.

"Hisan!"

The horse is immediately at our side. I kick and scream for him to release me, lift my head – and stop breathing. A pair of *glowing* red eyes peers out from the cave's darkness. We'd been standing right there only moments ago.

Another set appears when he throws me onto the saddle.

A third as he lifts himself up behind me.

I don't fight him anymore when the horse moves, knowing that the threat at my back is easier to handle than whatever is inside that cave. Whatever they are, they don't step into the light. They don't follow. But they watch.

"What in the Abyss are those things!" I yell, watching the desert whirl past us.

"Bahani."

Yoon digs his heels into Hisan's sides, his focus locked on the desert ahead. Every rough landing forces him to grimace, but he doesn't slow.

"Bahani?" I've heard that word many times over the last few days. The whispers of warning around the name from the mouths of everyone who has said them. Including those in the Blood Market. I remember the fear on everyone's faces when the slave runners led three of them into the Underground.

"We have to get to the other side of the river. We have to get rid of the scent."

Hisan barrels into the valley. The familiar slope calls to us, guiding us to the water. Hisan's hooves are in the river moments later. I look over my shoulder to Yoon, who scans the surrounding area.

"Do you think your clan is still here?"

"No. They'll follow their orders." He continues to search, leading Hisan through the current. "It isn't them I'm worried about right now." I feel him straighten behind me.

Got you.

"They're not my clan." He responds, slowly. Quietly.

"Whatever you say." I snarl back. "Head north." I say, looking towards the sun that is rising to my left. Which means we aren't heading in the direction that I now need to go.

"Don't think I forgot about Saedea."

"What?" His spine stiffens further.

"You heard me. Either take me there yourself or drop me off nearby."

"Out of the question." He scoffs.

"Fine." I make a move to leap from the saddle. The water will be refreshing anyway.

Yoon reacts instantly, gripping me to his chest. "What do you want me to do, Adessa? My machete is back there! You want me to take on an entire temple tribe and a *clan* by myself, with only two daggers?"

"Then point me in the right direction if you're so scared!"

"No!"

"You do not get to hold me hostage just because you deem me incapable of fending for myself!"

"That's not what it is!"

Hisan charges forward, his hooves barely skimming the jagged river rocks.

"I am not leaving her there!" I shout, thrashing against him.

"You don't understand!" His voice is desperate now. "We have to get –"

"No!" Red-hot anger blisters my skin. I know I'm not thinking clearly, but I can't help it. I refuse to leave her behind, especially now that I know she'll more than likely be dead if I do. I can't allow that. And the *last* thing I want to be doing right now is riding with a *Jidaani* who has a bounty on his head.

"These people aren't like the ones you've encountered before. Please understand! You may think that you can fight them. But even I know that I can't. We need a plan. I don't know if I can sneak in there. I've never been inside those walls before, this isn't like Kyr!"

I grit my teeth and swing my leg over the saddle. "I'll find her without you."

"You're missing the point!"

He growls in frustration, his strength pinning me in place. I feel the shudder in his muscles, the pain laced into every movement. Good.

"You want to face off against Neem again? You want to go into a territory ran by a tribe who has never been titled? Who has never been respected by others because of what they *do?* You think you'll make it out alive?"

"Nothing you say will change my mind! Let me go!"

"I can't!" He holds me steady while I rock back and forth. I'll throw myself into those rocks, I don't care. "What are you doing? There are Bahani around!"

I throw my elbow back, my aim sharp, unrelenting. I hit him right where I mean to, directly into the wound on his temple. Yoon's body jolts, a strangled groan rips from his throat. Hisan bucks beneath us, wild and furious with the chaos on his back. The world tilts.

The impact is hard, violent. I land on Yoon's chest, driving the breath from his lungs in a single, gasping wheeze as water rushes around us.

The air is warm, but I feel cold. Not from the water. From hatred. For him. For myself. I roll off of him, choking on my own breath, my body screaming in agony. My starving limbs, my sunburnt skin. The fact that I have no control over what is happening in my life. Everything weighs its heavy burden down around me as I sit in the river.

I don't move. I don't fight. I just sit there, trembling. *What am I doing?*

"Mystics, why!" Yoon groans, dragging himself upright, his head lolling side to side in a dizzy stretch. I stare at the water, too exhausted to answer. Too empty to care. My throat tightens while I silently beg myself not to cry. Not to give in to that weakness. I've always let my anger rule me. I never think. I only react, over and over again, leading myself into places I can't escape. Places like this. I clutch my arms around my ribs, shivering. I don't care how Yoon plans to punish me. Let him leave me here for all I care.

Let him hate me.

"She's just a kid." I whisper.

Water splashes beside me, indicating Yoon's finally on his feet. He could end this now. He could leave me here in the river, try to slit my throat, let the water wash away any evidence. I'd wake up eventually, then I'd be free of him too.

"It's my fault she's even mixed up in this." I continue, my thoughts unraveling. "If I'd realized she was following me –"

The words catch at the bottom of my throat. I can feel it leaking out of me; the guilt, the knowing. There's nothing I can do to make this right. I went from wishing for death to knowing I deserve it. It didn't take me very long to sink this low.

Now that I know she's alive...

Fuck Darde.

Fuck the Lapis.

I have to find her.

I hear Hisan trot back to us, shaking off his own frustrations with a sharp snort. I scowl at him for throwing us off, then direct my attention to Yoon. His hooded eyes betray him. I can feel something pained radiating from his look. Not because of his injuries, but because of whatever torment he holds within himself. The weight of what he chooses not to say. It's there, buried deep, but there all the same.

"I have to find her." I repeat, this time, aloud. "Even if I have to do it alone."

"You couldn't possibly know what you're asking of me."

"I'm not asking you to do anything. Show me where they've taken her and go on your merry way."

His exhale is daggered. "You can't be serious."

"I am going to the Sunce with or without you. Either way, the choice is your own." I straighten, feeling my limbs protest as I rise from the water.

A flicker of hesitation waits for me when I stand. Then, the worried crease between his brows deepens.

"If that's where you're going, then it's where I go too."

THIRTY-SIX

YOON

"The Mystics care not for us. Our fates are ours alone. Abandon each other and we will perish as a race." – 49th law of the one of the First Clans, Bahani. 1 T.A

"Is that Jax?"

Adessa's voice cuts through the silence in my head. I've been busy watching the desert, tracking each step forward, knowing it's bringing us closer to a place I don't want to cross into. The river is far behind us now, I can no longer hear the current. My throat feels raw, each swallow like shards of glass. Still, I need to conserve our water, I don't know when we'll find more. We're wandering into unfamiliar territory.

For a moment, I think Adessa's seeing a mirage. Her dehydrated mind could be playing tricks on her, as mine has been doing. But Hisan sees him too. My horse picks up speed, ears pricking toward his beloved Tagan, who stomps impatiently beside her master.

"Jax!"

I call out to him, feeling gratitude surge through me. He kneels in the sand, examining the same tracks I've been following. Relief rises first—but it's fleeting. It curdles into sorrow the moment I realize what his presence truly means. He's supposed to be heading to Jynn. He's supposed to be dealing with the problems I've unknowingly created.

"Yoon?" Jax answers back in disbelief, brushing his hands along his pants with a clap.

His grin brightens. Too bright for the dark circles under his eyes. When we reach him and Tagan, I jump from the saddle and smack him on the back. His gaze flickers over me.

"You changed shirts." He squints, inspecting the bloody mess on my temple. "Shit man, what happened to you?"

Then, he turns to Adessa. She shifts down from the saddle, attempting to use Hisan as a shield. My horse refuses, maintaining a petty amount of distance. Holding a grudge more than likely. I pull a sugarcane rod from my bag and shove it into her hand.

"What happened to *both* of you?"

"Got side-tracked." I mutter, hearing Adessa yelp as Hisan snaps at her fingers, greedily.

"Clearly." Jax snorts, brushing sand from his knee. I eye his own fresh injury. A dirtied bandage is wrapped around his arm, the cloth, stained pink.

"What happened to you?"

"Got – side-tracked." He says with a wink. "Those fucking Muhdams. Didn't know someone gave them access to bullets."

He slaps his arm with a grimace. "They never had any of those before you know who gave them..." His eyes shift back to Adessa. "Anyways, don't worry, the bullet went clean through."

I frown. Not because of the fact that Jax hinted towards *Tyg* being the one to give the Muhdams bullets, which will be a question for another time. I frown because he's not supposed to be *here*.

"You're supposed to be going to Jynn."

His smirk falters. "Ah." He throws a jeweled hand toward the wasteland. "That was the plan, wasn't it." His foot stirs the sand. "We barely made it out of Kyr. Every exit was blocked, thanks to *someone*. The alarms went off before Tagan and I were out of the city."

My chest tightens.

"We had to go *through.*" He lowers his voice and leans in. "They have explosives, those bastards." He wobbles back on his heels while my eyes squeeze with guilt at his admission.

"Couldn't find the camel. She must have run off. We had to lay low for a bit. Tagan was whipped in the stables. I had to tend to her."

My gaze drifts to the silver clay on her haunches.

"I did plan to head east. Really did. But then I saw these tracks and I thought I should follow them for a bit. I thought *you* would be heading to Jynn by now."

Adessa moves from her spot, relinquishing the last of the sugarcane from her hands.

"What tracks?" She asks, squinting at the divots in the sand. I'm not surprised she hasn't been paying attention to the tracks that *we* have been following as well, seeing how she barely remembers to cover up her own.

Jax hesitates. He must be remembering our last conversation. To be discreet. My secrets won't be kept for much longer anyway; Adessa is already too smart for my own good. I tip my head towards her, giving him silent acknowledgment. It's too late to try to hide anything more.

"Akhal-Teke. See how much larger they are than Tagan and Hisan's?"

"The golden horses."

Jax nods with twisted concern. Then, his face falls. "I see you've already had a run-in with them. That's Saedea's."

He points to the shawl around Adessa's neck. She closes the distance, desperation lining her posture.

"Did you see her?" I know she needs more reassurance that she's alive besides my words telling her she is.

"No. But if they're heading where I think they're heading, they'll keep her alive." My stomach sinks with understanding. "Do you know who has her?"

I hang my head, unwilling to share.

"They went by the names of Neem and Lee. And another one." Adessa turns in my direction and thumbs toward me. "He called him The Crazed."

Mystics I wish she didn't remember any of that.

Jax breathes in deeply, thoroughly disturbed by the sound of their names.

"Just them?"

I scoff, crossing my arms. *Just them.*

"Well, I suppose that's manageable."

"It is?" Adessa shoots me a daggered sneer. I turn to her in defense.

"Don't you see how well armed he is? Maybe if I still had my *machete* I wouldn't have told you no so easily!"

That's a lie, and we both know it. I still would have tried everything I could to keep her from wanting to go after Saedea.

"They saw you. That's how she knows their names?"

I nod, face tilting to the sky. Jax brushes against me again, voice low. "You healing okay?"

The burns on my shoulder pulse in response. "All but this one. But it went clean through."

Jax doesn't know the full extent of my healing, but he's known me as Jidaani for most of our lives. Which led us into many circumstances that put our lives at risk. And with that, came the knowledge that death didn't quite care for me.

Tyg knew it too. That was always my fear. That he would keep testing me. Pushing, prodding, until he proved something to himself. Something I didn't even understand.

"You know where they're heading?" I ask, hoping I won't have to break the news to him.

"I was planning to keep it a surprise for myself, but I have some theories."

Adessa clears her throat, impatience riding her movements. She pulls the map from her pocket and points to the area smudged with ash.

We watch Jax's expression fall. "You're sure?"

Adessa and I both nod.

He curses, spitting into the sand. "Well, that doesn't sound right."

"I heard them talking about it in Kyr. They've been ordered to go there."

He closes his eyes. "Well then it makes sense that they're bringing explosives."

A chill slides down my spine. "What are they bringing?" I ask, dumbfounded.

"The copper-wired boxes."

"The temple." The realization crackles through me like lightning, overwhelming in its weight. "That's impossible, that would be a breach in the contracts of the Firsts. He can't do that."

Jax picks at the wrapping around his arm. "I think Tyg believes he can get away with anything now."

"What does that mean?" Adessa cuts through the tension. "I've heard that name – Tyg. Who is he?"

"I'll tell you on the way." I beckon for her to mount Hisan again. "We need to keep moving before it gets dark."

Begrudgingly, she listens. I know she'll be waiting for my eventual answer. I plan to make her wait.

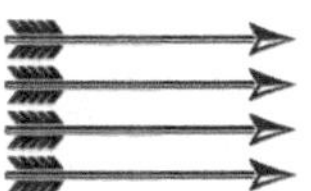

Jax rides alongside us, keeping his focus trained on the crater ahead, its jagged edge darkened by the sinking sun. The ancient cliffs surrounding us have crumbled with time, their edges fraying from centuries of a war that had nearly brought the world to its end. We navigate around it carefully, adjusting our path to avoid the slopes. My mind has been elsewhere; thankfully Jax's voice has been a welcome distraction, filling the silence with stories and exaggerated tales to keep Adessa from asking the questions we both don't want to answer.

He takes a moment to drink from his waterskin, leaving room for Adessa to take full advantage of the silence. She clears her throat, for the fifth time. I won't be able to stall any longer.

"Yes?" I ask, already regretting it. I nearly think Jax paused on purpose.

"What were you two talking about earlier? About the temple. And Tyg."

Jax smirks, turning his head away when he catches me silently begging him to distract her.

"I don't know how you heard that name." My fingernails dent the skin of my palms.

"I do. From the guards in Kyr. From that giant you killed. They all made it seem like he knew *you* too."

Lie. Lie. Lie.

"We can talk about the temple." I pivot, keeping my tone neutral, anticipating her to fight me on it. She doesn't. I wonder what she's thinking.

"Go on then." She tilts her chin slightly, challenging. "What is *Tyg* planning to do to the temple? What contract would that be breaching?"

My jaw tightens.

Why does she have to remember all of that?

I know deep down that she hasn't forgotten our conversation in the cave either.

I sigh, adjusting my spine. "I'll preface this by saying that what I'm about to tell you is common knowledge on the continent."

That's half-truth. The clans know. The people in their territories don't care enough to understand what holds their world together. But she doesn't need to realize that.

"During the Cull, when the world was burning, the First Clans rose from the chaos. In the Time After, they solidified into three ruling clans: The Jidaani, Bahani, and Nevadems."

I don't wait for her to confirm whether or not she knows this.

"There were other tribes that existed, of course, but the First Clans controlled the territories. The Sunce was one of those other tribes, but because of their – beliefs – they weren't allowed to expand. They weren't allowed to make decisions for the territory either. Same with the Muhdams. Their First Lord was insane. No one trusted him with land, so he built his city to keep everyone else out. Until his offspring eventually wanted to become merchants, formed the Blood Market, then the trade routes, but still, they were never granted allowance as one of the Firsts, so they were still unable to make territory decisions."

I try to peek around her to see her reaction. "No one has told you any of this?"

She shakes her head, searching. I push away the frustration I'm beginning to feel. She's traveled the entire continent without understanding what's at stake?

"Keep going." She prods. I suck in a breath.
"The Sunce have always had some land, for their temple and their people, to the north. Near The Barrens. Their temple has stood since the Cull, a relic of the old world. The First Clans made a pact. That no tribe within their territories would be threatened, no matter their beliefs. No one would stoop as low as the Elites once had. No war like before would ever happen again. Everyone agreed. They all gathered, they all signed a contract. And that contract lasted for generations."

"But you said territories were shifted. The Reversal." Her mind works quickly, gathering everything I've told her since.

Jax pulls Tagan back into step with us. "The Reversal was caused by the Jidaani. Their Zai –"

I clear my throat, a warning. Jax cuts himself off immediately. I can nearly hear Adessa rolling her eyes.

"I've already connected the markings I saw in Kyr to the Jidaani. And I already know that the men who have Saedea belong to them." She glares at Jax. "Burke and Aol too. Anything you want to tell me, Jax?"

He raises his brows, grinning as he shakes his head, throwing me a knowing look. I wish I could be anywhere but here right now.

"Tyg is Jidaani. I know that too. He must be their leader. Zaiem."
"Yes." I mumble.
"Your leader." She accuses.

"No."

I try to deflect, pushing Hisan into a trot. "We need to start looking for a place to camp before nightfall."

"Camp? No. We have to get there now."

Good, maybe I've distracted her.

"I know you don't want to wait, but it's not smart –"

"Need I remind you what happened the last time you chose rest over speed?"

I watch Jax's shoulder heave. He's enjoying this.

I ignore him. "We won't make it to the temple before them. They had a head start." My voice remains calm, steady, not wanting to spook her. "Saedea's life depends on us getting in there unseen. If we can. We need a strategy."

"But –"

"Believe me, they'll keep her alive. They have to. We'll get as close to the temple as we can. At dawn, we'll scout the area to get a better understanding of what we're working with. We need clear minds for this."

She doesn't answer, but I feel the tension in her shoulders ease slightly. At least she isn't about to swing at me.

"Your horses are faster than theirs. If we actually tried, don't you think we could catch up to them *before* they get to the temple?"

She's not letting this go easily. She's clearly blinded with the need to find Saedea. I can't say I blame her.

"If they realize we're tracking them, they will kill her. I promise you. Then they'll kill us."

"Three on three. Seems like good odds."

A strange heat sparks in my chest. Her confidence is maddening. Is she not afraid of anything?

"What if you're wrong?" She continues to challenge me. "What if they already killed her? She doesn't make being held hostage easy either, you remember."

Jax speaks up this time, allowing me a moment to shuffle my deflections. "They won't kill her."

Adessa whirls towards him, sneering. "And how can I trust that you know what you're talking about? This one lies to me all the time."

She points over her shoulder. To me.

Jax doesn't hesitate. "Because I used to belong to the Sunce."

His words make me suck in sharply, not truly understanding why he's choosing to admit his own truth. Maybe it's to save me from revealing anything about mine at the moment. His voice is quieter now, the weight of his admittance settling like ichor.

"My family name belongs to that tribe."

THIRTY-SEVEN

ADESSA

"If you ever find yourself lost, my daughter. Look to the hourglass. She will guide you."

Jax finds a decent spot for us to camp as the sun's last light bleeds from the sky. The silence during the remainder of our ride had been thick enough to slice through, but none of us dared break it. They fought earlier. Jax and Yoon. About what, I don't know. They kept their voices low, focusing outward, scanning the terrain, leaving me just far enough away to be out of earshot. But I know neither of them was happy with their conversation.

Now, Yoon has the audacity to look irritated as he buries the fire, shoving dry brush into the embers with a little too much force. Jax seems equally agitated, retwining an arrow, his scowl deepening with each precise motion.

"You coming?"

I hear Yoon ask in my direction. He sits back on his heels, watching the flames, rubbing dustings of flint and ash from his palms. He lifts his sleeve, absently prodding at the blister. The way he recoils tells me all I need to know. It's festering.

He catches me staring, gesturing toward the mat beside him. I obey, but only because I crave the warmth of the fire. Pulling Saedea's shawl tighter around me, I settle into the sand across from him and the fire instead.

"You get that in Kyr?" Jax asks, pausing the work on his arrows.

I nod, turning, plucking the shoe from my foot so I can mess with the wrappings, out of view. The wound has changed. The edges of the stitches are light pink. New skin. I'm not sure how uncomfortable it will be when the skin starts healing around the thread. Maybe I'll be able to rip it out later tonight without these two watching me.

"How's my stitching?"

Yoon's voice is teasing, but when I look up, he's already kneeling next to me. I shift the fabric back into place and inch away. Too slowly. He catches my heel. I inhale sharply when he tugs me forward, burning questions lining every crease of his face. But the accusations never come.

Instead, he draws his dagger and plucks the first few stitches free. It catches me off guard. I clutch the loose fabric of my pants. Every pull of the string sends a ferocious sting through my nerves. Every pinch brings tears to my vision, blurring his outline into the firelight beside him.

"Glad to see the tonic worked. Silver well spent."

Satisfied with his quick work, he lifts my foot, shifting to check the underside. It's a lot more tender than the top. The force of it makes me squeeze onto his forearm, willing him to stop, willing him to get it over with. He cracks a smile when I dig my fingernails in. My cheeks flush with heat.

"Looks like you need the tonic too. You should've gone back for it." I'm compelled to reach out and lift his sleeve even higher. The shadows cast by the fire make it look even worse. The swollen skin is taut and yellowing, glis-tening with infection. It reminds me too much of Aol's hand. He plucks another one of my stitches, forcing my hand to drop.

"Yeah, maybe I should have." His voice drops lower. "Should I have left you in the valley while I searched for it?" The tilt of his chin stirs something in me, and I fight the urge to smack him.

I roll my eyes, turning to Jax instead.

"Do *you* have something that can help?"

Jax doesn't answer right away. He laughs, one of those dry, almost bitter laughs that don't reach his eyes as he digs through one of Hisan's saddlebags.

"No, but I have this."

He tosses something in my direction, a wool bag the size of my hand. My jaw pulses, bracing for the next sting of pulled thread as I feel another stitch coming loose. Ignoring the discomfort, I focus on the ruffled edges of the bag, tearing it open. Inside, nestled in paper, is a small hoard of plump dates.

"I was saving those." Yoon chuckles, the handle of his dagger between his teeth as he carefully removes the last stitch. "She threw out my jerky."

"The buffalo ones?" Jax questions, sounding all too dramatic.

"Yep." He grins, sitting back on his heels, inspecting his work.

Then, with a flourish, he snatches the date from my fingers and pops it into his mouth. The seed bursts loudly when he spits it into the fire, the flames swallowing it greedily. I direct my sights to my foot instead of his arrogant gaze. Tiny pinpricks of blood dot the fresh skin, practically nothing compared to what the wound used to be. Pretty soon, it will only be a scar. A horrible memory like the rest of them.

Yoon's hand is steady as he replaces the date in my palm, then goes back to rewrapping my foot with care, slipping my foot back into the shoe. I catch Jax watching him, curiosity flickering behind his dark eyes while he chews on a date of his own.

Finally, mouth watering with anticipation, I tear into the temptation and bite the wrinkled skin. Sweetness floods my senses. I dig out the seed and bite down again, savoring the rich taste. It takes hold of my memories.

Of Isla.

Back when I'd eat my weight in dates. When Arthur, who took me in when I had nothing else, made sure we always had plenty; replacing trees that died without a second thought. The warmth of the sun, the sound of distant laughter, the days spent hanging around the gardens, waiting for the kitchen to finish preparing dinner. Those were the only moments in my life that hunger never familiarized itself with me.

My stomach growls in delight, the satisfaction of eating something so delicious briefly chases away the gnawing emptiness. Yoon smirks, settling in next to me, his eyes glinting with amusement.

"I see you two are getting along." Jax points to us, stretching out on his back on my other side. I'm trapped between them both now. One of clove. One of frankincense.

"I would hardly call it that." I snarl, lifting to my feet, moving to the opposite side of the fire, to the available mat, with the date bag in my hand. "Tell me, Jax. Do the Sunce tattoo their people's skin? Did you receive any markings while you were with them?"

"No markings." Jax frowns, side-eyeing Yoon. I hear Yoon release a breath of frustration.

"How about after you left? Have any from the *clan* you belong to?"
He shakes his head. "Nope."
Just as I thought, he's willing to lie too.
"So, what's the plan then?" I force the words out, needing a reason to distract myself.
"There isn't one."
I shoot a daring look at Yoon, whose attention is fixated on the stars.
"You're kidding."
"Jax knows the temple." He continues, shrugging. "We'll scout it, then find Saedea."

"That easy, huh?" I don't see either of them nod. "Merchants who don't like plans. Sounds a little odd, don't you think?" I'm left with a bitter taste in my mouth. I should save the rest of these dates.

"Merchants." Jax hums, indifferent. I glare at them both.

"Yes, that's what you two are, *right?* You're going to continue sticking with that, right?" I say the second sentence a little louder, forcing Yoon's attention. "And if we're caught while searching –"

"What do you mean, *we?*" Yoon announces, casually picking at his teeth.

"We. As in me and you two *merchants.*"

"You're not going anywhere near that temple."

My stomach rolls. I can feel anger flare at the base of my neck. "What do you mean? Of course I am."

"No. You'll stay with the horses."

"Like hell I am." I growl, my fists clenching involuntarily.

"This is not up for discussion." Yoon replies, deciding the matter alone. Jax bobs his head between us, making it seem like he's enjoying our argument. I can't help but laugh, almost maniacally so. It bubbles up from somewhere deep in my chest.

"If Jax weren't here, you wouldn't be so –"

"If Jax weren't here, I would have left you with Hisan regardless!"

His interruption makes me snap. He's so arrogant! My tongue clicks against my grinding jaw.

"And how would you have done that? Hm? Would you have tied me up?" I sneer, hardly holding back the rage threatening to boil over.

"If I had to."

The audacity!

It takes every ounce of control not to throw myself at him. "So, I really am your prisoner."

I watch his eyes narrow. Something shifts in his posture. His expression hardens as he contemplates meeting my challenge head-on.

"If that's what you want to keep thinking you are to me, then fine. I can make that happen."

I swallow the lump forming. I know I'm stuck because I wouldn't be able to take on both of them. Jax would absolutely stand in my way if I tried to do anything to this – liar. His unwanted words pop into our heated argument and it's like a knife dragging across my skin.

"Should I grab some rope?"

"If you try –" Energy crackles around me.

I start rising to my feet. Yoon matches me, cursing.

"Adessa."

It throws me off when he places a firm hand on the peak of my shoulder, pressing me down. It's not forceful. I don't let him see how much it rattles me. I swipe him away, the touch like fire on my skin.

"After everything that's happened, I would think it a blessing to stay behind."

He tries to soften his tone, but the edge is there. The smugness. If he weren't so solid, I would push him over. Make him feel how I feel.

"You're the one who's injured!" The words explode from my mouth, hotter than I intended. I shove my palm against his chest, watching him grimace. "Look at your shoulder! Why don't *you* stay with the horses, since you think it would be a blessing! You can give me your daggers."

"And what would I have to defend myself when I would have to come find *you?* Maybe I would have given you my machete and you *could* have come along, but I can't anymore because you tried to stab me with it! Do you know how much that thing cost me?"

Jax's laughter rings out, the sound of it grating my nerves. His eyes are on us, and there's something amused in his gaze as he watches the tension between Yoon and me.

"Jax will give me something."

The man raises his decorated wrists up, clicking his tongue with a shake of the head.

"Not a chance. Yoon has other weapons."

I relax my shoulders a bit, reminding myself that anger doesn't get me anywhere. Yoon seems to be doing the same. His fingers uncurl at his sides, the muscles in his neck no longer appear tight. We're both trying to calm the storm that is simmering, festering, below the surface.

Yoon breaks first. "Jax and I have been a team since we were young. I clearly don't have to worry about him. He was able to get a *horse* out of Kyr." His friend stands proud. "I could barely get *you* out. If you go with us –"

I scoff, does he really believe I wouldn't be any help? That I was more of a challenge getting out of the barred city than a *horse?*

"If anything happens to you –"

I ignore the feeling his sentiment gives me.

"If you honestly think that I will stay behind and wait, you really will have to tie me up."

"I won't." His response is urgent. And I can tell how much he hates saying it out loud. "You are free to make your own choices. Regardless of what I want."

My mouth suddenly feels dry.

"I only hope you make the right one."

I don't know how long we stare at each other. The space we share is thick with so many unsaid things. Uncertain lies. Things I'm not sure I want to understand. It's Jax who clears the air first, drawing my attention. He gestures for me to sit back down. Reluctantly, I slide back into my seat, watching the flames dance in the gaps of sand.

"Maybe I should tell you *why* Yoon doesn't want you to come along."

"Jax –"

His friend holds his hand up, settling across from me again. "It's a hard pill to swallow. For both of us." Jax sighs. "Saedea is going to be used as an offering, but the reality of it is worse. Much worse."

I don't like the way he says that. I don't like the way Yoon agrees with him either. Jax exhales, rubbing a hand over his jaw.

"Having you there might not be ideal because if we're caught, they might think *you're* an offering as well. And Yoon –" He looks to his friend. "Clearly, if that were to happen, he'd be running on emotion alone when we really need him to focus." He pauses, ignoring the look Yoon gives him. "Unless we plan for you to be a distraction –"

"No." Yoon cuts him off before he can finish. "If you're coming, you're not leaving my side."

I roll my eyes. Not daring to say anything that will make him take it back.

"Before you start listing all the reasons why he's wrong, let me say this very carefully." Jax rubs a thumb around his cuffed wrists. "Women in the Sunce are used for three things. Status. Servitude. Satiation."

A chill prickles my spine. "Satiation?"

"They don't believe in the Mystics. They never have."

I only knew the Tilidaans didn't worship the Mystics. They didn't worship anything but themselves. I never thought there were more tribes out there who didn't as well. Even in my homeland, non-believers were shunned.

"The Sunce take their worship even further than anything I've seen with the Mystics. Even the Muhdams don't take it as far as they do. They believe they need women for something else."

My stomach knots. "For what?"

"To satiate the God they created."

Yoon leans back huffing, his frustration clear. Jax continues to ignore him. He focuses only on me.

"What would a God need with their women?" I ask before I can stop myself. I don't want to know the answer.

Jax shifts. "The only way I can explain it is with a story."

He takes a drink from his canteen, gathering his thoughts. Offering me some water in return.

"In the Time Before, the Sunce used to believe in a matriarchy. The only monarchy on the continent whose bloodline could be traced back generations before the Cull. Queens ruled for centuries, their lineage blessed by a Goddess they called Mawu. A deity of the moon, of balance, stability. She granted the firstborn daughters rights to certain positions, the right to rule, to control, to build, and according to whispers I've heard, it was the most peaceful time in many histories on the continent."

The way he says *was* makes my skin itch.

"I'm not sure about the stories you've heard of the Cull, but I was raised with tales of the women turning against their own people. Forcing the men to finally rise up against their 'tyranny'. I never heard stories of what the Elites did. What those who governed the world did. I was only raised with the lies of what happened in my tribe. About how tensions began to grow all across the great continent because of the choices our female leaders made, how factions within the Sunce began demanding change. Ultimately, men who had spent their lives beneath the rule of women wanted power of their own. And when the Cull devastated the world, they saw their opportunity."

"Their first move was to rewrite history. A group of cultists – the First Grandfathers of the Sun, emerged from the catacombs beneath the ancient city, preaching that Mawu was all a lie. That the Goddess never existed. Instead, they claimed their true God was a deity named Mawuan. God of death. A male. They said the lies of Mawu's so-called compassion had doomed the world, and only through Mawaun's true rule, the Sunce would survive."

More brush is added to the fire. I listen to it hiss, realizing that I'm gripping my knees tightly enough to make my knuckles ache.

"The Queen tried to stop them from spreading the rumors. She led a hunt to imprison the cult's leaders, believing in mercy over execution. But that mercy was her downfall."

I don't need to hear the rest to know where he's going with this story.

"The cult gained followers. More than she had. When the Cull brought disease and starvation, the Sunce turned to the only people who claimed to have an answer. The First Grandfathers led a revolt, stormed the temple, and overthrew the Queen."

"They executed her in front of the Goddess's statue on the steps." Jax continues. "Then they turned to the priestesses. The ones who had served, according to them, the false Goddess, all their lives. They whipped them into obedience, forcing them to worship Mawuan instead. Any who refused were slaughtered. And then came their final decree. Every firstborn daughter from each family was to be sacrificed. To appease Mawuan. To keep his favor because the firstborn daughters had previously laid claim to control. This was a way for the cult to let the rest of the Sunce know that the bloodlines meant nothing. That it was time to begin anew."

An exasperated laugh escapes. "They originally wanted it to be *every* woman, but that would clearly not have been possible. So they compromised."

I raise my brow.

"I never said they were smart."

A sick feeling curls above my gut. I'm desperate to see how Yoon's reacting to the story. He lays back, staring up at the sky.

"They weren't allowed to expand. At the time, all of the unnecessary deaths didn't matter. But the rest of the clans, the Jidaani, Bahani and Nevadems thought the Sunce to be disgusting to even contemplate ridding themselves of the Mystics, the ones they all knew were the true Creators. So, they isolated them. From everything. Including the trade routes."

"I grew up not understanding that the Cull was created by the Elites, not by some insane God who demanded blood for payment of what happened to the world. Imagine my surprise when I realized that my tribe was the only one that thought like that."

He looks upwards, experiencing a memory.

"They overran the sanctuary, turning it into a prison. The cults' traditions became immediate law. My people were quickly brainwashed after that. And then their bloodline began, following the same monarchy rules as they had before, only with Kings instead of Queens."

He shakes his head. "The cycle of sacrifice became more intense, passed down through generations, becoming as natural to everyone as breathing. Their world had failed them, they had no other choice but to obey. By the time my mother was born, no one even questioned any of it anymore."

I can feel the shift in his tone. The way the story is no longer about *them* but *him*. "My mother's sister was sacrificed the day I was born." His tone is filled with the bitterness of acid. "A gift to Mawuan, to allow my mother an easy birth. To grant my access to the world through Mawuan's blessing." He mocks the words.

Yoon lifts his back up, resting on his elbows, watching his friend with concern.

"When I was a boy, things began to change slightly. A new King came to power. One who wanted progress. He allowed women more freedom. He slowed the rituals, believing that if the firstborns were given the chance to live, they would sacrifice themselves when it was necessary. For the good of their people, they would be willing participants. Mawuan would smile down on them for it. And there were many who volunteered for the 'greater good.'"

"The King re-established trade, dealt with Kyr from time to time, as well as the nomads in The Barrens. He signed a treaty with the First Clans, agreeing that they wouldn't desire anything other than peaceful trade for the things they desperately needed. And if they received that, they would bend to the territory laws. Everyone was apparently much happier. The Sunce began to thrive."

He leaves his sentence hanging. It forms a pit within me.

"But then he died. A sickness in the blood, they said. And the bloodline marked the next succeeding firstborn male. They crowned the King before his father was even lit on the pyre."

My gaze moves to the slow-burning flames in front of me.

"Now, this new King wasn't like his predecessor. Not in the slightest. He didn't want progress, he wanted power. His bloodlust was like that of the First Grandfather who decided it was his right to rule, the one who forced Mawaun's ideals down everyone's throats. The rituals returned in full. He severed ties with the other clans. He convinced our people that Mawuan was angry. That they had spent too many years in defiance. That the old King died because they weren't obeying."

"My mother." His energy feels hollow, following a deep, shattering sigh. "Killed my baby sister in front of me. In front of *everyone*."

My heart feels like it's stopped beating. The emotion in his voice rocks me to my core. I never knew the connection of a sibling. Even after my family had been torn from me, my own home destroyed, I can't imagine the pain he must have felt watching his mother take the life of his sister.

"That was the moment I knew I couldn't stay. I left my tribe that night and only looked back once. Well, until now." He takes a deep breath.

"Long story short. If you're asking *me* why I wouldn't want you to come along, it's because I would be worried about your safety too. It's been a lifetime since I left. I don't know what they're capable of now. I can-not promise you anything. All I can tell you is that Saedea reminds me of who my sister might have been. And for that, I'll do everything I can to bring her back."

I nod, feeling tears well into the pockets of my waterline. "Then you have to understand that I feel the same way. And that your story hasn't changed my mind about seeing this through."

Yoon sighs, holding his head in his hands. Jax moves his gaze to his friend.

"Well then all we can do tomorrow is hope that the Mystics favor us. And pray that Mawuan truly isn't real."

THIRTY-EIGHT

YOON

"I will never be one of you."

"We aren't them anymore, Yoon."

Jax speaks quietly, nearly swallowed by the night, pulling my attention away from Adessa's sleeping form.

"Yeah." I shrug, wishing that the water in his canteen truly was something stronger.

"Eyes the color of moss."

A smirk tugs at my lips as he repeats my mother's words. Words I once told him long ago. We laughed it off one drunken night together decades ago, intoxicated by nostalgia, trading secrets in the dim glow of a fire. His confession was raw, unfiltered truth. His life in the Sunce. His deepest regret laid bare. Mine was only a fragment of what I could have told him. A carefully chosen depiction, shielding the many truths I still keep for myself.

"Your shoulder doesn't look too good."

He suspects, in his own way, that I resist death differently than most. But he couldn't possibly grasp the full extent of it. No one could. Still, I feel it too. Something isn't right. The sweat clinging to my skin is proof enough. What's different about this wound than all the rest?

"I'll be fine. I always am."

He nods, deliberately. Acknowledging but not truly believing.

"I need to know who this new King is. If it's not Hafit, then who?" He scratches the side of his head, as if regretting saying the thought out loud.

"Do you remember anything else that you overheard in Kyr? Anything that might hint as to who he is?"

I shake my head. "I couldn't stick around to hear any more about it. Only that they sent a newbie up first with a few others."

Jax frowns while I continue trying to put the pieces together. "If the King falls when there is no one to claim the throne, then what happens?"

"I don't know. I don't think our history has ever seen something like that happen."

Their history. Jax's history.

His blood runs in that of Mawuan's monarchy. His drunken secret. The inescapable reality of it all. That my friend's lineage is tied to the Sunce throne. He was next in line. He was groomed to be its heir.

He did have a younger brother once. Hafit. But the boy had died years after Jax left. They barely knew each other.

Stories of the only heir to the throne dying followed the ears of many merchants we had been dealing with when we were stationed in Ferack.

"The heir is dead. Now their King will have to live forever."

The rumors didn't mean anything to those who were actually a part of the conversation, but they meant *everything* to Jax. So much so, that he pressured me into abandoning my duties that very day, leaving for too long to make the arduous journey to the Sunce, to watch the body of his brother burn on a pyre outside of the temple walls. Mostly out of a curiosity that wouldn't satisfy him. We got there just in time for the ending of their Death Rites, which according to Jax, traditionally lasted eight sunsets.

We stayed far enough away to keep Jax from being recognized, but close enough for him to see the King and Queen. To fill himself up with enough distaste to not want to return to that life, but not close enough to miss the familiarity. I didn't allow him to go any further than outside their gardens. Partly because I didn't want him to leave me. We'd been indoctrinated into the Jidaani together. I had no desire to return to Grandia without him.

"She still doesn't know who we really were?"

I shake my head, fingers drifting over the fabric on my thigh, knowing exactly what's etched into the skin beneath. "She'll find out soon enough."

"We aren't them anymore, Yoon," he says again, softer this time – like saying it twice might make it real.

I shudder. Not at the cold, but at the hopeful truth in those words. Of no longer being Jidaani. At the haunting fact that I ever truly was.

THIRTY-NINE

ADESSA

"Time waits for no mortal. History is made in the presence of Gods." – Sunce script, T.B. Date Unknown.

Before the sun crests the horizon, the men are already breaking down what little our camp has to offer. I woke moments earlier, jolting from a deep, dreamless sleep, my chest gripped with the fear that Yoon might have convinced Jax to leave me behind. That I'd open my eyes to an empty camp, nothing but fading hoofprints in the sand.

But they're still here. They waited.

Exhaling quietly, I watch them fasten their packs to straps along their horses' saddles. Beside me, the pouch that once held dates lies empty. I remember the last one, the way I ate it greedily, wondering if it would be the last treat I'll ever taste before walking into the unknown. I shade my eyes, glancing at Yoon, who has his smoothed hair re-tied into a knot at the top of his head. When I look at him, that unsettled feeling in my gut returns. I've learned more about Jax in a single night than I ever have about the man who claims to – never mind. There's no point in trying to understand the secrets of someone unwilling to share them.

"Ready?" Jax calls out, lifting a hand in greeting.

I roll my neck in response, loosening the coiled tension there and follow him towards the horses, deliberately avoiding Yoon's gaze, refusing to give him another excuse to bar me from going. Jax swings onto his saddle just as the scarred man extends a hand to me. I surprise both of us by taking it.

We ride through the empty desert all morning, the sky a soft purple, with the vultures circling high above as our only company. By afternoon, smooth alabaster buildings begin to rise from the horizon, their edges crumbling, much of their sides reduced to rubble. And yet, beyond the decay, the place still portrays some semblance of life. A fence surrounds the area, the wood stained an ashen black. It makes me think of Kyr. Another fenced-in city. Great.

We aren't on any road, which reinforces Jax's point; they've cut themselves off from the rest of the continent. Not once during our journey here have I seen signs of people. The path had been entirely abandoned. Now, the landscape has slightly changed. The surrounding area of the settlement flourishes in stark contrast to the desert, like an oasis pulled from another realm. Date palms sway in the wind, flowering cacti burst with color, a pool of water glistens softly under the sun's rays. Even from here, I can see a garden near the edge of the fence, with various vegetables thriving in a soil that shouldn't belong to this part of the desert. And beyond all of that, beyond the illusion of sustaining life, The Barren looms, ever-present to the east.

"Mawuan's symbol."

Yoon murmurs, pointing to two towering spires jutting into the sky from the heart of the compound. Their tips gleam gold. Painted suns encircle the structures, their golden rays smeared with streaks of red. Like bloody palm prints.

"I thought the Sunce people don't believe in the Mystics. Does Kyr worship the same God as them?" I ask carefully, not knowing what Yoon knows. The palm prints spark my memory of the arch in the prison. He shakes his head.

"No, but Jax likes to think their God stems from the Mystics all the same. They just use a different name. Maybe they picked up some rituals from each other."

We halt at the outskirts, taking cover behind the ruins left in the wake of the Cull.

"Elites used to govern this." Jax says, dismounting. I scan the area. He seems to be right. The buildings bear the weight of time. The only signs of change being minor repairs and the obvious budding garden outside.

Something isn't right.

Unlike Kyr, there aren't any guards that I can see patrolling the perimeter. No sign of the three men we've been tracking either. No trace of Saedea. For a brief moment, I wonder if they were ever heading here at all.

Jax rummages through his bag, arming himself with even more blades, as if he weren't already bristling with weapons. Yoon's fingers skim his bone daggers, their edges gleaming like fangs. I eye them, tempted to ask for one, but bite my tongue. Instead, I watch him pull a short sword from the fabric tied to his saddle. He secures it onto his back, replacing the lost machete, then turns to me. His gaze roams, scanning my body. Not in that slow, lingering way that makes my chest feel tight, but quickly, assessing.

"What?"

He shakes his head and unsheathes a dagger from his pack, hovering it between us. "You don't have a belt." He holds the handle out to me. "Here."

I hesitate.

"Take it before I change my mind."

I clamp my mouth shut and grab the hilt. The polished wood is smooth, fitting my grip perfectly. The blade itself gleams like gold.

"You'll lose that again." Yoon remarks, gesturing to the ring around my thumb. He tosses a length of leather cord into my palm, careful not to make contact – as if the thing will burn him.

"Don't want the raven following us."

A cold-clawed chill reaches my neck. *Do not lose it again.*

I furrow my brows, slipping the ring off and threading the leather through, securing it into a knot. I wrap the cord multiple times around my wrist, fashioning it into a makeshift bracelet. It lies flat against my skin, far more secure than it ever had been.

Jax clears his throat, smacking Tagan on the rear, forcing Yoon's attention away from my wrist. The mare bolts in the opposite direction of the temple. Hisan waits for his owner's signal, then chases after her when Yoon gives him a nod. We watch the two vanish into the valley. My heart flutters, knowing that we won't have an easy escape now. I can only hope they'll be within whistle range.

"Stay low. I'll be right beside you." Yoon whispers, positioning me in front of him.

Jax moves first, leading the charge. We follow, slipping toward the back edge of the fenceline, with slats that are thick and impossible to see through.

"Hear anything?"

Jax turns, shrugging. Yoon looks up, then jumps, latching onto the top ledge of the fence. Even with his injured shoulder, he hauls himself up, peering over the other side. Moments later, he drops down, rotating his arm.

"We'll have to go around, but there's an opening. Looks like it leads to the center." Yoon speaks with curiosity riding the tone. "There's no one in there."

"No one?" A shake of the head.

We move in a tight formation, rounding the corner. Sure enough, there's a gap in the fence. A man dressed entirely in white stands guard, an enormous weapon resting in his loosened palm.

"Is that –" Jax starts, edged with disbelief as he turns to us.

"It can't be."

Then, I recognize it too. The mace. I'd seen one just like it, gripped in the hands of a clansman. Lee.

"Shit." They both whisper in unison, offering an uneasy glance my way.

"I got him." Jax continues, already unwinding the wire from his belt. I crouch low, watching with pure anxiety as he approaches the guard. Silently. I can hardly hear his movements, can barely tell that a man is being strangled only a few paces away. *Jidaani. Jidaani.*

Suddenly, Yoon is too close. His presence is a bearing reminder of what I'm dealing with. What I've found myself in. All I wanted was to get to Darde. I try my best to create some distance between us, stress curling in my gut.

In a matter of breaths, Jax shows me that he's equally as efficient as Yoon. Perhaps not as – brutal – but efficient all the same. He drags the body to us, dumping it past where we came from. He brushes the sand smooth the entire way back, passing us again, erasing every trace leading up to the gap. Then, as if nothing happened, he waves us forward.

We slip through, stepping onto an empty path. The silence is suffocating. No murmur of voices, no footsteps, no wind stirring the emptiness. The area beyond the gate is bare. Buildings stand frozen in time on either side, their doors closed, their windows dark and hollow. It feels less like a compound and more like the husk of one, stripped of whatever souls once roamed its roads. Jax seems to be disturbed by this, falling back beside us.

"We know they're here. If Saedea was delivered, she'd be in the temple." His heads bobs in the direction of the spires. "Let's hope today isn't what I think it is."

"What do you mean by that?" I question, wary of the stark silence just as much as they are. We wander further down the path. Not even the smell of cooking oils fills the air. No early morning coffee. No cry of a baby. *Where is everyone?*

The temple is a massive, alabaster monolith crowned with what once might have been gold. Its towering spires are marked with the bloodied suns of Mawuan, a hundred steps lead to its entrance, flanked by two colossal statues of armored warriors. We're heading right for it, targets out in the open if anyone should see us.

"Wait, I see people." I whisper, leaning to the side, noticing white robes walking around and up the temple stairs.

"Priests." Jax mumbles, dragging us into a barrel-lined alcove to our right. "I think that we should have had a plan." Then, he laughs. *He laughs.* And Yoon laughs with him. And I immediately regret - everything.

"We're just going to find a way in, yeah?" Jax grins. "Or should we walk up those stairs and make a grand entrance?"

"What?" I ask, wide-eyed, wondering how we only have those two options.

"Find a way around." I answer first. "Right? We can't possibly –" I glance back at Yoon, whose eyes are set with determination. "Are either of you nervous at the fact that there's no one around?"

The two nod their heads.

"I'm worried that today is the day they... harvest." Jax replies, edging along the wall, leading us away from the stairs. "But it might work in our favor if we're smart."

"How so?"

"During harvest, everyone is distracted. The priests won't pay any mind, they're fulfilling their duties. And the people are – preparing themselves. I know where Saedea will be. Let's go."

Without another word, Jax steps out onto the path. Yoon grabs me, dragging me after him. He tugs Saedea's shawl up, covering the lower half of my face, as he had in Kyr. Then, without warning, he wrenches my wrists behind my back, locking my dagger into his belt.

"Don't fight me on this." He speaks into my hair.

My pulse spikes. "Yoon –"

"Pretend to be a willing sacrifice. It will help us blend in. In case we're seen.

His palm presses against my back, nudging me forward. I obey. Not because I trust him, but because the alternative of being *sacrificed* by these people is much worse. And if he thinks that this is our best option, I have to play along.

Jax leads the way, off-center to the temple, walking us through a barren market. Some of the meager stalls are closed, but the ones who are open show half-empty shelves. A few sacks of rice. Stray bolts of fabric. Stacked salt blocks. But nothing close to what a thriving community should look like. Especially with a thriving garden outside.

We hold our breaths as a pair of priests pass the crossroad, turning towards the temple steps, but not before turning to us. Their glazed expressions lift momentarily, moving between Jax and Yoon, then landing on me. Their suspicion fades almost instantly.

They think I'm an offering. I scowl at the thought.
I notice it then – their markings. Painted onto their skin, same as the ones scrawled on the fenceline, on the walls, on the temple spires.

Bloodied suns.

This is a cult. I remind myself. Not a clan. Not the Jidaani. The priests aren't armed. Jax is from here. For some reason, the knowledge of that doesn't make me as afraid as I should be. We press on, the last remnants of the marketplace fading into nothingness. The air shifts – thicker, heavier. The road becomes lined with husked buildings that seem to lean inward, as if whispering secrets to one another.

And then, the temple rises. It looms, impossibly pale against the sky, its alabaster walls streaked with stains, like something once bled down its surface and never quite faded. At its peak, the twin spires glare at us, the painted suns on them cracked and faded. Nesting birds circle their alcoves, resting in their thrones above the hollow city. Above the tower-ing steps, the entrance gapes like a hungry mouth.

"Oh no." Jax breathes.

I nearly collide into his back. My stomach knots alongside his worries as I peek over his shoulder. The symbols we all seem to dread come into view. Triangular markings slashed across the temple doors.
The black paint is thick and uneven – hurried. Desperate. The lines drip as if they were drawn in blood.

"Mystics' around." Yoon's voice is tight.

He shifts, tucking me closer against his chest. I'm too shocked to fight him. His hand releases mine, pushing the wooden handle of my dagger immediately back into my palm. His fingers linger, pressing on my fingertips as if to secure it more. A silent command.

"No turning back now." Jax growls, leading us along the side of the temple.

I almost wish I could change my mind.

Every instinct tells me to stop, to turn around, to reconsider. But Saedea is still somewhere in this place—at least, I hope she is. That hope is the only thing keeping my feet moving.

The further we go, the worse the unease settles in my chest. The warning signs are everywhere, yet these two are still willing to press forward without hesitation. That should give me confidence. Instead, it only makes me feel sick.

If something happens to any of us, it will be my fault.

Jax sprints to a low, open window on the first floor. Peeking inside, he scans the space, weighing something in his mind. Then, deciding it's safe enough, he hauls himself over.

We wait. For a shout. For movement. For proof that we aren't as alone as this place wants us to believe. But there's nothing. Moments later, Jax's shadowed form reappears, motioning us to him.

"No one's in here."

Yoon lifts me up and I slide through the open window, landing in a crouch with Jax's help. The air is stagnant and musty. It clings to my skin, heavy with the feeling of – loss. The room is stripped of life, save for a single water basin in the center, its metallic surface is pristine, like it's been polished. Although the rest of the floor looks like it hasn't been swept in centuries.

The wall in front of us is marked with Mawuan's symbol, stark against the light stone. The symbols are half-buried in new paint, covered by the jagged markings I've come to recognize. The ones I now associate with the clan of this territory. I'd be a fool not to make the connection.

"Have the Ramouz always been here?" Yoon asks, scanning the room as he keeps me firmly behind him.

"Ramouz?" I whisper.

"Jidaani markings." Jax answers without thinking. Then, immediately shrinks under Yoon's glare. "Oops."

I knew it.

"Finally some confirmation." I murmur. Yoon groans, running a hand over his face, but doesn't deny it. Jax busies himself, avoiding his friend's glare. He crouches, brushing dust away from the floor, plucking something from the stone. Gold glints between his fingertips. A coin. He turns it over, frowning.

"That's odd."

Then, we see them. Scattering across the ground, buried in the cracks and just below the surface of crumbled plaster, more coins glint dully in the dim light. There are dozens of them. Left behind, but for what?

"Who do you think is in charge now?" Jax rolls the coin.

Yoon smirks, playing along, holding up three fingers. He starts to count them down.

"Ty-"

A sound. Low and raw. Moaning. The kind that comes when pain is too immense to hold in. It cuts through the silence, slicing Yoon and Jax's twisted game in half. Their glances snap to each other, uncertainty written on both their faces. We are not alone.

The hallway ahead yields into an all-consuming darkness, swallowing what little light spills in from the singular window we crawled through. Cold drifts from its depths, slithering over my uncovered skin, curling up my spine.

Then, the smell hits. Rot.

Old. Settled. Familiar rot.

Like the prison I was in not that long ago.

FORTY

YOON

"Your Zaiem is your Father. Your Mother. Your comrades are your Brothers and your Sisters. The only family you have left is your clan. Obey. Obey. Obey." - Fifth Law of the Jidaani, etched in stone by Relik, the First Zaiem. Leader of the First Clan. 3,500 T.A

The closer we get, the more pungent the stench of piss and rust becomes. The walls press in around us, smooth and stark, the hallway narrowing like a throat about to swallow us whole. Groaning echoes along the alabaster, guiding us into an open space. I brace myself for the flicker of torchlight, but instead, a strange bluish glow seeps from above. The ceiling is lined with glass tubes. Inside them, something moves.

"Worms?" Jax mutters, his voice tight with confusion. We watch as the creatures shift through the clear pipes, their eerie blueish tint spilling across the room. The tubes weave through a network of tunnels along the base of the walls, casting shadows over the figures slumped against the stone.

A wall of men.

They are chained up in various positions, splayed out like trophies, each one covered in various stages of drying blood. The few who still cling consciousness barely resemble people. Adessa gasps, clamping a hand over her mouth. My hands move to my daggers on instinct. Jax lifts his broadsword, readying himself as well.

"Huh." I watch my friend step closer to one of the bodies. Then, he suddenly staggers back, alerted. "Jidaani."

The word barely registers. *They couldn't possibly be Jidaani.*

I move to one of the collapsed men on the ground. His arms are raised, wrists lashed to a metal bar above his head. His skin is a canvas of wounds, but there's no mistaking the Ramouz on his neck. A gash cleaves through it, bleeding slowly. It seems it's been doing so for a while.

A wet, gurgling cough makes me whip around. Another man, half-upright against his chains tugs weakly at the bar around his wrists.

"Not smart to bring a woman here." His voice is rough and ruined. "Mawuan likes em' too much." Another cough, blood flecking his bare chest. Four distinct markings rest right along his ribs. The world closes in around me.

"Lee?"

Through swollen eyes, the broad man lifts his gaze. A short, breathy sound escapes him. "Ha."

I drop to his side. "What happened?"

It's all I can manage to say to the man who once pulled me back from the edge of a death that was unwilling to claim me.

"You actually –" He wheezes. "Did come. You. Stupid. Bastard."

Adessa moves past me, scanning the bodies, searching. Neem isn't here. I know before she even says anything.

"Found Sadirh." Jax's tone is grim. He lifts the head of a bearded man, revealing the unmistakable mark on his forehead. The moment he lets go, the body slumps, lifeless.

"Why are there Jidaani here?" I press a palm against Lee's open wounds. His side is bashed in, his skin is slick with fresh and dried blood. I can't believe he's even awake. He makes a lazy gesture. A shrug.

"We weren't wanted."

Jax kneels beside me. "Who else is here?"

Lee's gaze drifts around the room. "Can't tell you who's alive or not. But there were eight of us. Five came –" A ragged rasp tears through him. "Before us. We didn't know."

I scan the bodies again. Six chained men.

"All of them are Jidaani?" Adessa asks quietly as she stands. Lee is barely able to bob his head in an answer.

"Yoon." His attention is back on me, heavy with something I don't want to name. "Why would you come here. I didn't think you would actually –"

"We're looking for someone. Someone you brought here." Jax pauses, latching his sights onto the other side of the room. The way we came in was not the only entrance. "You don't happen to know where the girl is, do you?"

Lee sputters, chest heaving. "The offering? You came for the offering?"

Adessa doesn't hesitate. She drives the tip of her blade into the side of Lee's neck. Places her foot directly on top of what appears to be his shattered leg. "Where is she?" She demands.

Lee moans, his mouth tilting into something that shouldn't be a smile. "Where you will be soon, I imagine."

The words slide over me like ice. I force myself not to push Adessa's hilt in, to ignore the warning from Lee by silencing him forever. Instead, I plead. "Lee."

Groggily, he lolls his head to the side.

"Who did this?"

The four-marked man shakes his head, lungs gurgling. I think back to Tyg. The fact that he sent his men here. He ordered them to bend the knee of the new King. He did this. I wonder if he knows of their tortures yet. Of what the Sunce have become capable of doing that no other clan has ever been able to do. To capture eight Jidaani. Impossible. It's impossible. If there wasn't going to be a war, there certainly would be now.

"What were your orders?" Jax asks. My mind is flooded.

"Kill the King." He spits, gliding slowly down the wall. "He isn't like his father."

Both Jax and I suck in a breath. I can feel the space closing in on us. My friend wavers, nearly falling back on his heels.

"What did you just say?" Jax stammers, holding onto his chest. Onto the beads he had made long ago for his sister. For the day she would arrive into his world. He would have given her those beads eventually, but he never got the chance.

Lee's breath rattles. "You heard me." His bruised eyes flutter shut, his body trembling with effort. "I told them you might come." A laugh. "But I didn't think you'd be stupid enough to actually do it. Didn't think Jax would either."

The mace. The empty streets.

"It's a trap." My voice hollows as I whirl around to the sound of footsteps in the corridor. Quiet, measured, heading straight for this room. I move towards Adessa immediately, pushing her behind me, but she sidesteps away, dagger poised. There's confidence in the way she holds it. A newfound resolve.

Jax staggers to the archway, his blade flashing under the eerie glow of the worms. He shakes off the fury trying to blind him and nods in my direction. I return the silent agreement. The footsteps halt right at the threshold, hidden in the shadows. For a moment, silence stretches taut; like whoever it is might turn back. Then, light flickers against the opposite wall. A shadow. A priest enters.

He's draped in white, his eyes locking onto mine. He hasn't noticed Jax yet.

"Who –" Jax's blade buries into his side before the word fully forms. The priest stumbles, hands shaking, the jugs he carries shattering as he collapses. Water spills across the stone, spreading towards us. Then, more pounding feet sound in the corridor.

"They have our weapons." Lee chokes out. "I think someone ratted us out.

The sounds stop short of the entrance. Then – *ping!*

Something small and black clatters into the center of the room. A blinding flash pierces the blue glow. Smoke pours from the box in thick waves. Jax sputters, and then a wet sound follows – a body hits the stone.

"Jax?" I call out, unable to see through the smoke.

"There's more of them!" I hear my friend answer back, in the throes of a fight.

I refuse to let go of Adessa, lifting my sword. A blade slashes the left side of my arm, the sting sharp and immediate. I swing my weapon forward, hitting something solid. A scream rips through the fog, belonging to the person I've struck.

To my right, tension pulls against me. Adessa is fighting someone too. I hear her grunt, followed by a sharp gasp. I react instantly, pulling her toward me. A second cut, this time against my thigh. My attacker stumbles as I drive my blade downwards, feeling muscle slip and falter to the floor.

"Are you hurt?" I ask, my voice frantic. She doesn't have time to answer. She's ripped from my grasp.

"Adessa!" I lunge forward, searching the haze, my fingertips brushing empty air. Pain sears through my side. I collapse.

Hands grab at my wrists, my weapon, prying it from my swollen grip. I can feel the daggers at my side being pried from my belt. I thrash wildly, twisting, grappling someone. I snap his neck. Another pair of hands are on me. Then another. They shove me to the ground, my lungs inhale dust. My left hand scrambles, feeling the bone handle of my dagger. It's there. It's within reach. I grab it.

Cold metal snaps around my wrist, someone wrenches my arm back right as I swing. I drive my blade forward. A shriek. I hit an eye. The soft flesh gives way. My mouth is sprayed with blood that doesn't belong to me as the body collapses on top.

Somewhere to my left, Jax shouts my name.

"Do you have Adessa?" I beg, straining towards his voice.

"No!" He yells back.

Movement behind me makes me hesitate. I can't see who I'm fighting. I take too long to decide. Someone yanks my still-cuffed hand, using the force to hurl me to the ground. A boot slams into my temple. Then again. The same area that had been injured only a night ago. I blink through the stars exploding across my vision. Another boot crushes my fingers. Jax yells for me in the foreground, but his words are cut short.

Incredible pain radiates throughout my neck. There is pressure on my back, the burns on my shoulder tear at the stretched, unhealing skin, reopening under the strain. Agony floods my sense. The last thing I hear before darkness claims me is the sound of my own ragged breath.

And Adessa's screams.

FORTY-ONE

YOON

"The hour of destiny is upon you. Upon all of us." – Excerpt from the fantastical writing of Hidaal, Copy Of Mystics, 2,400 T.A. Based from verbiage of The Script, Time Unknown.

"Bone!"

Her soft, honeyed voice calls out to me, wrapping around my entire being like warmth itself. It always does, especially on days like this. Bright. Golden. Endless. We are together. Finally. If only for today. Hopefully forever. It is a day that will live in my memories endlessly. The happiest day of my existence. The bone blades hum at my side in agreement.

"Where are you!" She laughs. The lilting sound I've craved for weeks. The same laugh that had once sent me searching through the unfamiliar marketplace of Halitia, desperate to find the woman it belonged to all those sunsets ago.

I splash against the river, making my presence known, grinning as her form emerges among the lilies. She matches my smile with one of her own and the sun bores down upon me.

"I knew I'd find you here." She carefully wades to me, the river meeting her knees.

"You're getting your dress wet." I say with a tilt of the head, watching her fiercely.

"I don't care." She laughs, making it known that she's hiding something behind her back.

"What are you hiding?" I ask, tucking her close when she finally reaches me, wrapping her into my arms. I resist the urge to kiss every inch of her. To never let her go. Her fingers slide into mine, warm and certain.

"For you."

I glance down to the object now resting in my palm. Nestled on the surface, is a ring. Jade.

"Might be a little too small." She smirks as I hold up the crudely formed circlet. "The priest who made it for me was no stoneworker."

Your destiny.

The words are clear. The Mystics, the priests, they've all told me as much. She is the one. Hearing the words confirms it further, as it always had from the moment we met. Like hers, my people are very much connected to our Creators. We've always listened to the voices that do not belong to our own.

"For my namesake." Her bright green eyes glimmer, so full of light that if I weren't already seated, it would bring me to my knees.

You love this woman, do you not?

I would scream my declaration across the valley, for all to hear, uncaring of what our people think of our union. Instead, I watch her slip the jade ring onto my finger. A perfect fit. She leans against my chest soon after, watching the river flow downstream.

"I have something for you too." I whisper against her hair.

Your destiny.

Around us, the world stills. At first, I believe it's only because I want it to. That I want this moment, this peace, forever.

But then the air shifts.

A nervous energy seeps into our quiet, little hollow by the water. A scent follows. Smoke. *No. No, no, no.*

I snap back into a reality that I am all too familiar with. None of this is real.

"Yoon?" *Yoon? I don't know that name –*

Until, I do. *I* am Yoon.

Adessa.

She looks up at me, pupils dilated when she notices where we are. She's here with me. She's in my dream with me. She's - conscious? I turn my attention to the tree across from us, to the raven who watches, clicking its beak towards the smoke. A circle of birds flies overhead, their wings slicing the air above us. They know what comes next.

I know what comes next.

The foreboding image of corpses splay out in my mind, ready to disrupt whatever peace I wished to feel. Is this how my nightmare starts?

I shift, holding Adessa in my arms, refusing to release her. My armor – I'm wearing the same armor I've worn in this dream on repeat. Nothing like the sanded colors I use to blend into the desert. A blue stone sits in the hilt of the curved broadsword beside me.

"Adessa?"

This is not Jade. I am not Bone. *Who are those people?*

"Please." Her eyes well up, spilling sadness down her rosy cheeks. I glance down, in horror, watching my ivory dagger sink into her belly. I can't let go of the handle. My other hand moves to the back of her head, cradling it.

"No. This isn't real. I would never –"

Your destiny.

"Chadron?" I call out, watching the smoke turn the sky to an ashen haze of orange. The raven caws. It's *his* voice. It has to be.

"Yoon. We need to end this."

Adessa's lips part, but the words are inside my head, paired with Chadron's in terrifying harmony. Her eyes roll back. Her body slackens. The hands that can't possibly belong to my own, finally release her. I feel the jade ring on my finger tighten, sealing into my flesh. The end of my blade slides from her stomach, its tip now angled towards my own.

"Adessa!" I weep for her, for what I've done as the dagger pierces me. Her blood is now mixed with my own. She sinks below the surface of the water. I scream, reaching for her.

Your destiny.

I begin to sink too. The air in my lungs is replaced with the river.

"This is not my destiny!" I roar into the depths, the thick bubbles rise to the surface. Above me, the river ignites in flames. "I do not claim this!"

Prove it.

FORTY-TWO

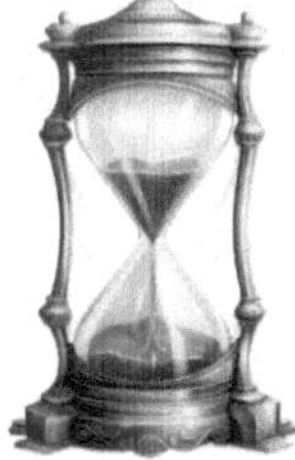

YOON

"You may never escape the sands of time, even if you beg."

"Until he's awake –"

I blink once. Twice. Light floods in from the massive windows at my back. It cuts through my vision like a blade. *Where am I?*

"Ah, perfect timing."

I shake my head, clearing the fog, only to feel instant pain. Warm, slick blood trickles down the expanse of my cheek. Iron binds my wrists, chaining me to the wall. I move my neck – too fast, feeling a sharp tenseness course through my body. I still, gritting my teeth. There's a gash on my arm. At my thigh. At least they're no longer bleeding, it seems. Pink flesh is starting to replace both gouges. *How long have I been out?*

To my right, I see Jax. He's hunched over in the corner, looking to be in the process of waking up as well. His abandoned shirt lies in a bloodstained pile beside him. A few cuts cover his bare chest in the shape of the Ramouz. Like it's mocking the three marks on his arm.

His side has been punctured with even, deliberate stab wounds. Crimson trickles down in thin, uneven lines that pool at his knees. At least he's breathing.

"I find it interesting that we've been given this gift of you three." The voice murmurs nearby. It's close, watching from across the room. "I'm grateful we were given a warning too. Imagine my surprise!"

Three.

My pulse kicks into a frantic rhythm, scanning the rest of the space in alarm. Adessa. My heart lurches when I see her. She's curled on her side, back facing me. Her chest rises and falls in slow movements, but she's alive. I inhale deeply, trying to settle the hate that seethes from my bones. My eyes snap up at the knowledge of being watched.

Two guards, dressed in hammered armor, block either side of the only entrance. To the left of the immense doorway, three men sit in waiting. Two in white, cross-legged on low, pale cushions. The third is between them, raised higher, casually leaning on what looks to be a throne.

He looks like Jax. Not quite the same, thinner, sharper features, and less hair. But the family resemblance is unmistakable. Unless Jax had another brother he never spoke of –

"What the fuck?" Jax. He lets out a violent, rasping laugh. My mind pieces together the impossibility. The man on the throne must be Hafit. The brother who is supposed to be dead.

"I watched your body burn!" Jax laughs again, a fractured, maniacal sound. His mouth foams from the force of it. There is a glimmer of pain there, wrenching him apart. My heart clenches at the sound of it, remembering the moment Jax had found out about his last remaining sibling. He had been so young. We both were.

"We both saw it!" Jax's teeth bare as he tries to say the words. We watched the pyre burn. Someone had been on it. Apparently, it wasn't Hafit.

"I mourned you!" He screams, bending over at the stomach, resting his forehead against the cold stone flooring. He *had* mourned. So much so, that he nearly drank himself into oblivion and set an Oasis on fire out of sheer spite on our way back to Grandia. He was next in line. If Hafit was dead, there would be no one to continue the Sunce monarchy. If Jax continued to call them his enemy, his tribe would have no bloodline left. It was an easy enough decision for him, to leave. To not look back. He wanted his people to burn alongside his brother. It did open up old wounds however, reminding him of why he left in the first place. Of Nadirra, his baby sister.

One good thing did come out of abandoning our duties in Ferack – in a surprisingly Jidaani sort of way. Tyg had to negotiate with their leader at the time, a lord who really had no right to control a city. The one desperate for help with guarding Ferack's borders from Nevadem scouts. The same leader who, the moment we tried to return, wasted no time ratting us out.

Tyg had to cut a deal with him, shifting the Red Line closer to Ferack's borders in exchange for our heads not being mounted on pikes. By morning, Jax was stripped of his title of router. Tyg made him Jiran of the Outliers instead.

And I had been introduced into my training as Tyg's assassin.

"If anyone can abandon their duties for ten days, sneak back in knowing the consequences, and still manage to survive the fallout – they damn well deserve more chances in this life."

Tyg never felt betrayed by us doing so. He respected it. As long as it was anyone other than him that we rebelled against, it didn't matter. We both received our first mark after that, at a very young age. It made us feel more than we ever should have felt.

Now, Jax's dead brother – his past, sits on a throne in front of us.

"Hafit –"

"Mawaun."

The name lands as sharp as the blade in his hand. As he rises, he shifts the weapon, showcasing it for all to see. The Deathbringer. Neem's scythe. I feel my stomach sink. Neem would not have given up his weapon willingly. It's an extension of himself. He would have lost everything for it. He *must* have lost everything for it. Yet, Jax's brother doesn't look to have a scratch on him, and neither do the others beside him.

"Mawuan?" Jax recoils instantly, as do I. Does his brother think he's a God?

Hafit sways, gliding forward with unnerving ease, stopping right in front of my friend. His voice is deep, strained, like it doesn't belong to him. Like he's making himself seem more threatening. Gold gleams around his fingers, circles of wealth on both hands. Chains spill from his neck, pooling at the center of his chest on top of loose, black fabric that drenches him from his collarbone to his sandals. The medallion at the end of the chain culminates in one final circlet of red metal. Mawuan's sigil. On his head, rests a golden crown that presses against the braids in his hair, decorated with small bones.

"Crazy," he muses. "How I was thinking about Hafit's long-lost brother not all that long ago. And now –" He grins. "Here you are. In my throne room."

The two priests turn their heads in eerie synchronization. The guards follow. All eyes are on Jax.

"What did you do with Jakesh?" Jax sputters, pulling against the restraints behind his back.

"Jakesh was not a King. He was *nothing*."

"He was the destroyer of peace, Hafit! He made his people's lives worse than they had ever been! And you're following in his footsteps?" Jax begs. "What did you do with him?"

"I killed the King! The monarchy of the Sunce ended when Hafit's brother abandoned them. There is no more King! Mawuan demanded change! I am their God!" Hafit's voice echoes off of every corner of the room.

Adessa stirs. My attention moves to her.

"A God?"

"*The* God." Hafit corrects. "My priests confirmed it." He moves a hand behind him, towards the two in white who raise their chins a little higher. "They had a plan for me."

"To fake your own death? To have our family – our father and mother mourn the loss of their entire bloodline?"

"Family! Ha!" His voice cracks like a whip. "A family that you destroyed!"

"They killed her, Hafit! What would you have me do?"

The crowned King pounds Neem's scythe into the ground, the sound rings through the chamber like a death knell. "Hafit is dead! He is merely a vessel! I am Mawuan! You are speaking to Mawuan!"

I scan the ceiling, the windows, searching for anything that could offer an escape. The guards took my daggers and my sword, I see that they've stripped Jax of all his weapons as well. They have to be around somewhere. Unless they dispersed them too, like they did with Lee's mace. I feel nothing but visceral anger at the knowledge of my daggers being in one of their hands.

My fingers tug against the iron cuffs, straining my arms forward. I can feel the nail in the wall loosen only slightly, powdered stone falls to the floor.

"Where is our mother?" Jax asks, lifting his head up again. His tone is now low, controlled. His eyes close, his body stills. I recognize this. He's centering himself, letting his rage solidify into something useful. I hope that means he's thinking of a plan.

"Alive. I've hidden her in the same cave I returned from before taking my rightful place among the Sunce."

The nail shifts again, a fraction. I keep tugging.

"You've been in hiding this entire time?" Jax sounds surprised. I wonder how long he'd been in those caves. No wonder he thinks he's a God. He's lost his mind.

Mawaun sighs, waving a dismissive hand as he paces back to his throne. The two priests both smirk behind their goblets, eyes flickering between each other with subtle amusement.

"I'm actually quite glad that you're here." He turns back, and an almost childlike delight dances across his expression. "I didn't think you would have joined the Jidaani after you betrayed us." He lets out a soft chuckle. "How ironic."

Adessa shifts again, groaning softly. My heart clenches. She's holding her stomach. Why? Is she hurt? I yank on the iron, watching the metal rod shift to the left. It has to be halfway out by now.

"And what are your plans with the Jidaani, *Mawaun?*" Jax teases. I can see one of his hands is now out of the restraint, but he keeps it hidden behind his back.

"Plans? They were the ones who came here! They wanted to make the King bow! They thought they could walk all over his kingdom! *My* kingdom!"

"Yoon?"

Hafit's voice is drowned out at the sound of my name on her tongue. She flips over carefully, holding her belly. *Where is she hurt?*

"Ah, the peace offering has finally woken up." He glances at his claw-like fingernails. "I've already received one of those, but I suppose I can make room for another. The harvest is always desiring more."

Hafit taps his fingers along the edge of his throne in boredom. The fact that he's talking about Adessa in any way lights my entire being ablaze.

"She isn't your offering, Hafit." I spit, finally joining whatever madness this is.

"An offering for *Mawaun* is an offering all the same." He shrugs.

"Where is the other girl?" Jax demands, motioning his head slightly backward when my eyes match his. He flexes his fingers, folding them into a fist, then gestures something that I can't understand, pointing towards the window behind us. It's a signal. I don't know what it could mean. Mystics' around, we should have come up with better signals. I remember we tried to a few times, it just never made sense.

Adessa is unshackled, watching me carefully. She might be able to help me pull the last of the nail out of the wall if we're quick. I could use it as a whip. I motion with my fingers, subtle, urgent.

Help me.

A small nod tells me she will. She begins to inch forward, glancing every so often at the 'King', who is still rambling on in a blur.

"You know, you've almost made us late. I sent that priest to prepare the alive ones, but since you killed him, I had to pull another from the altar room. That takes time. My temple is grand, you see. It's a long walk.

I don't know if you remember it." He clicks his jeweled fingers together, as if ticking the invisible time by.

"Late for what?" I press, anything to hold off the moment a little longer. Adessa is almost to me.

"Harvest." His smile widens, glassy-eyed with self-satisfaction. "Mawuan's first to be enjoyed in physical flesh." He gestures to his body, his robes. He twirls his scythe absently, lost in his own fantasy. His men remain fixated on Jax. Adessa inches closer, mere steps away from me now.

Then –

"Wait!" Hafit suddenly turns towards the doorway. Adessa freezes. I stop breathing altogether. I prevent myself from pulling against the chain, to add to the silence. "I have a surprise for you! In honor of Hafit's brother returning to see the Sunce thrive once more!"

He spins on his heels, motioning for the priests to open the doors, then faces Adessa, eyes blinking with recognition that she's moved.

"Take her." He commands his guards, who immediately obey his orders, relinquishing their posts at the door.

"No!" I shout, straining to be free of the wall, desperation saturating my bones.

"Ready her with the others. She will be a nice addition for the stone."

FORTY-THREE

ADESSA

"The Mystics will bless this unity. I know they will."

I don't make it close enough to Yoon before hands seize me. Rough, calloused fingers latch underneath my armpits, dragging me to my feet.

"Let her go!"

Yoon, he'll help me. He always does. But the terror twisting his face is telling me otherwise. His wrists are raw and bleeding against the cruel metal of his restraints. His shoulder wound has been torn open again, the dark crimson seeping through his shirt sleeve. A flash of guilt lances through me. I should have made him go back for the tonic. I never should have forced us to come here.

I thrash against my captors, but their grips hold firm, their nails bruise my skin like the same iron clamps bincing Yoon. Their hammered armor pounds against me as I try to fight them off. The one on my right dodges my wild kicks with infuriating ease, one of his hands shifts higher to press into the hinge of my jaw. He cracks the edge of his palm into my throat, a sharp strike that makes my breathing stutter. My vision dims for a second, but I fight with the need to focus.

"Hafit – Mawuan – listen to me!" Jax's voice is edged with something I can't name. He's free now, standing, his chest heaving as he stares at the man wearing the crude crown. I've never seen this anger from Jax. He lets his bindings fall to the floor. "I don't want to kill you."

A sick, rasping laugh heaves from the crowned man's chest. "You couldn't even if you tried."

And then, Jax is moving, lunging, his hands going for Hafit's throat. I want to stop him, to pull him back, because I see what comes through those immense doors. The priests step aside, a hateful grin spreading on both their faces.

Neem.

He lumbers into the room, his scrawny hands at his side, fresh wrappings on the wounds I helped create. His snakelike eyes scan the room with a smirk, landing on me. Landing on Yoon. Another man follows behind, one that I don't recognize. His bronzed hair is cropped short, Yoon's daggers at his hip.

"Neem?" Jax questions him for only a moment, then attacks Hafit regardless. They crash to the ground. Hafit scrambles for the scythe that clatters at his side, but Jax is faster. His hands clamp down around the man's throat, pressing hard. Harder. Hafit's eyes bulge, his golden chains twisting around his neck like a noose. He gasps, writhes.

Neem and the other one watch in bored amusement. As do the priests. As do the guards holding me. For a moment, I wonder if this was all a scheme, to kill this crowned man. Until Neem exhales with annoyance, grabs his scythe and bashes it into Jax's temple.

"Jax!" Yoon shouts as the sickening sound of the blunted edge hits bone. Jax's body slumps forward. I scream, the reaction tearing from my throat in something between fury and despair. Hafit rises slowly, coughing, straightening the crown that had shifted in the struggle. His expression twists into rage. He flourishes outward with a jeweled hand.

We watch in abject horror as Neem hands back *his* weapon.

"Hafit's brother is a fool." He mutters, looking down at Jax's unconscious body and sneering before kicking him over and over again. A hollow, fleshy thud.

"Mawuan! He is *your* brother!" Yoon's voice breaks, pleading.

"He is no brother of mine!"

One final, vicious kick sends Jax's body rolling. He doesn't stir.

"Restrain him! Make it tight this time!" Hafit – Mawuan – spits.

The man behind Neem obeys, coiling chains around Jax's wrists and ankles, latching him to the iron bar below the window. I fight harder, thrashing with everything I have left. It's not enough.

"Restrain her! Restrain all of them!" The crowned man screams at the top of his lungs. I can hear Yoon struggling with the nail in the wall, I can see that it's almost out. Plaster falls to the floor in an ashen pile.

A flash of white blurs across my vision as one of the old priests steps in front of me. A sharp pain explodes in my side. A hand, wrinkled and steady presses something against my ribs. A gold dagger – *my* dagger – finds itself buried deeply between my ribs. The short blade isn't deep enough, it was never meant to kill. But it is deep enough to burn. I can tell he's placed it strategically. My heart staggers at the sight of the polished wood protruding. Every ragged inhale presses and tears at my muscle.

My wide-eyed gaze wanders back to Yoon. He's sees it. His sight is locked onto the blood pooling at my side, dripping down to stain my dirty canvas shoes. His face contorts, his terror raw and unfiltered. My entire being stills at the sight of it.

A voice slithers through the air, a whisper that I know only I can hear. *Do they see each other?*

The tremor of knowing who the voice belongs to rolls through me. My nightmare. My mind itches with newfound fear. The walls seem to pulse, the room shrinking. Claws against my skin, nails raking through my mind. I feel like I'm drowning.

"Don't kill her yet!" Hafit snaps. "She needs to be prepared!"

"I am only readying her." The old man in front of me grins, with yellowed teeth and foul breath that wafts in my direction.

Prepared.

The word slams into me like a blow. My stomach churns. Hafit lifts the scythe, dragging the blade along Jax's chin, forcing his head up with the edge. The man still does not move.

"He does look a lot like Hafit's father, does he not?"

No one answers back.

A guard beside me snorts, shoving me forward. The motion wrenches the dagger against my ribs and a bright, white-hot pain splinters down my side. I bite my tongue so hard to prevent myself from screaming, I can taste blood from the marks left behind.

"If you make another move, I'll have them kill her now!" Hafit shouts.

Yoon stills instantly. His whole body locks up, muscles coiled tight with restraint. Neem laughs, a slow, slithering sound. He meanders toward the half-blind man, his every movement soaked in reveled humor.

"You made the wrong choice, Qa'id." He hisses, tilting his pointed chin in my direction, his slitted eyes narrowing. "Was it her that made you come here? Lee didn't think you would. But I did."

Yoon growls. "You're on the wrong side, Neem. To choose the Sunce over your own –"

The crack of Neem's palm silences him. The force snaps Yoon's head to the side, but he doesn't make a sound. His gaze only roams back to me.

"Please." I whisper, barely able to summon my voice. "I'll follow you." Each step rips the dagger deeper between my bones. My vision swims with dizziness. "I swear. Please – take it out –"

No one listens. My plea dissolves into rasping, uneven gasps. My waterline blurs, drowning the edges of the room.

"What are you waiting for? Tell Amira we're ready!" Hafit barks.

The second priest jolts into motion, moving for the door. His steps feel distant, like something I'm watching beneath the surface. Everything does. The room, the walls, the people – they're all stretching away. My feet slip on blood.

I meet Yoon's stare one last time. Those mismatched eyes sear into me, burning with unspoken words, with a war I can see him losing. He's debating. If he moves, if he fights, will the King make good on his threat? If he does nothing, will it kill him?

I almost laugh at the expression on his face. He looks like a man praying to Gods that have long since turned their backs. The Mystics won't interfere. They never do. He should stop wasting time on me. He should focus on saving himself. On saving Jax. He doesn't know that this pain is only temporary. That I *think* I'll survive. That I *hope* I will. But when I do... what will become of *him*?

The thought coils around my throat. What if this is the last time –

At least I'll finally be rid of him, right? That's the lie I've told myself, isn't it? That I'd be happy to be free of him. I blink at the room around me, knowing that it's steeped in ghosts, in the echoes of those who have knelt before this crude, towering throne and never risen again. The air is thick with the scent of old blood, clawing its way into the alabaster stone. Layered with it. A broken testament of all who have stood in this same position.

Bones are set into the walls, twisted into eerie, ritualistic patterns around the symbol of Mawu. Some are embedded so deeply that they seem to sprout from the stone itself. Others dangle above the windows, shifting slightly in an unseen breeze, clacking along the whispers of those they once belonged to. If Yoon and Jax are lucky, they'll join these ghosts quickly.

I'm forced forward again, moving past Jax, still unconscious on the floor. Toward the immense open doors that will seal my fate. I chose this. I forced them to come here. This is all my doing.

"Adessa!"

Yoon's voice tears through me – another plea, another wound in my chest that I can't endure. His face is the last thing I see before I'm dragged from the room of windows.

FORTY-FOUR

THEM

"Time. It is as cruel as we are."

"They are taunting us. They are *mocking* us."

Fists crash against the oak table in agreement, the sound reverberating like a war drum, steady and seething. The wood groans beneath the force, but it does not break. It cannot.

"They have been given assistance from the Exiled." The Hollow spits.

How unfair it is – this hundredth lifetime. *They* believe what should be savored has soured. What was once delicious, curdles on their tongues. And it is *his* fault.

"We must find the Exiled first." The Witness speaks, beckoning the blue flames closer to her palm. The fire twists in answer, curling towards her fingers like a beast eager to be tamed. "You were sent to hunt him down. Where is he?"

"He has not allowed his form to be revealed yet." I, the Keeper respond, tilting my hourglass back and forth, back and forth in a lazy rhythm.

"I have entered her dreams. I will find him." *Her* words scratch along the confines of our being.

The air shifts, shuddering with the weight of something vast, something terrible. The sky above becomes rotten with smoke. It bows. We bow. The three of us in the circle press our hands to our forms, tilting our heads downward – to the world below, to the creatures who scurry beneath our notice.

"Perhaps these mortals deserve our benevolence." I, the Keeper whisper, a mere sliver of a voice rippling through our collective mind like a stone dropped into still water.

"They have proven time and time again that they do not." The Hol-low scratches at the empty space where his chest would be if he still wore his human form.

"They have each other's artifacts." The Witness's whispers coil through the open cavern, rising, overlapping, merging in our heads. Uncertainty wades through the edges of those words. Impending, overwhelming, uncertainty.

"Not for much longer." The Tempest smiles, finally stepping out of the shadows, her grin stretching too far, splitting her face in two. "They have not seen each other yet. We will make them beg for death. Reveal to them who they truly are. What we wish for them to see. As we always have. He will have no choice but to reveal himself in the chaos we threaten. And then –"

Her sharpened teeth glint in the Witness's blue flames.

"We will burn this world to ash. Nothing left. Nothing more."

Nothing left. Nothing more.

ACKNOWLEDGMENTS

To my mom and dad, thank you for always supporting my dreams of becoming a writer, even when the stories were unusual, imaginative and odd. Your belief in me has been a steady guide.

To my brother-in-law and his family, thank you for your consistent encouragement and enthusiasm. Your support has meant more than words can express.

And to my dear friends, thank you for being my fiercest advocates, the voices that reminded me to keep going. Your unwavering encouragement has carried this book forward in more ways than one.

Another thank you to Karina @shepengul for designing Adessa's map, and Muhammed Waqas for creating the cover.

And to you, my readers, to everyone who gave this book a chance – thank you. There are a million stories in the world, and you chose to spend your time with mine, and that means everything. Stories are only half-alive without someone to hear them. Thank you for listening.

This story may have come from me, but it would never have come to life without all of you.

ABOUT THE AUTHOR

JJ has always lived in the in-between: between fantasy and reality, silence and story, dreaming and doing. A lifelong lover of strange worlds and sharp feelings, she writes to make sense of the beautiful and the broken. Often both at once.

This book began as a whisper, a flicker, a half-formed idea scribbled in a notebook. Given through dreams. It grew through late nights, too much espresso, and moments of doubt that turned into belief. JJ pours pieces of her heart into every page, chasing the magic that lives in quiet corners and untold truths.

When not writing, she can usually be found imagining conversations that haven't happened yet, dreaming of characters yet to be written and helping those in the world see themselves for who they truly are.

This is her long-awaited, debut novel –and the first of many stories she's ready to share with the world. She hopes you enjoy this book as much as she's enjoyed creating it.

Want to reach out? Follow @jjlaflin on Instagram!

Follow for expected release date and sneak peeks of Book Two in the Finality Series!

DICTIONARY

•- Akhali (Ah-ka-lee): Lead Akhal-Teke, granted the role by Zaiem of the Jidaani through Hayga

•- Akhal-Teke (Ah-kal The-kee): The Golden Horses, last breed of the continent, owned solely by the Jidaani

•- Ashwau (Ash-wao): Yoon's homeland, Far Eastern Territory of The Lapis

•- Bahani (Bay-ha-knee): Second of the First Clans, Leader: Geal

•- Blood Market: Market within the walls of Kyr, ran by the Muhdam Lord of Lords, coveted by all

•- Binehi (Bee-neh-hee): Of Bine: Mountain city of the West

•- Buzuq (Buh-zuk): A lute used by many harems to attract customers to their consorts

•- Dahue (Day-hew): River city, home of the last known Miners

•- Damire (Dah-meer): Ocean city, once owned by Tilidaans

•- Darde (Dar-d): City where the Elites fled during The Col lapse. Ruled by the Lapis

•- Deathbringer: Neem's scythe. Granted the title by the 30th Zaiem, Tyg

•- Death Rites: The process of burying the dead, as coded by the Mystics in the Hidra

•- Er Rada (Ehr-rah-dah): Former city of the Elites, now reduced to a marketplace town

•- Far North: The northern continent, Skeall as the capital

•- Farit (Fahr-eet): Large marketplace city, best known for opium dens

•- Ferack (Ferh-ack): Former city of the Elites, restored to near glory by Jidaan after expulsion of Nevadems during The Reversal

•- Geming (Geh-ming): Lower-Level city of Darde

•- Grandia (Grahnd-ee-uh): Home to Jidaan, from which the territory expands

•- Hayga (Hay-gah): Conquered trial of initiation to join the Jidaan

•- Hidaal (Hee-dahl): Prophet in the Time After, 2400 A.C

•- Honeyweed: A Mydizian herb known to treat the side effects of gout

•- Idane (Ee-dah-neh): Nearly abandoned now, by a plague that racked through years prior

•- Isla (Ee-sluh): Harem city in the north, new territory owned by the Tilidaan

•- Jidaani (Jih-dahn-knee): First of the First Clans, most feared clan on the continent. Leader: Tyg

•- Jiran (Jih-rahn): War leader

•- Jynn (Jin): Home to the Bahani, majorly, from which the territory expands

•- Kyr (Kee-uhr): Prison city, home to the Blood Market and Muhdams, from which the Underground centers

•- Majinka: Eastern continent city, where Tyg wants to expand once he has hold of Bahani lands

•- Malakiro (Mah-lah-kee-row): A Sunce word, used to de- scribe one's affliction of screwing goats

•- Mahudami (Mah-who-dahm-ee): A language only used by the Muhdams, stems from Arabic in the Time After

•- Mawu (Mah-woo): Goddess of the moon, stability, balance, life. No longer worshipped by the Sunce

•- Mawuan (Mah-oo-wahn): Death-God of the Sun, renewed spirit of Mawu. Now worshipped by the Sunce

•- Member of the Gid (Ghee-d): What the Muhdam lords call their highest ranking second born sons.

•- Mirit (Mee-rit): The port of which all travel to the Eastern continent goes through by way of the Dying Sea

•- Muhdam (Moo-dahm): Lords of the central, overseers of the largest merchant chain on the continent

•- Mydiza (My-dee-zah): The Eastern continent's port. Traders of spice and particularly opium

•- Nevadems (Neh-vah-dems): Third of the First Clans, owners of the Slave Runners

•- Qa'id (Kah-ee-d): Another term for leader, Jidaani used it for naming the second to their Zaiem

•- Qui Mehrijaan (Key-Mehr-ee-djan): The Great Abandonment

•- Ramouz (Rah-moo-z): Jidaani markings, given by the Zaiem, triangular in nature as an omen of the past

•- Red Line: The merchant's line, reformed by the 30th Zaiem, from which all trade and travel stems

•- Skeall (Skee-ahl): Adessa's homeland in the Far North

•- Sunce (Soon-tse): Jax's tribe, left out of the First Clans, but have not expanded to earn title

•- Teryal (Terh-yahl): Home of Aya and Tyg. largest shine pro- ducers for Yoon

•- The Barrens: Mountain lands of the north. territory run by the Bahani

•- The Collapse: Event that took place in 2300 T.B that led to the world collapsing due to the Elites

•- The Cull: Event that took place in 2350 T.B, led to 3/4 of the world's population to be wiped out entirely

•- The Elites: Those who ruled the world in the Time Before

•- The Firsts: The first generation after the Cull, from which every family line stems

•- The Hidra (Hee-drah): The Script, written by Hidaal in the year 2400 T.A

•- The Lapis (Lah-peez): All knowing ruler of Darde and the Eastern continent. Born of the Firsts who have Elite bloodline

•- The Mystics: Those who are the shapers, unknown creators of life and death, manipulators of the realm

•- The Reversal: Ten years prior, the borders change. The Jidaani undid all of the territory lines, pushing out the Bahani and Nevadems, breaching the contract of the First Clans.

•- The Time After/ T.A: The time after the Cull

•- The Time Before/ T.B: The time before the Cull

•- The Underground: Below the Blood Market, where slave runners profit, from which all rare item trade goes through

•- Tilidaan (Tee-lee-dahn): Pirates of Isla, origin unknown, although thought to have heritage from the Side That Is No More

•- Utar Line (Oo-tahr): Family line that can be traced all the way back before the Cull. Muhdam Royalty

•- U.F: United Front. Coalition preventing any and all further knowledge on technologies that will destroy the world after possible rebuild in the Time Before

•- Zaiem (Zah-eehm): Leader of the Jidaani